THE PRINCESS
DECEPTION

Visit us at www.boldstrokesbooks.com

By the Author

All In

Homecoming

Running With the Wind

The Princess Affair Novels

The Princess Affair

The Princess and the Prix

The Princess Deception

By Nell Stark and Trinity Tam: The everafter Series

everafter

nevermore

nightrise

sunfall

THE PRINCESS DECEPTION

by
Nell Stark

2018

ISBN 13: 978-1-62639-979-2

THIS TRADE PAPERBACK ORIGINAL IS PUBLISHED BY
BOLD STROKES BOOKS, INC.
P.O. BOX 249
VALLEY FALLS, NY 12185

FIRST EDITION: MAY 2018

CREDITS
EDITOR: CINDY CRESAP
PRODUCTION DESIGN: SUSAN RAMUNDO
COVER DESIGN BY SHERI (GRAPHICARTIST2020@HOTMAIL.COM)

Acknowledgments

William Shakespeare's *Twelfth Night* tells the story of Viola who, shipwrecked on the coast of a strange land, hides her "maiden weeds" and passes as male to survive. The experience of passing is familiar to me. As a card-carrying member of the "You're in the wrong bathroom" club, I can empathize somewhat with the difficulties Viola encounters as she performs the role of Cesario. I love *Twelfth Night* for its glorious, playful queerness, which persists all the way up until the final scene. Scholars call the play a comedy, and technically, they're right. Still, many queer readers can't help but heave a forlorn sigh when the cross-dressing woman turns out to be straight, after all. Tragic.

The Princess Deception is, among other things, a queer "revision" of *Twelfth Night*. It is also a contemporary lesbian romance. As such, it can't help but be inspired by the real life romance I'm privileged enough to live with my wife, Jane. She is my Muse, my cheerleading section, my rock, and my soulmate. I am so blessed by her love.

I am also privileged to be a part of the Bold Strokes Books family. If the zombie apocalypse breaks out, I'm confident that we'll find each other, form a commune, defeat the undead hordes, and continue printing quality queer literature.

Radclyffe knows how much her work means to me, and I will always be grateful for the opportunity to publish with her team. It's the best in the business, and I would like to thank all the hardworking people at BSB—Sandy, Ruth, Carsen, and others—for helping to market and release quality product year after year. Special thanks go to my editor, Cindy Cresap, who keeps me laughing and on my toes while she continues to teach me valuable lessons in how to grow as a writer.

Finally: I am profoundly grateful to my audience. As the saying goes: "every writer needs a reader." It's at once inspirational and humbling to envision you picking up this book. It belongs to you now.

Dedication

For Jane.

"With adorations, fertile tears,
With groans that thunder love, with sighs of fire"
—William Shakespeare, *Twelfth Night*

"Look in thy glass and tell the face thou viewest
Now is the time that face should form another."

—William Shakespeare, Sonnet III

"Conceal me what I am, and be my aid
For such disguise as haply shall become
The form of my intent."

—Viola, William Shakespeare, *Twelfth Night*

CHAPTER ONE

Brussels, Belgium

Her Royal Highness Princess Viola of Belgium had just raised her camera when her phone began to buzz. It was odd to be receiving a call at this hour, but after a moment's indecision, she ignored it. The light's perfection was fleeting, and if she didn't capture this shot now, she never would. She sighted through the viewfinder to where a single shoe lay discarded on the cobblestones, its patent leather gleaming beneath the early morning sun. Behind the shoe rose the edifice of a small fountain, one of the many in the city dedicated to a segment of the population who had lost their lives in the Second World War. As the fresh light streamed across the small square, it was refracted by the water droplets to create a rainbow arc that appeared to end in the shoe's gaping mouth.

It was a fantastic shot, made even better by the sharp toe and traditionally masculine buckle of the shoe. If it turned out, she would call it *Cinderello*. As she made her final adjustments, Viola wondered what had possessed the man to leave his footwear behind. Intoxication, probably—not nearly as interesting as the thought of a mistreated pauper, granted one wish by his fairy godfather.

After capturing several photos on her SLR, Viola grabbed her phone to snap a few digital shots. But when she powered up the screen, a prickle of unease settled between her shoulders. The missed call was from her mother.

"Your Royal Highness." Her bodyguard, Thijs, was always serious, but there was an urgency in his tone that intensified her apprehension.

She turned quickly. "What is it?"

"Your brother is in the hospital. We must return to the palace immediately."

"Sebastian?" Viola suddenly felt dizzy. She must have swayed on her feet because Thijs was instantly at her elbow, one hand supporting her. A flash of irritation at herself sliced through her panic, and she pulled away to face him. "What happened? Is he all right?"

Thijs looked from her to the street, his expression one of grim wariness. "We need to get in the car."

As though he had summoned it with those words, the Suburban used by her security detail swung around the nearest corner, then jolted to a halt. Viola tried to move quickly, but her limbs were strangely unresponsive. No sooner had she clumsily clambered into the vehicle, than Thijs jumped in behind her and the car rocketed away from the curb.

"Tell me what happened," she demanded. When he reached around her to buckle her in, she swatted his hand away. "I'll do that, damn it. Tell me."

"I've told you all I know."

Viola stared him down. The line of his jaw was as taut as a blade, but he returned her gaze steadily.

"You spoke with my parents?"

"With Ruben," he said, referring to the chief of security at the palace.

When another wave of panic crashed over her, it must have shown in her face, because he clasped her shoulder briefly.

"He is alive. Focus on that. We'll be back within moments and you'll know more very soon."

Viola didn't want his reassurances. She wanted the truth. "I'm calling my mother."

Her hands trembled as she extracted her phone, and the sensor refused to confirm her sweat-slicked fingerprint. Cursing, she bypassed it with her code. But the call went directly to her mother's voice mail, and when she tried her father, she got the same result.

A wave of nausea forced Viola to lean heavily against the leather seat. She closed her eyes and focused on taking slow, even breaths. Shock. She was in shock right now, but she had to get over it before she saw her parents. No matter what had happened, they would need her to be strong.

Sebastian had been in Paris last night at a high profile charity gala to benefit Syrian refugees, and as far as she knew, he had been planning to prolong the trip until his appearance in The Hague tomorrow to kick off the World Cup bid festivities. Had he been in a car accident? A shooting? Why hadn't she felt anything? Wasn't that how the twin bond was supposed to work?

The car slowed, then dipped and curved sharply. She kept her eyes shut as the realization washed over her: they weren't going in through the gates, but through the Catacombs. The secret underground route led both to the palace and to the nuclear fallout shelter that had been built beneath it during the Cold War. Her parents were committed to an honest and transparent monarchy whose comings and goings were a matter of public record, and their policy was to use the tunnels only in case of an emergency. Viola's panic ratcheted up another notch. The last time she had been in the Catacombs, terrorists had attacked the airport. Had they struck again? Was her entire family in danger?

"This way?" she managed to ask, hating the shiver in her voice.

"Ruben's orders." Thijs sounded as tense as she felt. "I don't know why."

The sinuous twists and turns were disorienting, and Viola fumbled for the handle on the door to brace herself against the motion. When the sour taste of bile filled her throat, she swallowed convulsively. She would *not* be ill. Not now.

Thankfully, the car's path straightened out within moments. As soon as the small parking alcove became visible, Viola unbuckled, ready to move. The uncertainty was torturous. Her head was pounding and her chest ached and she couldn't seem to catch her breath. But Sebastian was alive. For now, she had to stay focused on that simple fact. He was alive.

As she prepared to exit, Viola realized she didn't know the way. The door ahead led to an elevator. By going up, she would gain direct access to her parents' apartments. But the elevator could also access the underground bunker. She remembered the day of the airport terror, pacing the length of the bunker's main room while Sebastian sat at the small table holding their mother's hand. She remembered the whirlwind of her thoughts: gratitude that no one she knew had been injured in the attack, fear that another might be forthcoming, sorrow for the victims, guilt for the privilege that allowed her to feel secure when the rest of the nation did not. Over the hollow echo of her footsteps on the concrete floor, she had heard her father's vehement debate with Ruben over when they would be removed from lockdown. The people needed to see the royal family, he had argued. They needed reassurance and some measure of stability. None of them did anyone any good locked away in the dark.

That day, she had drawn comfort and strength from the presence of her family. Now, she didn't want to be sequestered away while Sebastian was in danger. She turned to Thijs, dreading his answer.

"Which way?"

When he pointed to his ear, she understood. He was still receiving instructions. She wrapped her arms around her chest, each passing moment an eternity of anxiety.

"Yes, sir," he finally said, pointing skyward for her benefit.

Up. Her relief lasted only seconds, before the formidable security measures between them and the elevator—including palm and retinal scans—offered a temporary distraction from all emotion. Once inside the elevator, she chafed at its slow progress and positioned herself in front of the doors. When Thijs moved to interpose himself between her and the metal, she glared at him. He backed off.

As the car slowed to a halt, Viola turned sideways and shouldered through the gap as soon as it was wide enough. One of Ruben's men was there to meet her, but she ran past him down the foyer. Voices emanated from the sitting room, and she turned into it sharply, dodging another man who was lingering in the doorway.

Her mother was seated on the sofa, her posture rigid. Tears streaked her pale cheeks, and she was fixated on her husband, who stood a few feet away, holding a phone to his ear.

The sight of their obvious distress broke Viola's heart and ratcheted up her own fear. Only when she dropped to her knees at her mother's feet did she notice her presence.

"Viola! Thank God." She clasped both of Viola's hands in hers, her lips trembling with suppressed emotion.

"What's happened to Sebastian? Where is he?"

"Your brother…" She choked off, eyes welling with tears that just as quickly spilled over. Before Viola could move, her father was there, wrapping his arms around her mother, who turned with a soft, heartbreaking gasp and buried her face in his chest. He rested his chin on the top of her head and gently smoothed her flowing, silver-tinged hair before finally turning to meet Viola's gaze. She watched as he pulled himself together and saw the effort required to compartmentalize his feelings.

"Very early this morning, Sebastian arrived at an emergency room in Paris. From there, he was rushed to the Hôpital Hôtel Dieu in critical condition, but the physician just called to tell us that he is now stable, though still unconscious. He—he overdosed. On heroin."

The shock was a punch to her chest, robbing her of breath. Dazed, she shook her head slowly. "What?"

"When he arrived, he was barely breathing. Fortunately, the physicians were able to administer an anti-overdose drug that saved his life."

Saved his life. The words ricocheted in her mind. Sebastian could have died. Would have died.

"From your reaction, it seems you are just as surprised as we are," her father said quietly.

"Yes, I—I had no idea." A wave of guilt joined her fear and shock. Why hadn't she noticed? As different as she and Sebastian were, there was no one on the planet to whom she was closer.

Their bond had formed in the womb, as much a part of each of them as their fingers and toes. As children, they had developed their own language. She thought of the silly little secrets they had kept together—but always from the rest of the world. Never from each other.

"Sebastian is the only one responsible for his own actions," her father said, the strain in his voice audible. "But if you do know anything that might be able to help the doctors treat him—such as how long he has been struggling with this…this addiction—please tell us. We won't be upset with you, Viola."

A rush of anger overwhelmed her as she realized he didn't trust her first answer. How, *how* could he doubt her, now of all times? She would have pulled away, but the misery reflected in his face caught at her, dissolving her rage as quickly as it had materialized. As the plea in his eyes and voice finally sank in, she squeezed her own eyes shut, but the tears seeped out anyway. No. This was not the time to lose control of her emotions. Her parents needed her to be strong. She needed *herself* to be strong.

When a soft hand cupped her cheek, she blinked furiously and focused on her mother.

"We love you," she said.

Viola swallowed hard as a fresh wave of tears threatened. "I know. I love you, too. And this is coming as an utter shock to me. I had no idea Seb was using heroin. I truly didn't. I would have tried to stop him, if I'd known. I swear it."

Her father leaned forward and covered her hand with his own. "We believe you. I hope you can understand why we had to push."

Viola nodded. As much as their mistrust stung, she had to focus on staying strong. Grasping for empathy, she tried to imagine herself in their position, but her mind recoiled from willingly embracing any more pain. All she could think of was Sebastian, lying supine and still in a hospital bed, all alone while machines marked the rhythm of his breathing.

She needed to be there, lending him strength. He had done the same for her after they were born one month prematurely, when he flourished but she languished. Mystified as to the cause of her weight loss and poor breathing, the doctors had finally put Sebastian into her incubator. Some innate fraternal instinct had prompted him to put one skinny arm around her tiny shoulders, and from that moment on, her health had improved. Every year on their birthday, her parents pulled the yellowing album off the shelf to show them the photograph and repeat the story. And every year, Sebastian rolled his eyes and joked that she still owed him one. Now, perhaps she could finally fulfill that debt.

She rested on her heels, barely registering the tightness in her legs, and looked from her mother to her father.

"I don't care what the visiting hours are. I need to see him. Now."

"I know." Her father glanced over one shoulder. "Ruben, is the helicopter standing by?"

"Yes, sir."

He squeezed Viola's hand. "You will go in the chopper with your mother. I will follow behind you in a car."

Viola opened her mouth to protest that they should all be together, but thought better of it when Ruben moved to her father's side. Security protocols dictated that the entire family could never travel together, and with Sebastian in critical condition, she knew Ruben would insist on splitting them up.

"Your Majesties," Ruben said into the silence. "Have you given any more thought to my earlier question?"

When her father closed his eyes and took a deep breath, Viola knew he was in danger of a rare burst of temper. Her mother stroked his arm gently, and Viola was struck by how they took turns caring for one another. It was beautiful.

"My answer is the same as it was," he said. "Take all reasonable precautions to keep Sebastian's condition private. Once we have seen him, we will reevaluate the situation."

"The paparazzi will not be reasonable." Ruben's tone was even and carried no note of command. At times, he was as much an advisor to her family as he was their security chief. "If word of this leaks before we make an announcement, we will be on the defensive."

Her father's shoulders tightened. "So be it." When he stood, his hands were clenched at his sides. "This is the life of my *son,* not a narrative to spin. Have your people process it as much as you like, but not another word to me about this until we've seen Sebastian."

His vehemence was as uncharacteristic as it was compelling, and Viola admired him more in that moment than she ever had. Following his lead, she got to her feet and reached out to her mother. The sooner they got to the hospital, the better.

CHAPTER TWO

A suburb of Paris, France

Duke's left knee twinged as she gave the bowl of eggs one final, wistful whisk and turned toward the stove top. She hadn't anticipated how much reprising this routine would hurt, though most of the pain had nothing to do with her most recent surgery. Smothering a grimace, she fell back on the mantra she had been repeating since her arrival: *Be thankful for your friends and your job.*

The scent of bacon radiated from the oven, a mouthwatering aroma that was only enhanced by the scent of frying garlic and potatoes as she wielded the spatula she'd found languishing in the back of a drawer. She was no longer useful to her friends as a teammate, but at least she could still cook for them.

The sound of footsteps on the stairs snapped her out of her spiral of self-pity. So far, her mantra hadn't been very effective. But when her ex-girlfriend Juno entered the room closely trailed by her now-girlfriend, Leslie, Duke managed a smile that wasn't entirely forced.

"It smells amazing in here." On her way to the refrigerator, Juno paused to plant a kiss on Duke's cheek, while Les slumped against the counter, blinking slowly at her surroundings.

"Coffee, Les?" Duke said.

"God, yes." Les's voice was still gritty with sleep. "Thanks."

If she had been anyone else, Duke would have teased her about her distaste for mornings. Duke had always been an early riser, one of many attributes she shared with Juno. Duke also refused to let the world see her uncoiffed, and her teammates had joked that she wore her makeup to bed. She didn't actually go that far, but neither did she feel comfortable looking less than polished. The girls had dubbed her "the Duchess" in a play on her surname, and while she had complained at first, she secretly didn't mind it at all. While not quite as fastidious in her own habits, Juno had understood her need to present a carefully controlled persona. But as refreshing as that common ground had been, Duke suspected their similarities had been the downfall of the relationship.

Les was nothing like either of them. Her boyish clothes were always rumpled, her short hair always tousled, and unless she was on a football pitch, she seemed in danger of dozing off. Duke silently scolded herself as she worked the French press. That last thought had been uncharitable. She might not understand Les's lackadaisical approach to life, but put her between a pair of goalposts, and she turned into Spider-Woman. That counted for a lot. And she seemed to make Juno happy in ways Duke had never managed to do.

"There you go," she said as she placed a steaming mug before the prodigy in question.

"Bless you."

As Duke retreated behind the counter to finish preparing the meal, Rosa joined them.

"How did we live without you?" she asked Duke by way of greeting, before helping herself to the coffee.

By the time the last of the four roommates, Cecilia, appeared, the kitchen was buzzing with energy. Even Les pitched in to set the table, and soon, the fruits of Duke's labor were being passed around the table. While the others piled their plates high, she ate sparingly and tried not to feel bitter about having to do so. Unlike her friends, she wouldn't be burning hundreds upon hundreds of calories this afternoon, and she refused to become one of those dried-up athletes who gained weight as soon as they retired.

Tradition and superstition dictated they not talk about the game ahead, and the conversation turned instead to Duke's new job.

"When do you have to leave tomorrow?" Rosa asked.

"My train's at nine, so I won't have time for a repeat performance," Duke said, trying out a grin.

Rosa elbowed her. "That's not why I was asking."

"But I'm devastated," Les said mournfully around a mouthful of potatoes.

"When is the actual event?" said Juno.

"Not until Sunday, but in the meantime, I have to meet with the Dutch authorities to get a press pass."

"What part of the bid process is this, anyway?" said Les. "I know they declared their intent or whatever last year, but now what happens?"

Duke wanted to tell them that they didn't have to show this kind of interest for her sake, but neither did she want to bring down the mood of the room. She also had no desire to subject herself to another lecture from Juno on how important it was to stay positive, which was exactly what she had earned the last time she'd made a self-deprecating comment about her new career.

"Usually, a bid is pretty dull: a lot of behind-the-scenes work that turns into a bureaucracy nightmare. All the paperwork culminates in the visit of a FIFA delegation that inspects each bidder's facilities and infrastructure before a final decision is made."

"That sounds marginally more exciting than watching paint dry," Juno said.

Duke smiled—more at Juno's inability to take her own advice than at the comparison. "Right? But Belgium and the Netherlands have decided to get creative and take things to the next level. The official visit only lasts a few days, but they're turning the whole month before FIFA shows up into a celebration of their football programs. The kickoff is Saturday."

"And you'll get to meet both royal families?" Rosa said.

"Maybe." Duke knew she should have been more excited about the prospect of hobnobbing with royalty, but she wasn't. These days, she didn't have the strength to muster enthusiasm about anything before it was absolutely necessary.

"Details, Duke," Rosa said. "Stop playing hard to get. We want to live vicariously!"

Rosa was smiling, her words unintended knives. Duke's chest constricted painfully and her pulse was suddenly racing and her hands had clenched into fists under the table without any conscious will. The idea that Rosa would want to give up her perfect knees and step into Duke's broken, useless body for *any* reason was beyond ludicrous. A few other words sprang to mind, too, and she took a long swallow of orange juice to stop herself from saying something she'd regret. To buy a little more time, she pretended to cough, then dabbed at her mouth.

"Sorry about that," she said, hoping they would impute the hoarseness of her voice to orange juice going down the wrong pipe, rather than the pressure of choking back rage at the weakness of her own ligaments. "Prince Sebastian is the face of the bid in Belgium, but King Maximilian has taken the lead in the Netherlands."

"Why not Prince Ernst?" Cecilia asked.

Les arched an eyebrow. "I had no idea you were such a royal fanatic, Ceci."

"I'm not a fanatic!" Cecilia protested.

"Haven't you ever wondered about the gossip magazines on the coffee table?" Juno said. "They're all hers."

"Not all," Rosa said. "Half are mine, and I'm not ashamed."

Duke barely heard their banter. She didn't know the answer to Cecilia's question, and she should. She hadn't done enough homework, and she knew it. Now they would, too. Before her chagrin could become full-blown self-loathing, she forced herself to move on. "Not sure why Ernst isn't on the front lines instead. I'll have to look into it."

Cecilia cut her a look. "Well, Sebastian is a total smoke show. Can you at least try to appreciate that for my sake?"

"And mine," Rosa chimed in.

For once, Duke laughed without having to force it. "I'll do my best."

"He's given himself a makeover this past year," Cecilia said. "Ever since he started dating Maria Fournier."

"The model?" Duke might not know much about the Dutch and Belgian royals, who weren't nearly as newsworthy as their British counterparts, but she had heard of Fournier, who had posed for a particularly provocative centerfold several months ago.

Les wrinkled her nose. "She's dating Sebastian and not his sister? That's disappointing."

"You have to let some beautiful women be straight, Leslie," Rosa said.

"Why?" Les deadpanned.

As Rosa rolled her eyes, the words sunk in. "Wait, what? Sebastian's sister is gay?"

When all four women looked at her as if she'd sprouted an extra head, Duke knew she was in for a lecture, after all.

"Where have you been?" Cecilia said. "She had a relationship with Dahlia last year. And I know you know who that is."

That much was true. Dahlia was one of those musical artists who didn't require a surname. Her biggest hit had been the unofficial anthem of the national team for Duke's final soccer season.

"The Belgian princess's name is Viola," Les added. "And they had broken up by the time the whole thing came to light."

Duke was stuck on the time stamp. No wonder she had missed that tidbit of gossip. Last year had been a blur of multiple surgeries followed by months of rehabilitation. While she had stayed in touch with her closest friends, she had avoided social media on all but her most masochistic days. Watching her number of followers slowly dwindle had been a daily blow to her ego. Reading about her teammates' exploits both on and off the pitch had opened up a new world of pain, the door to which she had only closed with the help of a sports therapist and an ongoing regimen of antidepressants.

"There were all the jokes you'd expect around Dahlia's tongue ring," Les continued.

Rosa nudged her playfully. "Trust you to remember that detail."

Smirking, Les was just about to offer a retort, when Juno cut her off and put an end to the banter.

"Really, Duke, you haven't done *any* research yet?" Her lips were drawn together in a thin line of displeasure. "You told me you were taking this job seriously, and I—"

"No." Duke swiveled to face her. "Don't you dare start." She didn't yell, but the words crackled with the simmering frustration that was always threatening to boil over. Clearly, Juno thought she was entitled to boss Duke around because she'd bullied her brother Toby into dropping Duke's name at Goal Sports Network. But Duke hadn't asked Juno for that favor, and she'd been appropriately grateful after she'd gotten the job. She wasn't going to let Juno use that currency now.

Duke watched as Juno's eyes narrowed and could tell the instant she decided not to heed the warning. But just as she was opening her mouth to fire a retort, Les gently rested her palm on Juno's forearm.

"Hey," she murmured. "Let it go."

Duke expected Juno to blow off her current girlfriend as easily as she'd disregarded Duke's own wishes when they were dating, but miraculously, Juno closed her eyes and took a deep breath.

Huh. Interesting. While she and Juno had only ever riled each other up, Les seemed somehow capable of helping her maintain a more even keel. Maybe there was more to the kid than her sexy swagger and "good hands."

Wanting to diffuse the tension that had filled the room, Duke pushed past her irritation at Juno. Maybe that was a sign of her own progress, because at one time, she would have wallowed in the feeling. Maybe.

"I've been saving my royal research for the train ride, but if you all feel like walking me through the high points, I wouldn't say no." She reached for her laptop. "Up to you."

"Are you kidding?" Cecilia said, gesturing to Rosa who had lit up like a Christmas tree. "This is our thing!"

"Yes—yes, it is." Rosa leaned forward conspiratorially. "So. Until recently, Sebastian was never one of the more interesting royals. He wasn't very attractive—"

"Always a little chubby," Cecilia chimed in.

Rosa seemed suddenly chagrined. "Not that appearance is everything, of course, but he was also kind of boring."

Cecilia nodded. "He was a golf pro for a while, but never highly ranked. There was a short-lived rumor that he and that princess of Monaco were dating—you know, the one who turned out to be gay—but obviously that wasn't true."

"Alix," Les interjected, her tone clearly conveying her disappointment at Cecilia's omission. "Her name is Alix."

Cecilia raised her hands. "Sorry! I sit corrected."

Duke, who had pulled up her article file when Cecilia began, was fleetingly thankful for her touch typing skills. "What prompted the change?" she asked, fingers flying over the keys as she hastily made note of their observations.

"No idea, but over the past year, Sebastian lost a lot of weight and started to be seen in the company of A-listers." Rosa shrugged. "He's finally had some sustained runs in the tabloids."

"Joy," Duke said, injecting every possible ounce of sarcasm into the word.

She might not have blue blood and a coat of arms, but for a time, she'd been American soccer royalty. Once the media began billing her as the second coming of Mia Hamm, Duke had been under just enough scrutiny to know how awful it could be: the invasive and inappropriate questions about her personal life, the digging and sifting through her social media presence in an effort to find anything that might topple her from her pedestal, the minute attention paid to where she ate and what she wore and who she was seen with. She had still been light years away from the A-list, but anyone with a camera phone could be an amateur paparazzo. Which was everyone.

And yet, there was a part of her that missed the attention—a part she'd been forced to acknowledge by the therapist she had finally agreed to see. Duke had always wanted to believe herself humble: a hard worker who cared more about results than the glory that attended them. It had taken more than a few heated debates with Dr. Pena before she'd recognized her humility as self-delusion.

"Sometimes," Pena had said into the shock of that epiphany, "when a significant change is required, you have to take yourself apart piece by piece—down to the very cornerstone of your identity—and then rebuild."

When Duke had asked how to recognize that cornerstone so she wouldn't accidentally throw it out with the rest of the debris, Pena had smiled and told her that was impossible.

"Your cornerstone is the most fundamental belief you have. The core value you can't abandon. The immovable object of your psyche."

"Hey, are you listening?" Juno's voice was accompanied by a nudge of her foot. "We're trying to help, you know."

"Sorry." Duke stifled a pretended yawn and rubbed delicately at her eyes, as though they were tired. They weren't, but the memory had made her tear up, and she didn't want anyone to notice. "I didn't sleep very well last night."

Rosa stood and squeezed her shoulder before beginning to clear the plates. "I'd be nervous about meeting royalty, too. But you're going to do great. You're smart and beautiful and charming—royalty in your own right. You'll always be our Duchess."

Duke smiled and told her she was sweet and then excused herself by claiming she had to visit the WC. As she left, she caught Juno's scrutinizing look and prayed she wouldn't follow. Duke quickened her pace, gained the threshold without incident, and locked the door with relief. The bathroom was tiny but private, and right now that was all that mattered. She braced her elbows on the sink and finally let the tears fall, registering the tiny plink of each drop on the ceramic surface. She wept silently, a skill she had cultivated in recent months.

It had been a mistake to come here. She'd had her misgivings, but Dr. Pena had convinced her that reconnecting with her friends—seeing them in the space they shared, going about their lives as she moved on with hers—would be good for her. Instead, all this visit had done was remind her of how much she had lost. She had ripped off the scab far too early.

As the tears finally began to slow, Duke focused on taking slow, even breaths. But when she tried running through one of Dr. Pena's meditation techniques, her chaotic mind refused to cooperate. The hours stretched ahead, interminable and tinged with the anticipation of pain. She didn't want to leave the house without her game bag.

She didn't want to part ways with her former teammates at the stadium entrance and watch them disappear behind the locker room door. She didn't want to be a spectator, cheering them on with rows and barriers between her and the pitch. Even sitting the bench would be preferable to sitting in the stands.

But what she wanted didn't matter. Her career was over, and the sooner she managed to accept it, the sooner she could find a way to move on. Today, she would find the strength to hide her grief and support her friends. Tomorrow, she would begin the first chapter of her new life in good faith with a good attitude.

Somehow.

CHAPTER THREE

Paris, France

Despite the beep of the heart monitor and the whoosh of the ventilator, an eerie hush pervaded Sebastian's room. It came from him, Viola realized—from the stillness of his body beneath the pale blanket. She tightened her grip on his hand as she watched her mother smooth his hair back from his forehead. Her fingers were trembling.

Viola forced herself not to look away. She had never seen someone intubated before, and while she understood that the procedure was necessary, the sight of the tube disappearing into his mouth filled her with horror. What must *he* be feeling—if he could feel at all? Had he regained consciousness since being admitted? As much as she wanted him lucid again, she hoped he hadn't woken alone and disoriented and in pain.

A selfish part of her wanted to flee the room, but she squared her shoulders against the panic. Sebastian needed her, and she would be damned if she gave in to cowardice now. After a hard swallow, she began to speak. At first, her voice was little more than a halting whisper, but the trickle of words grew stronger until they became a torrent, pouring out of her without conscious thought.

As she spoke to him, her mother moved to her side and took hold of her free hand. The gentle pressure anchored her, and Viola took strength from it, channeling that unspoken love into her words. She told Sebastian that she would always stand by him. She reminded him of all the ways he had taken care of her in the past and assured him that she would do the same for him in the present. She painted a picture of his best self, urging him to remember all the good he had already done in the world. She spoke of her pride in his accomplishments and her excitement for his future.

The tide of words slowed, then stopped. She felt hollowed out, drained. Her mother tugged her gently toward the chairs, and they sat.

"I'm so proud of you," she said.

But Viola shook her head. "I should have known."

Now that the initial shock had passed, the thought had become a painful mantra, drilling into her brain until the vibrations were all she could feel. How had Sebastian hidden his drug use from her? On the short ride to the hospital, she had found herself hoping that last night was the first time Sebastian had ever tried heroin, but she wasn't naive and could recognize her own wishful thinking. Denial was the first stage of grief, and she had to move past it if she was going to be able to help him.

Even so, the shock was difficult to absorb. She had never known him to be interested in drugs of any kind. As adolescents, they had tried marijuana together, and while Viola found the experience pleasurable, Sebastian had become paranoid. She had never seen him use it again. They had been at many parties where other drugs were circulating, and she had never seen him try those, either. But clearly, her knowledge was faulty.

If she had to guess, she would bet he started using shortly before he began losing weight. She distinctly remembered complimenting his appearance at a holiday party, when his new slim look had been accentuated by the cut of his brand new tuxedo. Why hadn't she realized that he'd lost too much, too quickly? How had she mistaken addiction for hard work and healthy choices?

Swiping at her lingering tears with her free hand, she forced herself to move past fruitless conjecture. What-ifs were of no use now.

Her mother placed one palm on her cheek and turned Viola's head until their eyes met. "You are not your brother's keeper," she said, unfallen tears shimmering in her eyes. Despite her reassurance, guilt saturated the words.

"Neither are you," Viola whispered.

The tears did fall and Viola's heart broke all over again at the sound of her mother's sob. She hugged her. It was all she could do, and the profound helplessness was overwhelming.

At the scrape of the door opening behind them, Viola turned to the welcome sight of her father. He joined their embrace, but Viola could sense his impatience to see Sebastian, and with a squeeze of his shoulder, she stepped out of his way. As she watched him smooth back the hair from Sebastian's forehead, she experienced a flash of anger at her brother. She should have realized something was wrong, but he also should have told them. Unlike so many other families, theirs wasn't fractured by ideological chasms or unhealed wounds from unresolved grudges. They were on good terms. They communicated well. No one would have judged him—they would only have tried to help. Why had he not reached out?

Why hadn't he at least confided in *her*?

When she realized she was blaming him, Viola's disgust at herself was punctuated by a bout of nausea so severe she thought she might actually be sick. She steadied herself against the wall and bowed her head in an effort to regain control. After a few deep breaths, she felt marginally better, but not enough to open her eyes. She concentrated on the bass rumble of her father's voice as he spoke to Sebastian, reminding him how strong he was and how much they all loved him.

The door opened. Cautiously, Viola straightened and turned. The man who entered was probably not much older than she was, but his badge proclaimed him a doctor.

"Good morning, Your Majesties," he said, inclining his head toward her parents before glancing in her direction. "And Your Highness. I am Lucas, one of the physicians assigned to Prince Sebastian. When you are ready, Dr. Charcot, the chief of cardiology, will be happy to speak with you in her office."

Viola looked to her father. His eyes were red-rimmed and his cheeks pale, but when he spoke, his voice was steady.

"Please, take us to her now."

Minutes later, Viola trailed her mother into the tidy office. It wasn't as large as she had expected, but the deceptively delicate spire of Sainte Chapelle filled the window, and beyond it, the thick ribbon of the Seine. Behind the nameplate on her desk, a middle-aged woman in a white lab coat stood as they entered and offered a shallow bow.

"Your Majesties, Your Highness. I am Jeanne Charcot. I have been overseeing your son's case since his arrival."

Viola was glad she wasn't required to speak. She kept hold of her mother's arm while her father stepped forward to shake Dr. Charcot's hand. "We are grateful beyond the power of expression for all you have done to care for Sebastian," he said. "What can you tell us about his condition?"

Dr. Charcot gestured to the chairs before her desk. "Please sit."

Only when Viola was off her feet did she realize how exhausted she was. It seemed as though years had elapsed since her early morning foray into the streets. She had slept well and risen before her alarm, relieved to see that the expected good weather had indeed materialized and eager to capture new perspectives of her native city. But the promise of the day had been shattered, and the horizons of her world had collapsed under the weight of her fear and guilt and grief. Sebastian had to pull though. He had to. She fixed her gaze on the physician. Beside her, she dimly noted the clasped hands of her parents, resting on her father's knee.

"Sebastian is currently suffering from a condition known as noncardiogenic pulmonary edema. He has a buildup of fluid in his lungs, which is causing him to have difficulty breathing. This accumulation of fluid is the result of an overdose of heroin, which depresses the respiratory system."

"Do—" Her father's voice cracked, and he cleared his throat. "Do you expect him to make a full recovery?"

"The next forty-eight hours will be critical," Dr. Charcot said. "Most patients in a similar condition are able to come off the ventilator within that time, unless they experience complications."

"What kind of complications might arise?" her mother asked, the strain of the question inflecting her words.

"A collapsed lung is possible, though unlikely in Sebastian's case. We must also be concerned about pneumonia."

Viola took a deep breath and forced herself to ask the question that had been haunting her since she had seen Sebastian, so still and unresponsive. "Is he likely to have any brain damage?"

When Dr. Charcot's sympathetic gaze met hers, Viola had her answer. In that moment, she vainly wished she could take back the question to shield her parents from the answer.

"That is a possibility. We do not know how long he was unconscious before he was brought to the ER."

Her mother turned to her father in confused distress. "But...can we not find out?"

When her father closed his eyes briefly, Viola realized he had been keeping some details from her mother. A sickening jolt of dread made it hard to swallow. What else did he know?

"Sebastian was brought to the hospital by a car service. The driver said he had been paid in cash—triple his normal price—to make the trip."

Viola watched the horrified comprehension dawn on her mother's face one moment after her own epiphany. Sebastian's companions—whoever they were—hadn't possessed the decency to personally ensure his safe arrival at the hospital. No doubt, they were trying to protect themselves.

"What is his treatment plan?" Viola asked, wanting to steer the conversation back toward pragmatics. It would do them no good right now to spend precious energy speculating about the circumstances of Sebastian's overdose.

"Now that Sebastian is stable, he has been scheduled for a CT scan," Dr. Charcot said. "That will give us a clearer picture of the existence or extent of any brain injuries."

"And when he wakes?" her father asked.

Viola appreciated his certainty. Yes. Sebastian would wake. He would be fine. Except, of course, he wouldn't. He would wake to the beginning of a lengthy battle against addiction.

"We can begin treating his withdrawal symptoms here, but he will need to be admitted to a detoxification and rehabilitation program as soon as possible." Dr. Charcot pushed a manila folder across her desk. "I have prepared a list of several such facilities that have my highest recommendation."

Her father took the file and opened it. Viola watched his eyes flicker as he scanned the page. When he looked up, his expression was one she had never seen before—sorrowful and dazed.

"I…" He exchanged a glance with her mother. "We know very little about such rehabilitation. What is the recommended protocol? What factors should we consider when making this decision?"

At that moment, Dr. Charcot's phone rang. She excused herself and answered. Her gaze returned to them briefly before she focused on her computer. Viola realized that her parents, their heads close together as they silently comforted one another, hadn't seemed to notice. Was this call about Sebastian? Had something changed in his status? Wanting to stand up and demand an immediate explanation, Viola gripped the arms of the chair and clamped her teeth together.

Dr. Charcot lowered the phone and moistened her lips. Viola thought the pressure of her fingers might splinter the plastic rods of the chair. Each second that passed was an excruciating eternity.

"I have good news," Dr. Charcot said into the silence. "Sebastian has regained consciousness."

A train in eastern France

Relief washed over Duke as the train lurched into motion, and she rolled her shoulders in a futile effort to loosen the tension lodged between her shoulder blades. If she had to be on the receiving end of one more ineffectively disguised pitying glance from her friends and former teammates, she thought she might scream. Soccer had been her life, all her life, but it wasn't anymore. Though she had learned that lesson already, this past week had only served to reinforce it.

The pity was hard to stomach, but the fear was even harder. Her friends were probably just as relieved by her absence as Duke was. She represented their worst nightmare: being struck down by injury in the prime of their career. Her presence reminded them that their status, goals, and financial security were as fragile as a tendon or ligament, as easily crushed as cartilage.

Duke closed her gritty eyes and rested her head against the cool glass of the window. She felt sluggish in body and mind, the product of both overindulgence and insomnia. She'd had just enough to drink last night to make her tipsy, but not enough to drown the hamster wheel of her brain.

Not so long ago, she had found it easy to relax her guard in the presence of her teammates. They had been her rock—she could trust them to watch her back, and to keep her secrets if she chose to engage in a tryst. Now, she was on the fringes of the close-knit community that had once been her family. Last night's party had included too many people she didn't know well enough to trust.

If Duke hadn't been so bone-weary from fighting off her own despair, she might still have risked a one-night stand with Isabelle, the Brazilian national team's starting goalkeeper who played second to Leslie on her club team. Isabelle's attempts at flirtation had been as terrible as her body was beautiful, but her assertiveness was exactly what Duke craved in a lover. In the old days, she would never have hesitated to accept such an offer. She had a powerful libido and no compunctions about seeking out liaisons whenever she was single. But when she was in a relationship, the strength of her drive often became an inconvenience. At times, she had even wished it away entirely.

Now that her wish had been granted, she wanted to take it back again. Without the spark of desire, she felt cold and empty. Better to burn too hot than to wonder if she would ever burn again.

A flood of light momentarily blinded her as the train emerged from the tunnels beneath the station. As soon as her eyes adjusted, she watched the urban landscape transition quickly into the rural. Low hills rose in the distance, and atop one hulked the ruined fortification of a castle. Delight temporarily chased away her melancholy. That castle was most likely older than her own country. She hadn't yet become so inured to Europe's charms that she took such a sight for granted.

After a few indulgent minutes, she reluctantly turned from the window and opened her laptop. This research wasn't going to do itself, and her blind spot when it came to royal gossip had been amply demonstrated by her friends. She opened a browser, gave herself a mental pep talk…and still felt her gaze pulled by the window.

Doing any research at all seemed useless. There was no way she would ever get close enough to one of the royals for a tête-à-tête. Still, if she didn't prepare for this job, she would never escape Juno's nagging words in her head, giving voice to Duke's own self-loathing.

Better to get it over with.

To sweeten the task, she allowed herself to start with Sebastian's sister. She, at least, sounded interesting. Sure enough, her friends had been right: Princess Viola of Belgium was best known for having briefly dated Dahlia. Most of the relevant articles were *about* Dahlia and mentioned Viola only in passing, but after some sifting, Duke finally found the original press release in which Viola had come out to the world. The release had been issued by the Belgian Crown, and one day later, a lengthy piece by Dahlia about bisexuality and her relationship with Viola appeared as the cover story for an entertainment magazine.

Intrigued despite herself, Duke double-checked the bylines. The cover story of a print magazine required plenty of advance work. That meant Dahlia had been interviewed and photographed weeks before the issue's due date. Duke skimmed the piece and found very few references to Viola. Dahlia did speak extensively of the pressure to conform to heteronormative standards and the tension placed on her relationship by her desire to come out publicly. She didn't speak of the relationship in the past tense.

The Crown's press release did. Her Royal Highness Princess Viola "had been" in a serious relationship with another woman, the release proclaimed, but that relationship "had ended." King Leopold, Queen Charlotte, and Prince Sebastian fully supported Viola, who was in the process of planning an advocacy campaign for LGBTQ+ issues. That was it. And one day later, Dahlia's glossy cover hit the shelves, featuring the titillating title: *My Alternative Royal*

Romance. The use of "alternative" made her skin prickle; although the word had enjoyed a recent comeback, it felt condescending in this context.

Duke noticed a few forum posts that, like her, had picked up on the timing of both announcements. These argued that Viola must have disagreed with Dahlia's decision to tell all, or she had learned about it at the very last minute. Generally, the posters applauded Dahlia's honesty while criticizing what they saw as Viola's duplicity.

At the bottom of her screen, one of the advertised links wanted to take her to the transcription of an interview with Princess Viola in the gallery featuring her most recent photography exhibition. Duke blinked at it, surprised that Viola was a serious enough photographer to have her own show. Perhaps it was a publicity stunt? Curious, she followed the digital breadcrumbs and discovered that Viola had taken her bachelor's degree from the prestigious University of the Arts in London, and her master's degree at the even more prestigious Royal College of Art. Two years prior, she had won the annually awarded Belgian Art Prize, and her exhibition in a prominent Parisian gallery last year was considered a success by most. There were, of course, plenty of naysayers who believed she would never have found success without the prestige of her last name—or technically, her lack thereof. Viola had three middle names, but no true surname. She was simply "of Belgium."

Duke's melancholy deepened at the thought of Viola's reality: she had grown up in the lap of luxury, but that very fact would always make her question her own accomplishments. Did they belong to her, or to her title? How must she feel to be better known for her royal status and her failed romance with Dahlia, than for her art? Duke had never been judged based on anything other than her merit. She could say that much, at least, despite the implosion of her career.

At her lowest moment, a few weeks after her second surgery, she had wished she'd never been born with an aptitude and love for soccer. But in the introspection that followed her anger, she finally realized just how much that aptitude had done for her. Without it, she wouldn't be on a train traversing the German landscape, but back in her tired West Texas hometown. Without it, she might have believed herself content to follow the path of her mother, her aunt, and her grammar school friends—to attract the attention of a sports hero (preferably the starting quarterback), marry him after high school, get pregnant, and take part-time jobs to supplement the family income.

Would she have even realized she was gay? Duke honestly wasn't sure. If any of her childhood peers had identified that way, they hadn't been out. Homosexuality was habitually denounced in the local pulpits. Any boy who preferred art to athletics, and any girl who couldn't juggle makeup and soccer balls with equal skill, was relegated to the lowest social caste. Duke wondered what her life would have been like had she chafed against the traditionally feminine presentation expected of her. Fortunately, she never had. As comfortable in a dress and heels as she was slide-tackling an opponent, she had never wrestled with any cognitive dissonance on that score.

Beginning in her teenage years, soccer had allowed her to travel far beyond the arid landscape of her community—first around the state, then the country, then the world. Much of that world had shocked her, initially. Duke rolled her eyes at the ghost of her reflection in the window, remembering how naive she had been. It hadn't taken long for her to realize that everything she had learned as "truth" was up for grabs, and that her family's way of understanding it was only one of many. She met girls of different ethnicities and religions who challenged the hierarchies and beliefs she'd been taught. And she also met girls who crushed on each other instead of on boys.

She could still remember their names: Lauren Kaplan and Jasmine Fox, one from northern California and the other from New Jersey. They had already been a couple when Duke had arrived to her first training camp for the U-18 national team. The first time she'd seen them holding hands on the bus, she hadn't been able to stop staring, feeling at once horrified and intrigued. Fortunately, they had been too wrapped up in each other to notice her scrutiny. Barely sixteen and the newest member of the squad, Duke had kept her mouth shut, waiting to see the others' reactions. The happy couple was subjected to some good-natured teasing, but that was it. The team didn't care about sexual orientation. They cared about winning.

That year, Duke persevered through each round of cuts to join the competitive squad. Over time, her Texas drawl became less pronounced. So did her bigotry. And then she went off to Chapel Hill with a full scholarship and fell in love with Rianna Gordon, the team captain. Now, when she thought of her childhood self, she felt as though she was living someone else's memories.

The deceleration of the train snapped her out of the reverie. As those disembarking in Bremen gathered their belongings, she forced her attention back to the screen. She had to move on in her research, but as she stared at the image of Princess Viola on her screen, she found herself wondering about *her* coming out story. Belgium was one of the most progressive countries in the world when it came to LGBT rights, but Viola had obviously made no public declaration about her sexuality until she was forced by Dahlia's hand. Was she ashamed?

Wanting a clearer sense of what Viola was like, she navigated to the video footage of the interview linked by the article. Sound blared from the speakers, and she jolted into action to mute them, then fished in her bag for her headphones. After an annoying advertisement in French for some kind of bizarre candy bar, the interview began. The princess was seated in a Louis XIV chair in what Duke guessed must be the press room of a Belgian palace. The Belgian royal seal marched repeatedly against the white background behind Viola.

Black slacks hugged her legs, and the fabric of her black jacket was slashed with irregular swaths of gold. Her snowy white shirt was open at the throat, an emerald pendant on a delicate gold chain resting in the hollow there. Auburn hair brushed against her collar, rising in shaggy layers to frame her freckled face.

She was beautiful and so was her voice—a low alto, rich and clear but pitched softly. As the interview continued, Duke got the distinct impression that Viola was struggling with some self-consciousness. Periodically, she tucked her hair behind her ears, even when there were no loose strands in evidence. It was a tell—a sign of her nerves. And yet, despite her reserved manner and that intriguing air of mild embarrassment, there was a subtle edginess to her that piqued Duke's interest. It was present in the corners of her mouth when she smiled, in the set of her shoulders, in the lean strength revealed by her crossed legs, in the loose curl of her fingers around the sculpted curve of the armrests. Princess Viola might not be the most confident person in public, but Duke had a feeling the opposite was true in private.

Desire stirred in her like dust on the floor of a forgotten chamber, suddenly unearthed. Discomfort followed on the heels of her surprise. She closed her eyes in confusion but opened them a moment later, not wanting to miss a moment of Viola on screen. Why couldn't Viola have been the one obsessed with sports, and her brother with art? Then, Duke might at least have something to look forward to, instead of simultaneously dreading every day on this assignment and fearing the insidious strength of that dread as it silently prompted her to self-sabotage. No. She would not be the kind of fool who threw away a second chance, just because it wasn't perfect.

"I began taking photographs because I enjoyed it," Viola was saying. "Only over time and with study did I realize the potential in all art to…" She cast her gaze up for a moment, clearly searching for the right English words. "To build bridges. We aren't born intolerant. We learn the prejudices we are taught and absorb the biases around us, to our detriment. Art is not only beautiful and powerful for its own sake. It also builds empathy, and in so doing, helps us unlearn our preconceived notions about others."

She offered the camera an intriguing half-smile that held a hint of self-deprecation. "I would never dare to suggest that my own art succeeds in this at all times. But if my photographs move someone, even once, to think about the world in a new way, I've succeeded."

That was a lofty mission, and Duke couldn't help but cynically wonder whether Princess Viola was speaking pretty words for the benefit of the public, or whether she was actually such an idealist.

She leaned closer to the screen, wondering if she could catch the hints of a lie in Viola's expression, just as the princess moistened her lips with the tip of her tongue. Oh, not fair. She was probably suffering from a dry mouth after so much speaking, but the movement was inexpressibly sensual, and it distracted Duke entirely from her mission.

Viola's interlocutor changed the subject by asking whether she ever worked in media other than photographs, and Duke listened avidly as she spoke about her interest in sketching and animation. She had also considered branching out into film. Duke wondered what it felt like to be creative in so many ways. She had no particular knack for photography—thank goodness for automatically focusing smartphones—and couldn't draw anything beyond a stick figure. And while she was a somewhat decent writer, she had no aptitude for creating her own material.

The interview ended, and the clatter of rain against the windows drew Duke's attention back to the outside world. The sky was dark in every direction, and it looked like they were heading into a front, rather than a passing storm. She hated the rain. It made her hair frizzy in a way that was thoroughly unattractive. Then again, what did that matter? She wasn't trying to attract anyone. Princess Viola would be off trying to save the world by taking pictures while Duke tried to get Sebastian to give her the time of day. All the focus and energy she had once sacrificed to soccer had to be channeled toward preserving this fledgling career. If she proved herself on this assignment, she would be given something more interesting and high profile. If she failed, she would have to reinvent herself yet again. The process had almost killed her the first time, and she didn't care to repeat it.

Maybe there was some kind of story hovering in Viola's background, and Duke would keep an ear out for any promising leads. But from what she could gather, the princess was uninvolved in the Belgian bid, and Duke needed to focus. With one final glance at the windswept landscape, she returned her focus to the screen and dutifully typed Sebastian's name into her browser.

CHAPTER FOUR

Paris, France

Viola's heart lurched as it always did when the helicopter lifted into the air, but this time, she felt as though she was leaving a piece of herself behind. In a way, of course, she was. Sebastian was not only her brother, but also her male *alter ego*, and walking out of his room had felt like amputating a limb.

It had also been a relief. As guilty as she felt at the realization, it was the truth. When Dr. Charcot had finally allowed them to see Sebastian, he had been in obvious pain. Each labored breath rattled in his lungs, and sweat slicked his forehead. Between brief periods of lucidity, he lapsed into confusion, groaning hoarsely as tremors wracked his body, contorting his limbs. Viola had held one shaking hand and forced herself to watch his torment, despite the terrible ache that hollowed out her chest.

"What is the matter?" her mother had asked, tears cascading down her cheeks. "Is he having seizures? Can you not *do* something?"

"He is experiencing withdrawal," Dr. Charcot had explained. "Muscle spasms are one of the symptoms. We have given him medication that will diminish the intensity of his discomfort."

Discomfort. It was far too mild a word for his agony. Viola shuddered at the memory, a pale echo of his convulsions. Her father rested one hand on her shoulder and squeezed gently. When she met his eyes, she saw all the pain and fear and sorrow of her own emotional state reflected. He said nothing, for which she was grateful.

A noisy helicopter was hardly the right place for any conversation she could imagine having right now.

She tightened her grip on the plastic bag given to her by one of the nurses that contained Sebastian's belongings. Once he was discharged, he would be transported to a private inpatient rehabilitation center in Switzerland. That much, her parents had decided, and she agreed with them. Sirona was a world-renowned, luxurious facility located in the Alps, but this would be no vacation for him. Family was only permitted to visit once per week, and clients were forbidden all other means of access to the outside world until their discharge.

Feeling her anxiety rise, she forcibly turned her mind toward the tasks facing her. She and her father were returning to Brussels briefly while her mother remained in Paris. While he held meetings as scheduled with the president of the Congo, Viola would meet with the personal secretary she shared with Sebastian to explain his situation and assume as many of his duties as she could. No decision had yet been made about what to tell the public, but the clock was ticking. In just over twenty-four hours, Sebastian was set to headline the launch event for Belgium's bid to host the World Cup. Unless some paparazzo ferreted out the truth in the meantime, they had one full day in which to decide what kind of announcement to make.

Her father wanted to wait until at least the following morning, when they could factor the most recent update from the hospital into their decision making. He thought they should be honest in broad strokes and say that Sebastian was in drug rehabilitation, but from what Viola could tell, he didn't have a contingency plan in case the entirety of the story ever emerged. Including the parts even they didn't know.

A fresh surge of anger accompanied thoughts of the "friends" who had abandoned her brother. A part of her wanted their names to be discovered and released so they could be dragged through the muck of social media. But that would mean releasing Sebastian's name and dragging him down with them. She didn't want that for him or for her family. He would be protected as long as he was in rehab, of course, but in some ways, the most difficult part of the process happened after he was released. Reintegrating into society—learning to live with his addiction instead of giving in to it—would be a battle. Sebastian would need peace and space, neither of which the media would give him. True privacy was an impossibility for any royal, but in that moment, Viola would have moved heaven and earth to grant him such a gift.

The helicopter's descent brought her back to herself. Thijs and André, Sebastian's chief security officer, disembarked first—a matter of habit, since the helipad was as secure as the rest of the palace. Within seconds, the pilot gave them the all-clear, and she followed her father onto the tarmac. Thijs was waiting for her, but André was on his way inside. She had seen Ruben speaking with him in a quiet corner of the hospital, and the rigid set of André's shoulders had been enough to clue her in to his mental state. He was in trouble. Sebastian had almost died on *his* watch.

"I will get away as quickly as possible," her father said. He stepped forward to embrace her. "Thank you for your help."

"See you soon, Dad." He didn't need to thank her, but she understood why he felt differently. He turned toward the stairs leading to the ground floor, shoulders bowed as though he faced a powerful headwind, and a wave of sympathy temporarily robbed her of breath. If she was feeling partly responsible for Sebastian's condition, how much heavier must that burden be for her father?

"Dad!" she called impulsively. He swiveled back toward her, shading his eyes against the sun. "I love you."

"I love you, Viola."

One of the helipad guards detached from their post to shadow him as he reached the landing. She watched him descend, feeling strangely forlorn. What was the matter with her? She had left her clingy childhood days far behind her. Perhaps these feelings were normal in a crisis.

"Your Royal Highness?" Thijs stood at her side. "Are you all right?" And then, appearing to recognize the stupidity of that question, he grimaced. "That is—"

"I'm fine," she said quickly. She had never made a habit of confiding her innermost thoughts to Thijs, and she certainly wasn't going to start now. As much to distract herself as him, she indulged her curiosity as they moved toward the door.

"How bad is this for André?"

His expression registered mild surprise before he managed to regain his customary impassivity. "It isn't good. Sebastian gave him the slip last night, and it appears this wasn't the first time."

She met his gaze in the reflective metal of the elevator doors. "You can't stop us from making mistakes."

"No," he agreed. "But we can protect you even when you do. And André failed to do that."

Viola didn't know how to answer him, and so she said nothing. She and Sebastian had enjoyed dodging their security details on a few memorable occasions as adolescents, but they had only ever gotten into minor scrapes that barely rated a captioned photo in one or another of the gossip rags. Their guards had always caught up with them eventually, and no real harm had been done.

Not so, last night. Not so for…months, if she had to guess, because it had been months since Sebastian had started losing weight. Had André truly turned a blind eye for that long? Or had Sebastian fooled him as effectively as he had hidden his secret from his family?

At the entrance to the wing of the palace that she shared with Sebastian, Thijs paused. "I need to make my report," he said. "Is there anything I can do for you? Anything or anyone I can send for?"

"No." Viola was looking forward to the opportunity to be as alone as she could be. There was always a guard posted outside their apartments, though none would follow her inside. But as he walked away, she felt a rush of guilt at brushing him off so brusquely. "Thijs—thank you. For your kindness today."

He turned and offered a shallow bow. "I am very sorry your family is going through this, Your Highness."

I am very sorry. How many times had she uttered that same phrase to some acquaintance or friend who was going through a difficult time? The words seemed so paltry now. But what could someone like Thijs do? What could anyone do, in the end, except Sebastian himself? No matter how compassionate or upset or assertive any of them became, only Sebastian had the key to his own recovery.

She had been with him an hour ago, but he felt so far away now. Bypassing the door to her own set of rooms, she entered Sebastian's instead. She was greeted by one of her own photos—a shot of him golfing in the St. Andrews Links tournament, just before his brief stint as a professional. She had captured him at the end of his swing as he followed through, the ball a white blur against the vivid blue sky. She remembered when he had decided to hang this picture here, remembered telling him he "didn't have to." The insinuation that he was placing her work in such a prominent position out of some sense of familial obligation had displeased him.

"Stop being self-deprecating," he had said. "It doesn't suit you and it won't sell your art."

He made those kinds of proclamations frequently—statements bordering on aphorism. Where did his confidence come from, and why could he lose it so easily in a sudden spiral of insecurity? How had he become so sure of himself, yet so vulnerable to the opinions of others? Part of his posturing at times might have derived from the expectation that a man—especially a prince—should know what he was about, even if he really didn't. She wondered if that stereotype had helped to lead him astray in his drug use. Perhaps he had believed himself in control, despite evidence to the contrary.

She walked past his sitting room and entered the bedroom. Decorated in muted shades of burgundy and gold, it was a tidy and comfortable space. The Belgian flag adorned the wall next to Sebastian's bed, and a signed photo of his favorite football player hung over his desk. On his dresser, a picture frame boasted three scenes from their childhood. Finding herself drawn to it, Viola was about to take a closer look when her phone buzzed with an incoming call.

But when she extracted the phone from her pocket, it was dark. The vibration, she realized, was coming from the bag holding Sebastian's clothes. His phone must be in there, too. She hadn't even thought to check.

Viola scrambled to grab the device before the caller hung up. The screen revealed a photo of a brown-haired man wearing glasses and a gray suit. She didn't recognize his face, but his name was familiar. What if this was one of the so-called friends Sebastian had been with last night? If she answered the phone as her brother, she might be able to learn more about what had happened to him.

There was no time to deliberate. She accepted the call and pitched her voice an octave lower than usual. "Hello?"

"Sebastian, we have a problem," Henri said. His voice was shrill with stress. "Mother of Pearl just canceled for tomorrow."

Viola's mind raced as she tried to make sense of what she was hearing. The World Cup event was tomorrow, which was probably what this Henri person was referring to. But what was Mother of Pearl? He hadn't been referring to the iridescent coating of seashells—that much was clear. She tried to remember what Sebastian had told her about the event, praying that her brain would make the necessary connection.

"Did you hear me?"

"Uh…" Desperate now, she tried to buy time. "What happened?"

"Food poisoning."

Viola cradled his phone against her neck and fumbled with her own, pulling up her web browser. She searched *Mother of Pearl World Cup,* a curse slipping out as her trembling fingers made typos.

"Jesus, are you still fucked up from last night?" Henri delivered the question in a harsh whisper.

Viola's heart seized. Last night. Henri knew something about where Sebastian had been, what he had done. But he hadn't mentioned the hospital, so he might not know the full story. Had he been with Sebastian, or only in communication with him?

"Uh, maybe," Viola said. She had to keep him talking without raising his suspicions. She took a gamble. "It was a rough one. I might need you to fill in some details."

"Not now." Henri's tone was exasperated and devoid of surprise. Whoever he was, Sebastian's overindulgence wasn't news to him. "This is a crisis! I need you to focus."

To get more information, she would have to play along. Viola looked down at her phone. She saw it near the top of the screen—a headline on some entertainment site about how Mother of Pearl was set to headline the opening festivities that would mark the launch of Belgium and the Netherlands's shared bid. That was it. Mother of Pearl was a band, and they had canceled. Henri needed Sebastian to help him find a replacement.

"I can handle this." Struck by her own epiphany, she forgot to modulate her voice, and the words came out at her own natural pitch. Wincing, she coughed hard to mask her mistake, then cleared her throat. "My sister knows DJ Smitten. Maybe she's free."

Henri's noisy sigh indicated his displeasure. "Beggars can't be choosers. She'll have to do. Let me know when you have confirmation?"

"I will," Viola said.

"Fine," Henri said. "See you in the morning. And…" he paused. "Take care of yourself. Tomorrow's a big day."

"Don't worry." Viola tried to sound confident and reassuring. "Everything's under control."

"Sure." Henri sounded anything but. "Talk to you later."

When the call disconnected, Viola sank onto the bed. A fresh wave of dizziness washed over her, and she closed her eyes, working to modulate her short, sharp breaths. She had to think this through. Should she go to her parents? Ruben would be able to track Henri down, but Henri would probably call his lawyer instead of sharing what he knew. Even if he agreed to be both cooperative and discreet, someone else could come out of the woodwork at any point with information powerful enough to start a scandal that would cast a pall over the Belgian-Dutch bid.

A surge of anxiety propelled her from the bed and she began to pace. Sebastian was a football fanatic, and the joint bid had been his idea. He had been working on the preparations for over a year, and the thought of his efforts coming to naught made Viola sick. She could see no way out. Her family could have found a way to dissemble about a short absence, but now, he would miss every moment of the month-long festivities he had been so instrumental in arranging.

When her head began to throb, she braced herself against the dresser in an attempt to stretch the taut muscles in her neck. Instead, the triptych picture frame caught her eye again, and she bent down for a closer look.

The first photograph displayed them as ten-year-olds, petting a giraffe at a wildlife sanctuary in South Africa. They were both wearing identical ponchos—she remembered the downpour they had weathered during a morning hike—and for a moment, she couldn't decipher who was who. Upon closer examination, of course, the truth revealed itself: her features had always been a touch narrower and sharper than his, and the awe in her gaze as she looked up into the giraffe's gentle face was at odds with his fierce expression of triumph—as though he had tamed the creature himself.

She picked up the frame, grief and nostalgia burning in her chest. The second photograph was a family portrait memorializing their trip to Antarctica—a gift to her and Sebastian on their thirteenth birthday. They were so thoroughly bundled up in fur-lined parkas that Viola doubted even her mother would be able to distinguish between them.

The final photo had been taken in the same year, somewhere in the Caribbean. They were on a small sailboat, Sebastian trimming the mainsail while Viola handled the jib. In swimsuits, they were easy to tell apart, but hair length and suit-cut aside, the resemblance was still uncanny. She peered down at him, selfishly wanting to erase the memories from this morning in the hospital: Sebastian suffering, frightened, weak. This younger version of her brother stared back at her with a carefree smile nearly identical to the one she recognized in the mirror. His nose was a hint wider than hers, but otherwise, Viola could have been looking at herself.

Her fingers went nerveless at the epiphany, and the frame fell to the floor. Automatically, she bent to pick it up. It was broken in several places and spiderweb cracks now marred the protective covering of the final picture, obscuring the faces below. Faces that were nearly identical. Faces that could *become* identical with only a few cosmetic changes.

What if? What if she could become her brother and impersonate him for the duration of his hospitalization? The World Cup bid would be saved, as would Sebastian's privacy. He could recover in peace, free from the attentions of the hovering paparazzi. And she might even be able to learn which of his so-called friends had put him into that car last night, alone and unconscious and on the cusp of suffocation.

No sooner had the plan begun to take shape in her mind than she realized she couldn't do it alone. At the very least, her security would have to know, and she didn't relish the prospect of trying to convince Thijs, with his unshakeable faith in rules and protocols. If he chose to interpret her plan as a risk to her own security, he would be justified in telling Ruben, who would promptly inform her parents.

Still holding the cracked frame, she paced the length of the room. How could she convince him? His impeccable professionalism had precluded any kind of friendship from developing between them, and his propriety gave her nothing to work with in terms of blackmail. She had no chips with which to bargain. Was that how Sebastian had flown under the radar for so long—by purchasing André's silence?

André. She could confide in him. He was in disgrace and likely riddled with guilt. He would want a chance to set it right. And as Sebastian's chief of security, he would be able to help her impersonate him. Together, they would find a way to ensure Thijs's loyalty.

She called him, but his phone went to voice mail. Maybe he was in a meeting. Maybe he had been fired and his phone confiscated. Thijs would know how to reach him, but she would have to tread carefully. He answered on the first ring.

"Your Highness? Are you all right?"

Why did he keep asking that? Of course she wasn't. "I want to speak with André."

"May I ask why?"

"You may ask."

He sighed when he realized she wasn't going to elaborate. "He's been placed on administrative leave."

The price of his negligence. Viola wasn't surprised. "Then he should be free to meet with me. I want to speak with him face-to-face. Today. Now."

"He may have already left the palace," Thijs said. "But I will see that he receives your message as soon as possible."

"Thank you."

When she disconnected the call, Viola threw open Sebastian's closet. A small, shrill voice in the back of her mind was screaming in panic at the folly of this nascent plan, but she ignored it. Instead, she took off her own shirt and pulled on one of his, then examined herself in the full-length mirror on the back of the door.

Not bad. It was roomy in the shoulders, but she didn't look completely ridiculous. A few months ago, any shirt of his would have hung from her frame—another reminder of all the weight he had lost, and what it meant. Pushing past the renewed surge of guilt, she narrowed her eyes at her reflection. Not bad, but also not ideal. To pull this off, she would need her own version of his wardrobe. That would necessitate a shopping trip, and she couldn't afford the risk of shopping for men's suits in public. She would invariably be spotted, and someone's tweet would turn into a tabloid headline that would lead to the discovery of Sebastian's condition. So, back to square one: finding someone to trust.

Her phone rang. She hesitated upon seeing an unfamiliar number, then answered. "Hello?"

"Your Royal Highness, this is André." His voice was slightly hoarse, his tone subdued. "Thijs said you wished to meet with me as soon as possible."

"Yes. Please."

"I'm outside your apartments, but—"

"I'm in Sebastian's. Feel free to let yourself in." She cradled the phone in the dip between her neck and shoulder, freeing both hands to frantically undo the buttons of her brother's shirt.

"I...can't. I no longer have my keys."

She should have guessed. Knowing Ruben, it was no surprise that the palace security did not take administrative leave lightly. "I'll come to the door in just a moment."

Viola disconnected the call and stuffed Sebastian's shirt back where it belonged. She opened the door to the familiar sight of André, dressed casually in jeans and a T-shirt. But the skin beneath his eyes was stained dark by fatigue, and his face wore a haunted expression she had never seen. His earpiece, subtle as it was designed to be, was conspicuously absent.

"May I come in?"

Only when he spoke did Viola realize her rudeness. "Yes, of course." She led André into Sebastian's office, and they sat at the small conference table. He looked at her directly but his fingers drummed softly on the tabletop. She found a grim satisfaction in his clear display of nerves.

"I need to know everything you do about Sebastian. Did you realize he had a problem?"

André flinched, but his gaze did not drop. "Yes."

Viola kept a firm grip on her anger. She wanted him to see it, but she couldn't let it consume her. "Why didn't you say anything?"

"I did."

"To whom?" Surprise eroded her control, and the words came out more harshly than intended.

"To him." André brought his hands to the table, palms open as if in supplication. "I knew he had been using hard drugs on and off for a while, but it started becoming more consistent—and more consistently heroin—about three months ago. I suggested that he talk with someone. I offered him a hotline number."

Viola leaned forward, her own hands knotted together, wanting so desperately to fill the gaps in her own knowledge of Sebastian that had been revealed by this crisis.

"What did he do?"

"He told me he would call. I don't know whether he ever did, but shortly after that conversation, he started dodging his guards. At first, he acted as though it was accidental. After I confronted him for the third time, he stopped pretending. Even when I increased his security detail, he managed to evade us—mostly because he had the help of his 'friends.'" André spat the word. "Last weekend, I told him that if he didn't check himself into a facility within the week, I would report on his activities to Ruben."

André's words were crystal clear, and yet they made no sense. He wasn't describing her brother. The Sebastian she knew rarely told anything more than a white lie and didn't have the urge or the need to sneak around. Until recently, he'd had a reputation for stodginess, mostly perpetuated by Princess Camille of Monaco, who had dated him briefly before deciding he was too "dull" for her tastes. The public had found the prospect of the union of two royal houses to be tantalizing, and the media had played up the glamour of the match. Once things went south, of course, the fickle entertainment world had enjoyed angsting over the breakup just as much.

Viola had done her best to cheer him up in the aftermath, and until now, she thought her efforts had helped. Within a few weeks, he had no longer seemed as melancholy. But what if he had been more affected by Camille's rejection than she realized, despite the brevity of their relationship? Had Viola failed him as a sister, a friend, a confidante? Had he first turned to heroin then?

"Your Royal Highness." André's address snapped her attention back to the present. "If I could relive the past few months, I would make very different choices. I am so very sorry for the role I played in enabling Sebastian's addiction and endangering his life. You know I have been placed on administrative leave, but if there is anything I can do to help him or you, I will do it."

His offer was a flare of hope illuminating her despair. Neither of them could change the past, but together, they might be able to improve Sebastian's future. Or, André would decide that her plan was insane and dangerous, and that the best way to get back into Ruben's good graces would be to report her. But there was no way to pull it off without him. Time to roll the dice.

"I have Sebastian's personal items from when he was admitted to the hospital, including his phone. An hour ago, Henri called him to—"

"Henri! Does he know anyth—" André caught himself. "I beg your pardon for the interruption, ma'am."

He was fairly vibrating with tension, and Viola needed to know why. "What were you going to ask me?"

"I believe Sebastian may have been with Henri last night. Did he say anything to that effect?"

"He said enough to confirm your suspicion."

André's posture grew even more rigid, if that were possible. "It's somewhere to start, at least. I'm surprised he told you anything. I thought he would have hung up as soon as you answered the phone."

Viola decided to confess what she had done before she said anything about what she intended to do. "I pretended to be Sebastian."

André stared at her blankly. "Excuse me?"

"I lowered my voice. It worked."

His expression became thoughtful. "That was clever. What did you learn?"

"It sounded as though Henri was with Sebastian for part of the night and knew he was, to quote him, 'fucked up.' But I don't think he was there when Sebastian lost consciousness. Henri didn't say anything about the hospital."

"Have you told Ruben?"

"No. And I don't plan to."

"What? Why not?"

André's shock was laced with anger. That meant he really did care about Sebastian, not just about his job. Viola swallowed hard. This was the crucial moment.

"Because I plan to keep pretending. And I need your help to do it."

André's mouth opened, then closed. As surprise gave way to comprehension, his eyes narrowed. "You want to impersonate Sebastian."

"Until he's out of rehab, yes. If my parents announce his condition, he won't have a moment's peace once he leaves the facility. If they don't announce it, they'll have to make excuses for Sebastian's disappearance from the public scene, and the media will ferret out the truth anyway." She leaned forward, silently willing his skepticism to yield to her logic. "If I impersonate him and am discovered, what's the worst that can happen? The world will learn a truth they were already bound to discover. And along the way, I might be able to learn what actually happened yesterday. Wouldn't you like to know who abandoned him to the mercy of an unknown driver while he was slowly asphyxiating? Because I sure as hell would."

André said nothing. She forced herself to hold his gaze while the silence grew and grew, until it seemed to suck all the oxygen from the room.

"If you're caught, you'll be dragged through the mud, too," he finally said. "The media might even make it worse for you than for him."

Viola hesitated, choosing her words carefully. "Right now, you're feeling guilt for what you didn't say. I feel guilt for what I didn't *see*. I'm his twin, André. I should have known. I'll do whatever it takes to protect him now. But I can't, without you." She extended one open hand across the table. "Will you help me make this right?"

For one long, agonizing moment, she thought he would refuse. When he finally reached out to clasp her hand, she exhaled sharply in relief.

"So," he said. "Where do we start?"

"The top priority is tomorrow's event in the Hague. I'll speak with Maes about filling in for Sebastian there—I don't want Maes to know our plan until it's too late for him to get in the way. Today, now, I need you to go shopping for me."

"Shopping." He laughed sharply. "This is crazy. You know that, right?"

Viola stood. "I know. And Thijs is going to be a problem."

For the first time since he had entered Sebastian's apartments, André smiled. "No, he won't. Leave him to me."

CHAPTER FIVE

The Hague, The Netherlands

The hotel wasn't anything to write home about, but Duke had slept in far worse places. She didn't unpack anything except her toiletries and the suit she needed for tomorrow. What would be the point? The exhibition match would wrap up late at night, and the next morning, she was booked for Brussels. At least there she would have a more permanent residence. Goal Sports had arranged for her to sublet the apartment of a reporter from its parent station who was on long-term assignment in Asia.

As she left the bathroom, her phone buzzed with a text message from Toby Hale. Duke wanted to grimace but needed to break the habit, especially where he was concerned. She was grateful to Juno for enlisting his help when it became clear she would need a new career, and equally grateful that he'd managed to get the network to offer her a job, even though a freelance reporting gig wasn't as high-profile as the commentator position Duke had hoped for. Still, it was something, and she had to start somewhere. She soon learned that Toby was one of those people who didn't do favors out of altruism, but to get a power trip. At every opportunity, he reminded her of just how generous he was being. And she suspected that he also enjoyed cashing in on the minor prestige of being seen with her.

At bar around corner from hotel. Fairy Ring. Stop by when u get in.

Duke didn't like feeling obligated, but she was also glad of the excuse to get out of her own head for a while. After reapplying her lip gloss, she was ready.

The bar in question was annexed to a so called "coffeehouse" of the same name. On her first trip to the Netherlands on the under-23 team, she hadn't understood why everyone else kept laughing about them. Finally, an older and wiser Rosa had taken pity and let her in on the secret: a coffeehouse in this country was a place that sold marijuana. Back then, none of them had dared to set foot inside, terrified that the secondhand smoke would contaminate their blood enough to register on one of the dreaded random drug tests.

Now, she didn't have to worry about that. The realization was strangely liberating. Still, she didn't want to try her very first drug without any backup, and she didn't trust Toby.

She found him in the bar section of the establishment, a half-filled stein of beer on the table before him and the end of a joint in his hand. He was sitting with two men she didn't know. Five years Juno's senior, Toby shared her hair color and the dimple on her chin, but the resemblance ended there. After a solid college soccer career, he'd been drafted by a Major League Soccer team, only to sit the bench. His entrée into journalism had been the result of helping Goal Sports break a story on doping, in which he'd played the inside man. Pushing through her uneasiness, Duke slid into the space across from him. He saluted her with his beer and introduced her to his friends, both corporate ex-pats. As they made mindless conversation, she could feel their attraction hanging in the air like smoke, suffocating her. The strangers argued over who would pay for the next round, and when it arrived, they began trading college sports stories in a clear game of one-upmanship.

Duke wished she'd had the foresight to take some pain relievers before leaving the hotel, because she was going to need them to combat the tension headache that was manifesting behind her eyes. Clearly, Toby had not divulged her sexuality to his buddies. As much as she appreciated his tactful silence, she was also certain it was self-serving. Intuition told her he didn't care at all about her privacy. No, he wanted them to think she was straight because of the effect it would have on his standing in their eyes.

As she pretended to care about the conversation, her mind churned over how to make her escape without offending Toby. If only she and her family weren't estranged, she could have texted one of them requesting a phone call. But they hadn't spoken in almost a year, and she couldn't ask Juno to rescue her from her own brother.

Claustrophobia rose up, sudden and suffocating, propelling her out of the chair before she could even try to resist it. All three men stared up at her with red-streaked eyes.

"Gentlemen, I need to visit the ladies'," she said, marveling that her voice could sound so calm while panic thrashed inside her chest. She retreated to the bathroom, grateful it was a single-person stall, and sat down on the toilet to run through one of Dr. Pena's relaxation exercises. Before her career change, she had never been victimized by these waves of anxiety, and she still wasn't used to them. Maybe she never would be.

As the grip of her panic began to ease, she tried a familiar reframing technique. Yes, one dream was lost to her, but she was embarking on a new adventure. Yes, she was uncomfortable, but no one ever improved without discomfort. How many of her childhood friends had ever left Texas, much less the United States? She was one of the lucky ones. Staying positive was the only way to seek out happiness.

And if the refrain sounded hollow right now, so be it. She would keep repeating it until she believed it.

Brussels, Belgium

Viola's guilt compounded every time her secretary thanked her for taking over Sebastian's duty in The Hague. Vincent Maes was relatively new to the secretariat, and she felt sorry for him now. His predecessor had been an unflappable septuagenarian whose family had served the crown for generations. Maes was high-strung, and this was an exceptionally bad day. Viola told him as little as she could get away with—Sebastian had taken ill and would not be able to fulfill his obligations in The Hague tomorrow—but his reaction was proportional to what had *really* happened.

"Will he be all right?" the bespectacled secretary had asked her nervously. And then he blanched. "But of course he will—I'm so very sorry for indulging in hyperbole, Your Highness, and—"

"The easiest solution," Viola had said, considering the act of interruption to be a kindness, in this case, "is for me to take over for him tomorrow. I have already informed my parents and King Maximilian of my attendance, and all I require at this point is a copy of Sebastian's itinerary and speech."

"Of course, yes, of course. I cannot tell you how much I appreciate your willingness to step in."

For a moment, Viola had feared he might stand there thanking her all day, but Maes retreated behind his desk to call his secretary with the request. What was the title for the secretary of a secretary, anyway? Sensing a hint of hysteria in the thought, she forced herself to focus on the pragmatics.

"I'll need his transportation changed to my name as well."

"Certainly, yes. He was booked on a commercial flight—first class, of course, leaving early tomorrow morning."

"That will be fine."

Now she watched him move, birdlike, around the office as he completed the preparations, and she silently apologized for what she was about to do. If he was anxious now, he was going to be a wreck once she had crossed the Rubicon by impersonating her brother. Her parents might understand after the initial shock passed, but they would still worry. Ruben, of course, would be livid. By going through with her plan, she was taking responsibility for all of that emotional damage. It was a sobering thought.

There was always the other choice: to forget this charade and follow her parents' lead, to gamble that they could control the narrative and its timing. But even if they succeeded, the world would learn about Sebastian's struggle at his most vulnerable moment. He would be temporarily protected by his rehabilitation facility, but he couldn't stay there forever. And the media might be able to solve the mystery of his overdose more quickly than Ruben's discreet inquiries could, in which case the monarchy would be on the defensive.

Her spiraling thoughts were stilled when Maes appeared before her, proffering a black dossier.

"Thank you," she said before he could launch back into his own professions of gratitude.

"Of course, Your Royal Highness. Should you need any other information, feel free to contact me at any time."

"I will." Viola left quickly, hurrying back through the corridors toward her own set of rooms. As she walked, she checked her phone for a message from André, but there was nothing. She hadn't heard from him since a brief text confirming that he had picked up the clothing items she needed. That was the low-hanging fruit. His next order of business was to inform Thijs of their plan in such a way as to ensure he didn't run straight to his superior. Viola had no idea how he planned to accomplish that, and André had refused to tell her. Her best guess was that Thijs owed him a favor—a big one. That, or André was resorting to blackmail. As much as her ignorance rankled, she suspected she should be grateful for it. There was more than one kind of protection.

Once in her apartment, she hesitated. Fatigue loomed like a wave, but she was much too keyed up to sleep, and there was far too much to accomplish in the next…she checked her watch. Twenty-two hours remained until the bid launch. She hadn't eaten since the early morning, but the thought of food held no appeal. Even so, she had to at least try. Performing Sebastian would be not only a mental challenge, but also a physical one. Fainting would ruin everything.

But as she began to dial the kitchen, her phone rang, accompanied by her father's image.

"Father? Is Sebastian—" She had been about to say "all right," but even if his condition had continued to improve, there was no way he was even close to all right. "Stable?" she finished.

"Yes." He sounded more tired than she had ever heard him. "I am nearly finished here. Will you be ready to leave within the hour?"

As much as she wanted to see Sebastian, she recoiled from the thought of returning to the hospital to watch over him as he moaned and sweated and trembled. Guilt followed hard on the heels of that revelation. How must her mother feel, who had been at his side all day? Still, it was a relief to realize she had an excuse to stay away.

"I want to be there, but I need to stay here." The words tasted sour. "I told Maes that Sebastian is ill but that I will fill in for him tomorrow. It's only a Band-Aid, but we'll have a little more time to decide what to do and say about his condition."

It was the truth, and yet it wasn't. All the doubt she had felt earlier returned to plague her, and for a moment, she considered abandoning the entire scheme. Was the benefit truly worth the cost? Not to herself—she was taking this on entirely of her own accord—but to those who would have to keep her secret?

"Good thinking," her father said, and the words held a hint of his characteristic warmth. "Stay and prepare. Get some sleep. I know Sebastian will thank you for stepping in. He…" His voice caught, and tears pricked Viola's eyes in empathy. "He has worked so hard on the bid."

And just like that, her doubts disappeared. Her father felt the same way she did—that all Sebastian's efforts shouldn't come to naught. She had heard his despair, and she could fix it. Part of it, anyway. Galvanized, she began to pace the room.

"I know he has. Let's not be hasty. I can continue to fill in for him."

While that was technically true, they both knew it wasn't a real solution. As soon as she appeared tomorrow, the bottom feeders around the periphery of the legitimate media would start sniffing for clues about Sebastian's illness. The longer he remained out of the public eye, the more attention his absence would receive. Real journalists with powerful networks of resources and contacts would join the hunt. And the house of cards her family was building would collapse.

"Thank you." Her father cleared his throat, and when he spoke again, there was no evidence of tears. "Do you have a message for your brother?"

There was so much she wanted to say, to ask, but it all boiled down to one thing. "Tell him I love him."

"I will."

The chime of her doorbell punctuated his promise. Only someone on her security staff could ring it, and she had a feeling she knew which one was insisting on speaking with her face-to-face at this moment.

"I have to go, Father. Be safe. I love you."

She waited to hear his, "You, too," before disconnecting the call. The screen below the foyer camera revealed both Thijs and André, and she quickly unlocked the door. As the men came inside, she looked closely at Thijs. His shoulders were hunched and his gaze, when she met it, was weary. He had always radiated competence and efficiency, but now he seemed...broken.

"Are we going to have a problem?"

He shook his head slightly. "No. I'm going to help you."

She couldn't help it—she had to know. "Why?"

"Because in this case, the end justifies the means."

Viola waited for him to elaborate, but he didn't. Well, fine. If he wanted to remain cryptic, so be it. She couldn't afford to waste time ferreting out his motives. His declaration of loyalty would have to be enough for now.

"Where would you like these, Your Royal Highness?" André asked into the silence, proffering two large shopping bags.

"Just there is fine. I'll take them back to my room later." As he obliged, she exhaled slowly, overwhelmed and uncertain of how to prioritize. Asking for help was not her strong suit, but she was going to have to swallow her pride. She gestured toward the kitchen. "Let's have something to drink."

She offered beer, but Thijs refused and looked askance at André when he accepted. Viola wanted to tell him not to be so judgmental, but the strain she saw on his face and heard in his voice dissuaded her from pushing him right now. Once they were all seated, she spread out her hands.

"I don't know where to begin and I want to hear your thoughts. At this point, all I know is that I need to review Sebastian's agenda and speech, and get a crash course in his perspective on football."

"After the speeches, you'll be taken to a VIP box to watch the exhibition game," André said. "You also need a list of the people on that invite list. Some you will know, but others you won't."

"Yes. Good." Viola pulled out her phone to take notes. "What else?"

"Social media," André said. "Maes's staff will continue to handle his scheduled tweets and posts, as he does yours. But Sebastian is more active off the cuff than you a—"

"Before any of that," Thijs interjected, "you need a haircut."

Viola couldn't believe she'd forgotten something so essential to her disguise. For one insane moment, she wanted to laugh—but as the sound bubbled up in her throat, she realized tears would not be far behind. Clamping her mouth shut, she fought to control her emotions.

"The question is whether the palace barbers are trustworthy," André mused.

"Too many people are going to be in on this secret as it is," Thijs said. "One of us should cut Her Royal Highness's hair."

André shook his head. "Sebastian doesn't get fifteen-euro cuts with electric clippers. He has a distinctive style. We need a professional."

"I trust Antonio," Viola said, hoping her voice didn't betray her internal struggle. Antonio DuBois was the younger of the Crown's two barbers. He was also gay. After she had come out so suddenly, propelled by Dahlia's betrayal, Antonio was one of the first people to offer support. She could still remember the unexpected card Thijs had delivered on his behalf while she was rehearsing her answers for a press conference following the family's announcement. In his carefully penned message, Antonio had applauded her courage and promised she would have the full support of every LGBTQ member of the palace staff. He had even rounded up their signatures, and whenever she thought of how much of his spare time he had freely devoted to the project, she experienced an echo of the same awe and gratitude that she had felt that day.

There were more names on the card than she had anticipated, and over the ensuing weeks, each approached her individually to declare their loyalty. It was as though she had suddenly discovered an inheritance—not of money, but of people. Of family.

"You're certain?" Thijs interrupted her thoughts.

"Yes."

"I'll make the call."

While they waited for Antonio to arrive, Viola reviewed the dossier Maes had provided. Conveniently, he had included a calendar for the entire month with the dates of Sebastian's appearances highlighted. Viola glanced through them quickly. Her own calendar held only one event she couldn't somehow avoid—the opening reception for an exhibition of her photography at a gallery in Prague, three weeks from now. Fortunately, Sebastian had no appearances on that particular day, so theoretically, she should be able to make it work.

"I'm going to need a wig," she murmured, hoping Antonio would be able to help.

When he arrived at the front door, Thijs ushered him into the kitchen where Viola was still concentrating on the documents before her. She looked up as they approached. He seemed ill at ease—no doubt because he had been summoned without any explanation—and she tried to smile reassuringly at him. Instead, his frown deepened.

"Hello, Antonio." She indicated the chair to her left. "Please, sit."

"Your Royal Highness, it is always a pleasure." He sat and rested his palms on the table. "Forgive my presumption, but…are you well?"

Again, that terrible laughter threatened. She swallowed it down, suddenly wishing for a mirror. Was all her fear and exhaustion and anxiety written plainly on her face?

"No, I'm not," she said, hearing the hoarseness in her own voice. "I need your help. But what I'm about to ask must be held in the strictest confidence, even from my parents. I can only assure you that I have my family's best interests at heart in making this request. May I count on your confidence?"

He didn't answer immediately, but his hesitation only increased her trust. What kind of person would make such a promise without thinking it through? She held his gaze steadily, and he finally nodded.

"Yes. Whatever the secret is, I'll keep it."

"Thank you." She took a deep breath. "Last night, Sebastian overdosed on heroin and almost died. He is in the hospital now, and as soon as he's stable enough, he'll be transferred to a rehab facility."

It was hard to say the words, and even harder to watch Antonio's reaction. But instead of the judgment she had feared, his expression betrayed only compassion.

"I'm so sorry," he said. "And so glad he will recover. How are your parents?"

It was hard for her to think of them—to remember their fear and sadness and confusion from this morning, and to imagine how they would react once her plan was in motion.

"They are relieved that Sebastian will pull through, but worried about his full recovery. He has a difficult road ahead."

Antonio nodded. "Yes. But he has your support, and that will make all the difference." He offered a lopsided smile. "It did for me."

It took several seconds for the import of his words to sink in, but when it did, Viola sat back in her chair, stunned. "You…?"

She trailed off, unable to complete the thought. He had been an addict? Was still one? Dully, she realized she didn't know the proper tense to use. "Thank you," she said instead. "Thank you for sharing that."

"You confided in me," he said, as if everyone repaid trust with trust.

"How are you now?" she asked, hoping he would understand that the question had nothing to do with his ability to do his job, and everything to do with Sebastian's prospects.

"I wish I could tell you the urge goes away." His gaze dropped briefly to the tabletop before he forced himself to meet her eyes. "But it doesn't. The craving is always there, some days worse than others. I've learned to manage it. I know Sebastian can, too."

His pragmatic confidence was exactly what she needed, and a small, detached part of her wondered whether he knew that. Was he manipulating her, reassuring her, or both? Did it really matter?

She searched his face for any signs of deceit but found nothing but openness and empathy.

"I hope you're right." Across the table, Thijs stirred, reminding her that she had not yet made her request of Antonio. She closed her eyes briefly, trying to focus her thoughts and gather her eloquence. "Sebastian has a very full calendar this month, as I'm sure you know. Obviously, he won't be able to keep his engagements, but it kills me to think that all his hard work on the bid might be threatened when news breaks about his overdose. Not to mention how hard it will be for him once he's back in the public eye."

Antonio nodded, and his hand moved as though he wanted to touch her arm, though he remembered himself before he did. "Unsolicited contact with a royal," the rule books called it—a breach of protocol and grounds for dismissal. She took a deep breath, hoping Antonio's own experience with addiction would make him amenable to what she was about to ask.

"I want to impersonate him, and I need your help to do it." Surprise flashed across his face, and she felt the need to clarify her motives. "Not to hide the truth from the public for its own sake, but to help Sebastian heal and keep our bid hopes alive."

"I understand." The corners of his mouth quirked. "It's a bold and courageous idea, ma'am."

Viola let one sharp peal of laughter escape. "It's madness, and everyone here knows it. In less than twelve hours, Sebastian needs to be in The Hague. My parents and Secretary Maes think I'm filling in for him as myself, but that's not my plan. I need you to cut and style my hair to look like his, and I need a wig so I can leave the palace as myself without suspicion."

"I can't have a wig ready from your own hair so soon, but while one is being made, I can get something that will work well enough in the short term." Antonio pressed his palms to the tabletop. "If you can give me a few minutes to collect my things, I'll have your hair cut within the hour."

Protocol demanded that he not stand before she formally dismissed him from her presence, and Viola used that power now to keep him where he was. Intuition told her she could trust him, but where had that intuition been while Sebastian had been spiraling into heroin abuse? She didn't fully trust it anymore, and the effect was paralyzing. But paralysis wasn't an option right now. If she was wandering in the wilderness without a compass, so be it. She had to take a calculated risk.

"No one else can know," she said, trying to make her voice firm.

"No one else will," he said, holding her gaze.

She wanted to look to Thijs and André for their reactions, but she couldn't use them as a crutch. "Thank you." She felt as though she should say more but didn't know what. Instead, she held out her hand, and he grasped it gently before getting to his feet. "Will you want to work here, or in the bathroom?"

He looked around the kitchen. "Here. I'll be back soon with everything I need."

Thijs walked him out, which left her in André's company. If she had been alone, Viola would have momentarily succumbed to the wave of fatigue urging her to sit, pillow her head on her arms, and rest her gritty eyes, just for a moment. Instead, she remained on her feet.

"Have you heard anything more from Sebastian's friends?" André asked into the silence.

"I haven't checked." After patting herself down, she realized Sebastian's phone was still in her bedroom. "Just a moment."

When she powered it on, her heart stuttered, a fresh spear of adrenaline lancing her fatigue. An hour ago, Maria Fournier had texted her brother. The daughter of a film director and an actress, Maria was an up-and-coming model. Over the past six months, she and Sebastian had engaged in an on-again, off-again romance. The tabloids loved their tempestuous relationship, in which Maria always seemed to be "storming off" about something. Whenever she saw a fresh headline, Viola reached out to her brother, but he always insisted there was nothing wrong and the incident had been overblown by the media. Viola had never pushed him, but now she wished she had.

She hurried back into the kitchen. "He has a text from Maria."

André's lip curled. "She's an enabler. What did she say?"

Viola clicked through to the text. *How are u feeling, baby? Worried I haven't heard from u.* She passed the phone to André, who showed it to Thijs upon his return.

"So worried she didn't send him a message all day." Viola welcomed the anger blazing in her chest, keeping the exhaustion at bay. "Do you think she knows he ended up in the hospital?"

"Yes, but that's just a hunch." André returned the phone to her. "What if you stick to the truth as much as possible? You woke up in the hospital without knowing how you got there..."

Viola picked up his thread. "...My parents were called, and I managed to convince them this was the first time I've tried heroin. They've put me in counseling and are watching me closely."

"That will give you a good excuse to limit your social engagements," Thijs said.

"Though I might have to rethink that strategy at some point, if we aren't getting answers." She watched Thijs bristle at the thought of putting herself in any kind of danger and forestalled his protest by holding up one hand. "I don't want to borrow trouble. I'll play dumb for now, and maybe, if she does know what happened, she'll let something slip."

"You'll see Henri tomorrow," André reminded her. "He might know more in person than he did on the phone."

The bright rush of anger was fading, under assault by the renewed strength of her fatigue. There was so much to do, so many goals to juggle. One misspoken word or unconscious action could doom her entire plan. Viola looked between the two men, knowing neither would blame her if she decided not to go through with it.

But she would blame herself. Sebastian deserved her best effort. Even if she failed, she would show him that he was worth the risk. Maybe that knowledge would help to guide him out of the dark maze of his addiction. Maybe not. Regardless, she had to try.

CHAPTER SIX

The Hague, The Netherlands

The Dutch princess was staring at her.

At first, Duke had assumed their gazes met by coincidence, but almost every time she raised her head from her notebook, the girl—Eveline, she reminded herself—was fixated on her.

Surreptitiously, she tried to catch her reflection in the screen of her phone. Was she having some sort of wardrobe or makeup malfunction? It didn't seem likely, especially since none of her colleagues in the press section had commented on her appearance, and she knew they weren't shy. There were only two possibilities: Eveline found her attractive or had recognized her. The former made her uncomfortable, as Duke knew from her research that the princess was barely sixteen. And while the latter seemed far-fetched, it wasn't impossible. Eveline's bio had mentioned her keen love of football and her membership on the under-eighteen Dutch squad. She might have seen Duke play during the last Women's World Cup, or watched one of the interviews or commercials in which she had been featured. Not so long ago, Duke had been a literal poster child for US Soccer, her glossy photo taped above the desk of many an aspirational young girl. She wondered how many times that poster had landed in a recycling bin last year.

"Cut it out," she muttered, needing to hear the words herself but hoping no one else had. She would *not* let her bitterness interfere with her work—especially not on the very first day. She had made that promise to herself, her friends, and to Dr. Pena.

Determined now, Duke looked back to the dais and kept her eyes trained on the Belgian contingent instead of the distracting Dutch. Prince Sebastian was seated closest to the podium, where the head of the Belgian Football Association was currently standing alongside his Dutch counterpart as they delivered a clichéd speech about football's role in facilitating social mobility.

To an extent, Duke believed their message—there were plenty of great stories about impoverished young footballers who rose through the ranks to become superstars—but she could also see the hypocrisy at its heart. In too many parts of the world, football was a luxury. In too many places, football reinforced the existing social hierarchy instead of challenging it. Most children living below the poverty line would never escape.

She refocused as the Dutch king, Maximilian, was introduced to the podium. He moved confidently toward it, smiling at the crowd—a genuine, infectious smile that charmed everyone in its path. His neatly trimmed hair and beard must once have matched Eveline's blond curls, but now they were streaked with gray. He delivered his speech first in Dutch and then in English. His charisma was both palpable and apparently effortless, and Duke had to remind herself to take notes. She was also recording the event on her phone, but her shorthand would help her remember what had impressed her at the time.

King Maximilian spoke eloquently about his hopes that this joint effort between Belgium and the Netherlands would reinforce the importance of collaboration within the European Union and beyond. "We must set aside our differences in the service of making progress together," he said in conclusion. "On our common ground, we shall work together to build castles that reach to the sky."

Duke suppressed the urge to roll her eyes at his sentimentality. Sky-high castles sounded lovely, but there would always be peasants barred from entering the gates. She turned to his audience, pressed up against the barricades before the stage. They were a diverse crowd, but most appeared spellbound by their own monarch. Their rapt expressions made her wish she weren't so jaded.

Maximilian concluded by inviting Sebastian to join him. The Belgian prince had continued to lose weight since his most recent photos, and the angularity of his clean-shaven face lent him an androgynous appeal to which even Duke was not immune. Bemused by her jolt of attraction, she watched Sebastian closely, curious to see how he differed from his sister.

His artfully mussed hair was the same shade as Viola's, though much shorter, and his freckles were not as numerous as hers. As he stepped up to the podium, he raised one hand to quiet the crowd, the other hand tracing the shell of his ear. Something about that gesture seemed familiar, but Duke couldn't quite place it. Sebastian began speaking in French, and he must have been nervous, because at first his voice cracked—starting high before dropping down to the register of a tenor. Thereafter, however, he appeared to acquit himself well, if the crowd's reaction was to be believed. She found out why they were hanging on his every word when he switched to English.

"My friends, we are gathered here to celebrate the greatest game on earth!" A fresh cheer greeted this proclamation, and Sebastian smiled tightly before he continued. "Over the next month, the Netherlands and Belgium will unite in a celebration of football at all levels. Now, I know that some of you watching this—perhaps even some of you here today—believe that King Maximilian and I are making too much of a fuss." His voice had become softer, conspiratorial. "Football is *just a game.* Why should our countries commit time, energy, and resources into seeking the World Cup bid?"

The crowd murmured, and Duke saw uncertainty reflected in the faces closest to her. Most of the people who had turned out for this event were probably soccer fanatics. Sebastian was forcing them to think about their priorities, and they didn't seem to appreciate the exercise. He held up one hand to quiet the crowd.

"This mentality is incorrect—and, I beg your pardon, unproductive—but you don't have to take it on faith. I can prove to you that the world's favorite sport is also one of its greatest tools."

His declaration met with enthusiastic applause. Duke was impressed by his manipulation of the crowd. The attendees had been distracted during the bland opening speeches, and King Maximilian had succeeded in grabbing their attention, but Sebastian was taking an academic approach in his oration. Duke hadn't expected that, given what she'd read of him. Then again, she should know better than to think it possible to form a real impression of someone from the articles in which they appeared online.

Plenty of news and speculation about *her* proliferated across the internet, but they told only a fraction of the truth. The most glaring omission was her sexuality. As far as all but her teammates and coaches were concerned, she was straight. And because she presented in a traditionally "feminine" way, most people didn't think to speculate about her orientation. As offended as Duke was by that stereotyping, she also had cause to be grateful for the camouflage it provided. As soon as a gay athlete threw open their closet, dozens of sponsorship doors slammed shut. She wouldn't have been able to earn nearly as much, had she been "out." Thanks to her many sponsorships, she had a solid nest egg that was making it possible for her to be independent during this transitional time.

Despite the obvious value of the pragmatic approach, Duke angsted over it even now. She knew how meaningful it would have been for the fans to see her publicly claim her lesbian identity. With one declaration, she might have been able to change someone's mind or even save someone's life. But she'd also had to think of herself. Her family had often lived paycheck to paycheck, and the church they attended every Sunday was unambiguous in its condemnation of homosexuality. So, she had played it safe, saving as much money as she could and revealing her sexuality only to her teammates.

"...there are hundreds of charities all over the globe using football as the vehicle to help build communities and foster peace in regions of high conflict," Sebastian was saying. "That's because football is transformative. Think about one child juggling a ball in a war-torn or poverty-stricken area. We aren't born suspicious of others. We learn the prejudices we are taught and absorb the biases around us, to our detriment. What if football can help us unlearn our preconceived notions?"

The line jarred her with its familiarity. His sister, Viola, had used it in the interview Duke had watched on the train. Then, she had been referring to the power and relevance of art. Sebastian must have stolen it from her. Again, his left hand rose to his temples in that quirky little gesture.

"Even as I speak," he continued, "there are charities working to create dialogue between societies in conflict through a program that brings the children of opposing factions together in training camps. As teammates, they learn to work together to achieve a shared purpose. They form friendships with people very different from themselves and recognize how much they have in common. They learn how to endure failure without giving up on their goals. They grow into a deeper understanding of their own strengths and challenges."

Only when Sebastian paused to survey the crowd did Duke realize she was hanging on his every word. She wasn't easily impressed, but his conviction was palpable and compelling. Her own experience fit right into his narrative. Soccer had been the means for her escape from the narrow borders of not only her town, but her entire upbringing. Soccer had helped her know and accept herself.

Until her body had failed. Soccer had elevated her status and prospects, only to sweep the legs out from under her.

The spike of grief took her breath away, and she clenched her teeth against a gasp. Daily, she fought against the dull ache of loss, but this pain was hot and sharp, darting inside her guard before she could register the threat. When her eyes burned with tears, Duke blinked rapidly, desperately trying to focus. She had work to do, and she refused to let these runaway emotions sabotage her on the first day of a new career.

"These very qualities," Sebastian was saying, "make football the perfect vehicle for philanthropic efforts to bring peace, harmony, and collaboration to communities in need. Over the next month, our campaign will be featuring one football-based charity each day on the website. We've also set up donation boxes in every hallway in this arena. Even a gift of one euro will help."

For the third time, his hand rose to trace the shell of the ear—and with all the suddenness of an electric shock, Duke realized where she had seen that gesture before. At several points throughout her interview, Viola had made the same movement to tuck her hair behind one ear. In her case it had been a clear sign of nerves, since half the time, her hair had needed no adjustment. But why would Sebastian make it? It was likely that twins developed similar mannerisms, but he didn't have long hair now—nor did he in any of the photographs she had ever seen of him.

This line of thinking culminated in an idea so ludicrous that she was hard-pressed not to laugh. Could Viola possibly be impersonating Sebastian? While insane, that would explain both his repeated gesture and his verbatim use of his line from a speech of Viola's. It would also explain why Sebastian looked thinner than he ever had. Duke stared at him through narrowed eyes, focusing on his height so she could compare it with other photographs.

"Football is good for us both personally and culturally," Sebastian said. "This is why both Belgium and the Netherlands are presenting our bids as a collaborative celebration. Here to kick off the party"—he paused to ensure everyone registered the pun—"are two of the most legendary footballers in the world: Please join me in welcoming our honorees of the day, Lucas Desmet and Frans Meijer!"

As he stepped away from the podium, Duke watched him move though narrowed eyes. He acknowledged the crowd with a wave before taking his seat. He started to cross one leg over the other, then evidently changed his mind. Was that some kind of meaningful shift in gender presentation, or was he simply uncomfortable in the portable chairs? Had she gone entirely off the deep end, or was there actually something to her suspicions? And if so, what motive did Viola have to take such a drastic action?

Duke didn't know if she could contrive a way to interact with him today, but if so, she would watch him closely. If not, she would continue her research at home, comparing photos and video footage of today with past appearances. Maybe she was hallucinating or jumping at shadows. Then again, maybe she had just stumbled across a story.

At the very least, spying on Prince Sebastian would provide a distraction from her own grief.

❖

The Hague, The Netherlands

Viola's head was pounding and her shoulders ached as she took her seat, ears still ringing with the audience's cheers. She started to cross her right leg over her left before remembering that Sebastian never sat that way. Raising her knee higher, she rested her right ankle on her left thigh and settled back against the seat. Within seconds, she wanted to change the uncomfortable position, but she would only draw attention to herself by fidgeting, and that was the last thing she needed. Plastering what she hoped was a bland, approving smile on her face, she tried to pay attention to the pair of football stars who now had command of the podium.

Fatigue pressed behind her eyes, kept at bay only by the force of adrenaline. The effort of performing Sebastian's posture and mannerisms was beyond exhausting. She had to process every phrase at the speed of light, lest she let slip verbiage that would betray her as an imposter. All the while, she had to remember to pitch her voice an octave lower than normal. Thankfully, her speaking role appeared to have gone off without a hitch—aside from her opening vocal stumble. No one had interrupted to denounce her as an imposter, though she supposed that was rather far-fetched.

Over the past twenty-four hours, her imagination had conjured a thousand horrific outcomes, and the relief of success lent weight to her exhaustion. All she wanted to do as soon as the speeches concluded was to catch the next plane to Paris and see Sebastian before he disappeared into the Swiss facility to battle his demons. But after this, there was the entire exhibition game to sit through while pretending she cared as much as he would have. And after that, there was the storm of her parents' reaction to weather, not to mention the possibility that some highly perceptive audience member would take to Twitter in the next few hours or try to sell their suspicions to a news source.

She wondered whether her mother and father were watching the live stream, and if so, how they were feeling. Would they understand what had compelled her, or would her actions drive a wedge in the midst of her family at the very moment they most needed to be a united front? And then a new thought occurred to her: if Sebastian were well enough, they might be watching the broadcast *with him*. Only days ago, she would have been confident enough in her knowledge of him to predict what he would think and feel about most topics. Now, she had no idea. Would he bless or curse her?

The footballers' speeches ended, and as they returned to their seats, she caught King Maximilian's eye. They rose as one and returned to the podium, where he thanked everyone who had contributed to this bi-national effort. Viola took a deep breath as he concluded. She had the punch line, and it was essential that she avoid a gaffe. While practicing it, she had tried to emulate the sonorous tones of her father, who always sounded so perfectly regal.

"We hereby formally declare our joint bid to host the 2030 FIFA World Cup." The amplified words rolled through the stadium in a voice she never would have recognized as her own. "Let the match begin!"

Thunderous applause greeted her declaration, and for a moment, Viola forgot the stakes, forgot her fatigue, forgot she was pretending. Around her, above her, tens of thousands of people were celebrating the project that had been her brother's brainchild. If only he could be here to feel this energy, she knew it would help him find the strength to fight his addiction.

And then the moment passed, and she was aware of Maximilian at her side. "A job well done," he murmured. "Shall we go?"

Together, they led the group down the stairs of the podium. Their joint security teams fell in beside them, and Maximilian's security chief directed them toward the tunnel that led into the bowels of the stadium. Viola focused on maintaining Sebastian's confident posture and stride, which she had practiced in front of Thijs and André this morning. Anxiety set in as she remembered that the most difficult part of this event was yet to come: for the next two hours, she would be in close quarters with VIPs, many of whom had interacted with Sebastian previously. Even those who didn't know him would expect him to be highly knowledgeable about football. She knew how the game was played, of course, and André had given her a crash course in Sebastian's favorite team and players. But the façade she had so painstakingly erected would crumble if she were pushed too hard.

As they entered the tunnel, Thijs fell into step beside her, mouth set in a grim line. He spoke so softly she could barely hear him. "Ruben just contacted me demanding an explanation."

A fresh spike of adrenaline lanced through her fatigue, and she bit down hard on her lower lip to keep from betraying her panic. "Tell him I'll be in Paris as scheduled and he'll have one then," she said, the words far more courageous than she felt.

"Very well." He reached for his phone, but a sudden thought prompted Viola to grasp his arm and lean closer.

"And tell him to tell my parents I love them."

He nodded once and stepped away. Heart pounding at the thought of their reaction, Viola tried unobtrusively to take a deep, steadying breath. She couldn't afford to worry about that when she still had to make it through the match.

"But why not, Papa?" The Dutch princess Eveline's youthful voice echoed in the tunnel, rising like a descant above the low masculine murmur. Her father shushed her, but she persisted. "She's my favorite player of all time!"

Viola watched Maximilian heave a sigh and was surprised when he turned back to engage *her*.

"Sebastian, Eveline has asked that we invite a member of the press corps to join us for the match. Until last year, she was an American professional football star and Eveline's favorite player. If you don't mind it, I will have my people verify her credentials and walk her up."

The thought of being caged in a room—however luxurious—with a reporter made Viola want to break out in hives, but she couldn't think of a logical reason to object. And when she glimpsed Eveline's hopeful expression, Viola couldn't bear to disappoint her.

"I don't mind at all," she said, hoping her nonchalance was believable.

Eveline smiled brilliantly in reply and hugged her father. "Thank you! Thank you both!"

As Viola trailed them into the elevator, Thijs again positioned himself next to her. She wanted to ask about his follow-up with Ruben, but the space was too cramped to have such a sensitive conversation. Instead, she mentally recapitulated her review session with André from the night before. They had agreed that the best strategy was for her to say as little as possible, and that meant knowing how to get each person talking. Between André's insights and Google, she had created a keyword for each person in the box, linking topics to names and faces. But there hadn't been time to study her notes in more than a cursory manner, and the insistent pounding of her head was a distraction.

Gritting her teeth, she gave herself a silent pep talk as she trailed Maximilian and Eveline—now chattering excitedly—along the corridor, praying her memory didn't fail her.

CHAPTER SEVEN

The Hague, The Netherlands

Duke watched wistfully as the podium party disappeared into the tunnel. Once the speeches ended, she had asked the two friendliest of her colleagues whether either of them had been able to gain access to the VIP suites. Her question was met with sharp laughter. Resigned to covering the match for the time being until she could think of some way to get herself upstairs, Duke was on her way to the press box entrance when a security guard abruptly barred her path. She looked up at him incredulously, feeling the stares of her fellow journalists as they passed her by. Was she in some kind of trouble?

"Ms. Duke?" he said.

"Yes. Is there a problem?"

"Her Royal Highness Princess Eveline of the Netherlands has requested your presence in her box."

Duke tried to cover up her shock with a cough. "I would be honored to join her," she managed.

"Please follow me."

As the guard led her to the elevator and then along the hallway, Duke tried to compose herself. Unlooked for, unsought, she was about to gain access to the inner sanctum precisely when she needed it. Surely, the Dutch and Belgian contingents were sharing a box, which meant Sebastian would be there as well. Eveline's interest—whatever its cause—had just given her the golden ticket. Had she known this would happen, she would have taken her preparation much more seriously, and she could practically hear Juno's chastising voice in her head. Caught flat-footed or not, she had to make the most of this opportunity.

The door to the box was flanked by two other guards. The male one took her camera and examined her bag while the female guard instructed her to extend her arms and then patted her down.

"You are not to take photos without express permission," her colleague said as he restored her items.

"I understand."

He inserted a key into a lock set high in the wall, and the door slid open. The room inside was a rectangle, its far wall composed of floor-to-ceiling windows looking out over the pitch. A full service bar ran the length of the wall to her left, and a buffet mirrored it on the right. Two rows of stadium-style seating faced the window, while the remainder of the space was filled with small tables ringed by upholstered chairs. Television screens hung in each corner, so that no matter where one stood, the game was visible.

"This way, Ms. Duke," said the guard who had found her on the field.

He led her across the room to a table populated by Eveline, her father, and a couple she didn't recognize. At their approach, Eveline looked up and smiled in delight. It was a childlike expression, open and eager. She hurried over, her father watching indulgently.

"Ms. Duke, it is an honor to meet you," she said in crisply accented English. "I am Eveline, and you are my very favorite football player."

Nostalgia flooded over Duke as she met Eveline's surprisingly firm grip. Once, she had been the daily recipient of tweets and emails and even letters to that effect, sent from girls all over America and beyond. By now, most of those girls had moved on to new idols. It was something, to still be the favorite footballer of the Dutch princess.

"Your Royal Highness, that is an honor to *me*," she said. "Thank you for your generous invitation."

"Please join us." Eveline indicated the table, where a member of the waitstaff was just pulling up another chair.

Shock struck Duke like an electric charge. The most she had expected was what had just happened: an introduction to the princess. To be asked to join her table was something else entirely. Since when did she have good luck?

"Thank you," she said, repeating the words when the waiter lingered to install her in the chair and take her drink order. And just like that, she was sitting between the reigning monarch of The Netherlands and his daughter.

"This is M—" Eveline began to introduce her to the table, only to stop short, color flushing her cheeks as she met Duke's eyes. "Ah. How would you prefer I...that is..."

The princess, Duke realized, knew about her antipathy to her own name, probably because Duke had mentioned it in a prominent interview several years ago and had later written a post about nicknames for the US Soccer blog. She felt a pang of guilt at Eveline's conflict: she didn't want to offend, but propriety demanded an introduction. Her father was frowning, and Duke jumped in before he could chastise his daughter for something that wasn't her fault.

"Princess Eveline knows I'm not fond of my given name," she explained, making sure to catch King Maximilian's eye. "You're very considerate," she said to Eveline, "but off the pitch, first names are a necessary evil."

That earned her a chuckle from the woman she didn't know, and Maximilian's frown dissolved. Relieved, she pressed on. "My name is Missy Duke, and I played on the American national team for several years. It's an honor and a pleasure to be here with you all."

Her smile renewed, Eveline took up the remainder of the introductions, and Duke nearly bit her own tongue when she realized that the other couple at the table was the prime minister of the Netherlands and her husband.

"You work as a reporter now?" Maximilian's tone was polite, but Duke could perceive his suspicion.

"That's correct, Your Majesty. My football career was sidelined by multiple injuries, and I had to retire." Duke had practiced that sentence in the privacy of her own bedroom over and over, slowly squeezing the bitterness out of each syllable, flattening the cadence of the words until her delivery was matter-of-fact. "I'm covering the bid process for Goal Sports Network, but I promise that everything you say is off the record unless you say otherwise."

Maximilian relaxed infinitesimally. "Good on both counts. And I wish you the best of luck in your new career."

"Thank you." The small part of Duke's mind that wasn't awestruck at being the personal guest of the Dutch royal family saw an opportunity here, and she forced herself to speak before her courage disappeared. "And if you wish to be interviewed about the bid at any point, I would be more than happy to oblige."

"You're welcome to interview me anytime you like," Eveline said, leaving Duke to wonder whether the girl had a crush on her after all, in addition to her obvious hero worship.

"I appreciate that, Your Royal Highness," Duke said. And then, because she was a terrible person not above manipulation, she flashed her most winning smile. "It would be very helpful to interview both you and a member of the Belgian contingent—Prince Sebastian, perhaps?"

Eveline's reaction was even better than Duke had hoped. She leapt at the hint and began to scour the crowd for him. When she caught sight of him near the buffet, she hastily excused herself.

"Your daughter is generous," Duke said to Maximilian, knowing parents always enjoyed being complimented on their children, "not to mention a fine footballer in her own right."

"You've seen her play?"

"Yes, sir. At last year's Algarve Cup." Eveline's inclusion on the Dutch squad had been a minor controversy—she was the youngest on the team by two years—but she put in a solid performance and the team returned to The Hague with the bronze trophy. The games had been streamed online, and Duke had watched every single one between her physical therapy appointments. Back then, she still nurtured the hope of returning to play professionally, and she had studied both her own team and the others with as much intensity as she conditioned the muscles around her knees.

The bad news would come weeks later, in a follow-up with her surgeon: despite all her hard work, her chance of re-injury was sufficiently high for him to strongly recommend retirement. She could leave professional soccer now and focus on maintaining her strength and flexibility in the hopes of minimizing arthritis as she aged, or she could continue to put her body through hell and risk needing total knee replacements in her forties.

"Don't you want to be able to run around after your kids, someday?" the surgeon had said.

As his office walls closed in around her, Duke had nodded numbly, even though she had no plans to bring children into the world. She didn't want arthritis at any age, and she certainly didn't want to spend her elderly years consigned to a walker or wheelchair. But neither had she wanted to give up on her dream—not when she had tasted it already, only to find it even sweeter than she could have imagined.

Now, watching any kind of soccer was painful. Glad to have her back to the windows, she kept her focus on the members of her table, away from the television screens. Dr. Pena had assured her that she wouldn't feel this way forever, but so far, the passage of time had brought with it no comfort.

Thankfully, Eveline's return halted the downward spiral of her grief, and Duke's inner turmoil disappeared entirely when she saw Sebastian trailing her. She observed his approach, watching closely for any sign that he was not who he claimed to be. He moved confidently, shoulders back and strides long, his expression at once attentive and guarded. If he was in fact his sister, Princess Viola was very good at replicating the external trappings of masculinity.

"Sebastian, this is Duke," said Eveline. "She's a football legend who played for the US and is now working for Goal to cover our bid. And she's going to interview me about it! She'd like to interview you, too, if you're willing."

Now that she'd had her first brush with royalty, Duke had expected to maintain her composure in Sebastian's presence, but the moment he turned the full weight of his attention on her, she felt herself go starstruck. The planes and curves of his face were reminiscent of a Greek sculpture, and there was something indefinable in his carriage that commanded her respect. It wasn't latent arrogance—she wouldn't have respected that—but rather a subtle confidence in his bearing that drew her attention. For the space of several heartbeats, it didn't matter whether "he" was actually "she," and why. All that mattered was his presence, and her proximity to it.

She might have stood there in awkward silence forever had she not caught the flare of appreciation in his gaze. All in a rush, her ulterior motives for being here came surging back. Duke inspired attraction frequently enough to recognize it when she saw it, and she had learned to pick up on its nuances. The interest of most men was inflected with an assertiveness and entitlement that she found rather off-putting, while most women tended to convey a more aesthetic appreciation, less laced with predatory undertones. Right now, Sebastian was looking at her the way women did, and her nerves jangled at the scrutiny. Still, it wasn't definitive proof that he was actually Viola in disguise. She needed more data points.

"Your Royal Highness, I'm honored to meet you," she said, relieved when her voice remained steady.

Sebastian's palm was smooth and warm, his handshake firm. "The pleasure is mine," he said in a low, smooth voice. His accent, a cross between British and French, was pleasant to her ears.

He certainly didn't *sound* feminine, and doubt seeped into the cracks of her theory, adding confusion to her nerves. Had she misjudged, after all? Was she too ready to see smoke where there was no fire?

"I have met many dukes," he continued, "but none so beautiful as you."

Eveline shot her a sharp glance, clearly concerned that she would object to his teasing, but her worries were unfounded. To her own consternation, Duke felt color rush into her cheeks at his flattery. His hand retained her own, and as she tried to formulate a response, she prayed her palms wouldn't start sweating.

"You're kind to say so. 'Duke' is my surname, but as Eveline knows, I much prefer it to my given name."

"In that case, I promise not to push the issue." He released her with a faint smile. As he looked between her and Eveline, the tip of his tongue emerged to moisten his lips.

Realization crackled through Duke with all the certainty of a lightning strike, the storm of epiphany fast on its heels. She nearly gasped, clamping down on the sound at the very last second and praying her face hadn't betrayed her shock. She remembered Viola doing the exact same thing in that video, remembered the desire that had reawakened in her own blood at the simple sensuality of that unconscious act. This was it—the puzzle piece she had been waiting for. It was such a small thing, yet it banished all but the faintest shadows of her doubt.

As Eveline asked "Sebastian" about the change in performer for the postgame celebration, Duke's brain launched into overdrive. There had to be a story here—a big one—but she would need much more than a half-baked theory to break it. While she couldn't discount the possibility that Viola was impersonating her brother on a lark, or because she had lost some sort of bet, her instincts screamed that something scandalous had happened—something bad enough to warrant this magnitude of risk just to keep the details out of the news. In that case, "Sebastian" would be on his guard and unlikely to participate in any kind of activity that might endanger his cover. Then again, "Sebastian's" attraction to her seemed genuine. Maybe there was a way for her to use that interest to gain additional access to "him"?

No sooner had that ludicrous thought crossed Duke's mind than she rejected it. Even if she were reading "Sebastian's" cues correctly, the princess would surely sublimate any such feelings while her brother was in crisis. Still, perhaps Duke could use that attraction as incentive to gain an interview. She was a nobody in the press world. Only by making an impression today, right now, could she possibly entice "Sebastian" into a private conversation. And the best way to do that would be to appeal to his interests without raising any red flags that might suggest she had seen through his ruse.

But as she tried to think of some appropriate topic, her attention was caught by "Sebastian's" explanation of why Mother of Pearl, the original headliner of the postgame concert, had been replaced.

"I heard that DJ Smitten donated her performance today," Duke said. "Is that right?"

He nodded. "That was a pleasant surprise. She is a good friend of my sister, and now we are both in her debt."

Duke hid her surprise behind her drink. She couldn't have asked for a better opening if this were a film and she were its screenwriter. It was time to take a gamble. "Is your sister here today?" she said, watching his face closely. "I was impressed by her recent interview in Zurich at the opening of her exhibition there, and I'd like to tell her that myself."

If she hadn't been watching for it, Duke would have missed the sudden flare of his pupils. She'd taken enough psychology to know that such a change could indicate a dozen different feelings, but the very existence of a strong emotional response was telling enough to support her suspicions.

"No. Viola is not as much of a football fanatic as I am, but I will be sure to pass along your compliment." The words held a note of humor—another shred of evidence? Was Viola bemused by the necessity of referring to herself in the third person? "Perhaps you'll have the chance to meet her someday."

Duke felt her jaw drop and quickly tried to smother her shock. That last bit had been entirely unnecessary. Was Viola *flirting* with her? Despite…everything? The possibility was as tantalizing as it was surprising.

"I'd like that very much," Duke said, glad her reaction hadn't been out of the ordinary. After all, how often did an American commoner receive even a tacit invitation to meet a princess? Desperate to hold "Sebastian's" attention, she decided to push a little harder. "I was struck by the common thread of social justice in her interview and your speech today. I hope many people are convinced by what you said. I've experienced the life-changing power of football that you spoke of, firsthand."

"Sebastian" didn't look alarmed, but his focus intensified. Being the object of that focus felt like standing in a spotlight, and Duke automatically indulged in her own nervous habit—running her fingers through her hair. It was a kind of preening, and she knew it. But it was also generally effective, and when she caught "Sebastian's" gaze following the path of her hand, the triumph was sweet.

It evaporated in the next moment, when his attention was drawn by his phone. Upon glancing at the screen, a shutter fell over his expression. "I'd like to hear your story. Perhaps you can share it with me when we sit down for that interview Eveline has already arranged." He smiled at her, and Duke belatedly realized she had forgotten all about the Dutch princess.

"I'm needed by one of the coordinators of this event," he said. "But before I go: will you be in Brussels later this week, in advance of the 'Magic of Football' gala?"

"I arrive on Tuesday."

He reached into his breast pocket. "This is my secretary's information. He'll be able to set up an appointment."

Duke took the elegant card, scarcely able to believe her luck. "Thank you, Your Royal Highness," she managed.

"I'll look forward to seeing you soon," he said, before exchanging cheek kisses with Eveline and a handshake with her father. He spoke to them briefly in Dutch before moving away, and Duke wondered how many languages he knew. She forced herself not to watch him go, and instead turned back to Eveline.

"I'm in your debt," she said. "Is there someone I should contact to arrange *your* interview?"

"I have my schedule here," Eveline said, extracting her own phone. "Is tomorrow too soon?"

"Tomorrow is perfect."

As Eveline pulled up her calendar, Duke's head spun, despite the fact that she had barely touched her drink. She had just made the leap from unseasoned reporter to royal interviewer, all within the space of an hour. As if that wasn't overwhelming enough, she was almost certain that the Belgian monarchy was involved in a cover-up having something to do with the crown prince.

She managed to hold herself together while saying good-bye to Eveline, but immediately thereafter, she got a fresh drink from the bar and settled herself on one of the seats overlooking the field. Now, she had even more reasons not to want to watch this match. She was dying to get back to her hotel and do the research that would either confirm or deny her suspicions.

But Goal was expecting a full report on the game, and staying here was a no-brainer. This space was much more luxuriously appointed than the press box. As an added benefit, she could try to observe "Sebastian" surreptitiously in hopes of picking up additional clues. Just now, he was speaking with a dark-haired man who must be the Henri he had mentioned, and unless she was drastically misreading his body language, their conversation wasn't entirely comfortable. She didn't dare try to get closer, but if she angled her body just so, she could keep him in her peripheral vision and still mostly concentrate on the match.

Duke took the notebook and pen out of her purse and kept her eyes on the game while straining her ears to catch as many of the conversations around her as possible. Fortunately, she had long experience at remaining in a state of laser focus for ninety minutes. For a moment, she thought about trying to reengage "Sebastian" in conversation in an attempt to subtly ferret out what was going on. But there was always the risk that he might see right through her, and besides, she didn't need to be aggressive. They would see each other next week. He had promised, and Eveline was her witness.

For now, the best plan was to watch and wait. She had never been a particularly patient person, but month upon month of physical therapy had forced her to develop the fundamentals. Some things couldn't be rushed, like healing. Like this secret. Whatever it was.

❖

French air space

Viola spent the first half of the flight to Paris engaged in a mental civil war. Two-thirds of her brain were berating her for being a selfish, hormonally motivated fool, while the final third was stubbornly applauding her decision to see Duke again. Her image had somehow been burned on Viola's retinas: the long, golden curtain of her hair; the sensuous curve of her lips; the delicate contours of her collarbone; and the tan skin at her throat. Her eyes, dark green as the needles on a pine, and as piercing. "Hot" was too shallow a word to describe her, and even "gorgeous" seemed woefully inadequate.

Beautiful. Stunning. Those were better. Alluring, too, which was the root of the problem. Duke had been alluring enough to prompt Viola to throw caution to the winds and then spend the remainder of the evening distracted by the task of burying her mistake with inadequate justifications.

Granting Duke an interview would help keep up appearances, she told herself. Duke was clearly starstruck—and, she thought, attracted—so she would be easier to manipulate than a seasoned reporter. Controlling the narrative was paramount, and striking up a friendship with Duke would allow her access to the media—both for the purposes of spying on and influencing it.

They were good excuses. Some were even plausible. None were entirely true, and beneath the veneer of logic, all were as flimsy as cardboard. Really, what *had* she been thinking? Given the magnitude of her worry about Sebastian and the effort it took to impersonate him, it should have been impossible for her to get caught up in a momentary surge of lust—especially when that lust was a dead end. Even a one-night stand was out of the question. Duke looked like the quintessential "all-American girl." What's more, she thought Viola was Sebastian. She had to be straight, and unless Viola could convince her to be tied up and blindfolded, all layers of clothing had to stay on.

The eroticism of that image took her breath away, shame following close behind. Here she sat, on her way to the *hospital* to see her *brother,* fantasizing about a woman she'd just met? Disgusted, Viola forced her thoughts away from selfish topics.

Thijs sat next to her, and he was obviously in distress. His posture was ramrod straight, fingers clutching at his knees. He looked like a prisoner en route to his own execution. Guilt curdled in Viola's stomach. She was the cause of his tension. His career—his vocation—was to protect her family, even at the cost of his own life, and now he was facing the very real possibility of dismissal because he had gone along with her plan.

When she tucked a loose strand of hair behind one ear, she registered the unfamiliar tug of the wig at her temples. She had changed into it and her own clothes just a few minutes ago while Thijs told the pilot in no uncertain terms that if he so much as breathed a word of this to anyone, Ruben would ground him. Ironically, of course, that was his own greatest fear.

She wanted to speak with Thijs, but that would either mean taking off her headset and shouting over the sound of the engine, or opening up a communications channel audible by the pilot. Instead, she put one hand on his forearm and squeezed gently, hoping to convey some fraction of her gratitude. He turned his head to give her a tight-lipped smile that was probably meant to offer reassurance but instead revealed the magnitude of his anxiety. Viola silently vowed to do everything she could to ensure he kept his job.

When she had imagined this trip last night, she had pictured herself riddled with apprehension about her parents' reaction. But now that she was on her way to them, she felt unexpectedly at peace—albeit with an undercurrent of guilt about adding to their stress at such a difficult time. All she could hope was that her actions had convinced them that the problem of what to do or say publicly about Sebastian was now out of their hands. She was trying to give them, and him, a gift. With luck, they would recognize it.

Exhaustion loomed behind her eyes, tugging like a wave, and part of her wanted to give in. The rest of her knew she wouldn't be able to sleep until she had cleared the air with her parents and seen Sebastian. He would be moved to the rehabilitation facility in the morning, and at that point, her visits would be limited.

Her phone buzzed. No, not hers—*his*. Suddenly awake, Viola showed Thijs the screen. Maria again, this time with a single word: *FaceTime?*

Viola's fatigue ebbed as her adrenaline surged. *Can't. W/parents now*, she typed back. And then, because the most convincing lies were close to the truth, she added, *They want me 2 enter outpatient rehab.*

Thijs pulled off his headset and motioned for her to do the same. "Is that wise?" he said, his mouth as close to her ear as it was possible to be without touching. "What if she asks where?"

"Then we'll Google a likely facility," Viola said. "But I don't think she will." A burst of anger eradicated the last of her fatigue. "I don't think she cares enough."

Ugh. Are they insisting?

Viola stared down at the confirmation of her theory. Unbelievable. How could *anyone* be so callous, much less someone who claimed to have romantic feelings for Sebastian?

Not yet.

When can u get away? I want to see u.

Viola wanted to see Thijs's expression. He looked as disgusted as she felt. "Should I meet with her? She might let slip more in person than she would by text."

Thijs shot her an incredulous look. "Begging your pardon, ma'am," he said stiffly, "but she is your brother's *girlfriend.* How long do you think your disguise can hold?"

Viola was not about to share that she'd been contemplating the same question mere minutes ago, though with an entirely different audience in mind. Once again, she wrenched her thoughts away from Duke.

"It might work if we met in a public place and I couldn't stay long," she mused. "But I'm sure that's not what she means by 'seeing him.'"

"I agree," Thijs said. "And besides, how likely is it that she would 'let slip' anything useful in a public setting?"

Not yet. Am still being watched closely.

Viola typed the words but didn't hit "send." She wondered if that would sound strange to Maria. Sebastian was, after all, a grown man—a prince. There was little his family could do to force or constrain him. As much as it sickened her to imagine the duplicitous side of her brother, she had to think like him now.

Want to be w/u but need 2 play along and keep up appearances 4 a while.

Maria's reply came in the form of a pouting emoji.

"What does he see in this woman?" she muttered, pocketing the phone when the chopper began its descent.

As the spires of Paris grew more distinct, her mind continued to chew on the question. Self-validation, probably. Maria wanted Sebastian for all the wrong reasons, but she did want him, and that was powerful—especially after the difficult end to his relationship with Camille.

Ruben was waiting for them on the helipad, and Viola watched Thijs's jaw clench spasmodically. She prepared herself for the discomfort to come and realized that the recent text messages, as evidence of what could be gained from her impersonation of Sebastian, might just help both their cases. An odd silver lining, but she wasn't about to reject it.

"Good evening, Your Royal Highness," Ruben said, his face betraying no emotion. "If you would follow me, please. Your parents are conferring in a private waiting room and wish for you to join them."

He led them into the hospital and down several floors. The building was a beehive of activity, busy but well ordered. Fluorescent lights illuminated the hallways, white walls magnifying their brightness. Despite the atmosphere of brisk efficiency, Viola felt her nerves drawing tauter the deeper she was led into the maze. Somewhere nearby, Sebastian was lying in a bed, probably still in physical pain, and certainly in emotional distress. What would he say if he knew about her plan? She didn't intend to tell him—it would be a terrible distraction at this point in his process—and she hoped that when he did find out, he would understand.

Ruben paused before a nondescript door and rapped lightly. Viola heard her father's call for him to enter, and a lump materialized in her throat. She swallowed hard, suddenly angry at herself. She was brave enough to pretend to be her brother at a public event, but quailed at being called on the carpet by her own family? No. Squaring her shoulders, she entered the room to the sight of her mother, rising slowly from a chair near the window. Her father was already standing.

"Thank you, Ruben," her father said. "That will be all for the moment."

It was a clear dismissal. Viola could predict what would happen once Ruben left: while her parents lectured her about risk and responsibility, Ruben would take Thijs to another private room and ream him out about failing to stop—or at the very least, report—Viola's dangerous actions. The only way to keep those futures from unfolding was to speak up forcefully. Now.

"Ruben, Thijs, please stay."

Her father frowned and opened his mouth, but she held up one hand. "Father, I'm sorry to countermand you, but I have information you all need to hear. I realize you all may think I've been incredibly irresponsible, but I'm asking you to hear me out. Five minutes."

The words had taken all her air, and she pulled in a deep, steadying breath as her parents exchanged an inscrutable look.

"Very well." He gestured to the table. "Let's be seated."

Relieved at her victory, however minor, Viola moved to claim the seat to the right of her mother. When she lightly touched her shoulder in passing, her mother covered that hand with her own. Another promising sign, and Viola let a welcome surge of hope buoy her.

"I didn't leave the hospital yesterday intending to impersonate Sebastian," she began. "That happened by accident when I answered his phone. It was in the bag of his belongings that I brought to his room. But when it rang, I realized the caller might be one of his so-called friends who abandoned him, so I mimicked his voice when I answered it."

"Who was it?" Ruben asked, his words clipped.

"Henri. And either he didn't know very much, or he was pretending not to." Viola shifted her gaze to her parents. "The fact that I was able to fool him into believing I was Sebastian inspired me." She looked back to Ruben. "I asked André for help, and to his credit, he was willing to give it. He feels terrible, and I can empathize with that. I'm Sebastian's *twin*. I should have known something was wrong."

"We all feel that way, Viola," her father said quietly.

"The difference in André's case," Ruben put in, "is that he knew something was wrong and did nothing."

"He's helping me now," Viola countered. "And the first gambit worked. The bid kickoff event went well. No one outside the palace knows anything is amiss. I spoke with Henri in person earlier today but didn't raise his suspicions as far as I could tell." She took a deep breath. "And I've been texting with Maria."

Ruben leaned forward, his expression reminding her of a hawk, focused and deadly. "I am as certain as it is possible to be without incontrovertible proof that she was somehow involved in Sebastian's overdose. May I see your conversation?"

Viola reached into her bag and handed over Sebastian's phone, letting that action speak louder than any words of justification could. As Ruben scanned it, his lips pressed together so tightly they grew white. Silently, he handed it to her father, and her mother looked on. Her father made a disgusted sound, and her mother's face flushed with anger.

"I didn't see any messages dated earlier than yesterday," Ruben said.

"I checked." Viola remembered the dizzying surge of hope that had lifted her up late last night, only to be dashed when Sebastian's phone revealed nothing. "There's no record of any earlier conversation."

"Someone must have deleted any incriminating details." Her father's voice was flat.

It was only a hunch, but as Viola looked around the room, she realized they all believed it. Fighting against a tide of despair, she tried to think of a way forward.

"I can continue to..." she searched for the proper, diplomatic words but couldn't find them. "To string Maria along for a little while. She might let something slip."

Her mother returned the phone, then touched Viola's wig. Her eyes filled with tears, and her words, when they came, were faltering. "I don't know what to feel or say right now, except that I love you."

Unprepared for the magnitude of her reaction to those words, Viola couldn't hold back her sudden tears. Instead of wiping her face, she took her mother's hands. "I love you, Mom. We're going to get through this. I know you're probably angry with me, but everything I've done, I did to help Sebastian." She dared to glance at her father. "And so far, it's working."

Ruben looked between her and her parents. He rarely let any emotion show in his expression, but he was obviously conflicted now. "If I may, Your Majesty?" he said, sounding tentative for the first time Viola had known him. When her father nodded, he continued.

"Your Royal Highness, I wish you had called me the moment after your conversation with Henri. I wish you had proposed this plan *to* us instead of forcing us to react."

Viola wanted to object that he would never have agreed to it, but she forced herself to remain silent. He had listened to her, and now she needed to return that respect.

"However, I think I understand why you acted as you did. And no one can dispute your generous motives or your courage. The question before us now is how to proceed."

"I need to continue impersonating him." Viola spoke up before anyone else could. "I know he will be protected during his rehabilitation, but once he is back in the public eye, the scrutiny will be intense. I can spare him all the notoriety he would otherwise have. And I can ensure the bid, which he worked so hard on, isn't mired in a scandal."

"Or you could be found out." Her father's quiet voice sliced through the room. "And your actions will only serve to amplify the scandal."

Viola had already thought through this objection, and she had a ready response. "If I'm found out, I will take full responsibility. I'll tell the truth—that this was entirely my idea and that I acted without your knowledge." At his skeptical look, she pressed on. "I'm not naive. I know you both will come under fire, regardless of what I say. All I can hope is that you agree that the risk is worthwhile."

The ensuing silence grew more difficult to bear by the second, but she forced herself to let it continue undisturbed. She had said her piece, and they had listened. That was far from the worst-case scenario she had imagined.

Finally, her mother turned to face her. "Viola, you can't remotely imagine how upset and afraid I was when I heard what you had done, on top of—of everything else." The pain saturating her voice made it difficult to meet her too-bright eyes. "But I know that I can never fully understand the bond you share with Sebastian. Your closeness has always been a joy and a gift to me—a beautiful mystery I unwittingly helped create. What you have done for him, you did out of love, and I respect that. If you truly wish to continue this…performance, you have my support."

Her tears spilled their boundaries, and Viola clasped her hand in comfort and wordless thanks. When her father joined them, his palm warm and heavy atop her knuckles, she bit back a sob of relief.

"Thank you," she whispered. "Thank you for listening to me. I don't take that, or you, for granted."

"We love you, Viola," said her father. "And we are so proud of you."

A fresh wave of tears joined the tracks on her face, and she leaned into them both, drawing in their comfort and strength even as she projected her own. This familial closeness was so precious. She knew of so many people who had nothing like it—people who lived in perpetual fear of their parents' criticism and judgment. She had even felt that fear herself years ago—when, half-defiant and half-terrified, she had come out as a lesbian. Neither parent had so much as blinked before embracing her, while Sebastian, who had known her secret before even *she* did, stood by her side. He had been willing to fight for her then.

She was willing to fight for him now. His absence was palpable, the phantom pains of a missing limb, driving her to heal the wound by any means necessary.

"I beg your pardon," Ruben said at last, "but I would remind you that Sebastian will be transferred in the morning. Should he be made aware of the plan?"

The question startled Viola because she had not thought of it herself. It seemed her father had, however, because he shook his head.

"No. If we tell him, he will be distracted during his rehabilitation."

Viola was less certain. Surely, he was already distracted by the knowledge of what he was missing. "Has he asked about the bid at all?"

"Yes," her mother said. "He asked last night, and I told him you were representing him today."

"Then let's tell him that I'll continue to do so," Viola said. "That should ease some of his concern about his responsibilities without making him worry about my…charade."

"That's good." Her father stood a little stiffly. "We have a suite in a nearby hotel, Viola. Will you stay with us?"

"Yes. Thanks." But as they prepared to leave the room, another thought occurred to her. "Will I be able to see Sebastian before he leaves?"

Her mother slipped an arm around her waist. "It's all been arranged."

"Thank you." With the relief, her fatigue came roaring back. When they reached the door, her father tucked his arm beneath her mother's elbow. Leaning on each other, they made their way down the sterile corridors.

CHAPTER EIGHT

The Hague, The Netherlands

Duke burst into her hotel room, dropped her bag near the door, and went immediately to the sink. She filled a glass of water, watching her hand tremble as it held the cup. She drank quickly, clumsily, water slopping over the edge to dampen the neckline of her dress. Without bothering to pat herself dry, she grabbed her laptop and sank into the mound of pillows on the bed. She drummed her fingers against the keyboard during the precious seconds while the WiFi reconnected, and then she googled videos of Prince Sebastian.

The top search results were all from entertainment sites boasting footage of Sebastian "stepping out" with various A-listers: musicians, actors, sports stars. Duke clicked on a few in quick succession—most taken on phones by amateur paparazzi—and soon saw a pattern. Sebastian hobnobbed with all kinds of famous people, but in almost every video, the same woman was at his side: supermodel Maria Fournier. In her preliminary research on Sebastian, their relationship had been the most prominent piece of news about him, yet Fournier had been conspicuously absent today.

After a few more clicks, she returned to the search listings and navigated to the next page. She needed something up close, preferably with higher production values. The truth would be found in the subtle movements that distinguished one individual from another, no matter how much shared history they might possess.

Near the bottom of the second page, she found a BBC Sports interview with Sebastian about his decision to leave the world of professional golf two years ago. The interview had been conducted in the studio, and its crisp video and audio were exactly what she needed.

After listening to half the video, she paused it and then played her recording of "Sebastian's" speech this afternoon, listening for differences in their voices. Yes. The distinction was subtle, but present. Sebastian spoke slowly, sometimes even ponderously, while the cadence of Viola's voice was lighter and quicker. But on its own, that observation proved nothing. Between then and now, he could have worked with a speech coach to develop a more engaging speaking presence. She needed more.

Duke focused on the professional video and watched Sebastian's body language. He kept his hands on top of the table, fingers laced together. His hair was styled similarly to "his" look today, and at no point throughout the ten-minute interview did he make any move to tuck phantom strands behind his ear. Instead, his nervousness manifested in a slight tic beneath his left eye and a rather annoying tendency to clear his throat. Not even once did he moisten his lips with his tongue.

By the time the video ended, she was 99.9% certain that her theory was, in fact, reality. But two years was a fairly long time, and a person's mannerisms could change. Despite her own fatigue, she went back to the most recent search results and watched a few of the lower-quality videos. Now that she knew exactly what to look for, it would be easier to pick out the relevant mannerisms.

At last, Duke sat back in her chair and rubbed at her eyes. Nothing she'd seen had led her to doubt her own conclusions, but now she had more questions than ever, beginning with *why*. Why would Viola risk public notoriety to masquerade as her brother? After speaking with Viola—she couldn't think of him as "Sebastian" anymore—Duke couldn't believe the explanation was anything as asinine as a bet or dare. The likeliest reason was that something had happened to Sebastian that the Belgian royal family wanted to keep a secret. That meant there was a story to sniff out, and she was perfectly poised to do it.

But could she do it alone? Did she *want* to?

Her coattails, along with a healthy dose of luck, had allowed her access to Viola. If she played her cards well during their interview next week, she might be able to insert herself into Viola's entourage in some way. The problem was that hanging around her and hoping for a crumb to drop wasn't a game plan. She would also need to do some digging into the real Sebastian's recent movements. If she could find the point at which he dropped out of the public view and Viola took over, she would have some sense of when the crisis—assuming there was one—had occurred. But then what?

The questions boiled over in her brain, driving her out of the chair. She went to the window and drew back the curtains, dismayed to find herself looking at the illuminated scaffold of a massive construction project next door. Good thing she wouldn't be staying here long—she could only imagine the noise level during business hours.

Duke blocked out her "view" and began to pace. To get the missing puzzle pieces, she needed someone with access to the royals' social circle. She didn't have any direct connections who moved in that upper echelon, and the only indirect link she could think of was Kerry Donovan, whom one of her former teammates had known from playing soccer with her at Princeton. Kerry hadn't been good enough to break through to the national team, but what she lacked in soccer skill, she more than made up for in brains. She had earned a Rhodes scholarship and went off to Oxford after graduation—at which point she had caught the eye of Sasha, the British princess royal. They were living proof of how difficult it could be to keep a secret from the media; the stress of the exposure of their relationship had been nearly enough to drive them apart.

Duke was fairly confident she could use her soccer network to get a message to Kerry, but what would she say? *Dear Kerry, I'm a failed US Soccer player turned reporter, and I've just discovered that Princess Viola of Belgium is impersonating her brother. Have you heard anything through the royal grapevine about why Prince Sebastian is off the grid? Can you ask around for me? Breaking this story will do worlds for my journalism career.*

She paused in front of the mirror over the dresser and shook her head at her own reflection. Who was she kidding? The media had put Kerry through hell. She would be on Viola's side in this, not hers. A twinge of guilt needled her as she imagined Kerry's perspective, remembering from her own experience the suffocation while being hounded by fans who wanted to know all the gory details about her life.

But she wasn't a fan. She was a journalist. Investigation was her profession now. And she hadn't stooped so low as to purchase an incriminating photo from an amateur paparazzo, the way Sasha and Kerry had been discovered. She was following a trail of breadcrumbs that no one else had noticed. There wasn't anything unethical about *that*, was there?

For a moment, she considered confiding in one of her friends—not Juno, who was far too touchy, but maybe Rosa. Or even Leslie, who could be trusted to keep a cool head off the pitch. But what could they do, aside from being a sounding board? They had their own lives to live, and she had leaned on them too frequently in recent months. This career was hers to make or break—a test of her determination and resolve.

The face staring out from the mirror reflected all her doubt and confusion, and she grimaced at the lack of confidence she saw in herself. It was time to renounce this uncertainty and rise to her potential. *She* had been perceptive enough to notice Viola's mannerisms in "Sebastian's" behavior. *She* had managed to get an interview. If she didn't have the courage to follow through on this lead, she was already resigning herself to mediocrity. And she had never been mediocre.

Duke turned away from the mirror and back toward her desk. If she couldn't think of a way to get more information about Sebastian's recent whereabouts, maybe Toby could. And if she went to him with this story, promising to share the credit, she would settle the debt between them. It was a good solution—better than her other ideas. She had only to convince him that all the details added up.

It was nearly midnight, but he was a night owl. She grabbed her phone and called, drumming her fingers against the desk when it rang without answer.

"Toby, it's Duke," she said after his voice mail greeting "I need to talk to you about a story I just uncovered. It's urgent." She disconnected the call and was just typing out a text to the same effect when her phone began to buzz. The part of her that was miffed at his obvious screening was quickly overwhelmed by the magnitude of the revelation she had to share.

A wave of sound greeted her when she accepted the call: swells of music punctuated by incoherent shouts. Of course, he would still be painting the town red on a Sunday night.

"Toby. Thanks for calling back so quickly."

"No worries!" His joviality sounded forced, even without the benefit of being able to read his body language, and she guessed he didn't appreciate being interrupted but was trying to hide his frustration. "How's everything going over there?"

"I have a scoop. A big one."

"Oh yeah?"

The crystalline sound of breaking glass punctuated his skepticism, and the ensuing shouts were loud enough to make Duke wince and hold the phone away from her ear.

"You still there?"

"I'm here, I'm here." Toby's syllables slurred around the edges. "Go on and tell me."

His voice dripped with indulgence, and Duke felt her lips curl in a silent snarl. The bastard was condescending to her. She momentarily entertained the thought of offering a red herring while keeping the real news a secret. If Toby wasn't going to take her seriously, what use would he be?

Then again, she was untested, unproven. That didn't excuse his condescension, but it did explain the underlying skepticism. And none of it changed the fact that despite his being an ass, she still owed him.

"The Belgian prince is AWOL, and his sister is impersonating him."

"What?"

"Princess Viola is pretending to be Prince Sebastian. I don't know why."

"How sure are you?"

Duke swallowed another surge of irritation. He had no way of knowing whether she was trustworthy or prone to jumping at shadows. "I'm sure. I first noticed some inconsistent mannerisms of his at the event this afternoon, and then I had a face-to-face conversation with him tonight that only reinforced my theory."

"You had a…how the hell did you score that?"

Duke was absurdly pleased at the awe in his voice, but she tried to keep her own tone casual. "The Dutch princess recognized me and invited me to the VIP box."

"Holy shit."

"I'm interviewing her tomorrow and 'Sebastian' sometime later this week," Duke continued. "But I obviously can't come out and ask him whether he's actually his sister in disguise. I have to figure out why the real Sebastian is off the grid, and I don't know where to start. I need your help."

For a long moment, the only sounds she heard were those in the background: the muffled thump of the music and the indistinct blur of shouts and cheers. He was probably shocked, and she wished she could see his face—it would do her self-esteem some good.

"I'm coming back to the hotel right now," he said, the slur gone from his voice, as though her news had sobered him. "Show me everything."

❖

Paris, France

Viola forced herself to enter the hospital room ahead of her parents because she wanted so badly to hide behind them. The impulse made her angry, and the anger gave her courage.

Unlike the last time she had seen him, Sebastian was sitting up in bed. He was still connected to an IV drip, but there was some color in his cheeks, and his gaze seemed lucid. The moment he saw her, one corner of his mouth quirked in a clear attempt at a smile.

"Hi," she said softly, going to the chair at his bedside and clasping the hand not bound to the IV. It trembled in her grip, and she wondered how much pain he was in. "It's so good to see you. How are you feeling?"

"I'm okay," he said hoarsely. "Vi…" He trailed off before he could even start to finish his sentence, eyes welling. She blinked her own tears back, not wanting to burden him with her own grief.

"It's all right." She released his hand and grabbed two tissues from the nightstand. She had no idea what he needed to hear right now, and she only hoped it aligned with what she needed to say. "I love you. I want to do everything I can to help you get well. Okay?"

He blotted his cheeks, nodded, then swallowed hard. "Thanks. I just wish…I wish I could go back in time."

"I wish that, too," she said, aching for him, for her parents, for herself. "But since none of us can, we'll move forward together. We'll be strong for each other. Remember that story Mom likes to tell, about when I was moved to your incubator in the NICU and you put your arm around me?"

He nodded but didn't speak.

"Well, now it's my turn." Viola scooted her chair closer to the bed and leaned in to wrap her arm around his shoulders. "Lean on me. On us. We'll be your strength until you get your own back."

The tears came in earnest, now, streaming down his face, overwhelming his efforts to mop them up. When their father moved to her side and held out his handkerchief, Viola gently took the used tissues from Sebastian's hand and replaced it with the soft fabric, embroidered with their family crest. While she did her best to comfort him, their parents flanked her chair, offering their silent support.

Once he had regained control, Sebastian tried to return the handkerchief, but instead, their father gently closed Sebastian's hand around the cloth.

"Keep it, son," he said. "I only wish I had a clean one to give you."

"Thanks." Sebastian sat up straight and met each of their eyes in turn. "I want you to know how sorry I am for letting…this… happen. You're the most loving and supportive family in the world, and I don't feel like I deserve you." When their mother started to gainsay him, he held up one hand. "Please hear me out. I'll work hard in rehab, I promise. I'll make you proud." He choked a little on the last word but pushed on. "I love you."

Discomfited by the guilt and self-loathing she heard in his voice, Viola leaned forward, grabbing his attention. "We're here for you, no matter what," she said. "And we only want what's best for you. Work toward *that*. What's best for you."

A knock at the door drew their attention and Ruben entered, his expression apologetic. "Pardon the interruption, Your Majesties, Your Royal Highnesses. Sirona's transportation has arrived and the counselors are waiting nearby."

Panic flashed across Sebastian's face before he mastered himself, and Viola felt her heart break all over again. "We're allowed to send you letters," she said into the fraught silence. "I'll write one every day."

"And you'll continue filling in for me, with the bid campaign?" he said anxiously. "Whenever you can, I mean. I know it's a lot to ask—"

"Yes, of course," Viola said, willing her voice to remain smooth despite the sudden spike in her pulse. "I met with Maes yesterday to go over the details. We'll take care of everything. Don't worry about a single detail."

"We'll come to see you as frequently as we can," their father said, leaning over to embrace him.

"We love you so much," added their mother, hugging him in turn.

Ruben returned with a hospital nurse and the two counselors— one male, with streaks of gray in his neatly trimmed beard, and one female, who seemed to Viola to be near her age. After introductions were made, Viola stood to the side with her parents as the counselors spoke to Sebastian and the nurse detached him from the IV. Then there were documents to sign—his discharge papers and the contract with the rehabilitation center.

Viola watched the pen shake in his hand, feeling more helpless than she could ever remember. She hadn't been very religious in recent years, but she found herself praying now: that the treatment would help him, but more importantly, that he would find the strength to want to help himself.

The counselors helped him into a wheelchair, and then it was time to say their good-byes. When the door closed behind them, her mother sat on Sebastian's vacated bed and wept. Viola sat beside her, silently handing over tissue after tissue, while her father comforted her as best he could. When her tears finally ran dry, she let out a shaky sigh and grasped their hands in her own.

"I know this isn't our fault," she said. "But I keep wondering what we could have done differently."

The pain in her voice made Viola ache, and she hurried to stop her mother from descending into a spiral of self-recrimination. She could see her father gathering his own thoughts, but as Sebastian's twin who was *not* an addict, the answer would be more compelling coming from her.

"Mom, no. Please don't," she said, squeezing gently. "Addiction is a disease—ask any well-respected doctor. You didn't keep us in ignorance when we were young—you did everything you could to give us the information to make smart choices. And our family is close-knit and supportive of each other, so there's no logical reason for why Sebastian didn't come to us for help."

She took a deep breath. Her mother's expression still reflected her despair, and Viola prayed she could somehow reach her.

"Unfortunately, addiction isn't logical," she continued. "Yes, he made a choice to try heroin for the first time. But from what I've read, the drug started changing his brain immediately, making him feel as though he *needed* it. That's not your fault. That's not anyone's fault."

"But his life is stressful because of who he is," her mother said, agony inflecting every syllable. "He is always in the spotlight, always being watched, and that made him self-conscious about his image and contributed to his lack of confidence. Whoever introduced him to these drugs must have preyed on that insecurity."

Viola had never heard her mother summarize Sebastian's state of mind so succinctly, and her bluntness was surprising. So was the depth of her guilt. For a moment, it had sounded as though she regretted ever becoming part of the monarchy, with all its public responsibilities and expectations. Viola was sure she hadn't meant to hurt her father but wondered if that was an unintended consequence. Instead of pointing out her insult, she decided to take a more rational approach.

"Yes, Sebastian's life is stressful. But many other people lead even more stressful lives by most measures. Some are addicts. Some are not. We attend parties given by people drowning in money, where any drug is available. But even if we were a so-called 'normal' family of middle income, we would have plenty of access."

The uncertainty and pain in her mother's face made Viola want to weep like the little girl she could not afford to be right now. She knelt at her feet, linking their hands, hoping for the right words.

"There's nothing you could have done to stop this," she said, "but there's so much we can do now. Sebastian needs us more than he ever has. He needs us to be strong for him while he's struggling. The guilt you're feeling—is that going to give you strength? Or will it leach away at your confidence and make you weak?"

At first, no change appeared in her mother; she remained slumped where she sat, folding in on herself in her misery. But then, slowly, her shoulders straightened and she raised her face to Viola's. Her mother's expression was still suffused with sorrow, but beneath it was a steely determination that had been missing.

"You're right," she said with a tremulous smile. "I should learn to be more like you, my fierce, brave, sensitive child." She cupped Viola's face in her hands and bent to kiss her cheeks. The comforting familiarity of that gesture overwhelmed Viola's self-control, unleashing the tide of tears she had held back since entering the room.

Over the sounds of her own sobs, Viola heard the reassuring murmur of her mother, mingled with her father's deep baritone. Their arms came around her where she knelt, holding her through the storm of her own grief and fear.

CHAPTER NINE

Belvédère Castle, Brussels, Belgium

Thanks to soccer, Duke had visited countries from Canada to Qatar. She had marched in the opening and closing ceremonies of the summer Olympics. She had even been a guest of the White House. Touring the Rose Garden and shaking the president's hand in the Oval Office had been a surreal experience, and sometimes she still looked at the photographs just to make sure it had really happened. But as she caught her first glimpse of the Chateau de Belvédère, its pale rotunda rising above the distant trees, Duke thought she must have entered a fairytale.

She had been on the train from The Hague to Brussels yesterday morning, typing up her notes from her interview with Eveline, when she received a call from "Monsieur Maes, Secretary to Prince Sebastian," asking whether this was a convenient time to discuss a meeting with His Royal Highness. How she had managed to reply that, "Yes, thank you, this is a good time," without stammering, she still didn't know. Five minutes later, she had an appointment with Sebastian for the following afternoon, as well as an email detailing the palace protocols regarding photographs, video, and audio recordings.

"A car will be sent for you," Maes had concluded. "Please stay on the line to confirm your address with my assistant."

Duke had expected a higher end sedan—an Audi perhaps, or a BMW. Instead, as she left the front door of her new home away from home, she found a black and gold Rolls Royce Phantom idling at the curb. The driver was standing at the rear passenger's side door. At her approach, he opened it, bid her a good afternoon, and introduced himself as Tomas. If he noticed her stunned expression, he didn't let on.

Once Duke got over her initial awe, she decided to risk chatting up Tomas. Surely, he wouldn't think her curiosity to be odd, and he might give some useful detail away without realizing it. She asked him how long he had been in the royal family's employ (six years), which car he preferred to drive (His Royal Highness Prince Sebastian's Aston Martin), where he lived (in the chateau), and what that was like.

He paused before answering the question—not with the wariness of someone choosing his words diplomatically, but with an earnestness that made her believe he was grasping for the right ones.

"It is a privilege to serve the royal family," he said. "They do a great deal of good in this world, and I am honored to be able to help them, even in such a small way."

As Duke was reflecting on his loyalty, he politely changed the subject away from himself. "I understand you are a reporter for Goal?"

Duke felt a moment's surprise before she reflected that he must be part of the palace's security staff as well as a driver. That would make sense, and it would also explain his knowledge of her identity.

"I am." Duke could see part of his face in the mirror, and she watched him closely. "I met Sebastian this past weekend and he generously agreed to an interview."

Tomas did not so much as flinch when she mentioned the prince's name. "His efforts on the bid are a source of national pride."

"I can imagine. I hope it's successful."

That, she supposed, could be at least one reason why Viola had decided to masquerade as her brother—to keep the bid running smoothly. But that idea got her no closer to an explanation of why Sebastian couldn't attend to the bid himself. He could be very sick and want his privacy, but Duke doubted it. Why not make an illness public knowledge and have Viola substitute for him as herself? That would go a long way toward generating sympathy and admiration for the entire family and their effort, which would in turn be politically expedient.

The street culminated in a roundabout, its inner circle boasting an ornate stone monument that seemed at first glance to be the lopped-off spire of a cathedral. As the car curved around it, Duke realized it was larger than it first appeared and functioned as a pavilion, sheltering the statue of a man.

"The monument of Leopold I," Tomas said, "First King of the Belgians."

Duke had read about that quirk: the king and queen were titled "of the Belgians," indicating that they were bound to the Belgian people rather than to the territory of the country. It was an interesting distinction, especially since their children were the prince and princess "of Belgium." As the elder twin, Sebastian had another title—the one given him by virtue of his status as heir-apparent—the Duke of Brabant.

The car exited the roundabout and turned down a narrow road that was almost immediately barred by a wrought-iron gate. A woman emerged from the nearby guardhouse and exchanged a few words with Tomas, who let down the rear window.

"Good afternoon, Ms. Duke," she said, her accent sounding more German than French. "May I please see your identification?"

The guard took her passport into the small structure, presumably to check it against some kind of computer system. She returned a few minutes later and handed it back, only to ask Duke to step out of the car.

Duke's first reaction was surprise, followed by apprehension. Had there been some kind of red flag on her passport? Some of what she was feeling must have been visible, because the guard took it upon herself to explain that a brief body scan was protocol for all visitors. As she stood with her legs splayed and arms out, Duke wondered whether this particular measure was a response to the increase in terrorism over the past few years. She also wondered how Viola and her family felt, knowing they were targets. Was that something a person ever got used to? Somehow, Duke didn't think so.

"Enjoy your meeting with the prince, ma'am," the woman said.

Duke slid back into the car, a tiny kernel of doubt flowering in her mind. Unbidden, both Tomas and the guard had referred to "the prince," which suggested one of three possibilities: either she had entirely misjudged the situation, or Viola was fooling them as well (which seemed highly unlikely), or the monarchy's security team was all in cahoots about her charade.

Moments later, the tree-lined street gave way to a cleared space dominated by the chateau's blue-gray facade. Its square-shaped main building was bisected by two identical wings, one stretching to the east and another toward the west. A cupola, its dome made of the same stone as the rest of the palace, crowned the center of the roof. Tomas pulled the car up to the entrance, a gray granite staircase that led to a landing dominated by four white pillars carved in one of the Greek styles. A tall, lean man in a black suit, his ginger hair cropped close in a military-style haircut, stood at the top with his hands clasped behind his back.

Tomas opened her door. "Here you are, ma'am. One of His Royal Highness's guards is waiting for you, just there."

She murmured her thanks, swallowed hard against a rush of butterflies, and began the short climb.

"Ms. Duke." The man's handshake was firm. "Welcome to Belvedere Castle. I am Thijs. His Royal Highness is awaiting you in the small study."

"Thank you." Duke followed him into a spacious foyer, its marble floor gleaming in the light cast by a three-tier chandelier. Twin staircases made of dark brown wood and polished to a lustrous shine framed the entryway, leading to a narrow balcony on the second floor. Two arched corridors stretched out to either side, both above and below. A door stood open across the length of the chamber, allowing her a glimpse of what appeared to be some kind of sitting room, apportioned in rose and gold furniture. Thijs took the right staircase, turned into the hallway, and led her past several closed doors. By the time he paused in front of one, Duke guessed they must be near the end of the western wing.

When Thijs rapped lightly on the door, Duke heard a single syllable in response: "*Viens.*"

She trailed him into a room furnished with leather furniture, decorated in hues of black and gold. Two large windows looked out onto the immaculately manicured gardens. The left wall held a fireplace, before which were arranged a leather sofa and two leather chairs. The right wall side of the room boasted a similar seating arrangement, the centerpiece of which was the largest television screen Duke had seen outside of a sports bar.

Two desks were angled toward the windows, and Viola rose from the one on the left. Her attire was several degrees more casual than it had been at the exhibition match. Dressed in slim-fitting olive chinos and a black linen shirt with a banded collar, she looked entirely convincing—so much so that when a wave of desire broke over Duke, disorientation followed. Some intuitive part of her was responding to Viola as a woman, but it was beyond strange to look at the object of her attraction and see a man.

"Duke, it's good to see you." Viola turned to her escort. "Thank you, Thijs."

"Of course, sir." Like Tomas and the other guard, he didn't hesitate before using the male pronoun. Maybe that was a measure of their training and self-control, but Duke found herself thinking of another possibility. Just how long had Viola been at this charade? She could conceivably have been performing her brother's role for some time now, which would have given the palace staff time to acclimate to her performance and their role in it. She made a mental note to look up all the recent footage of Sebastian to pinpoint the moment Viola's impersonation began.

As Thijs let himself out, Viola gestured toward the far corner where a large wooden cabinet, its doors carved and painted with the royal seal, was topped by a silver tray that held an array of decanters. "May I offer you something to drink?"

Duke was sorely tempted, but it was only the midafternoon and she needed to keep her wits. "Sparkling water, please, if it isn't too much trouble."

Viola went to the cabinet and opened it, but she hesitated a moment before crouching down to peer inside. Had she been fighting her instincts, there? A woman wearing a dress would have had to bend from the waist. Had Duke just witnessed a meaningful moment of dysphoria, or was she manufacturing significance where there was none?

A hint of pride touched Viola's smile as she turned, holding two bottles. "No trouble, as you can see. Between this bar and my father's, I daresay we could entertain even the most esoteric cocktail request."

"That sounds like a challenge," Duke said, accepting the bottle. Viola had half-opened the cap in a chivalric gesture that felt at once antiquated and genuine. Was that a mannerism of Sebastian's that she was mimicking, or part of her own performance of masculinity?

Her smile widened. "You're welcome to take it as such." She indicated the cluster of chairs near the fireplace. "Shall we sit?"

Duke noticed that she thoughtfully took the seat with its back to the window, giving her the best view. "Thank you again for your generous invitation, Your Royal Highness," she said, once she was settled.

"Please, call me Sebastian. How are you enjoying your time in Brussels so far?"

"I only just arrived yesterday, but I look forward to exploring the city over the next few weeks."

She looked mildly surprised. "Weeks?"

"My assignment is to cover the duration of the bid. This will be my home base." Duke crossed one leg over the other, considering her next words. She needed to be poised and professional right now, but her instincts were driving her to *flirt*. She felt like a bird of paradise fighting the impulse to display its plumage. "If you have any suggestions for sightseeing or restaurants, I'd love to hear them."

Viola cocked her head. It was a mistake, though not a flashy one—the movement subtly enhanced her femininity.

"Are we on or off the record at the moment? If word gets out that I've recommended one attraction or dining establishment over another, it could wreak havoc with the local economy."

It was Duke's turn to be surprised, and it took her a moment to find the right words for her thoughts. "But you must have your favorite spots. Aren't they obvious at this point?"

"Yes, if you're paying attention—as the media does all too well." She softened the words with a slight smile. "But making conjectures about my preferences based on my behavior is quite different from publishing a list of my recommendations."

"I understand," Duke said, "And I can promise you that this conversation is off the record until you'd like it to be otherwise." She was impressed that Viola was so self-aware, and that her first instinct was to protect her city from the possible backlash of her inadvertent role as a social influencer. But before she could frame a question about how it felt to wield such power, Viola turned the tables.

"Then before we move on to official business, I meant what I said on Saturday, before we were interrupted. I would like to hear your story."

Between Eveline's interview and this moment, Duke had spent every spare second researching the Belgian twins and the World Cup bid festivities. She hadn't even remotely anticipated that Viola would remember that comment from their brief conversation, or that she would consider it important enough to follow up on. She wasn't prepared to talk about herself. Weren't royals supposed to be self-absorbed?

Viola must have sensed something of her internal conflict, because she reached out to touch Duke's shoulder—a barely-there caress that left her skin pebbled in its wake.

"I apologize if I'm being intrusive. You don't have to answer."

Duke saw compassion in her expression, and it struck her. "You're apologizing to a member of the press for your own intrusiveness? That's somewhat ironic."

Viola's short laugh had an edge to it. "Or empathetic."

With two words, Viola had neatly turned Duke's assumption on its head and exposed its adversarial perspective. Her confidence was completely in character for a prince, but Duke didn't think it was a performance. And that was very attractive.

"I can empathize, too," she said, wanting—no, *needing*—Viola to know she understood. "When I was still playing football professionally, I stood in the spotlight. It's nothing like the attention on you, but I know how it feels to be constantly watched and analyzed."

"It's a form of brutality," Viola said. "And it's utterly exhausting." Her gaze sharpened. "We are still off the record, correct?"

"As I said, until you tell me differently," Duke said without hesitation, hoping her alacrity would inspire Viola's trust. "You're in charge."

Viola's pupils flared and her jawline tensed, her face momentarily betraying a fierce hunger that left Duke feeling weak. Not the kind of weakness she hated—the helplessness of a broken body, the hopelessness of broken dreams—but the glorious surrender of desire. In that moment, Viola's lust was a dark fin breaking the water, and Duke wanted nothing more than to be devoured.

And then Viola sat back in her chair and sipped at her water, and the dark fin submerged. "I'll keep that in mind," she said, her tone betraying only amusement. "In which case, my earlier request still stands."

Duke took a long drink, as much to soothe her parched throat as to buy herself the time to regain some measure of control. When she thought she could trust her voice again, she began to sketch the outlines of her soccer career. It was a story she had told frequently, and while it always dredged up bad memories, she now had cause to be thankful for the repetition. The practiced words rolled off her tongue easily, even as a part of her still flailed in awe and bewilderment at finding herself sitting in a castle across from a princess pretending to be a prince.

Viola was an attentive listener, and miraculously, Duke found her nerves fading into the background. An unfamiliar urge took their place—the desire to round out her story by adding the dimension of her sexual orientation. She had never shared those details with anyone other than teammates, whom she trusted to protect her secrets, and she had likewise constricted her dating pool for the same reason. Although she hadn't dated anyone since her relationship with Juno ended over a year ago, Duke had remained close-lipped, out of habit if for no other reason.

Now, she found herself wanting to come clean—not for the sake of lofty ideals or activism, but because in admitting her sexuality, she could potentially attract *Viola's* attention even as she ostensibly conversed with her brother. The problem was that if she confessed to being a lesbian, she would have no excuse to flirt more aggressively with "Sebastian" and possibly make some use of the sparks between them. But if she said nothing, Viola would likely assume her to be straight and therefore unavailable.

It was a Catch-22...if Duke were being an idiot. She wasn't here to get a date with a princess; she was here to learn as much as possible in the service of exposing a cover-up. If allowing Viola to believe her to be straight was a means to that end, so be it.

Duke paused to clear her throat before launching into the conclusion of her narrative. As she spoke, she reminded herself to keep her eye on the prize.

Viola had learned the broad strokes of Duke's story from Eveline, but it was something else entirely to hear the echo of pain in Duke's voice as she chronicled the dream-shattering verdict handed down by her surgeons. That pain pulled at her, and she had to actively resist the impulse to reach out and clasp Duke's hand where it rested on the arm of the chair. Sebastian wouldn't do that.

"So as soon as it became clear that I'd never be able to play at that level again, I turned to journalism as an alternative career. A former teammate's brother helped me secure this job, and here I am—trying to earn my stripes." Duke paused, then laughed self-consciously, a faint flush blooming across her cheekbones. "It just occurred to me that 'earn my stripes' might be one of those strange American idioms. What I meant by it was that I don't have much credibility as a journalist and am in the stage of proving my worth. And that's it—that's my story."

Viola watched in sympathy as Duke drained the remainder of her glass. She tried to imagine how it would feel if she were somehow deprived of her creative spark—still able to take pictures to make memories, but unable to elevate that skill into an art form. It would be beyond awful. She concealed a shudder by leaning forward, resting her elbows between her knees as a man might do.

"I'm sorry for your loss," she said, torn between wanting to express that sympathy in less clichéd terms and needing to stay in character. Had she been able to react as herself, she would have said so much more, but most of the men she knew, her brother included, were laconic when it came to describing their emotions. For what felt like the thousandth time over the past week, she wondered whether men felt as constrained by the norms governing their behavior as she did emulating them.

Sebastian had shared more with her than he did with anyone—or so she had thought, at least, before his overdose. Had he chafed at the unwritten rules all his life, or were they so deeply ingrained that he never even questioned them? She had never thought to broach the topic. Her own coming out process had involved learning to ask those kinds of questions—but of herself, not of him.

Viola realized that Duke had spoken again, and she had missed every word. "Please excuse me," she said, and quickly cleared her throat when the words came out in a higher register than she'd intended. "I'm not following. Would you mind repeating that last?"

She hoped Duke would take the implied excuse—that Viola hadn't been able to fully understand her English—at face value rather than seeing through it to her distraction. Perhaps this had been a bad idea. She had thought it wise to interact with the media on her own terms—and if she were being honest with herself, had wanted an excuse to see Duke again—but if she couldn't maintain her focus, she risked making a mistake that Duke might detect.

"Of course," Duke said. "I'm sorry. Sometimes I don't enunciate very well. I was just trying to apologize for bringing down the mood."

Viola felt a stab of panic at the realization that she had no idea how Sebastian would respond to such a statement. Her retort about empathy earlier had been a mistake, an instance in which she'd allowed her true self to shine through. Did Sebastian abandon some of his usual reserve when he was alone in the presence of a beautiful woman? She had no way of knowing.

"No apologies necessary," she said lightly, deciding he would try to defuse the intensity of the conversation at this point. "We'll spend the remainder of our time together talking about happier topics."

Duke took the opening she'd supplied. "Such as your bid. Are you ready to go on the record?"

"Yes." Viola straightened her posture, determined to be more vigilant. Some of whatever she said next would make it into public. This was a different kind of test from the exhibition match. Interviews were usually her forte—she preferred the more intimate atmosphere to speaking in front of a crowd—and she had plenty of practice at phrasing her replies tactfully. But now, she needed to be doubly cautious of her phrasing, even as she maintained the lower key of her voice and Sebastian's physical mannerisms.

She also had to monitor her reactions to Duke. Viola was confident in her own ability to resist a purely physical attraction, but hearing Duke's full story from her own mouth had rendered her a fully three-dimensional being. Viola now found herself drawn to that extra dimension just as much as she was attracted to her face and body. Duke's tale of injury and setback might be in the past, but she was still very much in pain, and that pain called to her.

She would have to answer that call with friendship and nothing more, of course. Duke thought she was Sebastian. The chemistry Viola had already sensed between them was heterosexual in nature. She grimaced at the frivolity of her thoughts, then hastily smoothed her features before Duke looked up. Tension settled between her shoulder blades and she exhaled as unobtrusively as possible.

"Do you mind if I record our conversation?" Duke said, holding up her phone. "I'll stop anytime you'd like."

"That's fine."

Fortunately, Duke's first few questions were low-hanging fruit: why had Belgium chosen to submit a bid, why was it a shared bid with the Netherlands, and how that collaboration worked. Those topics presented no difficulty to Viola, and she concentrated instead on how to phrase and then deliver her answers. She put special emphasis on the positive economic impact of hosting the World Cup, as well as the power of football to unite not only both countries, but the various cultural and linguistic groups represented within them. This was politically fraught territory, but Sebastian had always confronted it frankly, and because of that, she felt confident in doing the same.

"There is longstanding tension between French and Flemish speakers in this country, but in certain ways, football already functions as a *lingua franca.* When you are supporting the same team, cheers in any language bind all together." Her rhetoric there was perhaps more flowery than Sebastian's usual, but Viola didn't think the error would be glaring. Still, she needed to stop herself from getting so caught up in her ideas that she gave no attention to her delivery of them.

"Recently, we have become even more diverse," she continued. "Belgium's immigration policy is a liberal one by design. It is part of our national identity, and I am proud of that. As our demographics shift, we must continue to find new ways of creating community and building consensus around our core values. Football, as a source of personal, regional, and national pride, can help with that mission."

When Duke didn't immediately follow up with her next question, Viola dared to look at her more closely. She had a peculiar expression on her face: surprise, mingled with…respect? As much as Viola appreciated the latter, she wondered at the former. Had Duke expected Sebastian to be some football-crazy playboy with no sense of the game's broader impact? Did she think a speechwriter had written his remarks at the exhibition game? He might not be as charismatic as some other princes, but he had a kind of pragmatic political savvy that had never come naturally to Viola, and his passion for sports extended to a deep interest in the business side of professional athletics.

Their gazes met, and unmistakable attraction flared in Duke's eyes. If Duke had underestimated her previously, she wasn't now. Viola was on the cusp of responding with what Dahlia had liked to call her "mysterious smile" when she caught herself. She transmuted the expression into something she hoped was less feminine and flirtatious, offering Duke a slight quirk of the lips before reaching for her water. When she sat back, Duke was ready with another question.

"Would you mind talking about why you oversaw the bid effort personally? It seems to me that you're deeply invested—not only as a public entity, but also as an individual."

It was a good question, and a challenging one. She wished she could stop time and call Sebastian—not because she couldn't think of an answer, but because she wanted to do him justice by offering the *right* one. But Sebastian's phone was in her nearby bedroom, and even if she called his rehabilitation facility, they would politely take a message—nothing more.

"As a member of the ruling family in a constitutional monarchy, my real power is limited," she began, hoping he would approve of where she planned to take this. "In many ways, this is liberating, because it frees me to think outside the traditional boxes to determine how I may best serve my country. During the most recent World Cup, Belgium advanced to the semi-finals and I was able to attend the match in person—such is my privilege. But all day, my social media feeds were filled with photographs and videos from all over this country. They showed Belgian flags flying proudly from every window, whether large or small."

Viola could hear her voice rising in pitch as she got caught up in both the manufactured memory and her own rhetoric. Sebastian had attended that particular match, of course, but she had not, and she had no idea what he'd been thinking.

"The pictures of Belgium from that day captured signs in Flemish, French, and German, all in support of our national team. As fortunate as I was to be sitting in the stands, halfway across the world, part of me wished I could be at home, surrounded by my countrymen, raising a glass of *geuze* in honor of those representing us on the pitch."

Duke's attention was riveted on her face, and Viola experienced an unexpected surge of triumph at having managed to captivate her, even while she was actively manufacturing a response to the challenging question. With difficulty, she focused on finishing her point.

"The idea came to me in that moment: that I should campaign for my country to host the tournament. But upon analysis, it became clear that alone, we could not support the infrastructure necessary for such a project. It was a natural next step to invite our close friends in the Netherlands to join our cause. We share a language, core values, and a passion for football. It was a perfect match, and I remain grateful to King Maximilian and his people for everything they have done to advance this team effort."

Duke, having apparently recovered her wits, asked a few more questions about the logistics of the Belgian-Dutch collaboration, forcing Viola to choose her words carefully. Over the few days, she had done her best to study everything Sebastian had on file about the bid, knowing that if she didn't understand the context of each event, she would be more likely to make errors. But even with André's and Maes's help, her knowledge was thin and peppered with gaps.

"Your shared bid encompasses many events over the coming month. Is there one about which you are particularly excited?"

Relieved that she had a clear answer this time, Viola leapt to reply. "I am grateful to all who have given their money, time, and work to the bid. The gala, which will be held at the *Palais Royale* this weekend, is an especially exciting event. It will be a spectacular fete honoring football's charitable efforts over quite literally a century. All proceeds will be donated to the seven charities our committee has chosen to feature. We're calling it 'The Magic of Football,' and the evening's entertainment will include performances of both large and close-up magicians."

"That sounds like so much fun," Duke said, her face alight with genuine interest. "Is the guest list as star-studded as I imagine?"

"Many people have been very generous," she said, unwilling to offer names while they were still on the record. "I have high hopes."

She expected Duke to push for specifics, but instead, she asked whether there was anything else she wished to add about the bid before their interview concluded.

"Only that if we are successful, we look forward to welcoming guests from around the world in a few years' time. I believe the global community will find us generous hosts."

"You certainly have been to me," Duke said. She reached over to end the recording, then slipped the phone into her purse. "We're back to being off the record. Thank you again for agreeing to this interview. I—" She dropped their eye contact, but only for a moment. "I meant what I said about your generosity. I'm virtually unknown in the journalism world, yet you opened your home to me during an incredibly busy time. I don't take any of that for granted."

Her candor was as appealing as it was surprising, and a fresh surge of attraction made Viola wish once again that they had met under different circumstances. For one insane instant, she found herself wanting to confess all to Duke: to level the walls between them in one decisive blow and solicit both her sympathy and her alliance.

But that was ridiculous—while she might know the facts of Duke's life, Viola hadn't the faintest clue about her trustworthiness and moral compass. Duke had just barely crossed the line between stranger and acquaintance, and it was pure insanity to want to trust her with a secret of this magnitude just because she *seemed* honest.

Instead, Viola knew she should seize the opportunity to dismiss Duke from her presence. But she simply didn't want to. Not yet. She had played Sebastian's part near perfectly. Didn't she deserve some kind of reward?

Before she could second-guess her own logic, Viola spoke. "I've enjoyed our time together. Now that your work is finished, will you have that drink?"

"Please," Duke said with a smile that transformed her from lovely to stunning.

Viola was glad she had an excuse to turn away, and she busied herself with collecting the appropriate materials from the bar cabinet until she regained faith in her self-control.

"I have one particular cocktail in mind," she said, "but it requires you not to be allergic to juniper berries or lemons. Will that be a problem?"

"I'm not allergic to lemons, but I wouldn't be able to pick a juniper berry out of a lineup." A frown creased the bridge of her nose. "Is that another of those troublesome American idioms? Because I can expl—"

"That one I know," Viola interjected, finding her self-consciousness endearing. "And you know more about juniper berries than you think. They are the key ingredient in gin."

"I'm ashamed to say I didn't know that," Duke said. "While I was playing football professionally, I never drank alcohol. My ignorance is embarrassing."

"Not at all." Viola paused to spoon ice into a mixing glass. Perhaps it was fanciful, but she imagined she could feel the warmth of Duke's gaze on her back. She wanted to confirm that suspicion but resolutely forced herself not to. "Do you think most of your friends who enjoy martinis know how gin is distilled?"

Duke laughed softly. "Good point."

Silence stretched between them then, broken only by the sounds of ice cubes cracking as Viola measured and poured the ingredients. It wasn't uncomfortable, exactly, but it did feel meaningful—inflected by the subtle tension of attraction.

"That's a beautiful photograph," Duke said suddenly. "The one above your head," she added, indicating the print framed above the bar cabinet as Viola looked to her for clarification.

She felt her own smile break free before she could remember to temper it, and she quickly looked down at the mixing glass to hide her face. The picture, which she had taken last year, was a still life. A glass of genever and the bottle from which it had been poured dominated the foreground, the pale amber liquid gleaming in the light. Behind it, she had posed a small, brightly burnished copper alembic still.

"I agree," she said lightly. "My sister took it."

Hopefully, Duke would interpret her smile as an expression of fraternal pride. Viola's heart was pounding faster than it had been, and not from apprehension. Duke had admired one of her photographs before she knew the identity of the artist. That fact pleased Viola immensely, and the strength of her reaction was rather embarrassing. Did her vanity know no bounds?

"The colors are stunning," Duke said. "Now that you know my ignorance, what is genever? Is it related to gin?"

"Yes, though it would be more accurate to say the converse," she explained. She held up a bottle of the same brand as the one in the photograph before pouring some into the glass. "The recipe evolved from the Flemish parts of Belgium, where people have been distilling juniper berries since the thirteenth century. They called the result *jenever,* and the name has stuck through time. We Belgians are very proud of it. And it's in the cocktail I'm making, so you won't have to be ignorant any longer."

Viola forestalled any further questions by capping and shaking the glass over her shoulder. Her usual vigor was somewhat constrained by her chest binder, but the mild discomfort was a welcome reminder that she had to remain cautious. She poured the mixture into two hand-blown coupe glasses, their thin double stems twining like vines, then reached for the small glass jar she'd removed from the cabinet's spice rack.

"Is that some kind of spice you're adding?"

The muted sound of Duke's heels against the thin rug heralded her approach, but Viola still nearly stopped breathing when she felt Duke's breath against the shell of her ear as she leaned in to look. The skin on her forearms pebbled, and Viola prayed Duke didn't notice.

"Finely ground cayenne pepper." Viola took one careful step back before she faced Duke and extended one of the glasses. "And here you are: a Dutch Razorblade." She was careful not to let their fingertips touch.

Duke raised her drink. "Would you mind teaching me how to toast properly? I don't know what Belgians say."

There was a note of coyness in her voice that roused the sharper edge of Viola's desire—the urge to possess, to *take,* that had frightened her until she met Dahlia. Naturally submissive sexually, Dahlia had encouraged Viola's assertiveness, and the liberation Viola had found in Dahlia's arms had been intoxicating.

Too intoxicating. Learning to trust and express some of her more dominant urges had, ironically, been a kind of surrender—the kind that bared her soul, exposing her all the more to Dahlia's manipulations. As much as one part of her exulted in the fantasy of Duke yielding beneath her, another part trumpeted alarm at falling under someone else's spell.

But Viola wasn't the naive woman she had been. In fact, she wasn't a woman at all, as far as Duke was concerned. Duke had accepted her performance of Sebastian without the slightest sign of suspicion. As long as their flirtation remained playful—and exclusively verbal—Viola didn't need to be troubled.

"The most common toast is *santé*," she said, "which essentially means, 'May you have good health.'"

"*Santé*, then," Duke said. "Do we clink glasses?"

"No. Though in the Netherlands, it is customary to clink beer glasses. There, you say *proost.*"

Duke laughed—a pleasant sound, like the glitter of starlight on water. "I should take notes."

"Oh? Are we back on the record?" Viola smiled briefly to show she was joking.

"Not unless you'd like to be."

There it was again—the flirtatious note underlying what would otherwise have been a simple sentiment. Fleetingly, Viola wondered whether Duke might possibly be bisexual. Maybe, once this was all over, she could contrive to "meet" Duke as herself, and—

Had she been alone, she might have slapped herself. This persistent line of thinking was ridiculous. It didn't matter whether she might or might not be able to court Duke once her brother had returned to his public duties. What mattered was making sure she maintained her facade until then, at all cost.

Viola returned her attention to Duke in time to catch her first sip of the cocktail. "What do you think?"

"Delicious." Duke smiled at her in what seemed to be genuine delight. "I especially appreciate the 'kick' of the cayenne."

"You enjoy the heat, then?" Viola wanted to take the words back as soon as she spoke them, but some part of her refused to be silenced. The rest of her was intrigued by how Duke would answer.

"Oh, yes. Vanilla is my least favorite flavor."

Viola drank from her own glass, as much to mask what her face might give away as to soothe her suddenly parched throat. *That* was a tantalizing answer, and one that pushed all her buttons.

"Shall we sit?" she said, once she was certain she could master her expression.

Duke returned to her chair, and as she crossed one leg over the other, Viola admired their shapely curves. She might not play football any longer, but she clearly still kept herself in prime physical condition, and Viola could imagine the strength of those legs wrapped around her waist as she—

"Would it be possible for me to meet your sister, if she's at home?"

The question shattered Viola's fantasy as a chill of fear filled the void left by her arousal. There was no need to panic, she reminded herself. It was an innocent question with an easy answer.

"I hope that's not too presumptuous a request," Duke continued, "but if not, I'd like to tell her how much I enjoy her photography."

"And she would like to hear it," Viola said. "Unfortunately, she is not at home, but I will be sure she receives the message."

"Thank you." Duke offered a quick smile. "I'm curious: how did you choose the charities associated with the bid?"

Relieved at the change of subject, and that she knew the answer, Viola relaxed into the embrace of her chair. "The bid committee collaborated on the decision. We wanted a mix of well established charities with a proven track record and relatively new organizations trying promising approaches."

"It's a great idea," Duke said, then wrinkled her nose slightly. "I know that might sound like I'm pandering, but I do mean it. The philanthropic side of the bid encourages more people to get involved and changes the mission of the entire process."

Pleased, but not wanting to betray how much, Viola asked, "How so?"

"Because no one has to feel self-indulgent about participating in all your festivities," Duke said. "The point of these events isn't only to earn the right to host the World Cup, but also to increase support for the work of the associated charities. I've heard you speak twice now about how football can change the world, but that might sound like lip service if you weren't putting your money where your mouth is, so to speak."

"I believe in the mission," Viola said. "But you're correct that it's also expedient."

This time, Duke's smile was wider. "I think you've just given me the topic of my next article. The focus on charity is a large part of what makes your bid so distinctive."

An idea entered Viola's mind, and like the bid, it was also both self-indulgent and expedient. "In that case, would you like to attend the gala?"

Duke's sculpted eyebrows rose. "Very much. Unfortunately, the price of a ticket is out of my range by several zeroes."

Viola had to laugh. "Shall we trade and barter, then? An article about the bid's emphasis on charity in exchange for one ticket?"

"I accept."

When Duke leaned forward, extending her free hand, Viola's first thought was that she wanted to seal the promise with much more than a handshake. Still, the prospect of touching her, however platonically, was so appealing that Viola knew she shouldn't. Still, she could hardly ignore the invitation. Plastering what she hoped was a cordial but reserved expression on her face, Viola reached out.

Duke's palm was warm and smooth, and Viola was nearly overwhelmed by the urge to stroke her thumb across the soft web of skin between her thumb and forefinger. Instead, she disengaged as quickly as she could without jerking away, then drained her cocktail and looked ostentatiously at her watch.

"Sadly, I've run out of time," she said. "I'm due at the palace to examine the final preparations."

"Of course." Duke tossed back her own drink, and something about the movement—perhaps the way it bared the pale skin of her throat—made Viola's mouth go dry all over again. She moistened her lips with her tongue.

"This has been pleasant, as well as useful," she said as she stood and went to the door. She opened it to find one of the palace guards waiting attentively. "If you give Ricard here your contact information, he will send you a gala ticket."

"I'll do that." Duke's arm brushed hers as she crossed the threshold, and Viola tried to pretend she was unaffected. "I look forward to seeing you soon."

"Good-bye."

Viola closed the door and leaned against it, rubbing her temples in slow circles. Her heart still pounded and her skin still hummed, and she should *not* have invited Duke to torment her even further by attending the gala. She hadn't been able to help herself, and not even a dozen plausible excuses of expedience could make up for her weakness.

Still, Duke's promise of an article would be helpful, and perhaps she could transmute her own selfishness into generosity by ensuring that her friends benefitted from Duke's presence. She could introduce Duke to Alix, the Monegasque princess whose not-for-profit, Rising Sun, had recently formed a spin-off organization focused on empowering women through football. The new charity, Eclipse, was chaired by another of Viola's friends: Kerry, Duchess of Kent, wife of Sasha, the Princess Royal of the United Kingdom. If Viola steered Duke toward them, she could at least ease her own conscience. And she would be so busy at the gala that she probably wouldn't exchange more than a few words with Duke.

The gala would be her most challenging performance yet. Most of the attendees knew her brother, and she had yet to memorize the names and faces of those who would expect personal attention from Sebastian. She crossed the room to the window and perched on the seat, allowing herself just a moment to look out over the perfectly ordered gardens and wish that her own circumstances weren't so chaotic.

They didn't have to be. She had chosen this road, and now she needed to follow it to its conclusion. With a soft exhale, she stood and turned her back on the symmetry outside, focusing instead on what had to be done.

CHAPTER TEN

Palais Royale de Bruxelles

Viola examined her reflection critically from the top down, hoping the detail-oriented task would distract from her anxiety. Antonio had touched up her hair an hour ago; trimmed very short on the back and sides, it was significantly longer on top. He had spiked it dramatically before mussing it to create a less severe, though still fashionable, look.

Her tuxedo jacket was black, but Antonio had advised her to go with peak lapels rather than the traditional shawl. The sharp, uplifted corners would, he claimed, make her look taller. She needed all the help she could get in that department: her shoes did have an inch of platform (anything more had been conspicuous), but she was still an inch shy of Sebastian's height. No one had noticed at the exhibition match, and hopefully the same would hold true tonight. But this was also her "reunion" with Maria, and Viola worried that someone who spent so much time literally on Sebastian's arm would perceive the disparity.

As one of the hosts of the gala, Viola would be busy with official responsibilities, and it shouldn't be too difficult to keep Maria at a distance for the duration. It was the after-party that worried her— itself an official event, hosted by Zonde, one of Brussels's most prominent nightclubs. But in a text last night, Maria had suggested that as soon as he'd put in an appearance, he should give his security team the slip so they could attend a "Lorelei party." Viola didn't know what that was, but far more disturbing was the fact that none of her security team did, either. Maria's offer had precipitated an emergency meeting that had kept them all awake into the early hours of the morning. The question under debate was whether Viola should pretend to lose her guards and accompany Maria to the party to gather information. As much as Viola wanted to learn the truth, she had been apprehensive about the risk involved to her cover. Her primary purpose in impersonating Sebastian was to protect his quality of life, after all. Any details she could ferret out were icing on the cake; Ruben had his own people investigating the events leading up to Sebastian's arrival at the hospital, and he would put one of them on the trail of this "Lorelei."

Still, she had felt like a coward until Ruben, Thijs, and André had each separately expressed the same opinion—that it was far too dangerous for her to be "alone" with Sebastian's close friends. The after-party itself would be enough of a challenge. Now, with guests already arriving for the gala, the three of them were in the antechamber of Sebastian's office, waiting on her to do one final run-through of the plan for the evening.

They could wait a few more minutes. She brushed a dark thread from her crisp white shirt, its black buttons winking in the light of the overhead lamp. Beneath it, she wore a white undershirt, the entire purpose of which was to hide her chest binder. It wasn't the most comfortable garment on the planet, but then again, if she'd been alive a century and a half ago, she would have been strapped into corsets on a daily basis. Put in perspective, the binder wasn't so bad. It was also guaranteed to remain in place, so she didn't need to worry about it now that it was covered up.

The packing cock was a different story. Antonio had been the one to recommend it a few days ago, when they were discussing her fashion choices for this evening. His logic was that slim-fitting tuxedo pants would require at least the hint of a bulge. More importantly to Viola, it might help her fool Maria. She wouldn't put it past Sebastian's girlfriend to find a subtle way to grope "him" at some point this evening, and now she was prepared for that eventuality.

When she thought of how Thijs's face had turned a deep scarlet during that particular conversation, she had to smile. Ultimately, she had ordered André to acquire a few different models; he hadn't been thrilled, but he couldn't complain. As far as she was concerned, the most awkward part of the experience had been trying on each "packer" with the slacks and comparing herself to recent photographs of Sebastian. Staring intently at pictures of her brother's crotch was *not* something she ever wanted to do again.

Viola ran her fingers over the slight prominence. That awkwardness notwithstanding, she had been pleasantly surprised by how the packer made her feel. Something about it was sexy, though she hadn't yet pinned down what. Maybe it was the light pressure between her thighs that never quite let her forget its existence, or the mild exhibitionism of the bulge itself. Maybe she would do a few self-portraits with it on, once this entire ordeal was over and she could go back to performing only herself.

The buzz of her watch pulled her attention away. She was out of time. She met her reflection's eyes and straightened her shoulders. "Once more unto the breach," she quoted, pleased that Sebastian's pitch came almost naturally now.

The three men stood when she entered the room, and she waved them back into her seats. Ruben and André obeyed, but Thijs approached her, palm outstretched.

"A lavalier microphone, ma'am," he said, "and an ear bud. So we can hear your conversations and offer assistance as needed. May I?"

"They won't interfere with the other microphone, when I'm delivering my speech?"

"No. We tested it."

"Thank you." As he secured the microphone on the inside of her lapel, Viola looked over his shoulder to the others. "Are there any last-minute changes?"

"None, Your Royal Highness," Ruben said. "You will serve as the master of ceremonies at the gala as planned and afterward make an appearance at the club."

"That's still the part I'm most worried about," Viola admitted.

"We'll stay close," Thijs said. "You'll have the kind of over-protection you usually hate."

"I'll be appreciative tonight," she said, holding perfectly still as he inserted the ear bud.

"If you feel threatened, frightened, or uncertain, say 'chimera' and we will extract you immediately," Ruben said.

Viola caught herself before making a joke about safe words. "Chimera," she repeated instead. "Not the easiest of terms to slip into a sentence, but I'll think of something."

Once the electronic equipment had been tested, she followed Ruben into the corridor, Thijs and Andre taking up flanking positions just behind her. The cocktail hour prior to the gala's commencement had already begun, but the royal family would make a fashionably late appearance. By the time Viola reached the greenroom—so called not only because its walls and furniture were various shades of green, but because it served as a staging area for any official function held in the state rooms beyond—her parents were waiting, and she greeted them with cheek kisses.

"Are you certain about this?" her mother whispered as a member of the staff fastened a larger, visible microphone to her other lapel.

"Yes," Viola said with a firmness she didn't entirely feel.

Her father squeezed her elbow in a silent show of support, then nodded to Robert DeClerq, the head butler, who waited before the double doors that led to the Empire Room. Fastidious in his etiquette, DeClerq bowed before turning to grasp the bronze handles. The muffled notes of a trumpet fanfare became brazen as he pushed, and Viola heard the whisper of fabric, magnified over two hundred times, as the attendees turned to watch their entrance.

"His Majesty, Leopold Albert Louis Baudoin, King of the Belgians! Her Majesty, Charlotte, Queen of the Belgians! His Royal Highness, Sebastian Philippe Gabriel Nicolas, Prince of Belgium!"

Viola was glad she could enter one step behind her parents. She might be the MC of this event, but for now, they could serve as her shield. The crowd parted before them, and they made their way to the far end of the room, where a small dais was raised a meter above the ground. It held only a small, highly polished wooden table on which three filled champagne flutes waited to be claimed. Viola positioned herself between her parents and looked out at those gathered, glittering in their tuxedos and gowns.

She only realized she was looking for Duke once she spotted her. The black one-shoulder dress fell past her knees, but a slit in its side bared her left leg to mid thigh, revealing tanned skin and the elegant contours of her toned legs. The natural wave of Duke's golden hair had been enhanced, and it curled over her shoulders in a luxuriant mass that made Viola's fingers itch with the desire to comb through it, preferably while Duke's face was buried between—

Oh, no. No. She was not going to get trapped by a fantasy and forget all about her mission tonight. She was not going to let a beautiful face and perfect body distract her when the stakes were so high. Resolutely, she focused on her parents' opening words, considering how best to connect her own speech with theirs, and forced her gaze away from where Duke was standing. When her father concluded, she stepped forward.

"It is that promise of a stronger, united global community that has brought you here this evening," she began, before returning to the now-memorized script she and Maes had co-written. "Football isn't only an interest shared across the globe, but also a means for positive change. The charities you are supporting tonight have proven that football can help to heal broken communities, jumpstart economies, and promote social justice. We honor and celebrate their fine work, as we also commit to supporting them in their future endeavors. The 'magic' they work daily transforms lives.

"You are empowering that magic by joining us tonight. Our performers have also donated their performances, and we are grateful to them for that gift. Throughout the course of the evening, there will be opportunities to purchase raffle tickets, and three fortunate winners will receive a two-night stay in a VIP suite at a Four Seasons hotel of your choice—anywhere in the world. Other excellent prizes will be auctioned after dinner."

Viola turned to accept a glass of champagne from her mother, then raised it high. "To those who have worked tirelessly to harness the magic of football to promote positive change. *Santé!*"

The room filled with an echo of her toast as the audience returned the sentiment, and Viola sipped with them, relieved to have gotten through the opening of the gala without any hiccups. As she left the dais with her parents, her father murmured, "Well done," and her mother squeezed her arm lightly. She drew strength from their support, knowing the most challenging part of the evening lay ahead.

The first task at hand was for her family to greet the other royals in attendance, beginning with King Maximilian; his wife, Juliana; and Eveline. Wilhemina, the Grand Duchess of Luxembourg and Viola's second cousin, never missed a good party, and her consort, Francis, used any excuse to flaunt his passion for philanthropy. Nervous about being detected, Viola tried to keep them talking as much as possible while they exchanged pleasantries. It was a relief when her father swooped in to distract them with a question about the forthcoming northern European trade summit.

No sooner had she breathed a sigh of relief at having successfully weathered that gauntlet, then she caught sight of Princess Sasha arm in arm with her wife, Kerry. They were headed in her direction, and behind them were two others she recognized well: Alix, Princess of Monaco; and her girlfriend, Thalia d'Angelis, the only female Formula One driver currently racing.

When Viola's ill-advised romance with Dahlia had ended, catapulting her from the closet into the limelight, both Sasha and Alix had reached out to her with messages of support and an invitation to temporarily escape the storm of controversy by spending a weekend at Alix's family home on Lake Como. Since then, they had made a point to continue to see each other socially whenever possible. Sasha had unofficially dubbed their coterie the Queer Royals' Club.

Before Sebastian's hospitalization, Viola had been looking forward to reuniting with the four of them at this gala. Recently, she had even contemplated letting them in on her secret. She knew she could count on their support, but what if one of them let something slip while in public, or when a loose-lipped or ethically dubious staffer was within hearing? It was safer to keep her own mouth shut, and so she had texted them this morning with the news that she had come down with the flu and wouldn't be able to attend the festivities. At least she hadn't needed to feign her own disappointment.

There was no reason for them to be suspicious of her excuse, but Viola was still concerned about interacting with them as Sebastian. They were all intelligent, perceptive women, and their queerness made them more attuned to the performativity of gender than many people were. Her goal was to keep their conversation tonight as brief as possible. This was also an opportunity to move forward with her plan of introducing Duke. Hopefully, they would all keep one another occupied for the remainder of the night—though Viola couldn't quite suppress the thrill she felt at having the opportunity, however brief, to interact with Duke now.

She raised her glass to her lips, using it as a shield. "Thijs," she murmured into the lavalier mic. "Find Missy Duke and bring her here."

"Why?"

"No time," she breathed and took a quick sip as the four women drew closer.

"Sebastian!" Sasha's voice rang out like a bell, clear and pure. Viola turned, composing her lips in a friendly, though somewhat distant, smile. She suspected her brother had carried a torch for Sasha when they were all adolescents, though that didn't exactly make him unique. Viola had, too, though in that barely realized way that had made her own true desires a secret even from herself.

Suspicions aside, Viola knew for a fact that Alix had piqued Sebastian's interest last year. She had worried about that crush, coming as it did on the heels of his breakup with Alix's older sister. Had he truly been interested in Alix, or had he wanted an excuse to remain close (in some strange way) to Camille? She didn't know and probably never would. Fleetingly, she wondered whether Sebastian felt at all self-conscious that two of the women he'd fancied had turned out to be queer. Statistically speaking, that wasn't odd, but had the coincidence demoralized him further?

Then they were upon her, and she exchanged cheek kisses as quickly as possible, lest they detect her lack of stubble.

"Thank you for being here tonight," she said, concentrating even more than usual on the timbre of her voice. She turned her gaze on Alix, whose charity was one of the featured organizations. "I'm glad we could honor Rising Sun's impressive accomplishments."

"As am I," she said, "though I would be remiss if I didn't credit Kerry. Eclipse, the football 'arm' of the organization, is her brainchild entirely."

"Now you've done it," Thalia said. "These lot turn into a mutual admiration society with very little provocation."

"I beg your pardon!" Sasha's twitching lips belied her outraged tone.

When Viola felt herself wanting to join in their banter, she clamped her teeth together, uncertain of how Sebastian would react. He would try to be charming, she guessed, but sometimes his efforts were too transparent to be altogether comfortable. Perhaps the best strategy was to invoke Viola herself, which would hopefully redirect their attention and minimize their scrutiny.

"While I'm fortunate enough to have you all here," she said, pouring on some of that awkward charm, "Viola is so disappointed that she couldn't attend tonight. She has reminded me at least five times today to give her love to you all."

This precipitated a chorus of well-wishes mingled with expressions of dismay that Viola found highly gratifying. Sasha demanded to know the status of "the patient," and Viola found herself fabricating a range of symptoms that she desperately hoped would not raise any red flags for Alix, who was trained as a physician. Fortunately, before she could inadvertently give herself the measles and mumps as well as the flu, Thijs appeared with Duke in tow, and Viola immediately changed her tack.

"I'm glad you could join us," she said, turning to Duke just in time to catch the end of what had clearly been a once-over. As Viola held her gaze, a blush spread across Duke's cheeks. That clear evidence of her attraction was enough to make Viola feel even more self-conscious as she leaned in for the obligatory greeting kisses and caught the faint—and utterly distracting—scent of rose blossoms. "These are people you should meet. Duke, may I introduce you to Alix, Princess of Monaco; Thalia d'Angelis; Princess Sasha of Kent; and her wife, Kerry, Duchess of Kent."

Viola knew that Kerry had played football in college, which was why she had mentioned her last. Kerry and Duke hadn't appeared to recognize each other on sight, but perhaps they had mutual friends in America.

"Duke, is it?" Sasha's head was tilted slightly, much like a bird's. "That's an interesting name."

"It's my surname, Your Royal Highness," Duke said. Viola had to admire her poise. Despite having been hustled across the room to meet two princesses, a Formula One driver, and a duchess, she exuded self-confidence—though it was tempered by a charming note of bashfulness, as though part of her was pleasantly stunned by her good fortune. "Sebastian knows that I'm not fond of my given name and is demonstrating his chivalry in withholding it from you."

Duke was flirting with "him." Viola knew it, and so did the others—Sasha raised her eyebrows, Kerry looked bemused, and Alix and Thalia shared a meaningful glance.

"Duke is a professional football player turned journalist," Viola said, determined to spin this situation to her advantage before one of them took it into her head to start teasing—or worse, matchmaking. "She will be writing a feature on the gala, and I'm sure she would be interested in speaking with each of you about your work with Rising Sun and Eclipse."

"Of course!" Kerry turned to Duke. "You scored the game winner to get the US into the finals of this past World Cup."

"That's me." Duke's answering smile was tinged with pain, presumably at Kerry's reference to her now-defunct career.

Viola had to fight against the urge to touch her bare arm—not in flirtation, but with the intent to soothe, and to convey her sympathy. But that would be a mistake. The entire point of bringing Duke here had been to escape *all* of them, and now that she had her opening, she didn't want to take it? That was ridiculous. The longer Viola spent in the company of these women, the more likely it became that she would betray herself.

"Please excuse me," she said. "I'm afraid I'm needed elsewhere at the moment, but I hope to see you all at the after-party."

No sooner had she moved off, congratulating herself on accomplishing two goals simultaneously by using Duke as a distraction for the QRC and thereby also eliminating Duke as a distraction for *herself*, than Thijs's voice filled her ears.

"Your Royal Highness, Maria is approaching from your nine o'clock. I'm proceeding as planned."

Viola didn't respond. She couldn't very well appear to be talking to herself in the midst of her own gala, and that very fact had motivated the construction of several preordained courses of action designed for various scenarios. "Plan Maria" involved Viola acknowledging Sebastian's girlfriend and talking with her briefly before being "interrupted" by one of her parents (or, in extremis, a member of her security) who would need "him" elsewhere. Maria could hardly fault "him" for being in high demand, though from what Viola knew of her, she might do so anyway. Viola didn't change her trajectory or her attention, but she silently prepared for Maria's assault.

"Why hello, stranger." The words were accompanied by a warm hand on her shoulder.

Viola turned and looked into Maria's eyes. She noted their constricted pupils and wondered whether Maria was already high. Anger rose in her at the thought, but she tamped it down and summoned the smile she had practiced in the mirror: uncertain, but with a tinge of eagerness that should mollify Maria's ego.

"Maria," she said, taking in her appearance. "You look beautiful."

That much was true. Her hair was plaited in two elaborate braids that met behind her head, merging like two rivers above a dark blond waterfall. The style accentuated the angles of her face and collarbones, the pale expanse of her neck and throat.

"Words are cheap," she said coyly. "Show me." She wrapped her arms around Viola's neck and drew her down. "I've missed you, baby," she added in a throaty whisper before joining their lips.

Viola had tried to prepare for this moment, but how could she? She had no idea—and negative desire to know—how her brother's kissing technique compared to her own. The only possible course of action was to be herself and be ready to explain away any differences Maria chanced to remark upon.

Her pliant mouth tasted like overripe strawberries. Viola had assumed that, public as it was, the kiss would be brief, but Maria held her close and parted her lips, clearly wanting to send a message to any onlookers. Viola slipped her tongue just inside to tangle with Maria's, hoping she would be distracted enough to ease her grip. The ploy worked, and Viola promptly ended the kiss, stepping away before Maria could regroup. Her mouth framed a pout.

"That's all I get after so long?"

"Sebastian?"

Her mother's voice reached out with the promise of rescue, and Viola turned to her gratefully. Her mother's face betrayed no hint of her deception—she looked every inch the confident queen, at her ease in polite society. Upon noticing Maria, she feigned surprise so well that for an instant, Viola thought she must truly not have seen her. But of course she had: she was following through on the plan.

"Oh, Maria, my apologies," her mother said with perfect civility. "But I'm afraid I must abscond with Sebastian." She looked to Viola. "The Japanese ambassador would like a word before we announce dinner."

"Of course." Viola did her best to affect disappointment, and as she kissed Maria's cheek, she murmured an apology.

She linked arms with her mother, and once they were several paces away, thanked her in a barely audible whisper.

"It was the least I could do. How are you bearing up?"

"That was uncomfortable," Viola admitted. "But I don't think I raised any red flags."

Her mother paused to pluck two fresh glasses of champagne from a proffered tray and handed one to Viola. "You are an extraordinary person, Vi. And you are doing an amazing job. Sometimes, when I look at you, I forget it *is* you, and—" Her eyes filled with tears and she closed her hand convulsively on Viola's arm.

Viola thought she knew what had prompted the display of emotion. When her mother saw "Sebastian" across the room, she momentarily forgot that her son was in fact hundreds of kilometers away in a rehabilitation facility.

"He's safe," she said, bending her head to ensure the words weren't overheard, "and so far, he seems to be doing well. We're going to get through this—all of us, together."

"Yes." Her mother cleared her throat delicately, then managed a smile. "You should know that the Japanese ambassador does wish to speak with you, though the urgency was fabricated."

"There's no time like the present," Viola said, surreptitiously watching the crowd around them. From what she could tell, no one appeared to have picked up on her mother's distress.

Fatigue pressed against the backs of her eyes as they crossed the room, but Viola tried to ignore it. She still had to make it through dinner, the auction, and the after-party. As difficult as this performance might be, she reminded herself, it couldn't hold a candle to the battle her brother was fighting. She would do her part. She could be that strong.

CHAPTER ELEVEN

Brussels, Belgium

"Ready?" Thijs asked as the car pulled to the curb in front of Zonde. The word meant "sin," in Dutch, and the club played up all the relevant associations by dubbing itself "The Hottest Spot in Brussels." It had been open for a year, but Viola had only patronized it once, near the end of her relationship with Dahlia. They had argued that night—Viola had wanted to spend a quiet evening at home, but Dahlia had pressured her into going out—and the sour memory hadn't made Viola eager to return.

She didn't feel anything close to ready, but she nodded to Thijs and stepped outside before her courage failed. Flashbulbs filled the night with bursts of incandescence that illuminated the club's entrance. Its double doors were framed by an alcove painted in shades of crimson, and a projector created the illusion of orange flames flickering against the walls. To her left, a line of people wrapped around the side of the building, awaiting their chance to rub shoulders with royalty, celebrity, and wealth. Their cover charge was five hundred euro, and every cent of profit would be split between the gala's featured charities. Despite the weight of her exhaustion and the prick of anxiety, Viola felt her mood lift at the thought of how much more money would be raised to supplement the proceeds of the gala.

"Welcome, Your Royal Highness." The man who greeted them wore a white tuxedo, accentuating his mahogany skin. His bald head gleamed in the faux firelight as he made a bow. "It is an honor to host you this evening."

Viola shook his hand firmly, thankful for André's preparation. Sebastian and Henri had met with Raoul Lejeune, the club owner, several weeks ago. "Raoul, the honor is mine. I hope you know how much I appreciate your generous support."

"I'm glad we could partner in this. Allow me to show you to your table." When Raoul signaled, two of his guards led them inside.

The heavy fragrance of incense greeted Viola as she crossed the threshold, and as her eyes adjusted to the darkness, she saw two bouquets smoldering in sconces flanking the door. The bouncers turned sharply, leading them to a spiraling staircase designated "VIP," illuminated by red light lanterns hanging overhead. They emerged onto a landing that telescoped into a narrow hallway leading deeper into the building, lit by torches set into the stone walls at regular intervals. The music was faint here, its prominent bass line thumping like a heartbeat.

"Your grotto has all the amenities you requested," Raoul said, "and if there is anything else you require, you need only speak with Claire, who will be serving you tonight."

The corridor curved back and forth on itself sinuously before opening onto the upper level of the arena, a narrow ring looking out over the dance floor. It was called the Pit, and Viola took a moment to lean over the wrought iron railing and look down onto the mass of writhing bodies below. The first of the night's DJs was spinning on a raised dais in the center of the floor. The club's ceiling was a massive domed screen. Patterns of light flickered across its surface in synchrony with the music.

As Viola looked over the crowd, her gaze was caught by a woman, her chiseled arms raised over her head as she danced, her golden hair glittering in the rapid pulse of the strobe. She turned just enough for Viola to glimpse her profile.

It was Duke.

Of course it was. With difficulty, Viola held back the hysterical laugh threatening to bubble up from her chest. Even when she didn't immediately recognize Duke, she was somehow drawn to her. At the moment, she was dancing with a broad-shouldered man Viola didn't recognize. When he reached out to clasp Duke's waist, she allowed it for only a few seconds before sliding out of his grasp. Viola felt her teeth clenching and relaxed her jaw. She didn't need to get angry on Duke's behalf. Clearly, she could handle herself.

"If you would like to dance," Raoul said at her elbow, shouting now to be heard over both the thundering beat and the roar of the crowd, "I will be glad to provide an escort to the designated VIP area."

"No, thank you. I'd like to sit for the moment."

Viola turned her back on the spectacle below, wrenching her thoughts away from Duke as she was approached by Henri. As he had in Amsterdam, Henri was coordinating the entertainment at this event, and thankfully, there had been no last-minute crises. Viola thanked him for all he'd done and prepared to move on, but Henri stopped her with a hand on her shoulder.

"Maria is looking for you." He leaned closer. "In case you hadn't heard, there's a Lorelei party tonight." His brows rose in a gesture clearly meant to convey some kind of meaning, but without any more information about this mysterious Lorelei, Viola remained in the dark.

"Thanks," she said, hoping it was a safe reply. His eyes narrowed slightly, but he only nodded before continuing in his original direction.

Their group moved more slowly now as the guards worked to clear a path through the press of people. All attendees at the gala had been granted access to this level, and she paused to greet several of those she had not been able to speak with earlier in the evening. It was nearly impossible to conduct any kind of real conversation over the DJ, and that could only work in her favor. Still, it was a relief when they reached their "grotto," a deep alcove in the wall that held several couches and tables, demarcated by a chain and a pair of crimson curtains.

Raoul introduced Claire, whose black dress barely came to mid thigh, its neckline plunging into her cleavage. The prevalence of the "magic" theme was much less pronounced here than it had been at the palace, and Claire's single concession to it was a top hat, which she wore at a jaunty angle. When she assured Viola that she would be happy to meet her every need, Viola suspected she was quite serious.

"Would you prefer the curtains open or drawn?" she asked, somehow making the question sound like a proposition.

"Leave one drawn and the other open," Viola said, wanting some shelter but also needing to be accessible. She settled herself in a corner of the nearest couch, at the back of the alcove but visible to passers-by. As soon as she was seated, a woman in a dress that matched the shade of the curtains—also wearing a top hat—stepped forward to open the magnum of Cristal chilling on the table before her, while another approached with a large platter of oysters.

"Maria is here." Thijs's voice in her ear drew her attention away from the lavish refreshments. "With a friend. Stephanie."

This, too, was part of the plan—André stood at the chain separating the alcove from the rest of the club and refused entry to anyone unless she approved them. Thijs was his backup, and the one responsible for relaying the identity of each visitor. Viola looked up to the sight of a clearly frustrated Maria, who was gesticulating sharply in the face of an implacable André. Stephanie, an Italian supermodel, stood beside her looking bored. Viola mentally braced herself for her second round with Maria. This time there were no parents present to intervene. Instead, she was going to have to play the knight in shining armor herself. She rose and walked quickly toward the curtain.

"It's fine, André. Let them pass."

"Thank you," Maria said acidly as he undid the chain.

Viola kissed her, ensuring it was only a quick peck this time, then nodded to Stephanie. "Please, sit. Allow me to get you some champagne. She turned to Claire. "Three glasses, please."

"What the hell was that all about?" Maria said as she settled into the space Viola had vacated, while Stephanie took one of the chairs across the low table. Viola sat beside Maria and forced herself to rest one hand on the warm skin above her knee. It was disconcerting, and more than ironic, to have to overcome her desire *not* to touch a woman.

"I'm sorry," she said. "My security is tight this evening."

"That's a drag," Stephanie said, holding an e-cigarette to her lips and giggling at her own pun. "Though I suppose it's hard to blame them. I'm glad to see you back on your feet, Prince Charming." She turned to Maria with a pout. "How is your boyfriend becoming *better* looking over time?"

Viola caught the quick, warning glance Maria directed toward Stephanie, and her mind spun. Stephanie knew she hadn't been well. Either she had been present when Sebastian overdosed, or Maria had told her what had happened.

When Maria perceived Viola's attention, she flashed her teeth in a too-bright smile and linked their arms together. "It's true, you know," she said, reaching for her champagne. "You just keep getting hotter."

"Lovebirds." Stephanie drank deeply from her champagne. "This soirée is very cute, Sebastian, but how long do you have to stay? Lorelei has something big planned in Ixelles later. Doors open at midnight."

"I already told him," Maria said, a note of petulance creeping into her voice.

"I want to get out of here," Viola said, making a show of craning her neck to look over Stephanie's head. "But with my security this tight, I don't know how I'll manage without a miracle."

Stephanie rolled her eyes. "They need to relax. For that matter, *you* need to relax." She leaned in conspiratorially. "I have Ox in my bag, if you'd like to take the edge off. Consider it an amuse-bouche for the feast later." Once again, she laughed at her own joke.

This was far from the first time that Viola had been offered drugs in a club, and she was accustomed to brushing away the offers without difficulty. Her single experience with Ecstasy several years ago had been intensely enjoyable in the moment, but in the days that followed, she had been dogged by irritability and a temporary depression worse than anything she'd ever felt at the wrong time of the month. The side effects had convinced her to swear off all drugs except the occasional marijuana joint.

But right now, she wasn't herself. She was Sebastian—a heroin addict who should be craving any kind of opioid. She couldn't just say no. She had to make it look difficult.

"Oh God, do you?" Maria said, looking around surreptitiously before holding out one hand. "Please, I'm dying here. I'll owe you."

"You already do," Stephanie said pointedly, but she extracted a small prescription bottle from her purse and shook two blue pills into her palm. Maria tossed one back, draining her champagne in the process.

"I shouldn't," said Viola, staring down at the pill perched on the pale peach tip of Maria's fingers, hoping her expression could be interpreted as desirous when she actually felt rather sick. She had to come up with an excuse, and fast.

"Oh, bullshit," Stephanie said cheerfully. "Of course you should."

"I want to." Viola licked her lips out of necessity. Ironically, the strain was making her mouth as dry as the oxycodone would have done. "But I've agreed to random drug tests. I can't."

"You've what?" Maria hissed. "Why would you do that?"

"To keep the peace. It was that, or do the outpatient rehab."

The crowd roared as the DJ began to play a new song, and Stephanie turned toward the curtain. "Lovebirds, that's my cue," she said, no doubt hoping to escape what was quickly becoming an uncomfortable situation. "I'll be on the dance floor."

Once she left, Maria plucked the pill from Viola's fingertips and deftly stowed it beneath the rouge pad in her makeup kit. It was a practiced motion, and for a moment, Viola felt sorry for her. Then, Maria turned back to her with an accusatory look.

"Why are you letting your family bully you?" she said. "They can't control you unless you allow them to."

Viola's charitable feelings subsided as quickly as they had come. She bent her head and rubbed her eyes in an attempt to gain control over her outrage, but in the end, her efforts were useless. She couldn't possibly remain calm in the face of Maria's callousness, and maybe that was all right. Appropriate, even.

"I could have *died*." Viola raised her head, letting all the anguish she felt over Sebastian's close call color her words.

The frustration drained from Maria's face, and she reached out to squeeze Viola's forearm lightly. It was the most human response Viola had seen from her tonight, and her anger softened just a little.

"When I woke up in the hospital, I had no idea how I'd gotten there or where I'd been the night before," Viola said, hoping to capitalize on Maria's willingness to actually listen. "The last thing I remember is leaving the fundraiser with you. Do *you* remember anything after that? Where we went next? Who else we were with?"

Maria's hand remained on her arm, but as Viola spoke, her caresses stilled and her gaze dropped to the tabletop. "We got high in the car," she said so quietly Viola had to strain to hear her. "The H must have been stronger than usual, because I don't remember anything else, either."

"What is your next memory?" Viola persisted.

When Maria looked up, Viola found herself momentarily enthralled by the vivid blue of her eyes, as alluring as the Mediterranean.

"Waking up in Stephanie's suite. I was lying on the sofa with all my clothes on, all the lights on, and the television spouting an infomercial."

Her sudden laugh sliced through Viola's attraction, revealing it to be only a mirage. How could Maria be *laughing* right now, when her boyfriend had just asked for her help in reconstructing the night he'd nearly asphyxiated to death from an overdose? Her anger returned, even stronger than before, and for one terrifying, liberating moment, she thought the rage washing through her would overspill its bounds. A significant part of her wanted nothing more than to surrender to it. She would cause a terrible scene and blow her own cover, but at least the boiling pressure in her chest would have found a vent.

Maria clearly didn't see any sign of Viola's internal struggle, because instead of asking what was wrong, she nuzzled Viola's neck. "I'm sorry you're dealing with so much shit right now," she murmured. Her hand touched Viola's knee, then slid slowly toward her groin. When her fingers brushed the bulge of the packing cock, Viola didn't have to fake a gasp. Even the muted pressure of Maria's fingers woke her desire. But as her body reacted to the sensation, her mind rebelled.

"Let's forget it all," Maria continued, her voice a seductive purr. "Find a way out of here so we can be *free*."

Through the queasy thunder of her arousal, Viola could hear what Maria was doing. She was preying on Sebastian's pain, using it as a reason for him to return to drug use. It was a circular argument, and both a mental and physical trap. She wasn't just enabling Sebastian—she was goading him. Egging him on.

A fresh spike of anger burned through her arousal. "I really can't," she said and carefully moved Maria's hand away.

Her demeanor shifted from coy to pouting with a speed that revealed her fickleness. "But at the gala you said—"

"I said I would *try*." Viola jerked her head toward the far corner of the alcove. "André was put on probation after what happened to me, and now he won't let me out of his sight. My guard is triple what it was."

When those sea-blue eyes shone with moisture, Viola found herself wanting to laugh. They were so obviously conjured, so clearly crocodile tears.

"But what about *us*?" Maria asked, her voice quavering delicately in a way Viola suspected had worked to manipulate her brother many times in the past. "How can we have any fun like this?"

"Maybe *we* can't." Viola stared hard into Maria's eyes and let a hint of her anger surface. "Enjoy the party. Fill me in on what I missed tomorrow."

Maria made an exasperated sound and stood quickly. "Fine." She drained her second glass of champagne and cocked one hip. "But don't expect me to miss all the fun just because you won't play."

As Maria stalked out of the grotto and disappeared into the crowd, Viola exhaled slowly in relief. She didn't know what Maria meant by the threat, but it probably involved giving herself license to indulge however she wished tonight. Viola was happy to remain in ignorance about the particulars. But just as she was about to sink back onto the couch, a man in a navy tux hailed "him" by name and waved from beyond the rope. His arm was wrapped around a stunning Asian woman who smiled in recognition.

"He-ey, Sebastian!" the man called, revealing his American origins. "Glad to see you're feeling better!"

"Dave Morris," Thijs's voice fed her the details she needed before she could panic. "Finance whiz and entrepreneur. His girlfriend, Daisy Ma, is a vice president at Credit Suisse."

"Thanks, Dave," Viola called with an answering wave. "Hello, Daisy. Want to come in?"

"Maybe later. Headed to the dance floor. Join us!"

"Soon." Viola punctuated her lie with a smile, and off they went. They seemed nice enough, but clearly Dave at least knew something. She angled her body away from her entrance and pretended to check her phone.

"Thijs, are you keeping a list of everyone who refers to Sebastian's health?"

"Yes. How are you holding up?"

"Exhausted." She was starting to feel as though everyone else in the club was aware of what had happened to Sebastian but were plotting to keep it a secret from him.

When Thijs didn't reply, she thought he might be biting his tongue to keep from saying, "I told you so." She kept her eyes down, not wanting to meet his gaze or anyone else's. A few minutes. She just needed a few minutes to gather her strength.

"Ms. Duke is here asking for you, sir," Thijs said suddenly.

Viola's head snapped up before she could stop herself. Indeed, there she was: tan skin glowing with a light sheen of sweat, hair glittering as though it truly were spun gold, a hopeful quirk to her lips that Viola found wholly endearing.

There was no good reason to speak with her, and plenty of good reasons to actively avoid a conversation. Duke could know nothing about Sebastian's overdose, and Viola's growing attraction to her was at best a distraction and at worst, duplicitous. But ironically, in Duke's presence, she could relax her pretense. She still had to perform Sebastian, of course, but she didn't have to embody the persona expected by Maria or Henri or Dave. She could be more herself. She could spare a little time, couldn't she? A few, precious moments of relative sanity?

"Send her in," she said. When Thijs sighed meaningfully into his microphone, she ignored him.

❖

Zonde nightclub, Brussels, Belgium

By all rights, Duke should have been having fun. She was in the so-called "hottest nightclub in Brussels," surrounded by blue bloods and celebrities. But Toby would not keep his hands off her, and his persistence was getting old. She had gotten him in here by flirting with the bouncer, and this was how he repaid her? Deftly, she spun away from his next attempt to grab hold of her hips, pleased when her knee didn't twinge. Side-to-side movements were still dicey.

She glanced up and faltered when she saw Viola, bracketed by her security entourage, moving through the press of people above. She got Toby's attention, and they both watched as Viola disappeared from view, presumably into one of the VIP "grottos." Duke mentally marked the spot, then beckoned Toby into a corner. The likelihood of gleaning anything useful from Viola in this situation was slim, as she would be in high demand, and they both agreed their energy would be better spent observing their quarry than trying to get close.

For a while, they staked out a table near "Sebastian's" grotto, where they observed the comings and goings of his friends. A few minutes ago, Maria had stalked out of the grotto, face flushed in anger and perhaps embarrassment. Even more interesting was the most recent visitor, an American man who fortuitously made a comment about how glad he was to see "Sebastian" feeling better.

"Maybe he actually has been sick?" Duke said to Toby, leaning in just close enough for her words to carry. "Maybe he's *still* sick, and the family doesn't want anyone to know?" The thought made her uncomfortable. Blowing the lid off a scandal was one thing, but exposing someone's serious illness was something else entirely.

"Maybe." The thought didn't seem to bother Toby. "You could try getting tight with one of his friends to see if they might let the cat out." He nudged her with his shoulder. "Even the guys. Flirt, but drop in a word or two about past girlfriends. They'll assume you're bisexual, and you'll become even hotter."

Duke barely resisted the urge to slap him. "What are you going to do?"

"I'm going after Maria," Toby said, jerking his head toward the nearest bar, where Maria was talking with another woman and gesticulating so vehemently that the man nearest her moved back to protect his cocktail. "She doesn't look happy. Maybe her tongue will loosen up after a few drinks." His quick, predatory grin was all the evidence Duke needed that he was hoping she might do more than talk.

She watched as he sidled up to her and turned on his "charm." He was more subtle than a used car salesman, but only by a slim margin. Still, whatever he said made Maria turn with a smile, so either he was particularly charismatic tonight, or her good sense was compromised. Given what she had heard of Maria, it was probably the latter.

For a while, Duke lingered at the table, watching the crowd while she considered what to do next. She wanted to go to Viola, and the hypocrisy of that desire put a sour taste in her mouth. She had been angry at Toby for encouraging her to pretend an interest in "Sebastian's" friends, but wasn't she doing essentially the same thing when it came to Viola?

It was a disturbing thought, but it didn't quite feel accurate. Yes, she was pretending not to know that "Sebastian" was actually his sister in disguise. But her attraction to the woman beneath the masculine persona wasn't feigned. The more she interacted with Viola, the more intrigued she became. That realization should have been frightening. Instead, it motivated her to give up the table and follow the railing until she stood opposite the royal grotto, hoping for a glimpse.

Viola was sitting on a leather couch near the back of the space, her tuxedo blending into the shadows cast by the wall sconces. Her head was bowed over her phone. Even without seeing her face, Duke could tell from the set of her shoulders that she was exhausted. She allowed that wave of sympathy to carry her to the invisible border separating the grotto from the main room, where she spoke briefly with the security guard, a man she did not recognize. Thijs lurked nearby, his face an expressionless mask, as usual.

In the next moment, the guard was stepping aside and waving her through. She glanced at the wire over his right ear as she passed. Presumably, Viola decided who was allowed in, and they must be communicating over that headpiece. It would have been a simple matter for Viola to turn her away, but she hadn't. Why?

Their eyes met and Duke offered a small smile before crossing the distance between them. Viola stood and pulled out the chair next to hers, perfectly chivalrous. Her acting skills were improving—nothing about her behavior raised any kind of red flags.

"Duke, welcome. Please, sit."

"Thank you, Your Royal Highness." As she took the proffered chair, Duke couldn't seem to stop her gaze from drifting down the length of Viola's body, even though Viola had caught her out doing the same thing at the reception. Despite being prepared for the prominence in Viola's slacks, the sight of it sent a fresh jolt of excitement down her spine. She was a lesbian, for heaven's sake. Why did she find the sight of a packing cock arousing?

More importantly, why was she even asking that question? Now she wanted to slap *herself.* Sexuality was far more complex than most of the labels would have it seem—she knew that from plenty of her teammates' experiences. And even she, who rarely felt even a glimmer of attraction to men, had enjoyed using sex toys with most of her girlfriends. Now that she considered it, what she found so arousing about Viola's package was the prospect of revealing it for an accessory, and then pulling it aside to—

"No need to stand, or sit, on formality," Viola said, jolting her out of the fantasy into which her brain had been sinking. "Sebastian, please."

At least all this blushing she was doing in "Sebastian's" presence would only serve to reinforce the appearance of her attraction to him. So far, that hadn't worked against her, though she was still convinced that a subtle approach was best. She felt like a tightrope walker, balancing on the thin edge between nurturing the tiny spark between them, and fanning it into a flame that would prompt Viola's withdrawal.

"Sebastian," she said, allowing herself to savor the syllables. "Congratulations on the success of the gala. You're pleased, I hope?"

"I am." Viola signaled for the waiting attendant to pour a glass of champagne, and Duke accepted it with a murmur of gratitude. "Did you enjoy it?"

"Very much. I wanted to thank you in person for introducing me to Sasha, Kerry, Alix, and Thalia." She raised her glass. "Santé."

"Santé," Viola said, the warmth in her expression leading Duke to believe that she, too, was flashing back to their interview at Belvedere. "And you're welcome. Did you have a good conversation?"

"Yes. I've decided to write an article about Rising Sun and Eclipse," she elaborated, wanting Viola to know her intentions, especially since these women were her friends. "Both organizations do such good work, and not enough Americans know they exist. I certainly didn't, and I should at least have been aware of Eclipse."

"Don't be too hard on yourself," Viola said. "Alix founded Rising Sun last year, and Eclipse has only existed since January."

The timing did explain her ignorance, and Duke felt a pang at the memory of how she had avoided any soccer-related topics during her rehabilitation. If not for some very persistent teammates, she would have become a total recluse.

"I didn't realize," she said. "That makes their accomplishments even more impressive."

But Viola was looking at her quizzically. "You seemed to be… in pain, just now," she said. "Are you all right?"

"I'm fine," Duke said automatically. But what did it mean that Viola was watching her so closely? Was she suspicious? Attracted? Regardless, Duke knew she would have to be even more cautious about her reactions, now. "Just a bad memory that I should keep in the past where it belongs."

"An interesting philosophy. But how can we learn from the past if we ignore our memories?"

Duke considered the question, even as a small part of her brain flailed in disbelief that she was having a quasi-philosophical discussion with the cross-dressing princess of Belgium. "Some memories have a shelf life," she finally said. "An expiration date, beyond which they aren't useful."

Viola smiled—a true smile. Her own, and it was beautiful. *She* was beautiful. And then, as abruptly as it had materialized, her mouth straightened and her gaze slid away from Duke, to some point beyond her. Clearly, one of her guards had just diverted her attention. Duke turned to see a man about her age in a navy tux, waiting with clear impatience just outside the chain.

"I'm sorry," Viola said, and her regret sounded genuine. "I need to speak with Henri."

"I understand," Duke said, trying to toe the line between revealing a hint of her disappointment and betraying its full magnitude. She set her unfinished glass on the table. "Thank you for making the time for me."

She was turning to go when Viola caught her hand.

"Wait," Viola said, her voice low and urgent. "Will you be in Amsterdam later this week for the music festival?"

"Yes." Duke went still as Viola laced the tips of their fingers together. The touch scorched her, pleasure sparking under her skin and between her legs. She held her breath against the gasp that wanted to escape her lips.

"I'd like to continue this conversation," Viola said. "We can meet there. Give Thijs your phone number—the red-head in the far corner." Her confident demeanor slipped ever so slightly. "Will you?"

"Yes," Duke said again. She wanted to say it over and over and over again, where Viola was concerned. While naked, in bed. But when she realized Viola had literally reduced her to monosyllables, she made an effort to assert herself. "I'll look forward to hearing from you."

"Good." Viola squeezed her fingers lightly, her gaze intent. Duke wondered if she had a sense of just how much she was affecting her. Did Viola feel it too: the tension between them, like the charge in the air before a thunderstorm?

"Good night," Duke whispered.

As she left the grotto, Henri passed her, looking anxious. She knew she should care about that, but she simply couldn't. The frenzied atmosphere of the club was suddenly claustrophobic, the persistent pulse of her desire uncomfortable. She could stay and try to sate it with someone else, but the thought held no appeal.

She didn't want "someone." She wanted Viola.

CHAPTER TWELVE

Brussels, Belgium

The vibration of Duke's phone was an earthquake from the perspective of her coffee cup. She stared down into the tiny tsunami, watching its ripples slosh against the rim. Fatigue pulled at her eyelids, born of a restless night. She had slept, but fitfully, waking over and over again, unable to find a comfortable position. She didn't yet feel ready to interact with another human being, even by text message, and so avoided looking at her phone.

Until she remembered that Viola now had her number. Galvanized, she powered up the screen, only to sag in disappointment. Toby.

r u home?

Duke was surprised Toby was already awake. It was nearly ten o'clock in the morning, but given his plans for the previous evening, she had expected him to be recovering for most of the day.

Yes, she typed back.

B there in 15.

Duke turned back to her laptop, where she was currently agonizing over her description of the gala's auction. The words were not coming easily today. Thoughts of Viola, tinged with lingering threads of desire, continued to distract her. It almost seemed as though the universe was punishing her for *not* overindulging herself last night, and that made no sense at all.

When her buzzer sounded, she was grateful for the interruption, despite her increasing discomfort in Toby's presence.

As soon as she opened the door, he barged past her and headed straight for the bar, where he poured himself a generous helping of Craig's whiskey. Whiskey, at ten in the morning? She was about to ask what was the matter, when he turned to face her.

"I got it." His eyes glittered, and that's when she noticed how dark they were. His pupils had almost entirely swallowed the hazel irises he shared with Juno. Drugs could cause pupil dilation, she knew, but that was the extent of her knowledge. What had he taken? Was he still high?

"Got what?" she said carefully.

"The missing piece." He polished off half the drink in one swallow. She almost snapped back at him to get on with it and tell her, but she didn't want to antagonize him, especially if he wasn't sober.

"By the way, it was brilliant of you to get to 'Sebastian,'" he continued. "Seeing you two made Maria even more jealous. Without that little push, I don't think she would've invited me to the party."

"The party?"

His expression became secretive. "The *real* after-party. It was insane." He licked his lips. "I've never had Molly that pure. We fucked for hou—"

"Spare me the details, please," Duke said, wishing she could erase what she'd already heard. Her sleep-deprived brain was struggling to keep up with his erratic commentary. If she was following him correctly, Maria had seen her speaking with "Sebastian," became jealous, and cheated on him with Toby after they had attended a party.

"My sister never told me you were a prude," he said, taking the armchair.

"I'm not," she fired back, unable to keep herself from rising to his bait, but managing to cut herself off before she could say something she would regret. "You said you got information?"

"Suit yourself." He swallowed the rest of the drink, then drummed his fingers on the chair's armrest in a parody of dramatic anticipation. "Sebastian overdosed on heroin a few weeks ago, badly enough to be hospitalized."

The knowledge struck her like a physical blow, and she reeled as she absorbed it. Toby's analogy was spot-on. He had uncovered *the* missing fragment of the puzzle, the part that clarified where every other piece belonged.

"Once I got that out of her, the floodgates opened and Maria started bitching about Sebastian's parents tightening their grip on him. She said they threatened to expose his addiction if he didn't get help and change his behavior, but I'm willing to bet that's a line she was fed by Viola." He shook his head. "Maria has no fucking clue that she's being duped, by the way. Unreal."

Still stunned, Duke scrambled to follow his logic. "What do you think Viola's covering up—that he's still in the hospital?"

"Or in rehab." Toby shrugged. "That would be my guess."

Duke leaned back heavily against the sofa. His theory made perfect sense. And either way, Viola was impersonating him to protect his privacy during his recovery.

She was amazing.

No sooner had Duke registered the thought, then a wave of guilt crashed down on top of it. For weeks now, Viola had put her own life entirely on hold to help her brother. A fraction of her motives might be selfish—any scandal about him would embroil the entire family, to a certain extent—but Duke knew intuitively that Viola hadn't been motivated by any sense of self-preservation. Quite the opposite: in playing the role of her brother, she was courting personal disaster to a much greater degree than if the story of his overdose had broken weeks ago.

Now, she and Toby had what they needed to reveal Viola's deception, but the prospect of actually doing so no longer felt like a golden ticket. Fool's gold, more like. This wasn't some ridiculous story about celebrity privilege and excess that deserved to be brought into the light of day. This was a story about a man succumbing to the disease of addiction, and the lengths to which his family would go in getting him the help he needed. Viola's impersonation of her brother was no titillating scandal—it was an act of heroism.

"I'm going to Paris," Toby said. "This afternoon."

"Why?" Duke asked, wondering if she had missed some earlier comment during her introspection. Her mind was roiling and her stomach had begun to echo her mental disquiet.

"Oh, right, forgot to tell you that part." Toby's smug expression gave the lie to his words. He was on a power trip, she realized— parceling out his knowledge in meager bites to remind her that she was beholden to him. As annoying as his behavior was, right now she did need him—or more accurately, what he knew—so she stayed quiet.

"When Maria was talking about Sebastian's overdose, she let slip that they'd been in Paris at the time. I'm going to start with the highest ranked hospitals and do some digging. You should keep trying on this end."

Now he was giving her orders? Duke wanted to set him down a few pegs—to remind him that without her, he never would have known this story existed—but she was afraid that if she alienated him, he would be less forthcoming.

"I will," she said her voice as devoid of inflection as she could make it. She stood, hoping he would get the hint. "Let me know what you uncover in Paris."

"Of course," Toby said lightly, as though he hadn't already demonstrated a penchant for withholding information. He rose slowly with a luxuriant stretch, and Duke almost laughed in his face. Did he think he was being clever? This was textbook passive-aggressive behavior.

"I'll be in touch," he said as he opened the door.

"Safe trip."

When he was gone, Duke returned to the living room and poured her own glass of whiskey, silently reminding herself to buy Craig a new bottle before she left. This assignment had never been anything but temporary, yet the space between her breasts ached with a dull, hollow sensation at the thought of blowing the lid off this story and then blithely moving on in the wake of the chaos they would leave behind. What would happen to Viola and her brother?

Might he relapse, under the stress? And how would the scandal affect the Belgian-Dutch bid?

Her phone vibrated again, and she reached for it, grateful for the interruption. Her heart lurched into triple time at the unfamiliar number and the words beneath them.

Good morning. This is Sebastian.

Hi :), Duke replied, guilt and anticipation making her even queasier.

Are you free Wed. late afternoon?

Yes.

There's a quiet bar I like. Sterrenlicht. 1600hr?

Duke blinked at the screen in pleased disbelief. "Am I being asked on a date?" she said, needing to hear the insane words aloud. There was only one way she could think of to find out.

Perfect. Is this meeting on the record, or off?

Viola's reply was a long time coming. The thought of her agonizing over how to respond would have been highly gratifying, had Duke been able to forget that as an accomplice in Toby's crusade to expose the full truth about Sebastian's overdose, she was implicitly betraying his sister.

Off.

One word. One syllable. Was it purely informational, as it appeared to be on the surface? Or flirtatious, as it appeared to be in context? Did it matter? Flirtation could go nowhere while Viola retained her disguise, and after her exposure, she would want nothing to do with Duke.

The pain of that thought prompted her to knock back the rest of the whiskey. Its burn had no effect on her misgivings. She picked up her phone and navigated to Toby's contact information, then paused. If she shared her second thoughts with him, would he listen? Would he be angry? Vindictive? Did she want to risk his vengeance before she had the full story?

It was better to wait. He would ferret out whatever could be discovered in Paris, and then she would make a more informed decision about how to move forward. And if, in the meantime, Princess Viola asked her out on a date, she would accept.

See you soon.

❖

Switzerland

Viola walked along the gravel path, wishing she could fully appreciate Sirona's extensive garden. She didn't take its beauty for granted, and she was beyond grateful to be able to explore it with Sebastian at her side. But she had a difficult task ahead of her, and the prospect was making her nervous.

When the director had informed her parents that Sebastian would likely be discharged within the next fortnight, her mother had suggested that they tell him about Viola's impersonation. If he was upset, she reasoned, he would have both time and the support of the counselors to work through his reaction. It was a good idea, and her father and Ruben had both agreed to it, but Viola was still worried. In the end, she had suggested that she tell Sebastian alone, allowing their parents to serve as a support network if he reacted negatively.

The path ended at a stone fountain in the shape of a swan. The spray of the water created tiny rainbows in the air, and Viola watched them shimmer and dance as she tried to gather her courage.

"I've dutifully tried every art activity," Sebastian was saying, "but I'm still hopeless at all of them. All the predisposition for creativity was on the chromosomes that went to you."

She smiled, and most of it wasn't forced. Genetic jokes had long been a staple between them. "You're creative in other ways. I've seen that firsthand, in the way you organized the bid events."

His answering smile seemed genuine, but it faded quickly. "How has all of that been going? I know I'm not supposed to worry about it, and in the beginning, everything was so hard, I didn't have the energy or the concentration." He paused to swallow, and sympathy welled up in her at his admission. "But now that I can see the light at the end of the tunnel, I find myself thinking more and more about it. And about what I'm going to face when I leave here. Is there…is there anything you can tell me?"

He had just offered her the perfect segue. She stopped and turned to look him full in the face, silently praying that what she was about to say wouldn't lead to some sort of setback in his progress. "Yes. But I'm worried it will be difficult to hear."

"That sounds serious," he said, with a lightness she knew was feigned. "Shall we sit?"

She sank down onto the stone bench he indicated, then angled her body so she could face him, and the impact of her confession, head on. "I love you," she said. "Everything I've done comes back to that. I hope you can believe it, even if you are angry."

He squeezed her shoulder gently. "I know you do, and I thank God for it every day. It's all right, Vi. Whatever you have to tell me, I'm not going to shatter."

His mention of God surprised her. Neither she nor Sebastian had ever been particularly religious. As was traditional for generations of Belgian monarchs, their parents had raised them as Roman Catholics but had encouraged them to make their own decisions about what they believed prior to confirmation. Viola wondered whether Sebastian had embraced a more spiritual perspective over the past several weeks. She wanted to know the kind of person he wanted to become, so she could do everything in her power to help. But this was not the time for that conversation.

"I did take on your bid responsibilities, but I didn't tell you the whole truth." She took a deep breath. "I haven't been filling in as myself. I've been pretending to be you."

He blinked at her. "You've been...I'm sorry?"

She reached up with both hands to undo her wig, and when she pulled it away, his jaw went slack.

"It was my idea," she said, feeling a sense of urgency to make him understand her motivation now that the secret was out. "I bullied André and Thijs into helping me impersonate you at the exhibition match. Mom and Dad had no idea. Ruben was furious. But it worked, and we realized that if I could keep up the pretense, we could stop a scandal from happening while possibly learning more about what happened to you on the night you arrived at the hospital."

He reached out to touch her shorn hair, his fingers trembling. "I—I don't know what to say."

He looked confused and shocked and a little lost, and Viola ached for him. "I understand if you're upset. I take full responsibility." When his silence continued, she feared this had been a mistake. "I need to put the wig back on, now. It's important that no one else see me like this."

His frown deepened, then disappeared. "You could be discovered," he said.

"Yes. So far, so good, but it's still a possibility." She reached for his hand and was relieved when he didn't flinch at her touch. "I'm sorry this is hard to hear. Do you...did I make the wrong decision?"

Silence descended between them, broken only by the cheerful chip of birdsong in the nearby trees and the faint silvery sound of water rushing from the mouth of the swan into the basin below. Viola took shallow breaths as she watched him think, desperately hoping he could reach some measure of acceptance.

"I don't think so," he finally said. "I understand your reasons. It's just so strange to think that in the eyes of the world, I've continued living my everyday life, when really, I've been...here."

The surge of relief made her dizzy. "That makes sense," she said, making every effort to keep her voice low and gentle. "I'll tell you anything you want to know. Answer any question you have. Today, or any time. No more secrets."

"No more secrets," he agreed. He looked away from her, and she followed his gaze to where a staff member was approaching them. "Good thing you put the wig back on. Looks like our time is up."

Sebastian squeezed her hand gently, then disengaged and stood. After a moment, he turned back to her. "I do have one question now. Have you had to interact with Maria?"

Viola had prepared herself for this question, but she still felt herself blush. "I've seen her twice, only briefly. I did kiss her on both occasions. And I'm afraid she's been angry with me—that is, you—since the gala." She made a snap decision not to tell him why unless he asked for details. Instead, she studied his reaction, worried this new information might change his perspective. "I'm sorry. For all of it."

"I'm not sure I am," he said. "I've been thinking a lot about our relationship, and it's never been healthy."

"I'm inclined to agree, but only you can know for sure." She lowered her voice as the staff member drew closer. "Write to me, when you think of other questions."

He nodded as the uniformed man stepped into the clearing around the foundation. Viola recognized him as one of the two counselors who had been in Paris to help transport Sebastian. That terrible morning felt like years ago, rather than mere weeks.

"Your Royal Highnesses," he said, "my apology for the interruption. Your parents must leave within the hour and were hoping to spend some additional time with Prince Sebastian."

"Of course," Sebastian said as he rose from the bench. "Ready to go?"

Buoyed by his lack of anger or recrimination, Viola smiled. For the first time in far too long, she felt truly optimistic. Next week, she had her art exhibit in Prague, and the week after that, the FIFA delegation would arrive. If he was home by then, Sebastian might even be able to greet them himself. There was much to be hopeful about, and even more to be thankful for.

"Ready when you are," she said.

CHAPTER THIRTEEN

Amsterdam, The Netherlands

Duke paused outside the cheerful facade of *Sterrenlicht,* where Viola was waiting, and tried to calm her rising nerves. Anticipation at seeing Viola again warred with trepidation about her own subterfuge and the morality of breaking Sebastian's story. Was she allowing her feelings to compromise her mission? Maybe. But if the mission had become unethical, her feelings were steering her in the right direction.

There was a significant part of her that wanted to confess all to Viola: to reveal all her cards and lay down the burden of secrecy and guilt that was becoming heavier by the day. With an effort, she pushed the thought away and examined her reflection in her compact mirror. The day was warm, and she had chosen a cheerful orange dress patterned with white sunbursts, its scoop-shaped neckline revealing a hint of cleavage. She had spent more time than usual curling her hair, and it fell over her shoulders in sumptuous waves. She looked good. She could be confident.

As soon as Duke stepped inside and gave her name, the hostess personally directed up two flights of stairs to a spacious outdoor patio overlooking the harbor. Viola was sitting at a small table near the railing, while Thijs and André sat at the two tables flanking hers. Brightly colored clusters of tulips nestled in small glass jars decorated each surface. Wearing jeans, a black T-shirt, and a gray cap, Viola was dressed more casually than Duke had ever seen her.

Even when she had believed Viola's ruse, Duke had found "Sebastian" attractive. But now, every time they were together—and even more frequently when they were apart—Duke found herself picturing Viola as she was underneath her disguise. There were several photos from the net to help her imagination: a few shots of her in form-fitting gowns, and an entire series of her in the Maldives, sunbathing and wave crashing in a bikini.

The latter had clearly been captured by a paparazzo, and a part of Duke felt guilty for looking at them at all. The rest of her was grateful they existed and ashamed of the sentiment. It was a truth universally acknowledged that Viola should always be wearing a bikini. The red streaks in her auburn hair had glowed in the sun, creating a striking contrast with her pale, freckled skin. Her body was tall and slender, her contours an intoxicating blend of angles and curves.

Breathtaking. That's what she was. Duke wanted to unwrap Sebastian and find Viola beneath his trappings.

When she realized how quickly her thoughts had spiraled out of control, Duke blinked hard in a surreptitious attempt to clear her head. She was descending into truly dangerous territory now, and she had to take control herself if she was going to get anything useful out of this conversation.

As the hostess's shadow fell over Viola, she turned.

"Duke." Her smile was a genuine one—a far cry from the tight, controlled expression to which Duke had grown accustomed. "I'm glad you're here. Please, sit."

"This is a beautiful spot," Duke said, indicating the expanse of water.

"I'm glad you're pleased." Viola leaned across the table in a conspiratorial gesture. "Do you like my disguise?"

Duke's heart stopped. Her disguise? Had Viola somehow discovered what she and Toby were about? But how? After a panicked moment, she decided to play dumb.

"Disguise?"

Viola gestured to herself. "My casual incognito look."

Relief made Duke laugh more loudly than she otherwise would have. "I see. It suits you very well, I think."

"It's certainly more comfortable than a suit," Viola said. She passed a menu to Duke. "I got one in English. My treat, so pay no attention to price."

Duke was about to protest that they were in the Netherlands and should therefore "go Dutch," when she realized Viola probably wouldn't recognize the idiom.

"That's generous of you." She took the laminated sheet of paper and perused it quickly. "I'm not familiar with any of the beers on draft. Do you have a recommendation?"

When Viola sat back in her chair and crossed her arms over her chest, Duke's rebellious mind flashed to what was hiding underneath the T-shirt. She must be wearing a binder, to keep her breasts so well disguised. Duke had always felt constricted by sports bras, and she could only imagine how uncomfortable a tighter garment must be. With a painful intensity, she wanted to drag Viola somewhere private, peel off her shirt, and free her breasts from their compression. She would cradle them in her palms, supporting them gently, cherishing them as they remembered their true shape. And then she would kiss their tips, gently pulling the nipples between her li—

"Duke?" Her name was accompanied by the light brush of Viola's fingers across her knuckles.

Duke felt herself blush. "I'm sorry. The menu distracted me." It was a poor excuse, since she had clearly been staring at Viola's torso, but she pushed on. "Would you mind repeating what I missed?"

"I asked whether you trust me."

The unexpected intimacy of the question rendered Duke incapable of an immediate reply.

Did she trust Viola? All she could think was that Viola shouldn't be so trusting of her. Hoping the melancholy thought was not reflected in her face, she let the menu fall to the table top. The question held an edge of flirtation, and she could work with that.

"You've put me in an impossible position."

"Oh? How so?"

There was a hint of coyness to the question that gave Duke a welcome boost of confidence. "We still don't know each other very well. If I say 'yes,' I'll seem easy. But if I say 'no,' I might offend you."

"You're right. Forgive me, and allow me to be more specific: do you trust me to order your drink?"

"Yes," Duke said, warmed by the smile that curved Viola's lips before she mastered her expression into something more masculine. That reaction made her want more. What would happen if she dialed up the intensity of her flirtation? "I'm happy to put myself in your hands."

Duke watched the effects of her deliberately inflammatory words with satisfaction. Viola's gaze sharpened, her eyes narrowed, and her fingers twitched restlessly against the tablecloth. When she swallowed hard before finally speaking, Duke knew her instincts had been right: in sensual matters, Viola enjoyed taking control. Duke had just set herself up as eager and willing to follow Viola's lead, and that had clearly pushed her buttons. It seemed to be all she could do to collect her wits right now.

"Good," Viola said hoarsely. She turned to flag down a member of the staff. There were, Duke noticed, two hovering just out of earshot. Viola conversed briefly with the woman in Dutch.

"What did you choose?" Duke asked when she had left.

"I'm not going to tell you."

"Not even a hint?"

"I want it to be a surprise."

"Why?"

"Why not?" Viola arched one brow. "You said you trusted me to order your drink. Start trusting. In fact, close your eyes."

The note of command in Viola's voice made Duke want to obey, but she refused to be a pushover. "You're not even going to let me *see* the beer?"

"Close. Your. Eyes."

Duke was usually adept at snappy comebacks, but the air of challenge in Viola's expression ratcheted up her desire, leaving her mouth dry and her wits scattered. She did as she was told. As the world went dark, her other senses sharpened. The harsh cry of a seagull pierced the air, and beneath it, she heard the soft lapping of the bay against the pylons below, like the drones of a bagpipe. The delicate aroma of the tulips on the table top was a balm to her taut nerves, and she inhaled deeply to steady them.

When a light, spicy cologne sliced through the scent, she struggled not to open her eyes. That was Viola's scent—or rather, Sebastian's. If Viola was close enough for Duke to detect it, that meant she was very close indeed.

Brisk footsteps approached. Viola murmured something Duke didn't understand, and then she felt the table's surface vibrate slightly in concert with a light clinking sound. Had the waitress returned with her drink? How ridiculous must she look? As embarrassment flooded her, she felt her color rise. Still, the shame didn't override her desire to follow Viola's instructions.

"Your drink has arrived," Viola said into the silence. "I'll hold it up to your mouth so you can take a sip. Then, you may open your eyes."

"How thoughtful of you," Duke said, injecting as much sarcasm as she could into the words, lest she betray just how much Viola's assertiveness was affecting her.

"You're enjoying this as much as I am," Viola said.

Duke kept her mouth shut until she felt the cool edge of the glass against her skin. She parted her lips, but for several heartbeats, nothing happened. Was Viola teasing her? But just as Duke had made up her mind to pull back, liquid trickled across her tongue. The beer was pleasantly hoppy without being bitter, and notes of mango and grapefruit materialized mid-taste.

She didn't open her eyes right away—let Viola be the one to wait, for once—but when she did, the sight that greeted her was highly gratifying. Viola was staring at her intently, as though mesmerized by some kind of magic spell. No one had ever looked at Duke that way in all her life, and she didn't want the moment to end.

But it did. A shutter fell over Viola's expression and she gently returned the glass to the table. "What do you think?"

"I like it," Duke said, referring to so much more than the beer. "Very much."

"I'm glad." Viola sipped from her own glass and turned to look at the harbor.

Her profile seemed more angular with the addition of the cap. Duke pictured how she would look with hair that fell to her shoulders, as Viola had worn it in that video she'd watched on the train. A fresh surge of arousal washed over her, and she drank deeply as Viola turned away from the water, lest her face betray her.

"Did you enjoy Zonde?" Viola's tone was cooler than it had been. She was trying to steer them back onto more stable ground. It was the smartest course to take, but Duke found she wanted nothing to do with it. And then guilt consumed her, because if *she* was tired of pretending, how exhausted must Viola be?

She played along. They spoke about the club and the gala for a while, but Viola said nothing noteworthy or surprising. She made no reference at all to what Toby had referred to as the "real" after-party, and Duke couldn't think of a way to bring it up that wouldn't seem suspicious.

Viola ordered another round. As they conversed, Duke felt herself growing more comfortable with her, despite the duplicity on both sides of their equation. A part of that sense of ease might, of course, derive from the effects of the beer—it was strong, and her tolerance was still low after years of abstaining. Yet another sacrifice offered to the capricious soccer gods. Had it all been worthwhile? She held her breath at the thought, expecting the customary spike of pain, but it failed to materialize. Maybe that was because without her soccer career, Eveline would never have recognized her, and she wouldn't be sitting here with Viola right now.

Over time, a welcome lassitude settled over Duke's body like a blanket, and she felt the tension in her neck begin to ease. The harbor below was dotted with moored sailboats, and she found herself captivated by the view. The dance of the sunlight on the water looked the way bells sounded, crystalline and bright. Their dialogue had lapsed, but not uncomfortably. The silence was warm and full of promise.

"You have a beautiful smile," Viola said, surprising Duke from her reverie. It was a rather bold thing for a woman impersonating her brother to say to another woman, and the flush creeping up Viola's neck gave the impression that the words had been unpremeditated.

Duke was torn between an answer that would put them back on safer ground and one that would encourage flirtation, but the moment their eyes met, all coherent thought left her head. Viola was smiling too—a small, soft smile that somehow accentuated her femininity. Once again, Duke ached to tell her she knew her secret. She took a long sip, buying herself a few seconds to regain her self-control.

"Thank you." It was a relatively safe response—an acknowledgement of the compliment, and perhaps a tacit encouragement, but no more.

"As I was on my way here," Viola said, "I realized that most of our conversations have been about me and my life. I want to know more about you."

The pleasure Duke felt at this admission somehow eclipsed her self-consciousness. More alert now, she traced a curling pattern in the condensation on her glass and tried for nonchalance.

"What would you like to know?"

Viola smiled faintly. "We skipped over the basics. Where are you from? What is your family like?"

A gnawing twinge of anxiety drove away Duke's pleasure at Viola's interest. Should she play it safe by glossing over the personal details, or encourage Viola's trust by being honest? Last week, she had rejected the idea of coming out, but in this moment, every instinct was prompting her to tell the full story.

"I was born and raised in a small town in western Texas," Duke said, starting with the safe details even as a detached part of her continued to strategize. "The economy is built around drilling oil and raising cattle, and my father owns the local feed store. I'm the youngest of five. The expectation in my family has always been that after high school—secondary school, I think you'd call it—my brothers would help my father with the store, and my sisters and I would marry and start families of our own. But my aptitude for soccer—football, sorry—paved a road to a different kind of life."

Viola's gaze was hypnotic, and the clear interest she conveyed inspired Duke to throw caution to the winds. "I've been estranged from them for almost a year. Once it became clear that I wouldn't be able to play professionally anymore, they expected me to return home and live the life football had interrupted: marry a local boy, start a family, coach a few local teams." Duke took another sip as she prepared for the psychological impact of reliving the stress of the ensuing conflict. "When I came out to them and revealed my previous relationship with a teammate, they reacted...badly."

Only when Viola reached across the table to touch her forearm did Duke realize her fingers were clenched in a tight fist and her shoulders were taut with strain.

"I remember how anxious my sister was when she came out to our family." Viola's voice was low and soft. "To have your own parents turn on you in that way must have been so difficult."

She didn't hesitate at all when speaking of herself in the third person. Duke nodded in reply, her admiration for Viola's performance intertwining with the very real comfort offered by her words. The swirl of emotion was confusing. So distracted was she by her own thoughts that she didn't notice Viola reaching out until one fingertip stroked the skin between her eyes.

"I'm sorry," Viola said quietly. "I didn't mean to put you in a position to have to tell that story."

Desire rose in Duke at the intensity of Viola's gaze, and she struggled not to look away. "I chose to tell it," she managed.

"True."

Duke watched Viola's lips purse slightly as she formed the word. She wondered whether they were as soft as they looked. She wondered how Viola would kiss and whether she would take the lead and how her tongue would—

At that moment, the tongue in question darted out to moisten her lips. A sharp ache manifested between Duke's thighs, and her heart stuttered furiously. The adrenaline surge pushed back against her arousal, creating the space for rational thought. What was happening here? They were both grown adults who knew where this kind of flirtation could lead, and Viola wouldn't dare attempt to maintain her disguise in the bedroom—would she? Even the remote possibility was a strangely alluring prospect, but Duke couldn't imagine Viola would take that risk. Why was she letting it go on for so long? Was she a merciless tease, or could she not help herself?

"What is it?" Viola asked. "You're looking at me oddly."

"I—it's nothing. I'm sorry." Flustered and tongue-tied, Duke embraced the distraction offered by a flash of color in the harbor. When, moments later, a squadron of bright sails came into view, she pointed. "What is that?"

"A regatta," Viola said after a moment. "Do you sail?"

Duke shook her head, forcing herself to keep her attention on the race.

"I do. Perhaps you'd like to join me some time?"

Duke had to look at her then, and she knew she wasn't imagining the spark that flared between them. "All right," she said, marveling that her voice was steady when the rest of her was trembling.

Viola leaned closer. Her eyes were very dark, and they asserted a magnetism Duke felt helpless to resist.

"You said you came out to your parents, but you never mentioned how you identify. Are you interested in men as well as women?"

In a far off part of her mind, panic struck like chain lightning, jagged and continuous. This was it—this was the moment she had dreaded. And yet, the storm remained distant—held at bay, she realized, by the field of energy that crackled between them. Should she lie?

No. She was so tired of lying, if only by omission. She saw the swirling attraction in Viola's eyes and made her confession.

"I'm attracted to you."

Surprise and delight surfaced in Viola's shifting expression until she wrestled her face under control. Empowered by what she had seen, Duke shifted the position of her hand until she could intertwine their fingers again. It felt even better than the last time.

"I want to kiss you," Viola said, the rough edge to her voice betraying her desire.

It would have been a simple matter for Duke to close the space between them, but she didn't want to initiate. She wanted to surrender to Viola, and she couldn't—not really—until the air was clean between them.

"I want you to kiss me. But—"

"We've had a few drinks," Viola finished for her. When she released her hand, Duke had to clamp her mouth shut to keep from betraying her dismay. Viola offered a slight smile. "The first time should be sober."

"Yes," Duke managed after the sharp apex of her disappointment had faded. Sobriety was, she thought, probably more important to Viola than ever.

In a decisive motion perfectly in keeping with her disguise, Viola threw back the remainder of her beer in three long swallows.

"Once the festival is over, I'll join my father at a Northern European trade summit in Oslo," she said. "I return to Brussels next Tuesday night. Will you be there?"

"Yes," Duke said, trying to hide her dismay at the prospect of waiting so long for another time when they could be alone.

"Would you like to join me for dinner?" Viola spoke lightly, but the underlying edge to her words convinced Duke that Viola cared deeply about her response.

"I'd love to."

"I'll make a reservation and confirm by text." Viola folded her napkin and put it on the table. "Any allergies or dislikes?"

"No allergies," Duke said, entranced by the competent and efficient movement of Viola's hands. She wanted those fingers inside her. *Now.* She coughed and cleared her throat. "I'm a fairly adventurous eater. I'm sure I'll enjoy whatever you choose."

"You're putting yourself in my hands again, then?" Viola's tone was light, but the intensity of her gaze revealed how much she cared about Duke's answer.

"Yes." Duke didn't look away. Viola's eyes held a hint of gold today. Duke wanted to fall into them as Viola loomed above her, stroking deep—

When her reason caught up with the fantasy, Duke felt her cheeks go hot. She looked away.

"Don't," Viola said, and then her fingers touched Duke's jaw. Gently but firmly, she applied pressure until Duke had to meet her eyes again. "Tell me what you were thinking."

As much as Duke wanted to surrender, she *needed* to assert her own independence. "Maybe when we have dinner."

Viola laughed, the sound low and full of promise. When she stroked her thumb across Duke's mouth, Duke reacted instinctually, parting her lips and swirling her tongue against the pad. From Viola's quick intake of breath, she hadn't been expecting that. Good.

"You're pushing my self-control to its limits," Viola said. "It's time for me to go."

The frank admission ratcheted up Duke's arousal even further. "Should I apologize?"

"No. But you should let me offer you a ride to your hotel."

When Duke stood, she did feel a bit wobbly. It probably had more to do with adrenaline than alcohol, but she wasn't about to reject Viola's chivalric gesture. "All right."

Viola let Duke precede her into the car, then slid in beside her, leaving the middle seat empty. Maybe it was her altered brain, but Duke felt as though the space between them ached with shared desire. She fussed with the strap on her purse for a moment as a thread of guilt asserted itself into the tangled mess that was her emotional state. Nothing about this situation was simple. Both she and Viola were trying to fool the other. Even so, Duke couldn't escape the nagging feeling that she was taking terrible advantage of Viola.

"Are you all right?" Viola asked, frowning. "Do you feel sick?"

"No." Despite the guilt, Duke wanted so badly to touch her. "It's proving more difficult than I expected *not* to kiss you."

Viola raised her hand as though to reach toward Duke, then let it fall again. When she murmured something to herself in French, Duke didn't ask for a translation. Better she not know. Viola turned her attention to the window, but Duke couldn't look away. Whether she wore feminine or masculine clothing, she was beautiful. And yet, her beauty paled in comparison to the brightness of her courage and strength.

That's when it came to her. She couldn't do this. She could not break this story. She wouldn't.

What good could it possibly do? Wherever Sebastian was now, he was at the beginning of a long and difficult road to recovery.

Duke wanted to help Viola keep him safe, not throw him and her to the metaphorical wolves. It was such an obvious and easy decision, in the end. How had she not come to it sooner?

Viola stirred, and Duke turned her own face away, lest she somehow betray her thoughts. The story would die, and Sebastian would eventually make it out of rehab, and Duke would find a way to connect with Viola when she was playing herself and not her brother. Yes.

And they would all live happily ever after.

❖

Amsterdam, The Netherlands

The following evening, Duke opened her hotel door for Toby, already dreading what she would hear. His texts had been annoyingly mysterious, boasting of "epic news" that would, he promised "pull the whole thing together." She was almost positive that meant he wanted to break the story as soon as possible, and she was nervous about the confrontation they were about to have.

He arrived brandishing an elegant blue box branded with the Johnny Walker imprimatur and a taut, predatory smile that filled Duke with dread. He must have discovered something new—something that was important enough to warrant buying a two-hundred-dollar bottle of scotch. Trying to remain nonchalant, Duke raised her eyebrows as he set the box on her dresser and opened it with a flourish.

"What are we celebrating?" she said, keeping her tone light.

"Get some glasses," he said. "I got something big in Paris."

She did her best to wait patiently as he poured, knowing he was enjoying the chance to string her along. She didn't want to give him the satisfaction.

"Cheers," she said mildly, as they settled into the chairs near the window. The aroma of the scotch was enticing, and it slid smoothly down her throat, leaving a pleasantly smoky taste behind that temporarily distracted her from her unease.

When he smacked his lips, she struggled to maintain a bland expression. Were Viola's perfect manners wearing off on her? More likely, her annoyance was a function of her increasing distaste for him.

He allowed the suspense to build until it was all she could do not to shout at him. Every silent second wound her nerves tighter and tighter. She should have realized this whole plan was a mistake, sooner. No—she should never have told him her theory about Viola to begin with. Regret and fear joined her tension, a braid fit to strangle her.

"I found someone at the hospital who was eager to flip," he said finally. "A disgruntled orderly passed over for promotion."

"And?" She leaned forward, hoping he would mistake her apprehension for enthusiasm.

"And we now have the exact date and time when Sebastian was admitted to the hospital, which means we can narrow our focus to figure out where he was and who he was with on the night of the overdose. And once we know that—" He snapped his fingers. "Case closed."

Duke shivered and made a show of going to the closet for a sweater, even though she wasn't cold. As she pulled it off the hanger, she fought down a wave of panic. Clearly, Toby wasn't going to give up. It might take him days or weeks to get the final puzzle pieces, but once he did, he would move quickly to expose Viola. Which meant *she* had to convince him to call off his hunt. Immediately.

She returned to her chair, took a long, fortifying sip, and steeled herself for the argument she was about to start. She only hoped he could be made to see the value of compassion.

"Toby…the more we learn about this whole situation, the less comfortable I am with making it public. Doesn't Sebastian deserve to recover in peace?"

He snorted. "He'll be fine. The orderly told me he got transferred to Sirona, one of those luxury rehab resorts. The place is in the middle of nowhere and probably as secure as Fort Knox."

"I'm sure you're right," Duke said, hoping that by acknowledging him in that way, he would be more open to what she had to say next. "But I was talking about after he comes home. It's going to be hard enough for him to readjust to his own life. Why should *we* make it harder on him?"

Toby was looking at her as though she'd grown three heads. "How is that my problem?"

Duke noted his change in pronoun, from the collective to the individual. As soon as she had lodged a real protest, he had switched from "we" to "me." It wasn't an encouraging sign, but she still had to try to get through to him. She wet her dry lips with another sip of scotch.

"It's *our* problem because we'd be instigating it by choosing to break this story."

Toby scoffed. "That's the most ridiculous—"

He wanted to deliver a lecture, but that didn't mean she had to listen. Better to nip his speech in the bud before he was able to convince himself with his own rhetoric.

"Stop. It's not ridiculous. I know I'm the one who came to you in the beginning with this lead, and believe me when I tell you how much I've appreciated your help while we've looked into it. You should take up investigative reporting—you're good at it. But now that we know the whole story, or close to it, we need to consider ethics."

Toby's eyes were narrow in clear skepticism and displeasure, and once again, she was reminded of how much she owed him. Sharing her lead had been a way of repaying, and ripping it out of his hands would make the playing field between them uneven again. But she wasn't going to allow that debt to overwhelm her moral compass.

"You suddenly think our plan is unethical?" The scorn in his voice made her feel small.

"Look," she said, battling her insecurity. "What if Sebastian had cancer? Would you feel comfortable breaking *that* news, if it was clear he didn't want the public to know? I wouldn't. Journalists have respected the privacy of people in similar situations. Drug addiction is a disease, too—ask any respected medical professional. But because most of the public doesn't see it that way, the ethics seem murkier. They're not."

Duke took a deep breath and plunged on. "Which means this has to end," she said, injecting her voice with all the confidence she didn't feel. "I'm ending it. Right now. We're not publishing the story, and we need to stop researching it immediately."

"Are you serious right now?" Toby said shrilly. "You want to let this whole thing go?"

"Yes."

He slammed back his scotch and got up to pour another. "Because of ethics," he said, an ugly note creeping into his voice, "or because of Viola?"

Duke kept her eyes locked on his, willing her expression to remain impassive. He was grasping at straws. He couldn't have any idea of how her feelings for Viola had changed and deepened, and she wasn't about to let him bluff her into an admission of sentimentality.

"Because of ethics," she said steadily. "Exposing them both crosses the line. It's not the right thing."

"Are you fucking kidding me?" He clutched the tumbler so hard she thought it might shatter. "It sure as hell is the right thing. We're sitting on a gold mine! Your precious princess took a gamble and lost. That's no one's fault but her own."

Duke wanted to throttle him. Instead, she dug her fingers into the back of the chair and tried to adopt a calm, rational tone. "Think about it. What good will we do by exposing her? Her family will be embarrassed and the attention might set Sebastian back."

Toby stared at her as though she were a bug he wanted to crush. Cheeks mottled, he pointed at her with the same hand that held his refreshed scotch, the golden liquid sloshing dangerously close to the rim.

"Does it look like I give a flying fuck about the Belgian royal family? They're filthy rich and can hide in one of their *several* castles until the news cycle finds something better to talk about. Breaking this story will make your career and mine."

He was probably right, but she didn't care. Breaking this story would break Viola's heart, and she wasn't going to be a party to that. Feeling her temperature rise, she stood and went to the window. As she had suspected, Toby was fundamentally selfish. He clearly didn't care about the public service aspect of journalism. To convince him, she needed to make him think it was in his own best interest to abandon this scoop.

"You could be right," she said slowly, "or we could be branded as mercenaries for violating the privacy of Belgium's first family." Some of the bullheadedness went out of his expression, and she prayed he was starting to listen. "I was hired to cover the bid, not write an exposé. I want to be a sports journalist, not work for TMZ. And you're a respected sports photographer. This story could *break* us, not make us. There will be others to tell that don't involve dubious ethics."

Silence greeted her appeal, and as it stretched on, she struggled not to reveal her discomfort. Toby was biting his lip and staring into his scotch. His restraint was surprising after the force of his earlier vehemence. Finally, the pressure between them became unbearable.

"Let's agree to let it go and focus on FIFA's visit next week," she said. "I'm working on a great piece about a few of the soccer charities that benefitted from the gala, and I bet you have the perfect photos to accompany it. I can even show you my draft right now, if you want."

Toby tossed back his drink in one long swallow. He set the glass down so hard Duke thought it must have cracked. For one long, agonizing moment, all was silent as she held his gaze. The liquor hadn't hit him yet, and his eyes were narrowed, focused.

"Fine. We'll do it your way."

Her relief was so powerful that it rendered her breathless for an instant. "Thank you," she said once she'd recovered, hoping to toe the line between desperate and nonchalant. "I know you took a few photos of Viola as Sebastian that you were planning to use in our article. You'll delete them?"

"Of course. No use in keeping them now." When he grabbed the bottle and moved toward the front door, Duke's relief intensified. The sooner he left, the sooner she could stop walking around on pins and needles. "Send me the draft of that piece you mentioned," he said without turning around. "I'll look at it tomorrow."

"Sounds good." She trailed behind him, and as he opened the door, she felt compelled to lightly touch his shoulder. They were friends, after all, and she had disappointed him.

"Thanks for understanding, Toby. Have a good night."

He turned back just enough for her to see his profile. "Yeah. You, too."

Once the door closed behind him, Duke slumped onto the couch, clutching at the nearest armrest as though it were an anchor. For a while there, she'd thought he was going to insist on going through with the original plan. He probably wouldn't forgive her right away, but maybe after a cooling off period, he'd understand her logic.

She leaned back, resting her head against the cushion to ease the tension in her neck. That had not been enjoyable—he was more than a little frightening when he was angry—and she was disturbed by how differently they saw the morality of the whole situation. Still, he had finally come around, and she was almost positive that she hadn't betrayed her growing feelings for Viola even after his baiting.

Success all around—and yet, it didn't feel like success. The tension-draining tide of relief never materialized. She was still keyed up, still apprehensive, still restless despite her fatigue.

Duke reached for her phone and pulled up her text messages, then selected the ones from "Sebastian." As she scrolled through their conversations, she smiled at the stilted quality of Viola's first few messages—a cautious formality that had not quite masked her growing interest. But something had loosened in her at *Sterrenlicht*, and thereafter, her texts became more playful. Time might have slowed to a crawl since Viola had departed for Oslo, but at least their communications had increased in frequency. Duke was slated to return to Brussels tomorrow, where she would spend the next few days trying to work while impatiently anticipating their dinner date.

She tucked her feet to one side and stared down at the photograph she had chosen for "Sebastian's" profile in her phone. It was one of the official photos from the gala of Viola as the master of ceremonies at the auction, one hand dipping into a top hat, poised to reveal a raffle winner. Viola had done her best to stoke the crowd's anticipation, and her gleaming eyes and teasing smile betrayed her confidence in her own success.

As eager as she was to see Viola in person again, the prospect was also worrisome. Now that she had convinced Toby to give up the expose, she had to confront her own next steps. Should she tell Viola everything that she and Toby knew? Or should she never let on that she knew Viola's secret, allowing her to take charge of how their relationship evolved?

The idea of Viola taking charge was thoroughly distracting, but Duke forced herself to put aside that kernel of fantasy until later. If she said nothing about Viola's charade and managed to retain her interest, Viola would presumably tell Sebastian once he returned from rehab. He could then arrange to "introduce" his sister to her, and Viola could court her, if she so chose. Duke felt a little dazed by the prospect of being courted by a princess.

She came crashing back to reality when she realized just how presumptive she was being. What if Viola was only interested in her as some kind of dalliance? And really, how could she want Duke for anything else? Viola's last relationship had been with a celebrity. Why would she choose a washed up soccer player for her next relationship?

Too disturbed to sit still, Duke rose and went to the window. The street below was fitfully illuminated by streetlamps, and she watched a couple walk hand in hand from one pool of light to the next. Their heads were bent toward each other. They looked happy, and that gave Duke something else to consider. In the best-case scenario, if Viola did decide she wanted a relationship, they would never be able to take a simple romantic walk. They would always be shadowed by security. And if they did make such a relationship public, the media's unforgiving spotlight would shine more harshly on Duke than it ever had before.

How ironic, to be worried about this when she'd been on the cusp of unleashing that spotlight on Viola and her family. Guilt crashed down, plunging her back into the heart of the dilemma: should she confess her knowledge of Viola's impersonation? Or should she try to forget she had ever known of Viola's sacrifice, and risk saying something incriminating when her guard was down?

Duke turned away from the window and took the dirty cups into the kitchen. She washed them slowly, considering the possibilities. In the long run, she finally decided, it was better for Viola to know the truth sooner rather than later. The fewer lies, the better. She would be surprised, and quite possibly angry, but Duke thought she might be able to mitigate that anger by explaining how she had put a stop to Toby's plans once she learned the full truth of Sebastian's condition. Surely, that would help.

She brushed her teeth methodically, staring at her reflection. As anxiety-producing as the prospect of "coming clean" was, she felt some measure of peace in having made a decision. What would her relationship with Viola be like, once the air between them was free of all deception? Duke shivered at the thought, but in anticipation. She wanted that. She wanted it more than she had wanted anything since her soccer career had ended.

CHAPTER FOURTEEN

Oslo, Sweden

Viola was awakened by a sharp knocking sound. She woke disoriented in a bed not her own and quickly sat up, looking for some clue to her surroundings. She found it in the notepad on the nightstand, monographed with the insignia of the Grand Hotel in Oslo. The trade summit.

As the knocking returned, more loudly this time, she glanced at the clock in confusion. It was just shy of seven, and as she had no pressing engagements this morning, she had set her alarm for eight. Her schedule was known to her security. Why were they making such a commotion?

She threw off the sheets and stalked, nude, across the room, pausing at the closet to pull the terrycloth robe from its hanger and wrap it around her body. She checked the peephole—Thijs—and threw open the door.

"What on earth is—" Words failed her when she caught sight of his bleak expression. "What happened?"

He stepped inside, then closed and bolted the door behind him. "Your Royal Highness, I wish I could be gentle with this news, but I can't." He closed his eyes for a moment, then opened them to meet her gaze. "You've been caught out. We all have." He held out a piece of paper. "Skim this quickly, please. We leave for Brussels within the hour."

Viola's heart thumped painfully as panic ripped through her, constricting her lungs and making her head pound. "Caught out?" she whispered.

Thijs's hand was at her elbow. "Are you—"

"How many times do I have to tell you I'm not some delicate fainting flower!" She pulled away from him and sat at the desk, then forced herself to look down at the paper. It was a printout of an article on the web. The headline read, *Crossdressing Belgian Princess Covers Up Twin's OD.*

Viola couldn't believe what she was seeing. Was this a nightmare? But no—one edge of the paper had nicked her index finger, and the sting of the narrow cut was all too real. Caught, after the lengths to which she, and so many others, had gone. Caught, after weeks of success. Caught, with the end of this charade in sight.

"How?"

"Look at the byline."

By Toby Hale and Missy Duke.

Viola read it again, and then a third time. She cursed, French and Dutch words mingling on her breath. No. No! This wasn't possible. Duke had been…what? Spying on her? Gathering information for this—this tawdry exposé? For how long? And how had she possibly put all the pieces together without Viola somehow detecting her snooping?

A powerful surge of anger drove the questions from her mind, and her hand clenched, crumpling one corner of the page. How dare she! She had seemed so compassionate, so solicitous. How dare she worm her way into Viola's good graces, then tear down everything she had so painstakingly built, exposing Sebastian to the nonexistent mercy of the media?

Guilt followed hard on the heels of her rage as she remembered her words to her parents in Paris. She had promised to take full responsibility, and she would deliver on that promise. She *was* responsible. If she hadn't kept finding excuses to see Duke and include her in the bid events, this would never have happened. She had succumbed to the spell of a pretty face and allowed herself to be led around by the nose. This disaster was entirely her fault.

Gritting her teeth so hard her jaw ached, Viola forced herself to skim the article. Most of the truth was there: Sebastian had overdosed on heroin in Paris, where he had been admitted to the Hôpital Hôtel Dieu (according to a former employee), and was now at the Sirona rehabilitation facility. For weeks, Viola had been impersonating him, "in an attempt," Duke had written, "to cover up the scandal." That particular phrase made Viola even angrier.

Two photographs had been placed in the middle of the article: one of Sebastian last year, and one of her from last week. The differences were noticeable, but not entirely conclusive, despite the arrows pointing out their height discrepancy. The nail in the coffin was a quote by Maria Fournier, who claimed to have become suspicious of "Sebastian" at the gala. If she truly had been Duke's leak, she was a better actor and more observant than Viola had given her credit for.

Viola leaned back heavily in the chair and closed her eyes. They were burning, and her chest felt as though it wanted to explode. *She* wanted to explode, but she had to think. Was there any way out of this? Could the palace try to deny it? If her father sent a helicopter to Sirona to collect Sebastian, and they all held a press conference together late this morning...

No. Not only would such a plan be a waste of time and resources, the idea of thrusting Sebastian into the public eye under such conditions was a recipe for relapse. There was no way to deny it. They were just going to have to manage the situation as best they could.

"I'm sorry," Thijs said, and despite having been against this plan from its inception, he sounded genuine. "I hope you know how much I respect you for what you tried to do."

She turned and looked up at him in surprise. "Even though you thought it was madness?"

"I never said that."

"You didn't have to."

He sighed and took a seat on the edge of her bed. She had never seen him look so defeated, and another barb of guilt pierced her as she realized her own actions were to blame.

"Your Royal Highness, I'm honored to hold this position, and I take it very seriously. I've always been suspicious of allowing any emotions to affect my judgment. But over the past few weeks, I've learned that sometimes, relying strictly on logic is just as faulty. Initially, yes, I thought your plan ridiculous, even dangerous. But since then, I've spoken with Antonio about his own addiction, and I was with you when you visited Sebastian. Everything you risked, you did to support him and to enable his hard work. Please believe me when I tell you that I can empathize with that motivation."

Viola stared at him. Thijs had never spoken that many words to her all at once, and suddenly, his reticence and formality made perfect sense. While many of his peers developed friendships with those whom they protected, Thijs had seen those emotional investments as potentially undermining his mission. His distance had been born of an effort at perfect professionalism.

"Thank you, Thijs," she whispered. Suddenly on the verge of tears, she blinked them back. "Thank you for everything. I'm glad we understand each other now."

He nodded gravely. "I hope, ma'am, that you can also understand why it's important that we return to Brussels right away. Once this story gains momentum, the press will find you quickly. It's better for everyone that you be under the palace's protection."

She nodded, thoughts racing again, feeling as though her mind were being torn in different directions. "And Sebastian?"

"Ruben thinks it best that he remain at Sirona for the moment. They have been alerted, and additional security has been dispatched for him."

"All right." She glanced back down at the paper, taking strength from a fresh surge of anger. "I'll go. But I need to see Duke once we're back in Brussels. We'll stop at her apartment on the way to the palace."

Her tone brooked no arguments, but Thijs tried anyway. "Your Royal Highness, please, that's—"

"I'm not changing my mind." Viola threw open the closet, debating what to wear. She had none of her own clothes, only Sebastian's. "I'm going to confront her," she said, settling on a light gray suit over a black linen shirt. No tie, and she refused to wear that damn breast binder, either. No more lies, no more games.

"And then I'm never going to see her again."

Brussels, Belgium

Duke woke twitching from a terrifying dream in which she had been trapped between two boulders, one ankle twisted and stuck, while a swarm of hornets stung her legs and arms and face repeatedly. She gasped for breath as the worst of the nightmare faded, only to realize that her phone was buzzing.

The hornet swarm.

Stabbing with her thumb, she answered it. "Hello?" she said, hoping she didn't sound too groggy.

"What the hell are you and my brother doing, Duke?" Juno was as angry as the hornets had been. "I thought you were supposed to be a serious reporter, not a yellow journalist!"

Duke might not yet be fully awake, but she had plenty of practice arguing with Juno. "What are you talking about?" she snapped back, glancing at the hotel's bedside clock and noting that it was barely past eight.

"What am I—" Juno's strangled laugh was incredulous. "I'm talking about the fact that you and Toby just published a trashy article exposing Prince Sebastian's drug addiction. And don't tell me 'the public deserves to know,' because *I* know you never believed that argument when it applied to *yourself* about being gay. God, Duke, I didn't think either of you were so cruel."

Duke froze in the act of swinging her legs over the edge of the bed. Was Juno telling the truth? Had Toby violated his promise and published the story? And put *her* name on it, too? "No. My God, no! Are you sure?"

"Yes," Juno said, though she now sounded uncertain. "I'm looking at the article right now. The byline has your name on it." Her burst of indignation seemed to have cooled into confusion. "What the hell is going on?"

Pain, anger, and fear buffeted Duke like the eyewall of a hurricane, flooding her with panic. She could easily guess why Toby had broken his word, but what exactly had he done, and why had he involved her in it? Had Viola seen this article? If she had, she would believe Duke had played her false the entire time, betraying her just when they were starting to grow close. The mere thought loosed a groan from her throat.

"Duke?" Juno's voice held a note of gentleness she hadn't heard in months. "Talk to me. Please?"

"I didn't write an article, and Toby promised—" Suddenly galvanized, she stumbled toward her desk and stabbed at her laptop's keyboard. "I have to see it. How do I find it?"

"Google Prince Sebastian."

Duke cradled her phone in the crook of her shoulder and neck. She could barely think, and her fingers trembled when she tried to type. "I—I'll call you back, okay?"

"No," Juno said quickly. "I'm staying on the line. You're scaring me."

Duke didn't reply. The top search result had to be what Juno was referring to: an article with a headline that read, *Crossdressing Belgian Princess Covers Up Twin's OD.* Her stomach roiled, and she swallowed hard as she clicked on the link. Sure enough, her own name stared back at her from the byline. She stared back at it in disbelief. No. This wasn't happening.

Except that it was. She read the first sentence, then the second. By the third, her eyes were blurring with tears. She felt them running down her cheeks, dripping from her chin. *No. No no no.* It was a useless mantra.

When she reached the end, her nausea sharpened into urgency. "I'm going to be sick," she muttered, and carefully set down her phone before bolting to the bathroom.

She fell to her knees before the toilet, clinging to the porcelain sides with one hand and grasping at her hair with the other. Her body jerked and heaved long after her stomach was empty. When the spasms subsided, she fumbled for the flush handle and finally registered the pain in her knees and legs, not yet fully healed from two surgeries and still unused to the pressure of kneeling. She reached for the edge of the sink and pulled herself up, wincing at both the pain and her own reflection. Mechanically, she washed her hands, splashed water on her face, and brushed her teeth before staggering back to the desk.

"Juno?" she croaked into the phone. "Still there?"

"Yes. Are you okay?"

"I threw up," Duke said. Her head was pounding, and to her own ears, she sounded like a vulnerable child. But she wasn't. She was an adult, and she had to take ownership of her mistakes.

"Tell us what's going on, Duchess." It was Leslie, her voice a soothing balm.

"We're all here for you," added Rosa.

"Me, too," Cecilia said. "We're going to FaceTime, okay?"

A moment later, Juno's face appeared. She offered a slight smile, then shifted the phone so Duke could see that all four of them were gathered at the kitchen table where she had served them breakfast, less than a month ago.

It felt like years had passed since that moment.

"I'm sorry I yelled at you," Juno said, her face once again dominating the screen. "I got carried away."

"She does that sometimes," Leslie said.

Duke felt her tears start again, but this time she was also smiling. "I know," she whispered. "But she always means well."

"Of course I do." Juno pretended to be exasperated. "So. Start from the beginning, okay?"

Duke did. She told them almost everything—from her research into Viola on the train, to noting Viola's mannerisms and phrases during "Sebastian's" speech in The Hague, to being welcomed into the royal circle thanks to her soccer résumé. How she had shared her theories with Toby and interviewed "Sebastian" and been invited to the gala. How Toby had gotten information out of Maria, and even more details from a disgruntled orderly. How she had expressed her doubts about the ethics of exposing Sebastian, and how Toby had promised to let the story go.

"That was two days ago," she said. "Juno, I hate to say this because he's your brother, but as soon as he left me, he must have started putting his own plan in motion."

"He's my half brother," Juno said, frowning. "And he's turned into a real asshole."

"Why would he put your name on the article when he knew you wanted nothing to do with it?" Rosa mused.

"He probably thought she'd thank him later," Cecilia said. "I'm sure he was paid well. But he hasn't tried to give you any money?"

"The cat would have been out of the bag if he had," Leslie pointed out.

"I'm not taking one red cent of any money," Duke said hotly. "But other than that, I don't know what to *do*!"

"Write a rebuttal," Rosa said. "Maybe that's not the right word for it, but do you see what I mean? Write your version of events. Show the world your side and where you stand."

Duke considered the suggestion. It had merit. She might even be able to get Goal to publish it on their sports page, since it was tangentially related to the bid. But would Viola believe it? Would she even read it?

"It's a good idea," she said. "Thanks. I just…I wish there was some way I could help Viola and Sebastian. The worst thing about this mess is the damage it'll do to them. I'm partially responsible, but I can't think of any way to help make it right."

Silence greeted this declaration. After a long moment, Leslie leaned in to the camera frame. "About that. You're sort of maybe falling for Viola, yes?"

Duke blinked at her. Falling for Viola? She wanted her and admired her, but had her feelings progressed past that point? Duke feared that they had. Oh, God. She couldn't process this on top of everything else. What was she going to do *now*?

"Sort of, maybe?" she said weakly, parroting Leslie's words.

They were received with a grin. "Thought so, from the way you've been taking about her. In that case—"

But Leslie's advice was interrupted by three sharp raps at the door, followed by a muffled, but familiar, voice. Viola's voice.

"Duke! I need to speak with you."

"She's here?" Duke whispered, as much to herself as to her friends. "I have to go."

She ended the call and crossed the room in a haze of anxiety and fear, desperately trying to think. She had had no idea what to say. The truth, of course—along with many apologies—but there was more than one way of phrasing the truth, and that phrasing might mean the difference between misunderstanding and forgiveness.

Damp with sweat, her hands slipped on the door handle. It opened on her second try, and only then did she realize that she was still wearing what she had slept in: a tank top and boxers, her bra conspicuously absent. Viola, on the other hand, was immaculate in a dark gray men's suit and black linen shirt. Its top two buttons were open, revealing a triangle of tan skin and just the barest hint of cleavage. The evidence that she was no longer in hiding hit Duke like a bucket of cold water.

She hastily brought her eyes back to Viola's, but not quickly enough. She had been caught.

"Like what you see?" Viola asked frostily.

"Ms. Duke," Thijs interjected before she could fumble for a reply. "I need to secure this apartment. Is that acceptable?"

Duke looked between them, feeling dizzy. "O—of course," she said. As Thijs inspected first the bathroom, then the bedroom, she tried desperately to compose herself. She was going to have to be her most articulate self to convince Viola of her side of the story, especially when the opposing perspective was so much easier to believe.

Thijs returned to the foyer within moments. "I'll be waiting just outside, ma'am," he said.

The door clicked shut behind him. Silence fell. Viola was standing at the window, looking out over the narrow side street. She had abandoned Sebastian's pomade and wore her short hair naturally. Duke wanted nothing more than to wrap her arms around Viola's waist and hold her, but she knew her touch would be unwelcome. Aimlessly, she prayed for the right words.

"Viola—"

The princess spun to face her. "Yes. That's right, Ms. Duke—I am Viola Victoria Hélene Thérese, Princess of Belgium. A fact which you seem to have known for quite some time."

Duke held her ground, though her instincts were screaming at her to retreat. Viola's anger crackled around her, an invisible aura. Somehow, that ferocity only enhanced her beauty.

"I didn't write that article," Duke said urgently, sensing she didn't have much time to try to prove herself. "I swear it. As soon as I understood your situation, I told Toby we couldn't go through with it."

"How convenient for you." Viola crossed her arms beneath her breasts. "Even if I did believe you—which I don't—you've just admitted to deceiving me throughout the duration of our acquaintance."

"I didn't know the reason!" Duke heard the anguish in her own voice and could only hope it would make an impact on Viola. "I only knew you were hiding something that had to do with your brother. I didn't know why. If I had, I would never have said anything to Toby. I can't possibly tell you how sorry I am."

"Sorry?" She laughed, but there was no humor in it. "That's rich. Tell it to Sebastian, who will be accosted by you people as soon as he leaves rehab. What do you think that stress will do to him?" She pointed one accusatorial finger at Duke. "That's what I was trying to prevent. Drug addiction is a disease, not a scandal!"

Duke wracked her brains for words, any words that might help. This conversation was spiraling out of control, and while she felt as though she deserved every single one of Viola's angry retorts, she wanted her to know that she had never intended to cause such pain.

"I regret not telling you," she said. "I should have told you I knew your identity right away. I certainly should have told you after Toby learned what happened by sleeping with Maria. But then he went to Paris and somehow discovered the hospital where Sebastian had been treated, and when he shared that information with me, I made him agree not to write anything, but he—"

"Wait." Viola's voice cracked like a whip. "Your friend Toby had sex with Maria Fournier, and she gave him the tip that led him to Paris?"

"Yes." Somewhere in her babble, Duke had clearly stumbled upon an item of importance, and she offered it up eagerly.

"Did Maria tell him how Sebastian came to be at the hospital?"

Duke frowned, desperately trying to remember what Toby had told her. He told her Sebastian had been hospitalized, but she couldn't remember hearing anything about the circumstances.

"If she did, he didn't tell me," she said. "Why is that important? Can I help?"

Viola looked at her coldly. "We don't know where Sebastian was that night. All we know is that he was dropped off at the hospital by a hired car shortly before dawn."

Duke felt her jaw drop. "Someone put him in a car by himself?"

"While he was unconscious and slowly asphyxiating, yes." Her lips twisted in a grimace. "Which is why I was doing everything in my power to protect him, because I never, *ever* want him to be in that situation again. And you—you made it worthless. Out of greed."

Reeling with guilt, Duke watched Viola walk toward the door. Would this be the last time she ever saw her? Duke thought she might be sick again. She couldn't leave it this way.

"Viola, please," she called. "I promise I'm telling the truth. I promise I wasn't motivated by greed. I promise I tried to protect you and Sebastian, though I'll be the first to admit that I did too little too late. I admire you so much for what you've done. I'll do anything I can think of to help."

With one hand on the door, Viola turned. "I don't want your promises, and I wouldn't trust them even if I did. Stay away from me, Ms. Duke. That's the only way you can help me now."

When the door clicked shut, Duke's strength gave out. She sank to the floor, staring at the lightly checkered pattern of the carpet, waiting for the numbness of shock to wear off. When it did, she wept freely, pulling her knees up to her chest as she leaned against the bed, shuddering with each sob. Why did everything she touch turn to ashes? First her soccer career, and now any hope she might have entertained about being a serious journalist. Not to mention her relationship with Viola.

She wept all the harder when she realized how self-serving she was being. No abstract, nefarious force was at work. She wasn't under some kind of ridiculous curse. Her soccer career had ended because of bad luck combined with narrow cruciate ligaments. Her journalism career, on the other hand, was in danger of ending because she had made selfish decisions rather than thinking first of ethicality. And Viola—Viola was suffering for those decisions. Viola and Sebastian both.

Meanwhile, she sat here on the floor of her hotel room, drowning in her own tears. No. There had to be something she could do. There just had to be. After struggling to her feet, she retrieved her phone and called Juno back.

"Duke!" Cecilia was in front of the camera when the call connected. "We were just debating whether sending a text would be too much of an interruption. How did it go?"

"Not great," Duke said thickly. "Awful, to be honest. She blames me, as she should. *I* blame me. I have to try to fix this somehow."

"While you're not entirely blameless," Juno acknowledged as she moved into the frame, "much of the responsibility falls squarely on the shoulders of my asshole half brother."

At her mention of Toby, Duke was reminded of Viola's interest in his dealings with Maria. "You know what else he did? Plied Sebastian's girlfriend with drinks, used her to gain information, and then slept with her."

"What?" Rosa sounded outraged.

"She's not blameless either," Duke said, "but it seems to me like she has a serious drug problem."

"And Toby exploited that," Juno said, her jaw tight. "When I see him next, I'm going to give him a piece of my mind!"

An idea was slowly forming in Duke's mind. "Would it be too much to ask you not to?" she said.

"What do you mean?"

"Toby probably has information he hasn't shared with me. Some of it might be really important." She scrubbed at her face with both hands. "The one thing I learned about Viola today, other than that she never wants to see me again, is that her family doesn't know how Sebastian overdosed. Someone put him in a car while he was unconscious and sent the car to the hospital."

"That's insane," Leslie murmured in the background.

"Toby got key information from Maria, and he was just in Paris, poking around. That's how he learned the name of Sebastian's rehab facility." As the idea coalesced, Duke stood. Her legs felt shaky, but she was unable to sit still. "What if he knows where Sebastian was when he overdosed, but he's withholding that information? It wouldn't be the first time."

"Why would he do that?" Juno asked.

Duke shook her head, then stopped when the movement made her dizzy. "I don't know. Insurance?"

"You mean like blackmail?" Cecilia was incredulous.

"I don't know," Duke said again, frustration mounting. "I'm probably grasping at straws, right? But they're all I have." She wanted to pace the room but didn't have the strength. Instead, she threw herself down on the bed. "Even if he does have more information, he'll never give it to me."

"True," Juno said, but the fierce edge to her voice halted Duke's descent into another round of self-recrimination. "But what if we take it?"

CHAPTER FIFTEEN

German Airspace

As the jet's ascent evened out, Viola reclined in her seat and closed her eyes. Sleep had not come easily in the days since the exposé had been published, and she didn't expect it to cooperate now, either, but she had to try. The reception to open her exhibition at the Tusarova Gallery in Prague was this afternoon, and it would be her first appearance in public since the press conference her family had held at the beginning of the week.

Realizing where her thoughts had gone, she tried to direct them into less anxiety-producing channels. Despite the media firestorm that had sprung up around her, temporary relief was in sight. Sasha had invited the Queer Royals' Club to Balmoral Castle next weekend, and Viola was counting down the days. Right now, nothing appealed more than the prospect of secluding herself in the company of friends who could empathize with almost every aspect of her plight. She only wished Sebastian had friends who were truly supportive. He would need to find a new social scene once he was released from Sirona in just a few days.

She had said as much to Sasha when they spoke, and with her typical insight, Sasha had offered the beginnings of a solution. She would have her brother, Arthur, reach out to Sebastian. Arthur and his wife Ashleigh were not heavy partiers—especially since the birth of their daughter—and they could help Sebastian find a new circle. Viola was still terribly worried about what would happen when he reentered society, especially during the first few weeks after his return to public life, when the media frenzy would be at its most intense.

Strangely, Sebastian was not as concerned. She and her parents had delivered the news of the exposé in person, but instead of falling to pieces as they had feared, his only reaction had been a long, slow exhale. He had turned to Viola, who was trying not to cringe in anticipation of his anger.

"Please don't look at me that way," he had said, his voice quiet but saturated with emotion. "You did everything you could to protect me—far above and beyond what most siblings would have done. It's not your fault you were discovered." He had even managed a wan smile. "I'd like some good to come of all this. Maybe it's for the best that the world knows about my addiction. In time, once I feel stronger, I'd like to be an advocate for drug awareness education and humane treatment policies."

"That's a great idea, son," their father had said warmly. "Though I agree there's no rush."

"Yes." Their mother, who sat beside him on the couch in the sun-filled sitting room of his suite, had squeezed his shoulders. "Please, take your time. The most important thing to us is that you stay safe and healthy."

Sebastian had smiled at them, then turned his solemn gaze on Viola. "That goes for you, too, Vi. You're under an awful lot of stress right now."

Viola had wanted to cry, but instead, she forced a smile. "I'll take care of myself. I promise."

So much for redirecting her thoughts. She was keeping that promise as best she could, but her body was betraying her with insomnia and a lack of appetite. Viola opened her eyes, sat up, and finished the sparkling water she'd requested at takeoff. Immediately, the stewardess was at her elbow.

"Another drink, Your Royal Highness?"

The very least she could do was stay hydrated. "The same, please."

When the woman left, Thijs sat in the chair facing hers. "May we talk about the security precautions this afternoon, ma'am?"

"Yes, of course," she said, bringing her chair back up to its seated position.

"I'm sorry," he said. "I was hoping you'd fallen asleep, but when I saw you were awake—"

"It's for the best."

She listened closely as Thijs explained the additional security measures that had been taken to protect her, and she paid special attention to the photographs and blueprint of the Tusarova that he spread out on the table between them as he discussed extraction plans and routes. All the while, she tried not to feel guilty about the additional taxpayer dollars being spent because of her notoriety. Her situation had deteriorated even further since the publication of Duke's solo article, in which she claimed Toby had sold their story all by himself, after she had asked him to abandon it. But if that were the case, why had he put her name on the exposé and split the money with her? Duke had been honest about that much, and about what she planned to do with it: give every cent to Eclipse. Privately, Kerry had confirmed the donation.

Deception, more like. It was a flashy, calculated move, and Viola saw right through it. Duke was clearly playing some strange kind of "good cop, bad cop" game with Toby, the end result of which was that they both got the infamy they wanted. The ethical side of journalism would probably exonerate Duke, and she could go on to have a perfectly legitimate career, while Toby could rise to prominence in the tabloids.

Unless, of course, Duke was telling the truth. In which case, she had tried to do the right thing shortly after realizing the stakes, and was in the end only guilty of trusting the wrong person.

"Viola?" Thijs had never used her name, and hearing him speak it now jolted Viola out of her reverie. She must have gone off on a mental tangent so extreme she hadn't heard his first few attempts at recapturing her attention.

"I'm so sorry. I'm afraid, I—I drifted off."

"Where?" he said, so kindly she wanted to cry.

"Nowhere worth returning to." She pressed two fingers to the bridge of her nose. It had been oddly difficult to retrain herself not to rub her eyes, now that she was back to wearing makeup. "Let me recap the extraction routes so you're sure I know them."

Once she was comfortable with the plan and its contingencies, and after urging her to sleep, Thijs returned to the back of the plane. Sleep was easier said than done, of course. The problem with sleep was that she had to relax to do it. And every time she relaxed, she started to seriously consider the idea that Duke might be telling the truth. During their brief time together, they had connected in a meaningful way, below the surface level, and Viola didn't want to think about that. Better to focus on the surface—on desire itself, rather than what lay beneath it. How could anything more powerful than lust ever flourish with so much mistrust between them, anyway?

I'm attracted to you.

Duke's answer in Amsterdam had been well phrased. Such a simple sentence, and yet it was haunting Viola because she thought it might actually be true. Duke had, after all, known her real identity when she said it.

Viola shifted uncomfortably as her rebellious body made its own wishes known. Thoughts of Duke were always accompanied by pangs of arousal, which made them doubly uncomfortable. She had done her best to ignore them, but perhaps that was the wrong approach. What if she needed to burn this need out of her, instead of sublimating it? Perhaps there would be some willing woman in Prague, and so what if she would be the first total stranger Viola had dared take to bed? She wasn't inexperienced in any other way.

She would have to see how everything unfolded tonight. If she saw someone intriguing, she would at least consider the possibility of a liaison.

Anything to purge herself of this lingering desire for Duke.

❖

Prague, Czechoslovakia

Duke opened the closet door and stared at its contents, wondering if her current mindset bore any similarities to how ancient warriors had felt before arming themselves for battle. She removed one dress, then another. Some "armor." Still, it was important for her to look her very best, since there was a chance that she would come face-to-face with Viola.

As much as she might wish otherwise, she couldn't imagine any conversation between them going well. But that was why, in addition to her armor, she had a weapon—a thick envelope filled with everything Juno had been able to glean from Toby's computer.

If turnabout was fair play, they had managed it beautifully. Juno had visited Duke in Brussels at the end of the week, and they had pretended to fight. She called Toby and asked to stay with him instead. He grudgingly agreed, and while he was asleep, she had searched through his computer for any notes he might have taken about Maria and his trip to Paris.

She'd found them, spending only long enough to confirm the relevant files weren't password-encrypted before copying them onto an external drive. When they sat down together the next morning to examine the contents, Duke had watched her grow more and more furious. Toby had kept a daily journal of his progress, and the extra dimensions it revealed were ugly.

"Sebastian overdosed at a 'Lorelei party'?" Juno had asked, pointing to the words. "What is that?"

"No idea." Duke's eyes strained to take in as much information as quickly as possible. "But it looks like Toby met with Lorelei, whoever she is, while he was in Paris." A phrase near the bottom of the screen suddenly caught Duke's attention. "Oh my God."

"What?"

"Hang on. I need to scroll down."

"But I'm not there ye—"

Duke held up one hand. "Wait. Please. Let me focus." The more she read, the harder her heart began to pound.

"What?" Juno asked more urgently.

"He made a deal," Duke said, hearing the disgust in her own voice. She scrolled back up to where Toby's notes on his meeting with Lorelei began. "Right there. Read that."

"Son of a bitch!" Juno said after a moment. She meant it, too—while she and Toby shared a father, his mother was, according to Juno, a gold digger. Either the flaw was genetic, or Toby had learned his own manipulation skills at his mother's knee.

Juno stood and began to pace the width of Craig's living room. "I can't believe this. No—I *can* believe it—I just can't believe I'm *related* to him. What kind of person bargains away information about someone's near death experience for lifetime party invitations?"

"A selfish one."

While Toby's notes about his meeting with Lorelei were sparse, they would be enough for a professional investigation team to work with. Duke's own anger at what Toby had done was tempered by a strain of relief that she now had something to share with Viola.

"All I know," she said when Juno's rant had finally lost steam, "is that I can't thank you enough."

"What will you do with this stuff?"

"Give it to Viola. After making several copies."

"But how are you going to get to her?" Juno had pressed. "Do you even know where she is? She's disappeared from the public eye since that press conference."

It was true—after her single press conference on the so-called "Princess Deception," as the media had dubbed the scandal, Viola had gone to ground. Duke thought of her constantly, wondering where she was, what she was doing, and whether she had read the rebuttal that Duke had published on Goal's website two days prior. She hoped so. Even if it didn't change Viola's mind, Duke needed her to know the truth.

"I don't know where she is right now," Duke had said. "But I know where she'll be this weekend. I'm even on the guest list."

That was how she now found herself perusing the contents of her closet at the Savoy Hotel in Prague, having brought enough clothing changes for almost a week despite only staying for two nights. She finally settled on a sky blue sleeveless sheath dress with a matching jacket, its portrait collar giving way to an envelope-style front. The outfit conveyed the kind of elegant professionalism to which Duke had always aspired, and wearing it always boosted her confidence.

She would need every ounce of that confidence today. As she put the envelope in her clutch and double-checked her makeup, she silently rehearsed the speech she had committed to memory. She only hoped she would be allowed to give it.

The Tusarova Gallery was on a street of the same name in the Holesovice neighborhood, cradled in the bend of the Vltaska River. While searching for hotel options, Duke had read a little about the district—a former manufacturing center, its factories and warehouses had been converted into living space, restaurants, and offices. This gentrification had been motivated by artists, and the neighborhood was now the site of some of Prague's finest galleries.

The bright and crisp morning had given way to an overcast afternoon. A cold breeze had picked up while she was getting dressed, and she huddled into what little warmth was provided by the thin jacket that matched her dress. She hadn't been thinking of the weather at all when she chose this outfit, but even if she had been smart enough to check the forecast, she wouldn't have changed her mind. There might be only the barest fraction of a chance that she would be allowed in the door, but in case she did come face-to-face with Viola tonight, Duke wanted to look her best.

The closer she got to the gallery, the more her heart rate increased. By the time she turned the corner and saw its marquee above a glossy chrome facade, every muscle in her body was taut with tension. She went to the end of the line and peered around those in front, hoping for a peek at the security. When she didn't recognize the guard, her spirits rose. Thijs would have recognized her on sight, but she didn't think this person would. If her name hadn't been flagged in some way, she should be fine.

As the person ahead of her in line was allowed into the gallery, she took a deep breath, plastered what she hoped was a pleasant smile on her face, and presented her ID. The man scanned it with his device, then frowned. Duke's hopes plummeted. He spoke into his wrist mic in French, but Duke caught Thijs's name and her throat went dry.

"Wait here," the guard said. "You must speak with my supervisor. He will join us momentarily."

Duke quailed at the thought of confronting him and almost turned to walk away. But the part of her that wanted to escape was the same conflict-avoidant part that had made excuses not to tell Viola that she knew her secret, the same part that had failed to recognize Toby's duplicity. She had been afraid of so much for so long, and what good had that done her? The tenuous foundation she had started to build in the world of journalism was falling apart. She was going to have to start over, and she might as well make a new beginning right here.

Desperation added fuel to her courage. Besides wanting Viola to know the truth about her own motives, Duke *needed* her to know about Lorelei. Even if Thijs didn't let Duke in, she might be able to convince him to give the envelope to Viola, especially if she mentioned that it contained valuable information about Sebastian.

By the time Thijs walked out of the gallery doors, determination outstripped Duke's fear, and she met his eyes as he approached.

"Hello, Thijs," she said, wanting the first words.

"Ms. Duke," he said evenly. "Please follow me."

He started back the way he'd come, and she hurried to catch up with him. She hadn't expected him to let her in. Had Viola changed her mind? That seemed like too much to hope, but why else would he not have thrown her out on her ear?

At the last moment, he turned down the alley beside the gallery. She hesitated, staring into the dimly lit, narrow space with a fresh surge of apprehension as she imagined herself lying broken and bloody at its far end. But that was ludicrous. Thijs was no thug, and he didn't consider her that kind of threat.

Did he?

She plunged into the alley and saw that he was waiting at a side door. Feeling rather silly, she followed him inside. They were in a small corridor, made even more cramped by large pieces of cardboard lying against each wall. Thijs ducked into a room on the right lit by two naked bulbs hanging from the ceiling. A quick look around revealed it to be storage space, presumably for art objects not in use or being prepared for relocation.

"I don't have much time," Thijs began. "And before you ask, our mutual friend is not aware of your presence here. She continues to block your messages and refuses to take your calls, but she did read your article. She claims not to believe it, but I do."

Duke blinked hard against the rush of tears inspired by his unexpected show of faith. "Thank you."

The muscles along his jawline flickered. "Do not mistake my meaning. Your behavior was naive and foolish. I can understand her anger at you. But I respect your recent courage. Perhaps in time, she will as well."

"I can only hope so," Duke said fervently.

"She not only needs time, but also space," Thijs said. "If she knew you were here, she would feel bullied. Hunted. That will not help. I am asking you politely to leave her be."

The implication was clear: next time, he wouldn't ask.

"I know she doesn't want to see me right now," Duke said, deciding it was prudent to omit Viola's name since Thijs had done so—presumably in case this conversation was overheard by one of the gallery staff. "But I have sensitive information she needs, and this was the only way I could think of to make absolutely sure it gets into her hands."

"Sensitive information?" He sounded skeptical, and she couldn't blame him. He might believe her article, but she was still pursuing Viola against her will, and that made her his adversary in this context.

When she moved closer, his eyes narrowed and he widened his stance. It hurt to know that he was reacting to her as he would to a potentially hostile individual, but she couldn't really blame him for that, either.

"Information about the night Sebastian overdosed," she said.

Thijs crossed his arms over his chest. "Why haven't you divulged this before?"

"Because I didn't have it. This was the one missing piece of the puzzle, and I didn't know how to get it. Toby Hale figured it out. He didn't tell me, but a friend helped me get to the information on his computer."

"If that's true, why haven't I already seen a headline?" Thijs said.

"Because in exchange for not going to the press, he gets access to a social scene he could never have reached before." Duke opened her purse and pulled out the thick envelope. "Please, give this to... her. It has the pieces she's missing."

As soon as Thijs took the package, Duke felt bereft. She had taken photos of Toby's notes and made a copy as well, and she trusted Thijs to do as she asked. But now, she was in the position of a poker player who had thrown down her cards without knowing if they could win. She had to wait and hope and try to pick up the pieces of her life—again.

"I will see that she gets this," Thijs said, pulling her attention back to the present. "And if she will not open it, I will give it to my supervisor."

"Thank you." Duke didn't want to go, but it was time. Somewhere nearby, she knew, Viola was standing in the heart of the gallery's public space, accepting congratulations and answering questions about her work. Duke wanted so badly to finally be in the same room as *her*, without the invisible web of deception keeping them separate. She wanted to watch—in person, not on video— Viola's hands move gracefully through the air as she spoke with humble passion about the inspiration and craft of her art. She wanted to see Viola smile at her without premeditation.

When Thijs gestured for her to precede him into the corridor, she knew she had been dismissed. But as she left the room, the door at the far end of the hall opened and a man dressed identically to Thijs stepped through, trailed by a silver-haired woman in a navy suit, who in turn was followed by... Viola.

Duke froze, drinking in the sight of her like a desert in a downpour. Her hair was styled in a dramatically different fashion from how she had worn it as Sebastian; swept up and away from her face, it emphasized her elegant cheekbones. Her dark gray dress clung to her breasts and torso, flaring slightly where it ended a few inches above her knees. Tan, subtly muscled legs culminated in ankle-high Doc Martens, and the industrial touch to her outfit made Duke's mouth go dry.

The woman in the navy suit had been in the middle of a sentence when the door opened, but she cut it short when the guard stopped abruptly, his hand dropping to the holster at his waist.

"*Qui êtes-vous!*" he demanded.

Duke had command of enough French to know that he was asking her identity. She opened her mouth to answer but found she couldn't speak. Her attention was riveted to Viola's face, which was, for once, an open book. Duke read surprise there, and a flash of desire quickly eclipsed by the protective umbra of anger.

"She is with me, Jacques," Thijs said in English, smoothly interposing himself between Duke and his colleague. "And she was just leaving. Please excuse us."

He put one hand on Duke's shoulder and forcibly steered her toward the alley exit. Dizzy with shock, she allowed herself to be led until the chill night air roused her from her stupor.

"Wait, no," she protested at the hollow sound of the door closing behind them. Freeing herself from his grip, she whirled to face him. "Now that I've seen her, I need to talk to her!"

"Absolutely not," Thijs said, his voice grating. "Do you have any idea whom she was speaking to? That was Celeste Deschamps, the owner of one of the top galleries in Paris. She must want to see one of the photographs Her Royal Highness chose not to display. Her art is the only part of her life that remains in her control, and I will protect it as I protect her."

Duke felt his words like a blow. Her first instinct was to become defensive—how dare he insinuate that she would act in such a way as to sabotage Viola's career? But with her next breath, the indignation evaporated. He was looking out for Viola's best interests. And he was right—without his intervention, she would have stormed back into the building with no regard for the impact her actions might have on Viola's professional life.

The thought sickened her. Exhaustion crashed down, pummeling her mind until every thought ached. She was becoming *more* selfish, not less. Somehow, the harder she tried to do the right thing, the worse she behaved. But what other option did she have? She had to keep trying to put one foot in front of the other, even if so far she had only succeeded in moving backward.

"I'm glad she has you in her life," Duke said, feeling the tears on her cheeks and not caring for once. "Good-bye."

She walked quickly back the length of the alley, feeling her steps waver and knowing Thijs must be witnessing her unsteadiness. She didn't care about that, either. How could she, when she had just seen her own motivation for coming here tonight exposed for the half-truth it was?

Turning into the chill wind, Duke walked in the vague direction of her hotel, perversely glad to feel the tiny pricks of pain against her cheeks as her tears turned to ice.

CHAPTER SIXTEEN

Prague, Czechoslovakia

Viola sat in the window seat of her suite at the Four Seasons, clutching her knees to her chest as twilight leached the pastel colors from the sky. Her brain was spinning faster than the earth's descent into night. At Thijs's insistence, she had read Duke's letter and the material it contained. Numbly, she had agreed that a copy should be sent to Ruben immediately. When Thijs had withdrawn to take care of that step, Viola had retreated to this spot to watch the wind shake loose the leaves from the trees.

She mistrusted everything about Duke, and she'd told Thijs as much. Until Ruben did some digging, they wouldn't know whether her information was any good. In the meantime, she refused to trust Duke's motives and her story about how she had acquired the intelligence. It had to be another ploy. What was that American saying? *Fool me once, shame on you. Fool me twice, shame on me.*

A thread of doubt tugged at her thoughts, making her head throb. Viola pressed her cheek to the cool glass, wishing the chill could reach her fevered thoughts. What if Duke was actually telling the truth? She had nothing left to lose, after all. That brief sighting of her in the narrow corridor of the art gallery's storage space had been a shock and a relief, all at once. If she closed her eyes, she could still see the expression on Duke's face—the anguish and hope that had been a voiceless, desperate plea. Could that kind of emotion be faked?

Of course it could. But by Duke?

That was the question haunting her—the question chipping away at the entire foundation of her logic. She didn't like it. Her anger was losing its momentum, and she didn't like that, either. It had only taken one quick glimpse of Duke to reignite her desire and compound her confusion. How, *how* could any part of her still want Duke, despite her deception and betrayal?

Darkness fell, her heart measuring out the seconds in hollow thuds. The ache in her chest expanded until she wanted to scream. Her skin was hot and tight, a prison she wanted to claw her way out of. She dug the blunt nails of one hand into the soft skin of her other wrist, but the small pricks of pain did nothing to clear her mind. These emotions were ridiculous, and she had to get rid of them. Short of turning to drugs, which she had sworn she would not do, she could think of only one way to purge herself of this terrible craving for Duke.

Thijs was housed with the rest of her security team in an adjoining suite and quickly answered her summons.

"Do you know where Duke is staying?"

He smothered his surprise, but not quickly enough. "The Savoy."

"Call her. Tell her you'll be paying her a visit in…how long will it take to get there?"

Thijs consulted his phone. "Twenty minutes."

"Tell her you'll be there within the hour."

"And what do you want me to do when I see her?"

"Wait. Preferably in the lobby, but outside her door if you insist." Viola stood, energized by her decision. "I'll be the one meeting with her, but I don't want her to know I'm coming."

Viola spent the short car ride in silence, staring out the window at the unfamiliar words as Prague's cityscape slid by. Thijs didn't ask what she planned to do, and Viola wondered if he had any inkling of her true intentions. Probably, but it was more comfortable to imagine him laboring under the misapprehension that all she wanted from Duke was another opportunity to dress her down.

In fact, she had every intention of taking Duke's dress *off*. She would wait for Duke's consent, of course, but once she had it, Viola planned to slake her own lust without mercy. Whether Duke's desire burned out with hers or only gained in intensity, she didn't care. Let Duke continue to pine after her—it would serve her right. After tonight, Viola intended never to see her again. And this time, she meant it.

Once they reached the Savoy, Thijs escorted her to within a few paces of Duke's door. They had agreed that she would remain in the hall, out of line of sight, while Thijs checked Duke's room. Then, he would leave and Viola would enter.

"I will wait in the lobby," he said quietly, "if you promise not to set foot outside the door without calling me up, and not to answer the door for anyone except me."

"I promise," she said. "Thank you."

He moved forward to knock, and she took another step to the side, hating how her pulse raced at the sound of Duke's greeting. Her voice sounded brittle with fatigue and anxiety, and Viola fought down the sympathy that rose in her. Duke didn't deserve it.

Thijs's inspection must have taken less than a minute, but it felt like an eternity. Only when Viola felt a twinge in her knuckles did she realize she was clenching both fists. She forced her hands to relax, then positioned herself directly in front of the door and closed her eyes, hoping to hear something of what was going on in the room. As she listened, the indistinct murmur of voices grew closer, one elevating in pitch.

"—hell is going on?" Duke was protesting. "You can't just… just waltz in here demanding to inspect my room and then lea—"

The door opened, and when Thijs stepped out of the way, Duke's vehement protest died on her lips. She had exchanged the elegant blue dress Viola had glimpsed at the gallery for a pair of mesh shorts and a dark tank top. The scant clothing revealed that she had lost weight she couldn't afford to lose. Dark smudges discolored the puffy skin beneath her red-rimmed eyes. Somehow, the changes only sharpened her beauty, lending it an edge that pierced through Viola's seething anger to the intricate layers beneath.

As they stared at one another, Duke's face drained of color, then flushed a deep crimson. Viola wanted to scream at her and fuck her and hold her and push her away and kiss her and watch over her while she slept. The conflicting impulses made her dizzy. Dizziness was weakness, and she couldn't afford that.

She stepped over the threshold, then secured the deadbolt on the door, taking a moment to steady herself against the constricting snare of her tangled emotions.

"You're really here," Duke whispered.

Viola took a deep breath before turning to face her. "What is that supposed to mean?"

"I've dreamed of you walking through that door a million times since I arrived."

Duke's painfully hopeful expression was welcome oxygen to Viola's simmering anger. It flared up, bright and hot, a filament lashing out from the surface of the sun. She dug the nails of both hands into her palms and relished the sting.

"This isn't the reunion scene of a romantic comedy," she said. "I'm so furious I can barely speak to you."

As the hope drained from Duke's face, Viola reminded herself that her anger was justified. Duke had played her and exploited her for selfish reasons. Well, turnabout was fair play.

"If you can't stand the sight of me," Duke said, unshed tears snarling her voice, "why did you come here?"

Viola didn't want to answer that question. Words could be dangerous. Words might be taken seriously. Words could be binding. Instead, she crossed the space between them, framed Duke's face with her palms, and kissed her.

It was not a gentle kiss. Viola took her mouth with all the combined ferocity of her fury and desire. Duke stiffened in surprise before melting beneath her, knees buckling as she surrendered. Viola slid one arm around her waist, holding her up as the kiss went on and on and began to change, softening into passion laced with a tenderness she didn't want to feel.

Viola ended the kiss and trailed her lips along Duke's jaw before closing them around the lobe of her ear. She sucked lightly and let her tongue flick against the delicate skin. Duke shuddered and moaned, and the sound of her abandon was the sound of triumph. Exhilaration sang through her, momentarily eclipsing every other emotion.

And then Duke pulled back, just far enough to see her expression. "Don't you think we should talk?"

"If we try to talk, I'll end up screaming at you." Viola curled her fingers into Duke's hair, watching her eyes go hazy when she pulled. Arousal shuddered through her, laced with the intoxication of power. Duke might have played her for a fool, but *she* was in control now. "I want to burn you out of my system and move on with my life."

The pain that twisted Duke's features was at odds with the stark desire in her gaze. "That's really all this is?"

Viola steadfastly ignored the echo of that distress that knifed through her own chest. To acknowledge it would be to give it power, and she refused to do that. Instead, she disengaged from the embrace and took one full step backward. Space opened between them like a chasm.

"Take it or leave it," she said, knowing the words would hurt. Wanting them to.

Duke's eyes welled with tears, but she blinked hard and shook her head once, violently, to dispel them. A soft, despairing laugh left her mouth. Viola's heartbeat thudded in her ears, her satisfaction at watching Duke suffer soured by an unexpected pang of guilt.

"I'll take whatever I can have with you," Duke said, her voice something between a whisper and a sob.

"Then take me to your bed." Viola watched the miracle of her own words as Duke's eyes glazed over. The threat of tenderness hovered at the edges of her mind, but she continued to resist. Tonight was not about the nascent feelings that had begun to sprout between them before Duke's betrayal. Tonight was about what could be burned away—lust, craving, appetite. The desire of the flesh, not of the spirit.

Still, when Duke extended her hand, Viola took it, allowing herself to be led in this much. When morning came, she wanted Duke to remember this wordless declaration of her own willingness.

The room was tiny, but the full-sized bed did have a wrought-iron headboard that insinuated all kinds of possibilities. Viola didn't want to think, and so she did not hesitate.

"Stand there," she said, pointing to a spot on the floor near the head of the bed, "and watch."

Viola took her time undressing. She started by kicking off her shoes, then trailed both hands up, up along her thighs, slipping beneath the hem of her dress to work her lace bikini down her legs. Duke's eyes, alight with desire, followed the trail of flexing fingers and freshly revealed skin. When Duke licked her lips, Viola's vision blurred on a tide of wanting. Fighting to regain her composure, she stepped out of her underwear and reached up to undo the small hook at the back of her dress.

"I have this need," she began—and then stopped, hating the vulnerability in her own voice. That flash of anger burned through the fog of her arousal, reminding her of the mission: to finally feel Duke yield, and to force this ridiculous spark between them to burn itself out.

Duke took one step forward. "Whatever you need from me," she said hoarsely, "is yours."

Already, her surrender was so sweet, but Viola wanted so much more. She turned, silently presenting Duke with her back, and couldn't keep from shivering as Duke's warm fingertips brushed her nape. She pulled the zipper down slowly, but when she turned the motion into a caress of Viola's hips, Viola moved forward, breaking the contact.

"The first thing I need," she said, easing the dress's collar off her shoulders, "is for you to choose a safe word."

Duke's face went slack with shock, and her gaze flicked around the room as if its corners held some clue as to what Viola would do. "Why?"

Slowly, Viola eased the dress down her arms and torso, shimmying slightly to push the material over her waist. When it pooled to the floor at her feet, she stepped over the puddle of fabric.

"Because," she said in what she hoped could pass as a conversational tone, "I'm going to fuck you until you beg me to stop. But I won't. Not until I hear that word."

Duke's quiet gasp struck Viola like an electric shock. She traced two fingers along Duke's jawline before dragging them across her lips. Duke kissed them swiftly, then opened her mouth to pull them inside. She hollowed her cheeks, sucking firmly as she swirled and fluttered her tongue. Viola felt a rush of wetness between her legs, and she pulled away, reaching down to smooth the moisture along the contours of her own sex. The first touch was sweeter than usual, the sensation only heightened by the sight of Duke's glazed eyes and stunned expression. She changed the focus of her fingers, circling lightly, and watched Duke swallow hard. When Viola stroked experimentally across her clitoris, gasping at the delicious pressure, Duke moved toward her.

Immediately, she removed her hand. "Don't you dare, until I say you can."

Duke made a strangled noise in the back of her throat, and Viola laughed. Teasing her was even better than she had imagined. She cupped her own breasts lightly in her palms, then flicked her nipples with each thumb and smiled when Duke's hands clenched. It felt good—so good—to be wanted with such ferocity.

"Tell me the word you've chosen."

"Soccer."

Viola spared a fleeting thought for its significance—despite her inability to play, Duke apparently still associated her sport with safety—before her reason was overruled by a single imperative: to *take*. She had what she needed: consent to proceed, and the mechanism to maintain that consent.

She repeated the word for both their benefits and took one long step closer. "You can say it right now, if you want to end this. Walk away before I do." Viola watched her barbs find their mark, taking satisfaction in Duke's visible flinch. "But I don't think you will. Because part of you believes that if we sleep together, something will change."

Duke's shoulders straightened and a gleam of defiance made her eyes only more alluring. "I'm fighting for *us* the only way I can."

Anger flared again. "You forfeited 'us' when you published that story."

"But I swear I didn't—"

"No," Viola said, injecting all her pent-up pain into that single syllable. "I didn't come here to have this argument again." Duke's eyes beseeched her silently, but she hardened herself against it. "Now, undress yourself. Don't rush."

Duke did as she was told, though even while trying to move slowly, she managed to rip a seam in her tank top as she raised it over her head. Her gaze was riveted to Viola's, and the need her eyes betrayed was intoxicating. As each inch of pale skin was revealed, Viola felt her own desire ratchet higher. Duke's breasts were larger than Viola's, though her nipples were smaller, and very pale.

Viola's mouth watered at the thought of licking and sucking them, forcing them to swell and darken, but she forced herself to stand still as Duke peeled her shorts down her chiseled legs. She had enough self-control to wait, and forcing Duke to do the same only heightened her arousal. But when Duke finally stepped out of the fabric and stood before her wearing only a black thong, Viola's patience snapped. She grabbed Duke's hips, devouring her mouth as she pushed her against the edge of the bed. Duke toppled onto it and Viola followed her down, never breaking the kiss. She slid one thigh between Duke's legs and permitted herself a moment of fierce triumph as wetness smeared her skin.

"So responsive," she murmured against the shell of Duke's ear, flicking lightly at the lobe.

"For you," Duke said, the final syllable eliding into a moan as Viola thrust against her.

Viola increased the pressure of her leg until she wrung a sharp cry from Duke's throat. Then she eased back, holding Duke's hips to the bed and kneeling between her legs.

"How badly do you want to taste me?" Viola said, exulting in the audible intake of breath that greeted her question.

"Please," Duke whispered, and she dared to trail her fingers along Viola's forearms until Viola grasped both hands and pushed them down to either side of her head.

"Keep them here until I say otherwise," she said fiercely, "or I'll get up and leave. Do you understand?"

"Yes," Duke stuttered, her voice hoarse as her hands clenched into fists. The tendons in her forearms flickered.

Viola lowered herself until her breast was in reach of Duke's mouth. Duke reared up and caught her nipple between her lips, swiping quickly with her tongue as though she feared Viola might pull away before Duke could truly taste her.

Good. She should be afraid. But as Duke's tongue swirled and circled, coaxing a soft moan from her throat, it was Viola's turn to feel trepidation at the intensity of her body's response. Never, never had she felt so good, so quickly. She was already throbbing, and as Duke sucked harder at her breasts, the ache between her legs deepened.

She sat up quickly, her nipple sliding from Duke's mouth with a deliciously wet sound, then moved up Duke's body until she had positioned her thighs over Duke's face. Duke's lips were parted in anticipation, her eyes silently pleading for Viola to take her pleasure.

"You want this?" Viola said, unashamed of her harsh breaths. "Beg me."

"Oh, please," Duke said, her tone as fervent as any religious adherent. "*Please* let me."

"Let you what?"

"Let me lick you." Duke's tongue swiped her lips in mimicry of her words. "Let me suck you. Please."

Viola looked up to the shadowed ceiling, pretending to consider the request. In actuality, Duke's pleading had already put her on the edge, and she was struggling against the rising tide of her own desire. But why not surrender? This night was about finally slaking her desire for Duke, and she could do that in any way she wished.

"For a little while," she said, before finally lowering herself onto Duke's waiting mouth.

Heat and warmth enveloped her as Duke kissed her intimately, gently fluttering her tongue as her hollowed lips created the most exquisite pleasure. Her senses reeling, Viola couldn't suppress a sharp cry. She had intended to tease herself and Duke, but her climax already loomed on the horizon.

Viola didn't want to stop. She didn't want to lose control, either, but there was no possible way she could pull back now. And she wanted nothing to do with the nagging sensation of guilt that plagued the back of her mind.

She gasped at the vibration of Duke's lips as she moaned. The knowledge that the folds of her own sex were muffling the sound only sharpened her desire. As she approached the brink, she clutched at the headboard, wrapping her fingers around its top rung. The iron was cool against her heated skin. Duke's talented mouth increased the suction, and as her tongue flickered with excruciatingly light touches, Viola tipped over the edge.

A flood of pleasure tore through her, almost painful in its intensity, sweeping her reason away. She clung to the railing as her body convulsed, over and over, driven to new heights of pleasure at the wet sounds of Duke's lips and tongue on her. Finally, as her climax ebbed, she pulled herself upright, lifting away from Duke's face to kneel on the bed beside her. Duke's face glistened with her wetness, her hips thrusting in shallow arcs that Viola was sure were involuntarily. She traced Duke's mouth with her thumb, then continued down her chin and along the smooth skin of her throat.

"Please," Duke panted. "Let me have you again."

When she licked her lips, provocatively savoring the evidence of Viola's passion, the tide of Viola's desire, which had never fully ebbed, tugged at her body as though she were a puppet on strings. For one precarious moment, she almost gave in.

But if she gave in, Duke might think her resolve was weakening—that her desire was more than a physical itch. She had scratched half that itch, and now it was time to make good on her promise: to shatter Duke with pleasure and then walk away.

"No," she said, and pinched Duke's nipple without warning. When she gasped and arched her back, Viola felt a different kind of pleasure—the power of control, strong and sharp. Duke lay helpless beneath her, and until she spoke her safe word, that was how she would remain.

She covered Duke's body with her own, burying both hands in her long hair, holding her firmly in place as she plundered her mouth in a bruising kiss. It was a heady thing to taste herself on Duke's lips. When Duke's thighs opened even further, she slid one leg between them and rocked down, firmly.

All finesse disappeared from Duke's kiss as she gasped, and Viola increased the pressure, thrusting in short, sharp bursts that made Duke writhe beneath her. She tightened her grasp on Duke's hair, tugging intermittently even as she set up a steady rhythm with her thigh. And then, without warning, she pulled her hands away and levered herself up, breaking all contact.

"Oh, please!" Duke's hands were clenched tightly, presumably to stop herself from reaching for Viola.

"Tell me what you want," Viola said, wanting Duke to hear the vocalization of her own desires.

"You." The word was a plea, a prayer. Duke's eyes were glazed with need, and her mouth glistened. She was utterly intoxicating, and Viola wanted to devour her. She slid down Duke's body and pushed her legs apart, then ran both thumbs along the soft, tender skin of her inner thighs. When Duke's hips leapt beneath her touch, she lifted her hands away.

"Don't move or I'll stop."

"Oh!" It was a beautiful sound, an agonized, ecstatic syllable. Duke's hazy eyes focused only with effort. "I won't. I promise. Please!"

Viola took her time, first caressing the warm folds of Duke's sex with her thumbs before pulling them apart to reveal the delicate whorls beneath. Duke's breaths came as harsh gasps, and when Viola finally touched her tongue to the swollen knot of nerves, Duke cried out. Viola didn't want her to be quiet. When Duke remembered this night, Viola wanted her to hear the echo of her own needy sounds.

Within seconds, Duke was diamond hard beneath her tongue. Viola kept the pressure light, delivering a series of teasing flicks until Duke cried out, throbbing with release. Viola smiled in triumph, then scratched lightly at Duke's thighs with her blunt nails.

"Again," she murmured. This time, she closed her lips around Duke's clitoris and sucked. Duke gasped her name as she writhed in pleasure, and Viola strengthened her grip on her legs. Increasing the suction, she reintroduced the tip of her tongue. When Duke shuddered violently, Viola stilled, relishing her strangled cry of dismay. She began again, then stopped, over and over and over until Duke was keening in need and even the lightest brush of her tongue pushed her back to the edge.

Without warning, Viola sucked hard, tonguing her swiftly, and clamped down on Duke's legs as she shattered. This time, her climax went on and on, wringing her out with its force. Viola exulted in the sensation of Duke's opening pulsing rhythmically against her chin, and she hummed in satisfaction, setting off another round of contractions. As the tension in Duke's body began to ease, Viola gentled her mouth but never stopped entirely, coaxing Duke's clitoris into a renewed state of arousal even as her aftershocks continued.

Viola raised her head gazing along the tawny planes of Duke's body, admiring the sweat-slicked ridges of her abdomen and the pale slopes of her breasts. "Again."

"Viola," Duke gasped. "No. Too sensitive. Can't."

"You will," Viola said, removing her right hand from Duke's thigh and shifting position enough to bring her fingers into play. She traced the petal-soft contours, pressing firmly then backing off, taking note of all the particularly sensitive places. Finally, she dipped two fingertips just barely inside, glorying in the rush of wetness that greeted her invasion.

"Oh my God," the words were guttural, strangled, torn from Duke's raw throat.

Slowly, so slowly, Viola pressed deeper, retreating slightly when she met resistance before pushing more firmly with added momentum. By the time her fingers were as deep as they could go, Duke was breathing harshly, her chest heaving. When Viola curled her fingers up, she groaned. When Viola lowered her head again, Duke's sharp cry was almost a scream.

Viola kept up a gentle pressure with her lips and tongue and began to thrust, shallowly at first. She curled her fingers on every pass, and as her strokes grew longer and firmer, Duke's internal muscles began to quiver. When she stilled her movements, and pulled her mouth away, Duke's sob of frustration was the sweetest sound she'd ever heard.

"Do you like it when I fuck you?"

"Y-es!" Duke's eyes were bruises, the dark pupils nearly swallowing her robin's egg irises.

"What if I told you I was going to stop right now and leave you like this?" Viola spoke casually, steadfastly pushing away the pang she felt at her own cruelty.

Duke's eyes went wide and she shook her head furiously. "No, please. Please don't leave me."

Please don't leave me.

For a moment, the words threatened to overwhelm Viola's defenses and lay bare the part of her that still cared for Duke, despite everything she had done. But then Duke's internal walls fluttered around her fingers, and Viola remembered why she was here: to purge her terrible desire in Duke's embrace. Without another word, she pulled almost all the way out, then thrust hard, sealing her lips around Duke's clitoris as she did.

Duke's orgasm gripped her fingers, her inner muscles convulsing rhythmically as Viola continued her deep strokes, drawing out every last ounce of pleasure with hands and tongue.

When Duke's body stilled, Viola got to her knees without withdrawing. She leaned over Duke, balancing carefully as she traced her mouth with the thumb of her free hand, then dipped inside. Duke's eyes flashed open at the intrusion, catching and holding Viola's gaze as she sucked on the fingertip, swirling her tongue and flicking against the sensitive pad. Renewed desire sliced through her keenly, and she pulled away, not wanting to be distracted.

Slowly, Viola began to thrust again, loosening the warm grip of the silken walls that had closed down around her fingers. She brought her moistened thumb to the juncture of Duke's thighs, rubbing lightly just above her clitoris as she began to stroke more firmly.

"Again," she whispered. When Duke bit her lower lip and shook her head, Viola raised her eyebrows, waiting for the word. Until she heard it, she was going to relish the vision of Duke beneath her, surrendering.

Incrementally, Viola increased the pressure of her thumb and the force of her thrusts, until Duke's clitoris was like a tiny stone and her internal muscles quivered in anticipation of release. Then, finally, Viola brought her over, circling firmly and thrusting hard. Duke's choked-off scream dissolved into a low moan that finally ended in a ragged gasp.

"Soccer!"

Viola stopped. She rested one palm on Duke's heaving abdomen and withdrew her fingers slowly, wanting to memorize the image of Duke in this moment: cheeks flushed, hair disheveled, sweat pooling in the hollow of her throat. Her sensuality made Viola ache, but she had to remember that Duke's beauty was only skin-deep. Forcing herself to push past the unwelcome tenderness, Viola left the bed and began to dress.

"Viola!" Duke struggled to raise herself onto one elbow. "Please."

She didn't have to finish the sentence. Viola knew what she meant: *please don't go.* But if she stayed, what then? There could be no trust between them beyond the safe word.

She made herself remember everything: the pain of reading the exposé, the humiliation of the press conference, the incessant fear that Sebastian would be unable to cope. For the last time, she met Duke's pleading gaze.

Without another word, she turned and left.

CHAPTER SEVENTEEN

Balmoral Castle, Scotland

Rain fell in sheets outside the bay window, the sound of its drumming on the balustrade adding an extra cadence to the music playing softly through the room's artfully concealed speakers. From her seat in a gloriously plush armchair, Viola smiled against the lip of her wine glass as she watched Sasha peruse the white cards with black lettering that had been cast down on the table before her like so many offerings before a goddess. The black card she had turned over at the beginning of the turn stared up at them, its white letters demanding they answer the all-important question: "What makes me horny?"

Viola was new to Cards Against Humanity, a party game of American origin that Kerry had imported into the European royal circles, but the rules were simple: each player had to choose a white card from their own hand to answer the question or fill in the blank presented by the black card. The "best" answer was decided exclusively by the player who had drawn the black card, so it was helpful to know that person's interests and sense of humor. Kerry was, of course, favored to win this round, though Thalia, who had gone to secondary school with Sasha, had a chance at scoring an upset.

Viola had known *of* both Sasha and Alix nearly all her life, and she had met them both at various royal functions since childhood.

But until recently, Alix had avoided any kind of limelight as though it carried the plague, whereas Sasha had deliberately attracted the attention of every paparazzo under the sun. Viola had been most comfortable staking out the unoccupied middle ground, unafraid of publicity when it was expedient, but also maintaining firm boundaries behind which she could retreat.

Those boundaries were in splinters now, and she was deeply grateful to Sasha for providing the unexpected sanctuary of Balmoral. Her morning flight from Brussels to the castle's private airfield had taken barely two hours, but when she emerged from the plane and took her first breath of Scottish Highlands air, she felt as though she had entered a parallel universe. Protected by the 50,000 acre estate in the heart of the Scottish Highlands, Viola felt safe for the first time in a fortnight.

A knock at the door roused her from her reverie. When Sasha invited whoever it was to come in, the doors opened to admit a man carrying a large tray and a woman with a bucket of champagne in each hand.

"Lovely, thank you," Sasha said, beckoning them forward.

"Owen and…Evie? Is that right?" Kerry jumped up to intercept them. "Let me help. That tray looks heavy."

"Thank you, ma'am," Evie said on Owen's behalf as she began pouring the champagne, flushing in evident delight that the Duchess of Kent (one of them, at least) had remembered her name. Beside her, the empty-handed Owen seemed bereft.

From her position, Viola could tell that Alix was hiding a smile behind her hand, and she bit her own lip to stifle her amusement. Sasha and Kerry had recently celebrated their first wedding anniversary, but apparently, Kerry was still adjusting to the privileges that attended nobility. Still, instead of teasing her wife when she returned to the sofa, Sasha leaned into her with a palpable fondness that made Viola's chest ache.

No. She had told herself over and over that she wasn't going to indulge in any kind of maudlin sentimentality. She and Duke had never stood a chance. They certainly couldn't compare to a happily married couple.

"I don't want to be a pain," Thalia said, "but would you mind if I pass on the champagne? This is going to sound precious, but it reminds me of work."

Viola experienced a moment of pure confusion before Alix's distinctly unladylike snort clued her in that Thalia had said something humorous. But what was the punch line? Thalia was a Formula One driver, not a champagne tester.

With that thought, she had her answer: the top three finishers of every Formula One grand prix received a magnum of champagne during the award presentation, which they dutifully shook up, uncorked, and sprayed all over one another. She didn't follow the sport religiously, but since Sasha had formed the QRC, Viola had made an effort to follow Thalia's progress. So far this season, she had finished on the podium more frequently than not.

"Woe is me," Alix intoned. "I'm so clever at driving cars around in circles that I'm obliged to guzzle champagne every week."

Thalia turned an expression of mock outrage first on her lover, and then on the rest of them. "Can you believe this? Do you see what I put up with? *None* of the tracks are circular. Not even one!"

Before someone else could launch a repartee, Kerry was back on her feet. "You like Scotch, right, Thalia? This place has an amazing collection. I'll go get some."

This time, Sasha succeeded in pulling her down. "You'll do no such thing. Stay." She looked to Owen. "Would you mind bringing up a representative selection, please?"

He hurriedly assented, seeming relieved, and Evie trailed him out the door carrying the unused flute. Viola was suddenly moved to propose a toast, and when she saw that Thalia still had wine in her glass, she hurried into action before anyone else could take the initiative.

"A toast," she began, "to the QRC. We all know how rare it is to find trustworthy, nonjudgmental friends. Even after only a few hours in your presence, I feel more relaxed than I have in weeks. I'm thankful to and for you all. Santé."

Unexpected tears bounced into her eyes, but if anyone noticed, they didn't remark on it. Fortunately, she was able to blink them away before they could fall. Until this storm of controversy—which, she reminded herself vehemently, she had brought upon herself— Viola had never been an easy crier. She resented it. Not that there was anything inherently negative about tears, of course, but people associated them with weakness, and right now she needed to be stronger than ever.

Her current sleep deficit was probably a contributing factor. Maybe she could talk with Alix alone at some point over the weekend about that, since she could offer advice as both a physician and a friend. It wouldn't be difficult to ask her own doctor for prescription medication, but she wanted to avoid bringing that kind of temptation into the palace now that Sebastian was home.

But Kerry was smiling at her, and Sasha had extended one hand, and Alix reached across the space between them to lightly touch her knee. They were, she realized as her palm met Sasha's, a different kind of family. One that she needed, though not, thankfully, as a replacement for her blood relations, the way so many queer people did. As a supplement, instead. Unlike everyone else on the planet, these four women understood every aspect of her—the lesbian, the royal, the artist—and how those facets joined to create her holistic self.

"Right back at you, Vi," Thalia said, voicing the sentiment that hung in the air between them.

Before the charged moment could dissolve into self-consciousness, Sasha cleared her throat. "Back to what makes me horny," she said, and Viola laughed in pure, unrestrained amusement for the first time in weeks. It felt so very good.

Sasha gathered up the white cards with a dramatic air. "First card: state dinners. Hmm. That's not entirely ludicrous—I do resort to fantasizing to endure the boring bits."

Kerry's startled expression made it clear that Sasha's answer wasn't what she expected.

"I take it you didn't know?" Viola said dryly.

"I had no idea," Kerry said, turning an evaluating gaze on her wife. "Maybe I should start marking my calendar."

"Care to elaborate on those fantasies, Sash?" Thalia's grin was devilish.

Alix gave her shoulder a light push. "You are incorrigible."

Thalia twisted to meet her gaze. "And you love it."

"There will be no elaboration," Sasha said imperiously, "except to say that Kerry features vividly in every single one."

Thalia hooted with laughter, raised her glass in their direction, and drained it. Viola sipped lightly at the champagne, which was very good: crisp and light, yet flavorful. Her head was starting to feel fuzzy, but for the first time in what felt like forever, she didn't have to keep her guard up. The relief was exhilarating, though it was tempered by the nagging sensation that she was something of a fifth wheel in the present company.

"Second card," Sasha said. "Jodhpurs. And it's true. I have been known to enjoy a fine pair of legs in jodhpurs."

That one had been Viola's, and she reached for the open wine bottle to avoid betraying the fact. Perhaps it was silly, but if she showed her hand (so to speak), she thought Sasha might choose her card out of pity. Perhaps Sasha's competitive spirit would outweigh her sympathy and solicitude, but then again, maybe not. Viola wanted to avoid putting that theory to the test.

"Let me guess," Alix teased. "Kerry's legs?"

"More, Thalia?" Viola held up the bottle. "You'll need to kill it since the rest of us have moved on to the bubbly."

Unsurprisingly, Thalia rose to the challenge. "I'll do my duty."

"Have you not ogled Kerry's legs?" Sasha was adorably indignant. She looked from Alix, to whom the question had apparently been addressed, to Thalia and Viola. "I demand that you all ogle Kerry's legs immediately!"

"You really don't have to," Kerry said.

Viola looked up to find Kerry's freckles masked by a vivid blush. She did have very nice legs—long and lean and contoured by muscle, as befitted an athlete. They were almost as nice as Duke's.

No sooner had the thought—and its accompanying memory of Duke's gloriously naked body—crossed her mind than she shoved it back into the dim recesses from which it had emerged and forced herself back to the present moment. She debated wading into the rhetorical fray, but Kerry looked embarrassed enough already.

She focused instead on emptying the wine bottle into Thalia's glass. Of everyone in the room, Viola had spent the least amount of time with her, and she was enjoying the opportunity to get to know her better. For all her competitive spirit, Thalia took a lighthearted approach to most topics off the racetrack. In that way, she was very good for Alix, who was naturally serious and tended to withdraw in social situations. Their relationship had also helped Alix find a new kind of self-confidence, along with the courage to come out publicly despite the disapproval of her family. As different as they were, they were perfect for each other.

Viola couldn't help feeling wistful. She and Duke might have had something similar, if only—No. Not again. Why couldn't she stop thinking about Duke? Why hadn't their night of passion been enough to purge her desire?

"Third card: spotted dick." Sasha made a show of rolling her eyes. "I should have seen that coming."

"Pun intended?" Thalia said, grinning devilishly.

Viola groaned as Kerry made a face, but Sasha lapsed into a giggling fit that made her sound ten years younger. Now, Viola could understand why she and Thalia had been friends in secondary school—each had a prominent mischievous streak—and she could only imagine the high jinks they'd gotten up to.

Alix had tried to clamp one hand over Thalia's mouth, but her efforts had been thwarted and they were now engaged in a wrestling match.

"Save it for the bedroom, ladies," Sasha said. "Fourth card, and, I might add, the winner—The Bodleian Library."

In confusion, Viola watched Sasha cock an eyebrow at Kerry, who blushed even more furiously than she had before. That must be Kerry's card. But how had Sasha known? And why on earth would one of the oldest libraries in Europe make Sasha—who had gotten in, and out of, Oxford University by the skin of her teeth—horny?

"Are you kidding me?" Thalia said into the silence. "You two made the beast with two backs in the Bodleian?"

"Thalia!" Alix said, aghast.

But when Sasha's face became suddenly expressionless, and Kerry chugged her entire glass of champagne, Viola realized the inference had been on target.

"What?" Thalia was saying. "She's red as a tomato. It's obvious."

As Kerry muttered a curse on her Irish heritage, Viola took pity and leaned forward to refill her flute.

"The white cards are awfully specific," was all she said, glancing at Sasha.

Sasha's mouth quirked. "Mm. I made my own. That's the beauty of this game."

"You've been making your own rules since I've known you," Thalia said fondly.

After some additional friendly teasing, they played several more rounds and killed two bottles of champagne before Sasha suggested they take a break.

"You only want to stop because you're winning," Kerry said fondly.

"Lies and slander!" Sasha retorted, drawing Kerry's arm around her shoulders and snuggling close.

A sudden gust of wind rattled the windowpanes, and Viola leaned instinctively toward the roaring fire, glad to be tucked away indoors with friends on such an inclement night. The flames leaping up from the fireplace licked against its stone flagons in a sensually mesmerizing way. They really did look like tongues, she mused through her champagne haze. Unbidden, the memory surfaced of Duke, her hair fanned out against the sheets as Viola rode her mouth and—

"Vi?" At Alix's light touch on her knee, she started.

"Oh, I'm sorry," she said, when she realized all four friends were looking at her. "I was drifting."

"You looked a little sad," Alix persisted. "Do you want to talk about it?"

Until now, they had—as if by prior arrangement—avoided any topic that might have raised the specter of her recent controversy. Viola started to say that no, she was just fine, thank you, though she appreciated their concern and support.

"I slept with her."

Viola felt as stunned as the rest of them looked, despite having been the one who had spoken. How had those words come out of her mouth?

"With whom, exactly?" Sasha finally said.

"Duke."

"Ah." Thankfully, there was no judgment in Sasha's gaze. Viola didn't think she could have borne it if there had been. "When?"

Viola explained Prague—the terrible stress she had been under, Duke's unexpected presence at the gallery and the information she had delivered, the confrontation at her hotel room.

"I was so angry at her, and so angry at myself for wanting her," she continued, "and I thought that I if I just gave in to that desire for one night, I could burn her out of my system." She laughed, but it held no humor. "And don't worry—she was a willing participant."

"Did it work?" Alix asked quietly.

Viola looked toward the window, where the storm outside was picking up force. It was echoed by the invisible storm in her mind, in her body. She still longed for Duke, and not only in the physical sense. "No."

"Sometimes," Thalia said, more serious than Viola had ever heard her, "our bodies know things our brains can't yet process."

"Give yourself some time," Kerry suggested. "This past month has been a whirlwind. A rollercoaster." She smiled slightly. "Choose your metaphor, but you've undergone tremendous upheaval."

"I'll try," Viola said, swallowing hard against another swell of emotion. "Thank you all. I didn't mean to come out with that confession just now, and I'm relieved you were the ones to hear it."

"Nothing you've said will leave this room," Sasha said.

"Please don't be afraid to tell us what's weighing on you," Alix added. "We've all been through difficult times, and while no one's circumstances are identical to another's, we're happy to help."

As grateful as she was for their support, Viola was more than ready to turn the discussion away from herself. "Do you know what I think will help?" she said, reaching toward the tray. "A chocolate-dipped strawberry."

"And more champagne," Sasha said, reaching for the final unopened bottle. "More champagne always helps."

The pop of the cork was drowned out by a peal of thunder that rattled the windows, then rolled ominously for several seconds.

"I think the universe just underlined your point," Kerry said, passing the newly filled glasses around.

Thalia rubbed her cheek against Alix's leg, then looked up into her eyes. "Thunderstorms always make me want to fu—"

"—Forget all those warnings you've heard about being outside when lightning is striking?" Alix said, neatly parrying her bluntness. "We all know how much of a daredevil you are, my love."

Viola might have been able to clamp down on her amusement if Sasha hadn't completely lost her composure, doubling over in a fresh fit of giggles that set them all off. It felt so good to let go and know that she was safe.

This time, when the thunder roared, it was barely audible beneath their laughter.

❖

A suburb of Paris, France

Duke gave the eggs another stir, then turned off the stove and checked on the bacon. She smiled as she remembered the first time she'd cooked bacon in the oven for Juno, and how confused she'd been. It was a Texas trick, she had explained, and after tasting the results, Juno had promptly converted.

"What are you smiling about?" As if summoned, Juno entered the room, towing a sleepy-eyed Leslie behind her.

"Morning," Duke said, mustering a drawl. "And I was thinking about the first time you saw me cook bacon in an oven."

It was the kind of comment that might have roused the jealousy of a possessive girlfriend, but Leslie only blinked. "What's the story?"

As Duke told it, Cecilia and Rosa entered the room. They set the table while the others made coffee and Duke put out the food. When everyone was seated, Duke raised her mug for a toast.

"You four have been the very best friends anyone could ask for. You've supported me, encouraged me, and tolerated me through my bitchiest times."

"Which were pretty damn bitchy," Juno said, before Leslie could shush her.

Duke didn't even feel a twinge at her teasing. "You've challenged me to be my best, then helped me when I fell along the way. You're my safe harbor in the storm. You're family. And I promise I'll always be there for you in return."

"Stop making me cry," Rosa said.

"Don't be afraid of happy tears," Leslie said philosophically. "They're good for you."

In that silly, heartfelt moment, Duke realized she loved them all—loved them in a gloriously uncomplicated way that was so much simpler than the romantic kind of love. If only it were enough.

"I love you," she said, laughing. And it was enough, just then, as the clinking of glass and ceramic filled the room, and they all dug in to the feast she had prepared.

Later, the conversation turned to less pleasant matters. A few days prior, FIFA had declared that they would no longer consider the Belgian-Dutch bid due to the "politically fraught" situation. The Belgian-Dutch bid team had promptly filed an appeal, and after some consideration, Duke had made a formal request of FIFA to testify in support of that appeal, despite the fact that she was in no way affiliated with the bid effort. In the process of submitting that request, she had taken her friends' advice to consult with the now-retired woman who had coached the US Women's National Team during Duke's time on the squad. She had a direct line to FIFA and promised she would see to it that Duke's request would be dutifully reviewed—though she could make no promises about the outcome. As yet, she had heard nothing.

"They have to let me testify," she said, even though of course, they didn't. "They just have to."

"And if they don't?" Rosa said gently.

Duke sighed and looked down at her bread crusts. "Whether they do or not, I'm going to try to get a meeting with Kerry

Donovan." She saw her friends look at each other in surprise. "I met her a few weeks ago at a gala in Brussels. Unless I've been blackballed, I think she might see me."

"But what do you want to talk to her about?" Cecilia asked.

"A career in journalism is obviously not for me," she said, holding up one hand when Juno tried to protest. "It's not what I want, long term. To be honest, I still have no idea what I *do* want, but in the meantime, I plan to stick to my strengths. I'm going to see if Eclipse has any openings."

"Eclipse?" Leslie's face was blank.

"The charity Kerry founded last year. It's all about strengthening communities through the development of girls' soccer and related infrastructure."

"It's a very good cause," Rosa said. "But are you sure you'll be happy?"

Duke shrugged as she stood to clear the table. "I'll be helping people who need it," she said. "That's going to make me a hell of a lot happier than I am right now."

CHAPTER EIGHTEEN

Brussels, Belgium

"I'm meeting a friend," Duke told the hostess at the Belladonna. "The reservation is under the name 'Donovan.'"

"Your friend has already arrived," the hostess said in crisply accented English. "Right this way."

Duke followed her up a small staircase to the second floor. The Belladonna was one of Brussels's most popular bars, according to the internet, but it was blessedly quiet in the late afternoon on a Monday. The hostess gestured to a table in the far corner, where one seat was already occupied by an androgynous figure in jeans and a white Oxford shirt, their short, crimson hair glowing in the lamplight.

Kerry rose as she approached and greeted her with two light cheek kisses. "It's good to see you, Duke."

"Likewise." Duke swallowed against the swell of emotion at the unexpected warmth in her greeting. "How are you?"

Kerry took the question to heart, showing her the latest picture of her niece, Princess Eleanor, and chatting briefly about a recent trip to Scotland with Sasha. But once the waitress returned with their drink orders, Kerry's gaze sharpened and she leaned forward.

"Now that we're unlikely to be interrupted for a while, shall we get down to business?"

Despite having just taken a sip, Duke's mouth went dry. "I really appreciate your taking the time for this meeting," she said, hoping she was on the right side of the line between gratitude and flattery. "I'm *persona non grata* in most circles right now. Especially the royal ones."

Kerry met her eyes in an evaluating stare, tracing patterns in the condensation on her glass. "I believe your article," she said. "And I asked around about you."

"You did?"

Kerry nodded. "Everyone I spoke to told the same story. Brilliant soccer player. Hard worker, reliable teammate. Bit of a diva, but not malicious. Never that."

To her horror, Duke felt her eyes welling up. She blinked rapidly, hoping Kerry wouldn't notice. "That's what they said?"

"Mm." She sat back in her chair. "I watched you play a few times, you know. I've seen the 'brilliant soccer player' part for myself."

"I—thanks." Duke didn't know what to say when that small bit of praise felt more meaningful than the positive feedback she'd received from any number of illustrious coaches.

"And I remember seeing the headline about your early retirement," Kerry continued. "You've been dealt a tough hand."

Duke had to look away because Kerry's sympathetic gaze made her want to break down and weep. That was *not* the impression she wanted to make. Despite the awkwardness, she kept her eyes averted until she was reasonably sure she could keep her act together.

"I'm trying not to think of it that way," she said hoarsely. "I played soccer at the highest possible level. How many people dream of that and never get the chance?"

Kerry grinned and raised her hand. "Present. But I can hardly complain when I ended up with a Rhodes scholarship."

Her lightheartedness eased the terrible pressure in Duke's throat. "Fair enough," she said, and actually managed a genuine smile. How long had it been?

"So," Kerry said after drinking from her beer, "your email mentioned an interest in Eclipse."

"Yes," Duke said, chagrined that she had managed to turn what was supposed to be a business meeting into a confessional. "I'd like to get involved. To join *your* team. Do you have any openings for an athletic director or coach or—or anything? I'm happy to travel anywhere you need me…" Realizing that she was babbling, she shut her mouth with a click.

"We do have a few open coaching spots," Kerry said, though there was a grave note to her voice that made Duke's pulse spike in preparation of bad news. "But you're overqualified, based on the credentials of the ones I've hired so far. And the position doesn't pay very much. Room and board are covered, but they won't be luxurious."

Duke blinked hard again, this time in surprise. Was Kerry saying what she thought she had heard: that there *were* open positions in Eclipse and the only stumbling block was the high caliber of her soccer credentials? Not the scandal she'd managed to cause?

"I don't care about being overqualified," she said. "And I don't care about the living conditions. I want to do it."

"Why?" Kerry's tone wasn't hostile, only curious. "Because you're setting yourself some kind of penance? Or because you actually want to work with girls who might never have touched a real soccer ball in their lives?"

The pointed question stung a little, but Duke refused to engage in any further deception. "Both. For the past two years, all I've managed to do is ruin things—first my own body, and now Viola's plan to help her brother. I need to do some good in the world. To build things up instead of tearing them apart."

"You're being too hard on yourself," Kerry said. When Duke opened her mouth to protest, Kerry shook her head. "I'm an Irish Catholic. Believe me when I say I understand guilt. But it's ridiculous to even suggest that you purposefully injured yourself. As for exposing Viola, you thought you'd convinced your colleague not to go through with it. You were wrong. That just means you misjudged his character."

Duke didn't want to be let off the hook. She knew, deep down, that she didn't deserve it. "I should have called it off sooner," she said.

Kerry regarded her silently, then took a long sip from her beer before she next spoke. "I see you're committed to self-flagellation."

Duke forced herself to smile. "I'll try to stop. I know it's not the most productive way of managing the situation. FIFA has allowed me to testify in support of the Dutch-Belgian bid, so at least there's something concrete I *can* do."

"That's great news," Kerry said, brightening. "I couldn't believe it when they made such a myopic decision. I'm sure your testimony will help."

Duke wasn't sure that confidence was warranted, but it certainly helped to hear. "I hope you're right."

"As for Eclipse," Kerry continued, "later today, I'll call my secretary and have her email you a list of the openings. You can have your pick."

"Thank you." The wave of relief was strong enough to make her dizzy. "I won't disappoint you, I promise."

"I'm not worried about that," Kerry said.

Hearing that someone else had such confidence in her was comforting and terrifying, all at once. Near tears again, Duke drank deeply from her glass, using the interlude to regain her composure. When she returned her gaze to Kerry, she was looking out the window as though she had sensed Duke's struggle. She probably had. Her attention seemed held by the busy street outside, and as she watched, she idly spun the ring on her left forefinger with her thumb. Her wedding ring.

Duke wondered if she was thinking about Sasha, and from the English princess, her own thoughts quickly leapt to Viola. The ache between her breasts intensified. Since that incendiary night together, she had heard nothing. Viola's silence suggested that she had been able to burn Duke out of her system, just as she'd intended. Clearly, all she'd ever felt was lust.

If only Duke could say the same. She had fallen, head over heels, with someone who despised her, and the only solution she could think of was to put as much distance between herself and Viola as possible. When Kerry's secretary did send her that list, she intended to choose the location that was geographically farthest from Belgium. Over time, her unrequited feelings would fade. That's what people said, anyway.

They certainly hadn't faded yet. No matter how much of a pep talk she gave her reflection each morning, by the afternoon, she found herself scouring social media and Google for any trace of information about what Viola was up to. She had found very little of substance. While people continued to discuss Sebastian's condition and her impersonation of him, Viola appeared to have dropped off the planet. Doubtless, she was keeping a low profile for the sake of her own sanity.

A sudden thought made Duke's hand tremble so hard the beer stein clattered against the tabletop. What if Kerry knew something? She and Sasha were friendly with Viola, and they might be in touch on a regular basis. Could it hurt to ask?

She could feel the beer going to her head, making her bold. Still, she hesitated. Kerry had already been very generous with her time and her help. And once Duke had decided on a coaching job, Kerry would be her supervisor. But if she didn't at least make an effort, wouldn't she regret it?

Duke imagined herself trudging back to her apartment without having asked the question burning on her lips, and she knew the answer was yes.

"I want to ask you something," she said, all in a rush before she could second-guess her decision. "You should, of course, feel free not to answer."

"I won't if I don't want to," Kerry said mildly. "Or if I can't."

"It's about Viola," Duke ventured.

Kerry said nothing, only waited expectantly.

"I think I'm in love with her."

Her eyebrows arched slightly, the only indication of her surprise. "You really mean that?"

"Yes." Duke licked dry lips. "I know she hates me, and of course I can't blame her. When we last saw each other, she told me not to contact her ever again, and I'm respecting her wishes. But..." she trailed off, not wanting to cast herself in the role of the victim.

"It's making you crazy," Kerry finished, her gaze compassionate. "I think I know how you feel."

Duke remembered the media firestorm that had erupted when Kerry and Sasha's relationship was revealed by the paparazzi. If anyone could even remotely empathize, it would be her.

"Yes," she said. "Have you...spoken with her?"

When Kerry nodded, a wash of adrenaline made Duke's skin pebble. Dozens of questions swarmed in her brain, and she forced herself to wait until she had found the right words before speaking. The last thing she wanted was for Kerry, who was in contact with Viola, to think she was completely insane.

"I don't want you to break any promises you might have made," she began, feeling as though she were tiptoeing through a rhetorical minefield, "but is there anything you can tell me?"

Kerry sat back in her chair, her expression thoughtful. "Sasha is closer to Viola than I am," she finally said, "but I have spoken with her a few times over the past fortnight. She's going through an exceptionally challenging time, as you can imagine. I'm not sure there's anything I can tell you that you hadn't already guessed at."

That was fair enough, but Duke—selfishly, she knew—wanted the answers she *couldn't* predict. Did Viola think of her, ever, with anything other than hate? Was there any part of her, however small, that wanted to see her again? Did she ever think back on their night together? If so, had she ever considered the possibility that their physical chemistry might be some cosmic sign of their compatibility?

Duke swallowed hard, tamping down the questions along with her frustration. Kerry had said what she could, or would, and Duke refused to press her—no matter how much she wanted to.

"I'm glad Viola has you and Sasha to talk to," she said. "I'm sure your support has helped her." She drained the last of her beer. "And thank you again for this meeting. You've helped me, too."

To her surprise, Kerry stood when she did and stepped forward for a quick hug.

"Don't lose faith," Kerry whispered, just before she pulled away. "I'll be in touch."

She resumed her seat, leaving Duke to thread her way through the maze of tables. Her thoughts were just as confused as the path she took. Was she meant to take heart from Kerry's parting words? Had Viola said anything to Kerry or Sasha that indicated she might not despise Duke, after all? Or was "Don't lose faith" only a platitude?

As Duke stepped out into the pleasantly cool evening, she tried to stay focused on what was important. Thanks to Kerry, she was no longer at loose ends. She would be able to do what she'd always been best at in the service of helping disadvantaged young women and their communities. So what if the pay wasn't great and the living conditions rustic? Right now, a simpler life dedicated to truly meaningful goals was exactly what she needed.

CHAPTER NINETEEN

Fédération Internationale de Football Association Headquarters, Zurich, Switzerland

As the clock chimed ten, Duke clamped down on the plastic armrests that caged her in, forcing herself to remain seated. She had been waiting for well over an hour now and desperately wanted to pace the length of the narrow antechamber to release some of her pent-up tension. But at any moment, the young man who had ushered her into this room and asked her to "wait for the committee" might return, and when he did, she wanted to appear calm, collected, and in control.

For what felt like the thousandth time, she wondered what was taking so long. Her appointment had been for nine o'clock. How could the committee be so far behind, this early in the morning?

And then the door finally did open, and Duke had her answer as Prince Sebastian followed the secretary into the waiting room, his bodyguard close on his heels. Suddenly, Duke couldn't breathe. Her heart stuttered, then began to gallop. The man said something to Sebastian in French before turning to Duke.

"My apologies for the delay, Ms. Duke. Unfortunately, we must ask you to wait a few minutes longer."

He disappeared back through the door before she could reply, leaving her to confront the man she had inadvertently betrayed. He was immaculately attired in a dark pinstripe suit, but his cheeks were gaunt and his eyes shadowed. He regarded her intently, but she couldn't detect any malice in his gaze. When his bodyguard made to step in front of him, he motioned the man aside, speaking to him quietly but firmly in French.

He came forward to meet her but did not extend his hand. "Ms. Duke. I am surprised to see you here."

"Your Royal Highness." She knew a deferential bow of her head was sufficient to acknowledge his rank, but instead, she made a careful curtsy. "I'm here because I lodged a formal request with FIFA that they reinstate the candidacy of the Belgian-Dutch bid, and they agreed to hear my testimony."

"Why?"

"Because their decision to disqualify your bid was unfair, and because I'm partially at fault for that decision."

He nodded. "I've read your article. I didn't know whether to believe it."

"Whether you do or not, it's the truth." Duke was feeling a little dizzy, and she forced herself to take a deep breath. After wanting time to speed up all morning, she now begged for it to slow. At any moment, she would be summoned into the room beyond. This was an unlooked for chance—maybe her *only* chance—to convince the real Sebastian of her sincerity.

"I am so very sorry for everything that I did to contribute to your…your current difficulties." She cursed herself for fumbling after the right words. "There is so much I wish I'd done differently. I hope someday you can believe that I did try to prevent the exposé from being written. I even thought I'd succeeded. If I could turn back time, I'd make very different decisions."

A slight twist to his lips—nearly a wince—was the only emotion he betrayed. "I understand that sentiment perfectly."

She felt the tiniest stirring of hope that he had established even a small connection between them. "My actions have hurt both you and your sister. I think the world of her, and I can't apologize enough for causing you both so much distress. If you can think of anything I can do, large or small, to help you in some way, I'll happily do it."

Across the room, the door opened. "I think you already are," Sebastian said as the FIFA undersecretary moved toward them.

He began to turn away. His profile, so similar to Viola's, made her ache with longing. "Your Royal Highness, please, one more thing," she said all in a rush, before she could think better of it. What, after all, did she have to lose? "How is your sister?"

Sebastian looked back over his shoulder. "Strong."

"The strongest woman I've ever met," Duke said fervently.

"Ms. Duke," said the undersecretary. "The committee will see you now."

"Thank you." As she followed him, Duke glanced back toward Sebastian. His shoulders were straight, his head high. He didn't turn.

He was strong, too. She only hoped he believed it.

Now, it was her turn to muster all the strength and eloquence at her disposal. Undoubtedly, he too had been trying to convince the FIFA committee to reinstate the bid. Maybe together, their testimony would be enough.

Belvedere Palace, Brussels, Belgium

Viola sat on the terrace, trying to admire the hue of the Chardonnay in her glass as it caught the orange light of the sunset. She was doing her best to enjoy this unseasonably warm autumn evening. It shouldn't have been difficult, especially since Sebastian was sitting across from her. Their parents had excused themselves a few minutes ago, after a family dinner over which Sebastian had related his experience testifying in front of the FIFA committee this morning. He had maintained his composure while recounting the conversation, but Viola could feel the tension radiating from his thin frame. Their parents had been quick to praise his efforts, and he had accepted their encouragement graciously, but Viola could tell that it pained him to linger on the subject. She glanced up at him, only to find that he was regarding her with a pensive expression. Her palms began to sweat. Something was wrong.

"There was one detail I left out of my account," he said.

"Oh?"

"I saw Missy Duke at FIFA Headquarters."

Stunned, Viola could only blink at him. She felt strangely short of breath.

"When I left the committee, I encountered Duke—you said that's what she prefers to be called?"

"Yes." She barely managed to force out the word.

"I met her in the waiting room. She spoke to me."

"What—" The word emerged as a croak. "What did she say?"

"She apologized. I was prepared to mistrust her, but she seemed genuine."

Viola bit back a cruel retort about how Sebastian should hardly trust his own judgment right now. The last thing he needed was to bear the brunt of an anger directed toward Duke and herself.

"She also told me she 'thinks the world of you,' and that she was terribly sorry for causing you so much pain."

Viola prayed he couldn't perceive the emotional rawness beneath the fragile shields she had constructed. "Apologies are just words."

"Maybe." Sebastian sounded thoughtful. "But the fact that she was there to testify to FIFA on behalf of the bid means something, don't you think?"

"What?"

"She was summoned to meet with the committee while we were talking. And before she left, she asked after you."

Viola's heart raced faster. "What did she say?"

"'How is your sister?'" He was watching her closely. She wondered what he saw, and whether she wanted to know.

"And what did you tell her?"

He smiled faintly. "All I said was, 'Strong.'"

Her eyes welled, and she looked away. "Thank you," she whispered.

When he touched her hand, she forced herself to meet his gaze. "To which she replied, 'The strongest woman I've ever met.'"

When Viola blinked in surprise, one of the tears spilled onto her cheek. She brushed it away in frustration. "That's what she said?"

"Verbatim." He moved his hand away. "There's something between you, isn't there?"

Viola wanted to look away again, but she forced herself not to. "There was," she said slowly. "It started with simple attraction, and for a while, I thought that's all it was." She laughed sharply. "I thought I couldn't act on that attraction because Duke believed me to be a man."

"When really, she knew all along," Sebastian realized. His eyebrows lifted. "That's…complicated. But what's the problem now?"

Viola stared at him incredulously. "The problem now is that she's the reason you had to spend the morning being interrogated by FIFA!"

"As I understand it, her colleague deserves most of the blame."

"You believe her? That she tried to stop the story from ever going public?"

"I think her presence in Zurich is all the proof we need," Sebastian said. "Don't you?"

Viola still couldn't believe what she was hearing. "But she hid her knowledge of my identity for *weeks.*"

Sebastian shrugged. "Was that really unethical, from her perspective? I don't like the press's intrusiveness any more than you do, but she didn't know what you were hiding."

Viola looked down into her wine glass. "By her own admission, she could have done more, sooner, to try to stop the story from breaking."

"Hindsight is always perfect," he said, offering a smile tinged with sadness that made her wonder how much *he* must wish to change the past. "Making that admission in the first place says a fair amount about her character."

Viola drummed her fingers against the table, no longer able to disguise her agitation. "Why are you taking her side in this?"

"I'm not. But from what I saw in her face this morning, she's enamored with you. And based on the reaction I'm getting from *you* right now, I'd say you feel the same." He leaned forward. "I'd like to think I've learned a few things about priorities over the past month. Why hold on to your anger when it's not even deserved? Why not see if whatever connection you shared in the past can amount to anything now?"

Why not? All the answers that came to Viola were reasons Sebastian had already dismantled. If *he* didn't feel any rancor toward Duke, despite the role she had played in his addiction becoming public information, why was she holding on to the grudge?

"We all have to move on now, Vi," he said quietly. "You, me, Mom, Dad, Ruben, André…we all have to stop blaming ourselves for what happened." He folded his napkin, pushed back his chair, and stood. "Go find Duke. See if that connection is real. And if she has any bi or straight friends who find sobriety sexy, I wouldn't mind an introduction."

She had to smile at that. He left her and she felt her smile fade as the sun sank beneath the horizon. Was he right? Had she been using her anger at Duke to avoid processing her own shortcomings and fears? What if that anger was mostly displaced self-loathing? She could hardly blame Duke for being perceptive, and they were both guilty of flirting under false pretenses. Since their single night together, Viola had only found herself more distracted, not less. Sebastian had seen in minutes what she had allowed her own anger and frustration to obscure for weeks: that Duke's heart was in the right place, and that Duke cared about her.

As all the reasons to keep her distance crumbled into dust, Viola was possessed of a growing urgency to see Duke as soon as possible. But was she still in Brussels?

Galvanized, she grabbed her phone and began scrolling through her contacts list, then cursed aloud, startling the staff member who had begun to clear their table. After a quick apology, she returned to her most immediate problem: she didn't have Duke's number. No one did—she had deleted it from Sebastian's phone before returning it to him. But Thijs would know how to get it.

He answered on the first ring. "Is everything all right, ma'am?"

"You might think this an odd request," she began, "but I need Missy Duke's cell number."

If he did think it odd, he didn't say. "Just a moment." He was as good as his word; mere seconds later, her phone vibrated with a text message. "You have it now."

"Thank you," she said. "And, Thijs—I might be going out in a little while."

To her relief, his voice remained neutral. "I'll have a car standing by, ma'am. Text me the address when you know it."

She thanked him again, then hung up and promptly created a new contact in her phone. She was in the process of typing Duke's first name when she stopped and erased it, leaving the field blank. Her hands trembled as she pulled up a new text message, and she braced them against her knees to steady herself.

Duke, this is Viola, she typed. *I'd like to speak with you. Tonight, if possible. Are you in Brussels and available?*

She read the words once, then again. They were overly formal, but she could hardly take a more casual approach until she knew exactly where they stood with one another. Her thumb hovered over the "Send" button. She thought of Duke's desperation at their confrontation in Amsterdam, of her impassioned plea in Prague that she was fighting for an "us." Viola had denied the possibility of it then, but she wanted it now.

Slowly, deliberately, she pressed her thumb to the screen, then swallowed the wine remaining in her glass. All she could do now was wait.

CHAPTER TWENTY

Brussels, Belgium

No sooner had she pulled on her floral print dress than Duke pulled it back off again, barely restraining herself from hurling it against the mirror. After receiving Viola's text and replying with Craig's address, she had jumped into the shower and shaved as quickly as she dared. Since then, she had been systematically going through her outfits, trying to find something that toed the line between overly formal and too casual. So far, nothing looked right, and Viola would be here within moments.

She reached for the next hanger and was just in the process of pulling the yellow halter top dress over her bra when the buzzer rang. After one hasty glance to make sure no straps were showing, Duke ran for the door. She opened it to find Thijs, looking professional as always in a dark suit. Viola stood half a pace behind him, dressed casually in a scoop-neck black shirt and hip-hugging jeans. The shirt clung to her breasts, and Duke's mouth went dry as she remembered the sensation of them pressed against her own chest as Viola moved against her. She swallowed hard.

"Hello," she said, and by some miracle, her voice didn't emerge sounding strangled. "Please, come in." She shut the door behind them and turned to Thijs. "I know you'll need to inspect the rooms.."

He nodded and moved deeper into the apartment, leaving Duke alone with Viola. When Duke met her eyes, she saw none of the anger that had defined their last encounter. In fact, she seemed uncharacteristically uncertain, even hesitant. Wanting to reassure her, Duke nearly touched her arm before thinking better of it. She needed to be patient. After all, she still had no idea why Viola had come here tonight.

"Can I offer you something to drink?" she said, fumbling for some semblance of normalcy to ease the tension. "Sparkling water? Wine? Beer?"

"Water, please." Viola trailed her into the kitchen, and Duke felt her gaze like a spotlight as she stood on her toes to reach for two glasses. As she was pouring, Thijs returned.

"All clear, Your Royal Highness. I will wait for you outside."

"Outside?" Duke knew what was outside Craig's apartment: a cramped landing from which two other doors led to his neighbors' residences. She desperately wanted to be alone with Viola, but the thought of Thijs leaning against the wall or sitting on the stairs wasn't something she could live with. "It's not very comfortable out there. You're welcome to stay inside."

In her peripheral vision, Duke saw Viola shake her head ever so slightly. That meant she wanted privacy. Did that also mean she wanted a repeat of what had happened in Prague? The thought at once aroused and discomfited Duke. As much as she wanted Viola physically, she needed so much more.

"I'll be quite all right, Ms. Duke," he said. "But thank you for your concern."

He left them in the kitchen. When the door clicked shut behind him, Viola cleared her throat. "Thank you for seeing me on such short notice."

Her lack of assertiveness inspired in Duke a protective impulse, the likes of which she had never felt before. Whatever Viola was going through, she was going to need some gentle handling.

"I'll always want to see you," Duke said. "Let's go into the living room where we can talk more comfortably."

She led the way into the small room with its single loveseat and twin armchairs. She chose one corner of the loveseat and was surprised when Viola claimed the other cushion. Hope blossomed in her chest, despite the pain that could very well be waiting on the other side. As Viola settled herself, Duke drank in every detail, from the feathered pixie cut of her hair, to the elegant lines of her legs.

"You're beautiful," she said. What was the use of playing it coy?

Viola arched one eyebrow, a hint of her fire returning with the expression. "I didn't come here for flattery."

Duke had expected to feel intimidated, but she didn't. Maybe it was because she had already lost Viola once. This visit from her was a gift, and all she could do now was be honest.

"I'm not flattering you. I'm telling the truth."

To that, Viola said nothing. The silence became uncomfortable, but Duke tamped down her self-consciousness. Whatever had inspired Viola to walk back into her life, Duke didn't want to ruin this moment by being impatient.

"You were in Zurich this morning," Viola said finally.

"Yes. I met your brother."

"That must have been strange."

"It was, a little," Duke acknowledged, wanting to tread lightly lest she reawaken Viola's anger. "I admire him, and I'm grateful he wanted to talk to me. But that was all I felt when I was with him—admiration and gratitude. It's always been different with you."

"Always?" Viola seemed suspicious of the claim.

"Since the very first time I heard you speak in The Hague," Duke said. "I'm not usually attracted to men. Imagine my confusion."

Viola actually laughed, and it was the most beautiful sound Duke had ever heard. "Sebastian was impressed with you."

"Oh?" Duke sensed there was more she wanted to say.

"He helped me realize I've been unfair to you. I was so angry, I couldn't see that for myself."

Duke held her gaze, though with difficulty. "I deserved it."

Viola shook her head. "No, I don't think you did. Not entirely."

Duke dared to move a few inches closer. "As soon as Toby uncovered Sebastian's hospitalization, I should have told you who I was, what I was doing. And I should have known he wouldn't just abandon an opportunity to make a quick buck."

Slowly, Viola reached out to bridge the remaining space between them, her hand coming to rest on the strip of skin between Duke's knee and the hem of her dress. The warmth of Viola's palm stirred Duke's desire, and she bit her bottom lip to stifle a moan. They were in the middle of a crucially important conversation. This was not the right time to let her body take over.

"I do wish you had told me your real purpose," Viola admitted. "But my brother was right when he told me that I was letting my emotions blind me to the facts. You couldn't have known Toby wouldn't honor his promise."

"I should have gues—"

"Shh."

To emphasize the point, Viola leaned in to kiss her. Stunned, Duke was barely able to return the kiss before Viola pulled away. Despite that loss, triumph sang through Duke like a fanfare.

"I've accepted your apology for what you could have controlled and chose not to," Viola said. "So, let's make a pact. You'll stop blaming yourself for Toby's mistakes, and I'll stop blaming myself for not being a strong enough actor to fool you in the first place."

Duke surprised herself by laughing. "You only had, what, a day's worth of preparation before we met? You did an amazing job, given the circumstances."

"I don't want to dwell on the past anymore. I'd like to talk about the future, instead."

"The future?" Duke knew she sounded like a parrot, but a part of her was still in shock that she and Viola were sitting on the same couch, and that Viola had just initiated a kiss. Now she wanted to talk about the future?

"In Prague, you said you wanted to fight for an 'us.'" Viola leaned closer as she spoke, and Duke mirrored her action, helplessly magnetized. "Is that still something you want?"

Duke's heart clattered against her ribs, and to her mortification, tears sprang to her eyes. "Yes," she said. "God, yes. *You* are what I want."

And then, because words would never be enough, she initiated a kiss of her own. The sensation of Viola's mouth against hers, firm yet soft, was a goad to her craving. She parted her lips, and their tongues met in a delicious swirl that made Duke's head spin. She lost herself in the kiss, some distant part of her hoping that Viola would be able to sense the authenticity of her desire, her delight, her need to affirm this fragile new connection.

When Duke felt the feather-light touch of Viola's fingers against her cheek, she pulled away. Viola's eyes remained closed for a long moment before they opened and focused on her.

"Why did you stop?" she sounded almost forlorn.

"Because as much as I want to spend the rest of tonight in your arms, we still need to talk." Duke took one of Viola's hands and cradled it in both of hers. "Over the past month, you've gone through emotional whiplash. I don't ever want to cause you pain again. Be honest with me now, and I promise I'll do the same. I thought I'd never see you again, but now you're here. What does that mean? What does 'us' mean to you?"

With her free hand, Viola caressed Duke's cheek. "I want you. As a lover, but as more than that, too." She wrinkled her nose. "I find most of the names for it rather awful: girlfriend, partner, significant other. I want what those names signify."

"What they signify?"

"A relationship." There was a vulnerability in Viola's gaze that convinced Duke she was genuine. "We somehow found our way to each other, despite the fact that we were both pretending."

"Yes," Duke said, sensing that Viola needed her affirmation. "It's amazing, really."

"I want to see what we can build together when all pretenses are set aside."

What we can build together. Duke felt light headed with relief and joy. Never, never in a million years, had she expected to hear these words from Viola tonight. "That's how you want me?"

"That's how I want you."

Viola was watching her reaction closely. She seemed more confident now, and Duke was glad to hear the certainty in her voice. But in the next moment, reality intruded, as she remembered the plan she had put in place.

"You should know that earlier this week, I signed a contract with Eclipse to do a three-month coaching and mentoring stint in Zimbabwe." She interlaced their fingers together, marveling at how right it felt to touch Viola this way, and wanting desperately not to lose this connection. "It starts next month. I don't want to leave just as we're trying to build a—an 'us,' but I need to honor that commitment."

Viola's expression was curious, but free from recrimination. "What made you decide on Eclipse?"

"I don't want to be a journalist," Duke said. "I can't play professional soccer. But I can coach and be a mentor. Eclipse will let me do both in places where there's a real need."

Viola nodded. "Three months?" At Duke's nod, she squeezed her fingers lightly. "I'll miss you, but you'll be doing amazing work. Would it be too distracting if I came to visit?"

The bolt of pure, unalloyed happiness that struck Duke reminded her of just how long it had been since she had felt any unsullied emotion. And now, that kind of joy was back in her life. Thanks to Viola.

"Yes, but you should anyway." Duke brushed a kiss across her knuckles. "I'm so glad you were willing to forgive me," she said, not caring about the waver in her voice. "For the first time in what feels like forever, I'm actually looking forward to the future."

"So am I." Viola became thoughtful. "Even at my angriest, I couldn't stop thinking about you. I talked about you with my friends, you know. Sasha and Kerry, Alix and Thalia. I didn't mean to bring you up, but we had too much champagne, and I suddenly blurted out that I'd slept with you."

"You—" Shocked, Duke leaned back against the cushions, her mind struggling to wrap itself around the idea that Viola had told two princesses, a duchess, and a celebrity athlete about their night together. After a moment, she realized Viola's bemusement had become concern.

"I'm sorry if I've upset you," Viola said. "I really didn't intend to say anything. And I didn't share any details, I promise."

"I'm not upset." This time, it was Duke's turn to reach out. She let one hand come to rest on Viola's thigh and stroked lightly, amazed all over again that this was something she could do in reality and not only in her imagination. "What was their reaction?"

"You made a positive first impression on them all at the gala," Viola said. "They were inclined to give you the benefit of the doubt, though instead of arguing with me, they focused on being supportive."

"They sound like good friends."

"They are. I think they helped me start to heal."

An idea popped into Duke's mind and she decided to voice it before she lost her courage. "Maybe we can all go on a triple date, someday?"

Viola laughed—a genuine laugh, free of any self recrimination. "We absolutely must." Her gaze grew speculative and she moved closer to Duke, until their legs were touching. "Thalia is better known for her outrageous statements than her pearls of wisdom, but she said something in Scotland that's stuck with me."

"Oh?" Duke felt herself go liquid at Viola's nearness. A delicious tension had just sprung up between them, making her weak in the best of ways.

"'Sometimes, our bodies know things our brains can't yet process.'" Viola leaned in to kiss one corner of her mouth. "I think she might be right."

"Prague?" Duke could only manage the single syllable. It was all she could do not to pull Viola's head down to hers and lose herself in another of those long, luxuriant kisses.

"Prague." Viola's voice was solemn.

"We should talk about it." Duke tried to sound firm and confident, despite her melting synapses.

Slowly, Viola settled one arm around her shoulder, pulling her closer. "To be honest, I'd rather repeat it than talk about it," she said, lightly resting her free hand in the space between Duke's breasts. "Though never again out of anger."

"And this time, you'll stay?" Duke hated how forlorn she sounded, but the memory of lying awake half the night sobbing after her hotel door had closed behind Viola was *not* something she wanted to dwell on, or ever repeat.

"Yes." Viola cocked her head. "Is that all that worries you? Not the...tone of what we did?"

Torn between the ache of arousal and the urgent need to clear the air between them, Duke was struggling to think clearly. "The tone. You mean, how dominant you were?"

"Yes." Viola's gaze was intent and unwavering, the warmth of her palm seeping through the thin cloth of the dress.

"Your dominance in bed," Duke began hoarsely, "is not the part of that night I regret." She licked her lips purely for the purposes of moistening them, but when Viola's eyes tracked to her mouth, a heady confidence filled her. "It's true—our bodies connected even when we couldn't communicate any other way. Now that we're doing a much better job of communicating, I wouldn't be opposed to exploring how our chemistry is affected."

When Viola smiled, Duke was gratified that her words, calculated to be at once meaningful and playful, had hit their mark. She moved her hand down to cup Duke's breast through the fabric. Duke's eyes fluttered shut at the possessive touch, but when Viola ran a thumb across her nipple, she gasped, refocusing.

"Your heart is beating so fast." With her free hand, she brought Duke's palm to her own chest. "Mine, too."

"Why?" Duke whispered, sensing a hidden depth behind the words.

"Because I want you. And because I'm falling for you." Viola's mouth quirked sensually. "That's the proper idiom, isn't it?"

Duke nodded, then licked her lips again. "I'm already in love with you," she said, and the words weren't nearly as frightening to say as she had thought they would be. "So you have some catching up to do."

"Challenge accepted." Viola disentangled herself from Duke, then stood. She held out one hand. "Come home with me. I want to make love with you."

As Viola conferred with Thijs, Duke quickly gathered everything she would need for an overnight trip and threw them into a small duffle. She focused on the small tasks to distract herself from the awe that threatened to overwhelm her. Viola had forgiven her. Viola wanted her. And ironically, she had Sebastian to thank for helping his sister finally see reason.

When she closed Craig's front door behind her, Viola took her bag and handed it to Thijs.

"That's really not necess—"

"I don't mind, Ms. Duke," he said mildly before leading them down the stairs.

This time, the waiting car was a Bentley. Thijs climbed into the front passenger seat while Viola held the back door for Duke. As soon as they were in motion, Viola activated the privacy partition. Once it was up, she held out her hand to Duke.

"They can't see us, and I can't wait any longer. Come here."

Duke went willingly, abandoning her seat belt to straddle Viola's legs. The position made her dress ride up on her thighs, and Viola murmured appreciatively as she reached around Duke's back to unzip the garment. When she pulled down the straps, Duke didn't protest. Viola's urgency was intoxicating, and Duke trusted she wouldn't do anything to embarrass her.

"Do you like being on top?" Viola asked as she divested Duke of her bra.

"Sometimes," Duke said breathlessly. "But usually that's where I'll want you."

"Oh, don't worry." Viola's tone was dark and seductive. "I'm still the one in charge."

She captured Duke's breasts in her hands and cradled them gently before flicking at the tips with both thumbs. Duke bit down hard on her lower lip to keep from crying out, and her hips surged against the deliciously rough fabric of Viola's jeans. Again and again, Viola tormented her nipples, until Duke thought she might climax.

Viola leaned close to suckle at Duke's earlobe. "Can you come this way?" she whispered.

"I never have," Duke said, hearing the tremor in her own voice and not caring in the slightest. "But you make me want to."

"Another time." Viola's expression was stark and hungry in the flickering city lights. "I'm not feeling patient tonight."

She brought one hand to the juncture of Duke's thighs and caressed her through the thin fabric of her underwear. This time, Duke wasn't fast enough to stifle her moan.

"Shh." Viola seemed amused by her lack of self-control. "The barrier isn't soundproof. I'm going to touch you now, but you must stay quiet, or I'll be forced to stop. Ready?"

Duke nodded frantically, her mind a blizzard of need, her lips clamped together tightly. When Viola twitched aside her underwear to find her swollen and throbbing, it was all Duke could do not to scream. Bracing herself with one arm against the back of the seat, she threaded her other hand through Viola's short hair, communicating via pressure what she couldn't say in words. *Yes. So good. More, more, more, oh God, don't stop!*

The pleasure tightened, pulsed, shattered. She came hard, hips thrusting furiously. Viola's smile was triumphant, but her hands were gentle when Duke collapsed against her, sated. As her wits slowly returned, Duke burrowed closer, craving the comfort of Viola's touch. When Thijs's voice came over the intercom, announcing their arrival in two minutes, Viola helped her back into the dress, though she pocketed Duke's bra.

At that, Duke felt a mild twinge of anxiety. "But what if we encounter your parents on our way in?"

Viola cupped her cheek in one hand. "Stop worrying. I'm sure they've retired for the night." She gave Duke a slow once-over that rekindled her desire. "Besides, it's not *that* obvious."

The car slowed, then halted. The door opened. Duke stepped out, and Thijs steadied her when she wobbled.

"Thank you," she said, forcing herself to meet his gaze. Thankfully, she saw no trace of judgment.

"I have her, Thijs," Viola said as she came around the car. She linked their arms together and tugged lightly. "This way."

Duke had expected to enter Belvédère Castle the same way as she had the first time, but instead, she found herself in an underground enclosure.

"Where are we?"

"The private entrance," Viola said. "Don't worry. My apartments are close by."

"Good." Duke remained glued to Viola's side throughout the elevator ride. She didn't count how many floors they ascended. She didn't care. All she could think of was worshipping Viola's body with her own, proving the truth of her love in a language deeper than words. She would offer herself up in any way Viola wanted. The thought made her shiver, and Viola tightened her hold.

Finally, the doors opened. Thijs bid them a good night, and Viola returned the sentiment. As she led them down a wide corridor, Duke felt as though she had stepped into a twenty-first century fairy tale. Tonight, she would make love to Viola in her own bed. In a castle. And for the first time, there would be no secrets between them.

Finally, Viola stopped before a door, inserted a key, and pushed it open. "Here."

Duke had the vague impression of a hallway, its walls lined with photographs, but Viola led her quickly into the bedroom. Duke glimpsed several abstract oil paintings before Viola adjusted the lights, casting the walls into shadow and illuminating the bed.

It was king-sized, a glorious monstrosity covered by a crimson duvet and matching pillows. Viola threw back the blanket to expose cream colored sheets.

"I want you so much, I can't stand it," she said, and at the tremor in her voice, Duke wanted to weep for joy.

She went to Viola and grasped her waist, tugging at the hem of her shirt. "You can have me as many times as you want. But please, *please* let me taste you, first."

Even in the dim light, Duke could see Viola's eyes darken. The hunger in them was like nothing she had ever witnessed. Its stark ferocity was sacred. Blessed by Viola's need, Duke waited only for permission.

"Yes," Viola breathed, and Duke pushed up her shirt while Viola worked frantically at the buttons on her jeans. By the time Duke had divested her of the garment, she was dressed only in a black lace bra and underwear, simple yet striking against her pale skin.

"I love you," Duke said. "I want you. And I intend to worship you."

Viola swallowed hard. Her mouth worked silently. And then, as Duke freed her breasts from the bra, she spoke. "Please."

That single, beautifully vulnerable syllable galvanized Duke into action. She tore at Viola's underwear until it fell to the floor, then tumbled her onto her own bed. The kiss was fierce, almost painful in its intensity. When Viola's hips surged, seeking relief, Duke held her gently down with both hands. The knowledge that she was giving Viola pleasure was a heady aphrodisiac.

"I'm going to put my mouth on you now."

Duke slid down Viola's body, urged her legs apart, and sealed her lips around Viola's throbbing clitoris. A harsh scream filled the room before it was extinguished in a gasp. Duke luxuriated in Viola's wetness, suckling and licking without a consistent rhythm. Once Viola was keening and shuddering, her body poised for release, Duke pulled away.

Viola clutched at her. "No! Please don't stop."

"I want to be inside you."

"Yes." Viola's head tossed against the pillow. "Now. *Please.*

Intoxicated by Viola's need, Duke pushed one finger slowly inside. She pulled back when she encountered some resistance but pushed forward again almost immediately. Slowly, Viola's body relaxed—opening to her, welcoming her. Once she was as deep as she could go, Duke returned her attention to Viola's clitoris. When she flicked at it lightly with her tongue, Viola surged from the bed.

Duke raised her head. "It's my turn to take care of you. Relax. Feel me."

She pushed deeper as she stroked Viola with her tongue, first licking, then swirling, then sucking. Only when Viola's pleas became truly desperate did she abandon her teasing strokes for slow, rhythmic thrusts and increase the pressure of her lips.

At the sensation of Viola's inner walls contracting, Duke moaned in pleasure, and when Viola called her name, Duke redoubled her efforts. One climax became a second, and then a third. Viola's body clamped down hard, holding her inside. When Viola finally lay quiescent, Duke pillowed her cheek on Viola's smooth, firm abdomen, imprinting Viola's taste and scent on her memory.

"You're beautiful, she whispered. "So beautiful."

"And exhausted." Viola managed to laugh weakly. "But you—you are amazing." She tugged lightly at Duke's hair. "Come up here."

Duke withdrew her fingers slowly, then pushed herself up to fall into Viola's open arms. "*We* are amazing," she amended.

When Viola smiled in unalloyed delight, Duke thought her heart might break from pure joy. Silently, she vowed to do anything in her power to put that expression on Viola's face every day. Preferably forever.

"Yes," Viola said. "Yes, we are."

Yes, Viola wanted her. Yes, Viola had forgiven her. Yes, Viola was willing to push through all the many obstacles that still faced them. Yes.

Viola's eyes were growing heavy, and Duke kissed each lid closed. "Sleep now," she said, falling in love all over again as Viola curled protectively around her. Duke shut her own eyes and slowly relaxed into Viola's embrace. This felt so good, so right.

For the first time in her life, Duke wanted nothing more than what she had, here and now. For the first time in her life, she knew peace.

EPILOGUE

Brussels, Belgium

Viola inspected her reflection and grimaced. Her hair was in that terribly awkward stage of growing out. It was too short to pull back or put up, but if she left it down, she looked sloppy and unkempt. Even Antonio could only do so much.

"Why are you frowning, lover?" Duke's voice came from behind her, and then her face appeared in the mirror as Viola felt her waist encircled. She relaxed against Duke and watched her own frustration melt away.

"My hair is terrible."

Duke rested her chin on Viola's shoulder and smiled. "No, it isn't. You have this wild, shaggy look about you that suits your artistic sensibilities."

Viola snorted. "You're good for my ego."

"I hope so." Duke's smile sharpened into an expression of determination. "But I also promised never to lie to you again. I meant that promise, and I meant what I just said. You're beautiful."

Viola turned away from the mirror, spinning in the circle of Duke's arms until she was facing her. She cupped Duke's face and kissed her—a deep, slow kiss that held the promise of so much more. When she finally pulled back, Duke's eyes were hazy.

"What was that for?" she whispered.

Viola cocked an eyebrow. "Do I need a reason?"

"No." Duke buried her face in the curve of Viola's neck, punctuating the word with a soft brush of her lips.

It was a submissive gesture, and Viola instinctively pulled Duke closer as a surge of possessiveness washed over her. They fit together so well. She didn't want to be separated, even if it was for a good cause. Fortunately, she had laid the groundwork for a few projects of her own that would allow her to see Duke frequently while she was in Zimbabwe. That was a surprise she was planning to reveal today. For all Duke knew, she would be boarding a commercial flight to Harare by herself tomorrow morning. In fact, she and Viola would be flying together on the Belgian royal jet.

"I'm going to miss you," Duke murmured against her skin.

"Have you taken up mind-reading?" Viola kissed the top of her head. "I was just thinking the same thing."

Duke pulled back just far enough to meet her eyes. "Really?"

At the note of insecurity in her voice, Viola decided it was time to come clean. "Yes. And there's something else I need to tell you."

She took Duke's hand and led her to the pair of chairs in front of the fireplace. Duke's expression held a mix of curiosity and wariness. Their relationship was still so new that Viola didn't feel offended by the latter. In time, they would become sure of one another.

"I'm accompanying you to Africa tomorrow."

Duke blinked, then smiled brilliantly. "That's a very pleasant surprise." She laced their fingers together. "What will you do while I'm working?"

"I'll stay in Harare to attend to some state business while you go on to Msango. But I'll join you there after a few days to do some photography for Eclipse." Viola squeezed Duke's fingers lightly. "I promise to be on my best behavior and not distract you…too much."

Duke shot her an imperious look. "You won't distract me at all. I'm a professional, and I won't let you. Not during the days, anyway."

"But at night?"

"We'll see."

Viola laughed. "I promise to do nothing to jeopardize your professionalism. I'm just glad I'll be able to see you in your element."

"Me, too." Duke's smile was soft and loving, and it made Viola want to coax her back into bed. But soon, they would join her parents for brunch, and there simply wasn't time. "How long will you be able to stay in Msango?"

"Three days. Then, I'll stop by the Congo before coming home."

"What will you do on the state visits?"

"I'll meet briefly with the presidents of both countries, and with our ambassadors there, but I'm most excited for the meetings I've arranged with the National Arts Council in Zimbabwe and a few grassroots women-centered initiatives in the Congo."

"You're amazing." The awe and pride in Duke's expression made Viola feel ten feet tall.

"So are you," Viola countered, knowing Duke didn't believe it yet, but hoping she might, one day. "You inspired me, you know."

"I inspired you? How?"

"I never felt all that passionate about public initiatives until I impersonated Sebastian," Viola said. Suddenly nervous, she licked her lips. What she was about to say was important, and she wanted it to come out perfectly. "I took on responsibilities here and there because I was expected to, but as an artist, I was always focused on my individual work. 'Becoming' him changed my perspective, and falling in love with you motivated me to act."

Duke looked dazed. "That last part," she said. "Would you mind repeating it?"

Viola brought Duke's fingers to her mouth for a kiss. "Maybe I should say it a different way. I love you, Duke. I love you. And once you've fulfilled your commitment to Eclipse, I want us to sit down together to make our own plans."

Duke's face was radiant. She stood and pulled Viola up from her chair for another embrace, threading her fingers through Viola's wild hair. Viola wrapped one arm around her waist and cupped the back of her neck with a gentle, worshipful touch.

"Our plans," Duke whispered. "Big, world-changing plans."

"Yes," Viola said. "They'll take years to come to fruition. Maybe even a lifetime. How would you feel about that?"

Duke pulled her head down for another kiss—a fierce, triumphant kiss that sparked every nerve in Viola's body and urged her to consummate the declarations she had just made. Without breaking the kiss, she began to back them toward the bed. Duke followed willingly for a few steps before suddenly coming to a halt.

"No," she gasped as she tore her lips away. "If we go to bed, we're not going to brunch, and I absolutely refuse to be the brazen hussy who tempts you away from family meals."

Viola had to laugh, and it felt so good. "Brazen hussy?"

"I'm sure it will sound even worse in French." Duke lowered her arms and freed herself from Viola's grip. "Let's go now, before that look in your eyes disintegrates my will."

They walked through the halls hand in hand while Viola entertained Duke with various translations—in both French and Dutch—of "brazen hussy." They were still laughing when they emerged into the solarium, a circular room with walls and ceiling made almost entirely of glass. Warm and bright, it was a cheerful space.

Her parents were already seated, and they welcomed both her and Duke with genuine smiles. Thankfully, they weren't interested in holding any kind of grudge—especially once Viola had explained Duke's role in discovering how Sebastian had overdosed, and Sebastian had described Duke's efforts in Zurich. It hadn't hurt that a few days after their testimonials, FIFA had reinstated the Belgian-Dutch bid. Duke had been self-conscious in their parents' presence at first, but as the weeks passed, she grew more and more comfortable.

"How are your preparations coming along for tomorrow?" her father asked Duke.

"Very well." Duke squeezed Viola's hand. "And I've just learned that Viola will be joining me for the flight, which was a welcome surprise."

"We'll miss you," her mother said. "Both of you. But we're proud of your good work."

"Where is Sebastian?" Viola said suddenly. A spike of fear lanced through her. She didn't want to alarm anyone, but since becoming sober, he tended to run early to his obligations, and he was most certainly late now.

Her father frowned. "I haven't heard from him yet tod—"

"Good morning!"

Sebastian's voice, clear and strong, filled her with relief. She turned to the sight of him striding toward them, his steps brisk and confident. He had gained some much-needed weight since leaving rehab, and his cheeks were no longer sunken. Today, his color was high, and as he approached, she could feel the energy crackling around him. She opened her mouth to ask what had happened, but he beat her to the punch.

"I'm sorry to be late. I was detained by a call, but I hope you'll forgive me when you hear the good news."

A heartbeat before he said the words, Viola knew. She gripped Duke's hand so hard it must have been painful, but Duke didn't flinch.

"The call was from FIFA," Sebastian continued. "We've won the bid."

Her mother gasped. Her father exclaimed in French. As disbelief turned to triumph, Viola leapt from her chair and threw herself at her brother, embracing him tightly before leaning back to grasp the lapels of his sports coat.

"You did it," she said fiercely. "I am so proud of you!"

"*We* did it." Sebastian's eyes were bright. "We did it together."

Viola nodded, suddenly unable to speak around the knot of emotions in her throat. She turned, needing to include Duke in their triumph, only to realize that Duke was weeping. Tears streamed down her cheeks, and when their eyes met, Duke buried her face in her palms.

"Go," Sebastian whispered, but she was already in motion.

"No, no," Duke said as she knelt before her and gently pulled her hands away. "Go back to Sebastian."

"I love you," Viola said, because it was true and it made Duke happy. When a smile flickered on her lips, Viola leaned in to kiss them lightly. In the background, she heard her parents telling Sebastian how happy they were, and how proud. "Tell me what you're feeling. Please."

"Relief, mostly."

"But?"

"But also some guilt and sadness. If I had made different choices, the bid would never have been endangered in the first place."

"Perhaps," Viola said. "But the choices you made brought you to me, and I'm grateful for that." When Duke's eyes widened, Viola gently squeezed her fingers. "And don't you dare ask me if I'm certain. I am."

"I love you," Duke murmured. "I love you so much."

Viola stood, then pulled her upright. "Thanks to you, I have everything I need. Your love. Sebastian in good health. The respect of my family. Purpose. I don't expect our life to be easy all the time, but I know it will be good."

"Oh," Duke said, the word saturated with emotion. "Please don't make me cry again."

"Only happy tears." Viola gently tugged her toward where Sebastian was being simultaneously embraced by their parents. "It's time to celebrate."

The End

About the Author

Nell Stark is an award-winning author of lesbian romance. In 2013, *The Princess Affair* was a Lambda Literary finalist in the romance category, and in 2010, *everafter* (with Trinity Tam) won a Goldie Award in the paranormal romance category. In addition to the *everafter* series, she has published five standalone romances: *Running With the Wind, Homecoming, The Princess Affair, The Princess and the Prix*, and *All In*.

By day, Nell is a professor of English at a college in the SUNY system. With their son and two dogs, she and Trinity live a stone's throw from the historic Stonewall Inn in New York City.

Books Available from Bold Strokes Books

Breakthrough by Kris Bryant. Falling for a sexy ranger is one thing, but is the possibility of love worth giving up the career Kennedy Wells has always dreamed of? (978-1-63555-179-2)

Certain Requirements by Elinor Zimmerman. Phoenix has always kept her love of kinky submission strictly behind the bedroom door and inside the bounds of romantic relationships, until she meets Kris Andersen. (978-1-63555-195-2)

Dark Euphoria by Ronica Black. When a high-profile case drops in Detective Maria Diaz's lap, she forges ahead only to discover this case, and her main suspect, aren't like any other. (978-1-63555-141-9)

Fore Play by Julie Cannon. Executive Leigh Marshall falls hard for Peyton Broader, her golf pro...and an ex-con. Will she risk sabotaging her career for love? (978-1-63555-102-0)

Love Came Calling by CA Popovich. Can a romantic looking for a long-term, committed relationship and a jaded cynic too busy for love conquer life's struggles and find their way to what matters most? (978-1-63555-205-8)

Outside the Law by Carsen Taite. Former sweethearts Tanner Cohen and Sydney Braswell must work together on a federal task force to see justice served, but will they choose to embrace their second chance at love? (978-1-63555-039-9)

The Princess Deception by Nell Stark. When journalist Missy Duke realizes Prince Sebastian is really his twin sister Viola in disguise, she plays along, but when sparks flare between them, will the double deception doom their fairy-tale romance? (978-1-62639-979-2)

The Smell of Rain by Cameron MacElvee. Reyha Arslan, a wise and elegant woman with a tragic past, shows Chrys that there's still beauty to embrace and reason to hope despite the world's cruelty. (978-1-63555-166-2)

The Talebearer by Sheri Lewis Wohl. Liz's visions show her the faces of the lost and the killers who took their lives. As one by one, the murdered are found, a stranger works to stop Liz before the serial killer is brought to justice. (978-1-63555-126-6)

White Wings Weeping by Lesley Davis. The world is full of discord and hatred, but how much of it is just human nature when an evil with sinister intent is invading people's hearts? (978-1-63555-191-4)

A Call Away by KC Richardson. Can a businesswoman from a big city find the answers she's looking for, and possibly love, on a small-town farm? (978-1-63555-025-2)

Berlin Hungers by Justine Saracen. Can the love between an RAF woman and the wife of a Luftwaffe pilot, former enemies, survive in besieged Berlin during the aftermath of World War II? (978-1-63555-116-7)

Blend by Georgia Beers. Lindsay and Piper are like night and day. Working together won't be easy, but not falling in love might prove the hardest job of all. (978-1-63555-189-1)

Hunger for You by Jenny Frame. Principe of an ancient vampire clan Byron Debrek must save her one true love from falling into the hands of her enemies and into the middle of a vampire war. (978-1-63555-168-6)

Mercy by Michelle Larkin. FBI Special Agent Mercy Parker and psychic ex-profiler Piper Vasey learn to love again as they race to stop a man with supernatural gifts who's bent on annihilating humankind. (978-1-63555-202-7)

Pride and Porters by Charlotte Greene. Will pride and prejudice prevent these modern-day lovers from living happily ever after? (978-1-63555-158-7)

Rocks and Stars by Sam Ledel. Kyle's struggle to own who she is and what she really wants may end up landing her on the bench and without the woman of her dreams. (978-1-63555-156-3)

The Boss of Her: Office Romance Novellas by Julie Cannon, Aurora Rey, and M. Ullrich. Going to work never felt so good. Three office romance novellas from talented writers Julie Cannon, Aurora Rey, and M. Ullrich. (978-1-63555-145-7)

The Deep End by Ellie Hart. When family ties become entangled in murder and deception, it's time to find a way out... (978-1-63555-288-1)

A Country Girl's Heart by Dena Blake. When Kat Jackson gets a second chance at love, following her heart will prove the hardest decision of all. (978-1-63555-134-1)

Dangerous Waters by Radclyffe. Life, death, and war on the home front. Two women join forces against a powerful opponent, nature itself. (978-1-63555-233-1)

Fury's Death by Brey Willows. When all we hold sacred fails, who will be there to save us? (978-1-63555-063-4)

It's Not a Date by Heather Blackmore. Kade's desire to keep things with Jen on a professional level is in Jen's best interest. Yet what's in Kade's best interest...is Jen. (978-1-63555-149-5)

Killer Winter by Kay Bigelow. Just when she thought things could get no worse, homicide Lieutenant Leah Samuels learns the woman she loves has betrayed her in devastating ways. (978-1-63555-177-8)

Score by MJ Williamz. Will an addiction to pain pills destroy Ronda's chance with the woman she loves or will she come out on top and score a happily ever after? (978-1-62639-807-8)

Spring's Wake by Aurora Rey. When wanderer Willa Lange falls for Provincetown B&B owner Nora Calhoun, will past hurts and a fifteen-year age gap keep them from finding love? (978-1-63555-035-1)

The Northwoods by Jane Hoppen. When Evelyn Bauer, disguised as her dead husband, George, travels to a Northwoods logging camp to work, she and the camp cook Sarah Bell forge a friendship fraught with both tenderness and turmoil. (978-1-63555-143-3)

Truth or Dare by C. Spencer. For a group of six lesbian friends, life changes course after one long snow-filled weekend. (978-1-63555-148-8)

A Heart to Call Home by Jeannie Levig. When Jessie Weldon returns to her hometown after thirty years, can she and her childhood crush Dakota Scott heal the tragic past that links them? (978-1-63555-059-7)

Children of the Healer by Barbara Ann Wright. Life becomes desperate for ex-soldier Cordelia Ross when the indigenous aliens of her planet are drawn into a civil war and old enemies linger in the shadows. Book Three of the Godfall Series. (978-1-63555-031-3)

Hearts Like Hers by Melissa Brayden. Coffee shop owner Autumn Primm is ready to cut loose and live a little, but is the baggage that comes with out-of-towner Kate Carpenter too heavy for anything long term? (978-1-63555-014-6)

Love at Cooper's Creek by Missouri Vaun. Shaw Daily flees corporate life to find solace in the rural Blue Ridge Mountains, but escapism eludes her when her attentions are captured by small town beauty Kate Elkins. (978-1-62639-960-0)

Somewhere Over Lorain Road by Bud Gundy. Over forty years after murder allegations shattered the Esker family, can Don Esker find the true killer and clear his dying father's name? (978-1-63555-124-2)

Twice in a Lifetime by PJ Trebelhorn. Detective Callie Burke can't deny the growing attraction to her late friend's widow, Taylor Fletcher, who also happens to own the bar where Callie's sister works. (978-1-63555-033-7)

Undiscovered Affinity by Jane Hardee. Will a no strings attached affair be enough to break Olivia's control and convince Cardic that love does exist? (978-1-63555-061-0)

Between Sand and Stardust by Tina Michele. Are the lifelong bonds of love strong enough to conquer time, distance, and heartache when Haven Thorne and Willa Bennette are given another chance at forever? (978-1-62639-940-2)

Charming the Vicar by Jenny Frame. When magician and atheist Finn Kane seeks refuge in an English village after a spiritual crisis, can local vicar Bridget Claremont restore her faith in life and love? (978-1-63555-029-0)

Data Capture by Jesse J. Thoma. Lola Walker is undercover on the hunt for cybercriminals while trying not to notice the woman who might be perfectly wrong for her for all the right reasons. (978-1-62639-985-3)

Epicurean Delights by Renee Roman. Ariana Marks had no idea a leisure swim would lead to being rescued, in more ways than one, by the charismatic Hudson Frost. (978-1-63555-100-6)

Heart of the Devil by Ali Vali. We know most of Cain and Emma Casey's story, but *Heart of the Devil* will take you back to where it began one fateful night with a tray loaded with beer. (978-1-63555-045-0)

Known Threat by Kara A. McLeod. When Special Agent Ryan O'Connor reluctantly questions who protects the Secret Service, she learns courage truly is found in unlikely places. Agent O'Connor Series #3. (978-1-63555-132-7)

Seer and the Shield by D. Jackson Leigh. Time is running out for the Dragon Horse Army while two unlikely heroines struggle to put aside their attraction and find a way to stop a deadly cult. Dragon Horse War, Book 3. (978-1-63555-170-9)

Sinister Justice by Steve Pickens. When a vigilante targets citizens of Jake Finnigan's hometown, Jake and his partner Sam fall under suspicion themselves as they investigate the murders. (978-1-63555-094-8)

The Universe Between Us by Jane C. Esther. Ana Mitchell must make the hardest choice of her life: the promise of new love Jolie Dann on Earth, or a humanity-saving mission to colonize Mars. (978-1-63555-106-8)

Touch by Kris Bryant. Can one touch heal a heart? (978-1-63555-084-9)